# DELLA'S
## HOUSE OF STYLE

# DELLA'S
## HOUSE OF STYLE

ROCHELLE ALERS · DONNA HILL
FELICIA MASON · FRANCIS RAY

ST. MARTIN'S GRIFFIN
NEW YORK

Published in the United States by St. Martin's Griffin, an imprint of St. Martin's Publishing Group

www.stmartins.com

Designed by Gabriel Guma

ISBN 978-1-250-83419-5 (trade paperback)

Our books may be purchased in bulk for promotional, educational, or business use. Please contact your local bookseller or the Macmillan Corporate and Premium Sales Department at 1-800-221-7945, extension 5442, or by email at MacmillanSpecialMarkets@macmillan.com.

First St. Martin's Griffin Edition: 2024

P1

# Contents

# It Could Happen to You

DONNA HILL

# CHAPTER ONE

Della was in a hurry, and she disliked rushing with a passion. It set a bad tone for her entire day. However, if she didn't rush she would be late and she disliked being late even more. The thing was, she wouldn't be rushing and on the verge of being late in the first place if she'd had a decent night's sleep. But that was another story. No time to dwell on it now.

She took a quick glance at herself in the hallway mirror. Not bad for a woman pushing past fifty, she thought, puckering her full lips. Her skin was clear and relatively wrinkle-free. She kept her body in shape with a weekly massage and plenty of exercise. And her hair, well . . . she was a walking advertisement for the famous 125th Street salon. She peered a bit closer and noticed a few new gray strands. She'd have to get Reggie to give her a quick rinse. If not, the next thing you know they'd sprout up like weeds in an untended garden. She'd been so busy lately, she hadn't noticed until now.

With her daughter Chauncie off on her honeymoon, she'd had to get back into the swing of running the shop. On top of that she'd had to make all the preparations for the grand opening of the club that she'd added onto the salon. Although all the work had been completed nearly three months earlier, by her son-in-law Drew and his construction company, Della wanted everything to be perfect. That took planning. And if there was one thing Della Frazier prided herself on, it was that she left no stone unturned. Especially since the former Rosie's Curl and Weave, which she'd previously managed, was now named Della's House of Style.

Della smiled. Louis Sweet had turned the shop over to her lock, stock, and barrel after he'd tripped head over heels in love with Elaine. Della would have never thought Louis would give up the business that he and Rosie—God rest her soul—had built together. But love makes you do crazy things, she thought wistfully. Love had turned her daughter's life completely around when she met Drew. Love had given Louis a second chance with Elaine. So many couples had met and fallen in love at the former Rosie's. It not only changed looks, it changed lives. She wondered if Della's would have the same magic touch.

She fluffed her hair one last time, grabbed her keys and purse, and hurried outside. Once behind the wheel of her Volvo, Della tried to settle herself down. Why was she so edgy? She pulled to a stop at a red light and tapped her manicured nails along the steering wheel.

Methodically she went over a mental checklist of all the possibilities. She knew Chauncie and Drew were fine. Chauncie called the night before last gushing about how happy she was in Hawaii, and promising to be back in time for the opening. The salon had been running smoothly. Business was booming. The new receptionist she'd hired was working out fine. The caterer and the decorators were taken care of. The staff seemed to be happy and excited about the opening.

She stepped down on the gas and zoomed across the intersection. She couldn't think of a thing that was amiss. Yet the feeling of impending disaster wouldn't leave her alone. That was the reason why she was behind schedule. She'd slept poorly, worrying—about what, she didn't know—and though she finally did get to sleep, she woke up late.

"Just take a breath and be cool, Della," she said aloud. "It's probably nothing." Maybe this was her introduction to menopause, or something. She supposed a hot flash would be next. *Oh, Lord.*

To keep her mind off the countless possibilities, especially thoughts about a major turning point in her life, she turned on the radio and Luther Vandross's cool crooning kept her company for the balance of the short drive. It was hard to imagine that sooner, rather than later, a major part of her womanhood would be a distant memory. But she didn't feel old, felt every bit as desirable as she'd always felt, maybe more so with maturity, and she could still turn a few heads when she set her mind to it. Yet, there was no denying that time waits for no one and not even a good hair dye can change that fact.

By the time she arrived at the shop, it was already in full swing. All five operators had customers beneath their skilled fingers and more were waiting along the row of cushioned seats.

The familiar scents of chemical relaxers, hair pomades, coffee, and perfumes greeted her. Flowing, light jazz from CD 101.9 FM filled the air and womanish laughter completed all the spaces.

As usual, Reggie held center court, decked out today in a lime green suit and matching shoes, the iridescent outfit protected by the required black smock. Only Reggie could get away with an outfit like that. His nimble fingers were as fast as his mouth as he applied a henna rinse and chatted nonstop about his latest weekend adventure.

"'Morning, Ms. Della," Cindy, the new part-time receptionist, greeted. "Full house today. Folks were waiting outside as soon as we opened."

"So I see," Della, said, placing her purse on the desk. "Any cancellations?"

"None. We even had a few walk-ins."

"Looks like it's going to be another long day," Della said on a breath, not at all displeased. When she'd officially taken over the business and changed its name, she'd worried about a loss of clientele. That was not the case. If anything, business seemed to have picked up.

"Any messages?"

Cindy reached beneath the desk to the tray where she kept the message slips.

"Just one, from a Mr. Hawkins."

Della frowned, trying to place the name. She took the pink slip of paper and studied the number as if it would somehow reveal something. Nothing clicked. "Did he say what he wanted?"

"No. Actually he was kind of rude. He just said it was personal and for you to return his call as soon as you came in."

That "trouble is coming" sensation rumbled around in her stomach again.

"Thanks, Cindy," she said absently. "I'll be in my office if you need me."

Della reclaimed her purse and headed to the back office, waving and greeting her staff and clients along the way. But her mind was on the slip of paper in her hand.

Once inside her small but ordered office, she closed the door and went directly to her desk.

Taking a seat, she stared at the number again, took a breath, and reached for the phone. It was answered on the second ring.

"Internal Revenue. Matt Hawkins speaking."

Matt Hawkins's voice could have been that of a sexy rhythm and blues singer. It was deep, dipping down to the core of her, stirring that part of her womanhood that had long gone unattended. But the pleasure ended there.

Internal Revenue! Damn. Her heart began to pound. She cleared her throat, her mind racing over any possible reason why Matt Hawkins, no matter how good he sounded, would be calling her.

"Uh, this is Della Frazier. I received a—"

"Yes, Ms. Frazier," he said, cutting her off. "I'd like to set up an appointment for you to come into the office within the next three days."

"What in the world for?" She heard the shuffling of papers and held her breath.

"According to my records it appears that improper tax papers were filed when the addition was added to your place of business. It appears that you owe us a great deal of money."

"Obviously there's been a mistake. I—"

"The IRS doesn't make mistakes, Ms. Frazier. Taxpayers do."

Della's neck snapped back. She held the phone away from her face and stared at it a moment as if it were a foreign object.

"Well you've made a mistake this time," she flung back, recovering quickly. Who the hell did he think he was, anyway?

"If you say so, Ms. Frazier. But the fact remains. You have a large tax debt, and if it's not straightened out to our satisfaction, we'll have to shut you down. And you may do some jail time in addition to a fine for tax evasion."

"What!"

"When would you like to come in? I have an opening tomorrow at ten, and the following day at two. The sooner the better," he added solicitously.

Della's hands shook. She couldn't think straight. This man was obviously going out of his mind. She'd heard and read the horror stories about innocent people getting caught in the web of the IRS. People had been ruined, their homes and businesses destroyed by a "mistake." *Lord have mercy.*

"Two o'clock sounds fine," she finally answered, attempting to sound stronger than she felt.

"I'll make a note. You'll need to bring all of your tax records for this year and last year and all of the paperwork relating to the additional space."

"Of course."

"Then I'll see you day after tomorrow at two. Please be on time. I have another appointment at four."

"I'm sure this error will be straightened out long before then." Della swore she heard him laugh.

"Have a nice day, Ms. Frazier."

Della listened to the dial tone for so long, the next sound she heard was the mechanical voice that warned her there was a phone off the hook.

Mindlessly, she returned the phone to its cradle. She covered her face with both hands and tried to get her thoughts in order.

Could this fool be right? No, that wasn't possible. She'd been handling the books for years and never made a mistake. They'd had Sid as their accountant for as long as she could remember, and he was as reliable as they come.

When Louis finally broke down and agreed to have the extension built, she'd gone over everything he'd given her. Chauncie had overseen the construction and Drew swore everything was up to code.

She looked helplessly around her office. What in the world could have happened?

"If it ain't one thing it's another," she mumbled, as Rosie—God rest her soul—would have said in a time of crisis.

Della tapped her nails in a steady drumbeat against the desktop. First things first, she decided, getting up from her seat.

She crossed the room and opened the file cabinets, pulling out the tax returns for the past two years along with a the folder marked "Lennox Construction." There had to be something in there that she'd missed.

But two hours later, she hadn't found a thing and she was two hours closer to her appointment with the dreamy voice of doom.

# CHAPTER TWO

Della had been holed up in her office for the better part of the day, something totally out of character for her, and it hadn't gone unnoticed.

"You seen Della today?" Misty asked, smoothing a Revlon perm into Ms. Lucille's flaming red hair.

"Not much," Reggie said with a huff, looking at Tanisha's head from several angles, trying to figure out what to do with the mangled job she did of coloring her own hair.

"Well, that's not like her," Misty continued, wanting to stir up something.

"It's like her today," Reggie said with attitude, refusing to get caught up in the gossip trap of Misty's big mouth. It was one thing to run your lips about your own business, but running it about others' was where he drew the line. Especially when it came to Della.

Della had been the one who went to bat for him when he first applied for the job fresh out of cosmetology school. She listened to him when he'd cried on her shoulders about his love affairs, and applauded his outlandish clothes. She'd been his friend, his surrogate mom, and his employer. And he damn sure wouldn't let the likes of this big-mouthed heifer put the badmouth on her. Even if she could hook up some hair.

"All I was sayin', Reggie, was that she's acting strange, that's all." She smoothed on the rest of the perm and combed it through in long, even strokes. "I just hope nothing's wrong, that's all I'm sayin'."

As much as he didn't want to agree with Ms. Thing, of all people, she was right, Reggie thought, squirting the last of the peroxide into Tanisha's hair, hoping to strip away the last of that hideous color. He gently massaged it through, as he pondered what to do about Della.

She had been acting strange today. It wasn't like her not to be right in the mix, talking with the customers, checking on the technicians, especially on a day that was as busy as the one they'd had. Usually, Della would have jumped in to do a head or two herself to cut down on the backlog. But he'd barely seen her all day.

"Come on, sugah," he said to Tanisha, snapping a plastic cap on her head. "Sit under the dryer for ten minutes." Reggie ushered her over to the dryer and set it on cool.

He returned to his station and took off his rubber gloves, tossing them into the trash with a flourish. He spun around, hands on hips, and surveyed the remaining group of waiting women. He had two more clients. One wanted an auburn rinse and the other blond. They both could wait.

———————

Della's eyes were beginning to cross. She'd looked at so many numbers and read so many letters and contracts that it was all one big blur.

She squeezed her eyes shut and massaged her temples with her thumbs.

The light tap on the door sounded like gunshots.

"Come in," she mumbled, briefly looking up to see Reggie saunter in.

"You look beat down, Ms. Dee. What's wrong?" He closed the door and came around to the side of her desk and sat on the edge.

Della shook her head as if to say it was nothing.

"Look, Ms. Dee, don't even try it. We've been friends for too long for you to pull the 'it's nothing' routine with me." He folded his arms, his signal that he wasn't budging until she spilled her guts.

Della sighed in resignation. "The shop's in trouble."

Reggie's finely plucked brows arched perfectly. "What kind of trouble?"

"Big trouble."

"Well, how do we get out of it? What do we need to do? If it's money, you know I'll pitch in," he ran on, his fingers furling and unfurling as he spoke. "I have some cash stashed away for a rainy day. You're welcome to it."

Della glanced up at him and her heart stirred. For all of Reggie's eccentricities and often outlandish proclamations, she could always depend on him in a crunch.

"I wish it was that simple, Reg." She blew out a long breath, a mixture of frustration and exhaustion. "The fact is, the IRS is on my tail."

His brows shot up again and stayed there. Della wanted to laugh, but it wasn't funny.

Reggie gave a slight shudder. "Just the thought of the IRS gives me the willies. What do they want with you? The thievin' SOBs."

Della ran down as much of her improbable circumstance as she was aware of. She punctuated her monologue with tosses of her mane of hair or a slap of her palm on the desk for emphasis. And when she really got worked up, she resorted to the age-old sucking of her teeth that came from so far back and so strong, the suction puckered her red lips for a full minute.

"This sounds like that rainy day I was talking about," Reggie mumbled. "Do you think you'll have to close the shop?"

"I hope not, Reg, but it's a possibility. And the grand opening of Della's Place will definitely have to be postponed. At least until I get this mess straightened out."

"Maybe Louis knows something. Have you tried to call him?"

"Louis and Elaine are on a two-month Caribbean cruise. I don't have the faintest idea how to contact him. And even if I did, I'd never intrude on them. When Louis turned the shop over to me, he washed his hands of the business. Right or wrong, I took on the good and the bad. It's my responsibility."

"Yeah, I hear ya. But all that responsibility ain't providing us with any answers."

Della pursed her lips in annoyance at the obvious.

"I'll figure something out," she mumbled, none too sure of her declaration.

Reggie hopped down from his perch. "I have two more clients and then I'm done for the day. Let's go for a drink and think."

The right side of Della's mouth curved. "I thought people drank so they *wouldn't* think."

"Whatever," he tossed out flippantly. "We could both use one." He turned toward the door. "See you in about an hour."

"And don't say anything to Ruthie. You know how she worries."

Reggie ran his fingers across his lips and sauntered out.

---

Matt Hawkins turned off his computer, returned his files to their proper slots, and prepared to leave, cutting his ten-hour day short. He was way ahead on his client list and felt he deserved the perk.

His office was immaculate. Every pen, pencil, and paper clip was in its place. Order was a passion with Matt Hawkins. He was known throughout the department as Take-No-Prisoners Hawkins because of his relentless pursuit of tax evaders. His success record was impeccable. He'd yet to lose a case.

But as he flicked off the light switch and locked his office door, he wondered how much his zeal had cost him.

Sure, he made great money, had some solid investments, owned his own home, traveled every summer—usually alone—drove the latest Lexus, and had a Jeep. But at the end of the day, that's all he had—*things.*

He'd been thinking like this a lot lately. Maybe it was midlife crisis setting in. Whatever it was, he couldn't shake it and he realized it again today when he'd spoken with that Frazier woman. On any other case he never would have given the client the opportunity to choose when she would come in. He made that decision. This time he'd been easy on the woman and he wasn't sure why.

He turned the key in the ignition, the smell of Coach leather enveloping him. He must be getting soft, he thought, pulling out into traffic. What other explanation could there be?

Moving along with the snail's pace of traffic, Matt had the sudden urge not to go home. The last thing he felt like being tonight was alone. Instead of taking his turn on Malcolm X Boulevard he decided that a few hours in a smoke-filled room and some down-home jazz was just the thing he needed. He went straight down 125th Street.

But when he stopped for a red light, the momentary lift he gave himself by deciding to go listen to some music began to slowly dissolve. Who was he kidding? He didn't any more want to listen to music in a club alone than he wanted to go home and be alone.

What had his life turned into?

"How can you look at yourself in the mirror?" his twenty-year-old daughter Lisa had recently asked him. "You seem to take some sort of pride in ruining people's lives. What kind of man are you?"

"The same man who busted his butt at this job you hate, to put you through college, buy you that car, and send alimony to your refuse-to-work mother. That's the kind of man I am," he said in his own defense. "One who takes care of his responsibilities."

"By any means necessary, Daddy?" she asked, a despondent edge to her voice.

The question had shocked as much as hurt him. He loved his daughter, blindly, and would do anything to see her happy. To realize that she thought so little of him had forced him to look at his life, at himself. He wasn't too sure he liked what he saw.

A car horn honked behind him, snapping him out of his musings. He looked up and the light was green. The two cars ahead of him were well across the intersection. He started to pull off when movement to his right caught his eye.

Maybe it was the eye-popping green outfit and matching shoes on the tall, model-thin man. But that wasn't what held his attention. It was the woman. She was stunning. At first he thought it was Diahann Carroll. But he couldn't imagine the famous star strolling down 125th

Street with that particular companion. Then again, you never could tell. However, gut instinct told him better. This woman was better looking than any Diahann Carroll.

She had a head full of tumbling auburn hair that gently brushed her shoulders and blew lightly in the spring breeze. The bronze-toned trenchcoat she wore didn't hide, but accented the cream-colored suit worn beneath it, the skirt hitting just above her knees.

And she wore heels! Real heels. Something women these days didn't do much of anymore. But he loved them. Loved what they did to a woman's legs. And her legs . . . every time she took a step they peeked out from behind the coat. Taunting, tempting . . .

The horn blasted again, seconds before a white Lincoln sped around him, the driver sticking his head out of the window long enough to let go of a few words he'd never want his mother to hear.

The squeal of tires must have caught the woman's attention and she turned briefly toward the sound. She had wide expressive eyes the color of cinnamon, and smooth, flawless skin to match.

In that instant he captured her face with the sensitivity and high speed of a camera shutter. The image would be engraved in his head forever.

The couple turned the corner and disappeared from view, but not from Matt Hawkins's mind.

For the rest of the night and into the morning, he thought of that woman and the incredible sensation he'd felt when he saw her. It was as if something that had been dormant inside of him had finally been awakened. He couldn't remember the last time, if ever, that just seeing a woman had made such an impact on him.

The following morning before going to work, he took the same route in the vain hope of spotting her. He didn't. He felt like a fool as he cruised down the avenue, but he couldn't help himself.

Finally, he accepted the futility of his actions and headed to his office. He was crazy to think he'd ever see her again.

# CHAPTER THREE

Della spent the next day at home, sitting at her kitchen table going over every scrap of paper, every canceled check. There was no way to be too prepared for the IRS. She only wished she knew what that fool Hawkins had in his nasty little file folder. At least then she'd know what she was up against.

She blew out a breath and pushed the papers aside, and reached for her cup of coffee. As soon as the liquid touched her lips, she screwed up her face in disgust.

"Yuck!" How long had she been sitting there? The once hot coffee was ice cold and full of grounds. She checked her watch. It was nearly noon. Damn, she'd been at this for nearly four hours. Slowly she rotated her neck to work out the kinks, stood, and stretched.

Resigned, she stared at the multitude of papers. There was nothing more she could do. She'd gone over every nook and cranny with an eagle eye. All she could hope for now was an earthquake.

Della slid the loose papers securely inside the folder, closed it, then placed it in her leather briefcase.

"Dammit!" she stomped her foot in frustration as tears welled in her eyes. She couldn't lose her shop. She'd dedicated more than ten years of her life to the business, and earned the right to call it Della's. Now, when it was truly hers, it could be snatched away in a finger pop.

Well, she damn sure wasn't going down without a fight. She wiped away the feeling-sorry-for-herself tears just as the phone rang.

Maybe it was Chauncie, she thought, and sniffed. She could sure use the sound of her daughter's voice right about now.

She pulled the gold clip earring from her right ear and picked up the phone.

"Hello."

"Della, it's Ruthie."

Della's stomach knotted for a quick minute. Ruthie never called her at home unless it was an emergency.

"Hi, Ruthie. Please don't tell me there's a problem. Don't know if I can handle it today." She pressed her thumbs to her temple.

"Well, shoot the messenger later—'cause we have trouble now," she said in a harsh whisper.

"What is it?"

"There's some man here claiming he's from the IRS." Her voice dropped a notch. "Doing an assessment of the premises."

"What!" Della's heart tried to jump out of her chest.

Ruthie cupped her hand over the mouthpiece. "You heard me. He strolled in here, flashed me some ID, and started sniffing around like a hound on the hunt."

"I'll be there in fifteen minutes. Walking out of the door right now." Della started to hang up, then stopped. "Ruthie!"

"Yeah . . ."

"Do any of the other staff know what's going on?" She held her breath.

"Don't think so, Dee. Maybe Reggie noticed him, but that's a different story. Everyone else is too busy. This place is jumping."

"Good. See you in a few."

———

Della sped down the Harlem streets, alternately praying and cussing. "Lord, please don't let those foul people take my shop. We've worked too hard and too long. Damn fool, probably a four-eyed loser with a pocket protector! Oh, Lord, forgive me. I didn't mean that."

She made her turn onto 125th Street and was stopped cold. There was a line of traffic all the way to the Triborough Bridge nearly eight blocks away. She wanted to scream, but all she could do was tap her foot and inch along. By the time she pulled up in front of the salon she was a ball of fury and raw nerves. She parked the car and snatched her purse from the passenger seat, then took a quick look in the mirror. Taking a deep breath of resolve, she got out and marched toward the shop.

M att knew he shouldn't have come to the shop. It was completely against policy, and if anyone ever found out, he could lose his job. But his compulsive nature steered him there for a peek at his next conquest. What could he have been thinking?

He looked around at what was now Della's Place, the questionable addition to the shop. There was no doubt that it was a fabulous combination café and nightclub. A great concept. Whoever had done the work did an incredible job, and whoever came up with the concept was a person with vision. Was it the mysterious Della Frazier? he wondered. Shaking his head, he walked quickly to the front of the shop. The sooner he was out of there the better.

He nodded briefly at Ruthie, who looked as if she wanted to make quick work of him with her haircutting scissors. He didn't intimidate easily—he couldn't, in his business—but that woman could put some fear in your heart.

Matt breezed by the rest of the women, who sized him up like an object on the auction block. Some discreetly peered from above the tops of magazines, others used no camouflage devices at all but boldly stared with winks and smiles, while one blatantly asked what was his hurry—to the delight of everyone.

By the time he'd thankfully reached the threshold of escape, he felt as if he'd been put on the Colonel Sanders rotisserie grill ready to be served up with a Coke. He couldn't get outside fast enough, and practically ran across the street to his car.

Matt was halfway across the street when he saw her again. He stopped dead in his tracks, blinking rapidly, sure that he was imagining things. But no, there she was, and she was heading straight for the shop!

He jumped as the blast of a car horn rudely reminded him that he was standing in the middle of two-way traffic. He jogged to the other side just in time to catch a glimpse of her walking through the doors of Della's.

He could kick himself for his lousy timing, but instead he kicked the tire. If he hadn't suddenly become so paranoid about being there in the first place, he'd still be inside. Damn. He couldn't very well go back, and knowing women and their hair, she was liable to be there for the rest of the afternoon.

Reluctantly, he got into his car. He didn't think he'd see her again. The better part of the previous night he'd thought about her. It wasn't just that drop-dead walk of hers, the lustrous hair, or the stylish clothes. This woman embodied femininity. Everything about her spoke self-assurance and confidence. Qualities sorely lacking in the few women he'd dated since his divorce.

Matt sat in his car for a few minutes in the vain hope that the mystery woman would reappear. No such luck.

———

Della hurried inside, briefly nodding to Cindy, but not stopping for messages. She went straight for Ruthie.

"Melody," Della said, taking her tempestuous stylist by the hand. "I need you to roller-set Ruthie's customer." Melody screwed up her face. "As a favor to me," Della cajoled, knowing that Melody needed to be stroked at every turn.

"No problem, Ms. Dee. Mine is ready for the dryer."

"Thanks, hon. You're a doll."

Della placed her hands on Ruthie's client's shoulders. "Ms. Clarke,

I need to borrow Ruthie for a minute," she said to the middle-aged woman. "I know you love Ruthie to do your hair, but I need to talk to her about something. My stylist Melody is going to set you. She's one of the best. And for your inconvenience I'll take ten dollars off the cost for today."

Lula Clarke looked up at Della and beamed in delight. "That's why I love this place, Della. You're always thinking about your customers. Thank you, dear."

"Not a problem. Just relax. Melody will be with you shortly."

Ruthie secured the black plastic cape around Ms. Clarke's shoulders, then followed Della to the back of the shop.

As soon as the door was closed to Della's office, Ruthie launched into her story.

"He just came in here like he owned the joint or something," Ruthie complained. "Strolling around and looking up and down at everything. But what he really seemed interested in was the back where the club is. He was in there for a long time." She folded her arms and tapped her foot.

Della paced.

"What the devil is going on, Dee? Why is the IRS snooping around?"

Della halted and blew out a breath, debating on how much she should say. But the fact was, Ruthie had been with the shop since the early days when Rosie and Louis were first starting out. She'd been a faithful employee and a diehard friend. It was Ruthie whom Della had depended on to look after her daughter Chauncie during her absence. Ruthie could run the shop with both hands tied behind her back. She deserved to know the truth.

"It seems that somehow or the other," Della began, "when the addition was put on the shop, some wrong tax papers were filed and we owe a ton of money."

"How could that be? Louis took care of everything."

"Maybe he didn't. Something must have slipped through the cracks. But I've gone over all the paperwork and I can't find the mistake."

"Have you talked to the accountant?"

"I've been trying to reach Sid since I got the call. All I'm getting is his answering machine."

"Hmm. I don't like the sound of this, Dee."

"Yeah, who you telling? I have an appointment at the IRS office tomorrow."

"You need me to go with you? 'Cause you know I will. Can't stand those SOBs anyhow." Her features bunched together in a knot.

"No. I can handle it. I'll just go in there and straighten this whole mess out. It's obviously a mistake," she added, no longer so certain.

"I sure as hell hope so. 'Cause if it ain't, we got problems, sister."

Della sat on the edge of her desk and looked at her friend. "Don't I know it."

# CHAPTER FOUR

As Della walked through the doors of the Internal Revenue office, she wondered if anyone heard her teeth chattering even as she recalled the brave speech she'd given her staff the night before.

"I just thought I should tell you all before you heard this someplace else."

She looked around at the rainbow of faces. Ruthie, her head technician; Jewel, the weave queen; Melody, whose cuts and styles were unsurpassed; Blaize, the braid diva; Tricia, the masseuse; Holly, the manicurist; Misty, the gossip; and, of course, Reggie.

Della cleared her throat. "The IRS is investigating the shop, the club in particular."

An offbeat chorus of "What?" and "Oh, no" bounced around the room.

Della held up her hand for quiet. "Listen, I'm going down to the office tomorrow and straighten this out."

"We'll go with you," Blaize announced.

"That's right," added Jewel. "Just close the shop tomorrow," she added swinging her waist-length weave around her narrow face.

Everyone nodded in agreement.

"You know I'll put this all in check in a heartbeat," Reggie said with a finger pop.

"No. Thanks. Believe me, I appreciate your support, but it's business as usual," Della stated. "I'll handle it. Louis turned this shop over to me.

He trusted me to keep things going and I will." She looked at each one in turn. "Now, you all have to trust me, too."

But as she walked toward the reception desk of the Internal Revenue office, she wondered if she was worthy of their trust.

"I'm here to see a Mr. Hawkins," Della announced at the desk.

The gray-haired woman looked as if she'd been in the sun too long. Her pale skin was a raw red punctuated by milky blue eyes. She gazed up at Della above a pair of half-frames.

"Name?" the woman asked blandly.

"Della Frazier."

The woman looked at Della for a full minute as if she didn't believe her. "You . . . you look so much like that actress. What's her name?"

Della knew exactly who she was talking about, but had no inclination to indulge the woman.

"I really don't know."

The woman angled her head to the right, then the left. Finally she shrugged her shoulders in defeat.

"I'll let him know you're here."

She picked up the phone and punched in a three-digit extension.

"Yes, Mr. Hawkins. There's a Ms. Frazier to see you. Yes." She hung up. "You can go in. Third door on the left."

"Thank you."

"Good luck," the woman said. "He's one of the tough ones," she added in a pseudo whisper.

Della's heart knocked as she forced a tight-lipped smile. She straightened her shoulders, took a breath of resolve, and strutted forward.

"I know," the woman shouted to Della's back. "Diana Ross!"

Della shook her head sadly and kept going.

———

Matt slipped on his suit jacket, pushed his coffee mug aside, and closed the case file he was working on.

He was in an especially foul mood today. He hadn't slept well, thinking about that woman and worrying about his reckless behavior of going to the shop. Every time he thought about it, he cringed. The only way to remedy it all was to stick it to this woman and get his frustrations out of his system. It was obvious from the documents he had that this Della Frazier woman was in deep trouble. He'd be finished with her one, two, three.

He stood at the tap on his door.

"Come in," he barked in his most intimidating voice.

Della swore her knees would give out as she opened the door. "Just keep it together, girl," she chanted to herself, and stepped inside.

When Matt looked up, he immediately knocked over his cup of coffee, jumping as if stuck with a pin.

Della instinctively rushed over to help him.

"Be careful, it will get all over your pants," she warned, snatching his white handkerchief from his jacket pocket to mop up the spill.

Matt was paralyzed with shock and embarrassment. He kept staring at Della as she fussed over the spill.

"Coffee is the worst stain," she muttered, dabbing at the soiled papers. "You'll have to dry these out separately, or they'll all stick together." She held up the forms and began to fan them back and forth.

The fanning snapped him out of his daze. He plucked the brown and white pages from her hand. "T-thank you." He cleared his throat. "Please have a seat . . . Ms. . . . ." His mind had gone blank.

"Frazier," Della offered, filling in the gap. And for the first time she took a real look at Matt Hawkins and her mouth went dry as dust. He wasn't some short, fat, bald man with a pocket protector. Matt Hawkins was Fine. With a capital *F*.

*Oh, Lord.* Della reached behind her, feeling for the chair. Slowly, she sat down and crossed her long legs.

Matt followed suit and forced his gaze to rise from her legs to her face, which was no better for his composure. His chest felt tight. This was her. The woman, sitting right in front of him. The same woman he'd fantasized about for the past two days. She was even more fantastic up close. What he wanted to do was reach across the desk and touch her face, see if it was as soft as it looked.

Instead he snapped open the folder marked "Frazier." He had a job to do.

"Ms. Frazier, according to our files you're personally liable for seventy-five thousand dollars in taxes."

"Seventy-five thousand dollars!" She sprang from her seat. "Now I know you've got to be kidding."

She was magnificent. The flash in her eyes, the arch of her long neck. "If I was kidding, Ms. Frazier, you wouldn't be here. Now, did you bring the forms I asked for, or should we skip all that and just set up a payment plan?"

Why, the arrogant—handsome—pompous—doll. How could anyone so incredibly good looking be such a coldhearted creep? Della seethed. She flashed him a look to kill and reached for her briefcase. Snatching it open, she grabbed the folder from inside and tossed it on his desk, then stared at him for a good thirty seconds, almost daring him to open it.

Casually, Matt pulled the thick accordion folder toward him and began taking out papers. "Have a seat, Ms. Frazier," he instructed, not looking at her. He dared not. All he could think about was the countless number of taxpayers who'd sat just where she was and virtually quaked in their boots. Not Della Frazier. And as much as he quietly resented her challenge of his authority and power, he couldn't help but admire her tenacity.

Della reluctantly sat down—hard—folded her arms, and tapped her foot with impatience. What she wanted to do was smack that smug look off of his gorgeous face. She was fuming. If she'd been a cartoon character, steam would have been coming out of her ears. But at the same time she was terrified. Terrified that this man had the power to ruin her and disrupt the lives of her entire staff and their families.

The minutes ticked by. The only sound in the office was the shuffling of forms and the rapid tapping of keys on the calculator as Matt continued to add up the numbers.

Periodically, Della stole a glance or two at him. His dark hair was cut close with faint sprinkles of gray at the temples. His birch brown skin was smooth, clean-shaven, with sharp cheekbones and dark deep-set eyes in sharp contrast to the snow white shirt and red power tie. And for someone with such an abusive mouth, it was actually full and rich. The kind of mouth you could sink into, allow it to explore you.

She watched his long fingers as they nimbly stroked the calculator keys, and wickedly wondered what they would feel like running along her skin.

Della shook her head, scattering her erotic marauding. She must be lonely, she thought, if she could spend an iota of time fantasizing about the likes of Matt Hawkins. She tapped her foot a bit faster. If Chauncie were in this predicament, she'd probably slip into one of her many roles and wiggle her way out of this mess. If things got too desperate, she may have to pull an Angela Bassett herself and just burn the joint down. She could see the headlines now: OWNER OF FAMED BEAUTY SALON TORCHES IRS OFFICE AS THOUSANDS OF TAXPAYERS CHEER HER ON!

Matt scrubbed his face with his hands before pushing the damning documents toward Della. He pressed his fingers against the bridge of his nose, then looked at her.

She quickly adjusted her expression to neutral.

Suddenly, his stomach muscles tightened when her face came into full focus and he had the overwhelming desire—need, almost—to ask her to dinner. But of course he couldn't. Why did they have to meet under these circumstances? From the instant he'd seen her, something inside of him had shifted, softened somehow. He had the irrational notion that she could be everything he'd been looking for. How crazy was that? He didn't even know this woman. And to top that off, she had tax problems. Major ones. According to everything he'd seen, Della Frazier was in serious trouble. She owed the government and it was up to him to get the money. That was his job. His responsibility. They didn't call him Take-No-Prisoners Hawkins for no reason. But for the first time in his career he felt no pride in his skills.

"I've compared your records with ours, Ms. Frazier and they don't match."

"So what does that mean?" Her heart began to rattle in her chest.

"It means that the burden of proof is on you, and until you can prove the IRS wrong, you owe us seventy-five thousand dollars." He said this all without the slightest bit of emotion in his voice, even though he suddenly felt sickened by what he was doing.

"I—I don't have seventy-five thousand! Where would I get that kind of money?" Her voice broke and her eyes filled.

"If you have property, a car, stocks, maybe you could liquidate them to pay off this debt," he offered by rote.

She looked at him as if he had two heads. "I'm a hardworking woman, not some CEO on Wall Street. I own a brownstone that cost me a ton of money in renovations and my car is five years old. I'd have to sell the shop. Those people, my staff, my friends who depend on me, will be out of work."

Matt tossed up his hands as if there were no more he could do. "Ms. Frazier, I'm sorry, but—"

Della practically leaped from her seat. "Sorry! You can sit there in your five-hundred-dollar suit, with your comfy government job, and say sorry to me when you're about to take away everything I've worked for over the past ten years of my life?" Tears of pure pain and rage spilled from her eyes. Her whole world was falling apart. "What am I going to do?" She looked him square in the eye. "How do you sleep at night?"

The stabbing pain of the past ripped at his gut. That was the same question his wife had asked when she and their daughter had walked out, and he felt powerless to stop them. When they left, all that was human in him left with them. He hadn't made the effort to change the man he was becoming soon enough. It had cost him his family—his reason for his relentless pursuit of rising up the ladder. He looked across at Della. He ached to wipe the tears from her eyes, stop the trembling of her beautiful mouth. Before he knew what he was doing, he'd come around the desk and put his arm around her shoulder, helping her back to her seat.

"Maybe there's some way to work this out."

"How?" she cried, sniffing back her tears.

What he was about to do went against every rule he'd been trained to uphold. His eyes roved the room as if searching for answers. He looked into Della's eyes. "I'll find a way," he finally said. "I—I can't promise you anything, but at least I can hold off any levies against you—for a while."

Della swallowed down the knot in her throat. "A while? How long is a while?"

Slowly Matt moved his arm away. "A few weeks at best."

Della wiped her eyes and sat up straighter. "So you're going to give me a few weeks to either come up with the money or give up my business? It that what you're saying?"

"Maybe there's something that both of us missed. Something we can come up with—together."

Della's eyes widened, then narrowed in suspicion. "Together?"

What was he saying—doing? Better yet, why? He took a breath of resolve and nodded. "Yes. Together."

# CHAPTER FIVE

Hey, maybe she wouldn't have to burn the place down after all, Della mused as she pulled away from the infamous office building.

She was definitely feeling better now than she had a few hours ago. Truth be told, she almost felt like smiling. But in the words of Rosie, "Don't count the roosters in the henhouse, count the eggs." Or something like that. She was never sure what that meant, but it seemed to fit every situation.

She drove by the Apollo Theater, barely noticing the marquee for Amateur Night. Hmm. He actually said he was going to help. But did he really mean it? Or was he just running his mouth to throw her into a false sense of security before he came swooping down on her? Everything she'd ever heard or read about the IRS was negative. They didn't give you a break. This guy definitely clouded all of her preconceived notions.

He'd promised to call the following day and they'd set up a time to get together. He almost made it sound like a date instead of a life-or-death business meeting. And though she'd be loath to admit it to anyone under threat of a bad peroxide rinse, she was actually looking forward to seeing him again.

As much as she may detest what he did for a living, she couldn't deny the magnetic pull she felt for him. Beneath that stiff, corporate, by-the-book exterior, she sensed that he could be a decent man—was a decent man. He had to have some kind of soul to do what he was doing for her. Didn't he?

---

M att paced back and forth across his office floor. He'd committed the cardinal or maybe the carnal sin of his profession: crossing the line from business to personal. That never boded well. But he couldn't seem to help himself.

Della Frazier wasn't like any other client. He wanted to know her and for some reason he didn't want her to walk out of there believing he was the coldhearted heel he'd built his reputation upon.

He wiped his face with his hand. What had he done? If anyone ever found—

"Hey, man. You about ready to cut out?"

Matt's head snapped toward the door. He'd been so absorbed in his dilemma, he hadn't heard Paul come in.

He and Paul Marshall started at the agency two months apart, nearly fifteen years ago. They'd both risen up the ladder and were secure in their positions as senior examiners. But that's where the similarity ended.

Paul had a wife and three great kids. They went on vacations together, planned their lives together. Where Matt dealt with individual client cases, Paul handled corporate accounts. There was an easiness about Paul, an openness. He hadn't let the nature of his job steal his humanity, and never took the same pleasure in winning as Matt did.

"You need more than that job," Paul had said to him as they banged bodies and mixed sweat on his backyard basketball court. "If I didn't have Janet and the kids," he puffed, charging toward the basket, "the job would throw me over the edge, make me crazed and bitter." He leaped for the layup with Matt's long arms right in his face. "I don't want to see that for you," he groaned, and slammed the ball through the hoop.

It was probably too late for him. He'd let his job consume him. He seemed to take out his loneliness and frustrations on anyone who walked through the doors of his office. Except today.

"Yeah, sure," Matt finally said now to Paul. "It's that time already, huh?"

"Janet and the kids went to her mother's for the weekend. I thought I'd hang out at the Lenox Lounge for a while. How 'bout it?"

Hmm. He had nothing to rush home to. "Sure. Sounds great."

"Then let's roll."

---

B y the time Matt and Paul arrived at the famed Lenox Lounge, the after-work crowd was in full swing. Smoke clouds hovered like halos over heads, the band was warming up, and singles mingled like old friends.

Matt and Paul squeezed in at the bar and placed their orders, then took their Coronas to an empty booth in the back where the stage was set up for the band. Dim was the de rigueur of the Lenox Lounge, punctuated by hazy red light bulbs and red leather booths—all of which had seen better days. Their table rocked unsteadily with the beat of the music.

Paul laughed good-naturedly as he clasped his drink to keep it from taking a short dive into his lap. "Some things never change," he said, sipping his brew.

"In some circles this place would be considered seedy." Matt chuckled. "But that's what gives the lounge its character," he added with Harlem gusto.

They tapped bottle necks. "To the Lenox Lounge, whose music can't be topped," Paul toasted.

"May many more springs sprout from their chairs," Matt added, easing over to avoid a painful accident.

Paul bobbed his head to the music and checked out the clientele, then turned to Matt.

"So, what's been happening, man? You seem a little offbeat the past couple of days. Everything cool?"

Matt took a long swallow of his beer. "Yeah, yeah. Guess I'm a little overworked."

"Not you. Not the Hawkman, swooping down on unsuspecting tax-payers," Paul said with light-hearted amusement.

Any other time Matt would have laughed, would have thought it was funny. Not tonight. He wasn't quite sure what it was that he wanted to say, but he knew he needed to talk, sort out his feelings.

"You ever think about what we do, Paul?"

Paul's bottle of beer halted just before it reached his mouth. "What do you mean?"

Matt shrugged. "You know, do you ever look at some of the destruction we cause to people's lives?"

Paul's eyebrows flicked for a moment in thought.

"I can't. If I did, I would have quit a long time ago. Do I ever feel guilty or bad about the mistakes that people make and we benefit from? Yeah. Absolutely." He took a sip of beer. "That's one of the reasons why I got out of individual cases and moved to corporate. At least then I can look at it as a 'thing' and not a person." He glanced at Matt. "Why, what's going on? Don't tell me you're starting to believe all those awful rumors about the IRS," he joked, attempting to lighten the suddenly somber mood.

Matt looked away. "Maybe they're not rumors at all," he said dully.

"What's gotten into you, man? This doesn't sound like you."

Matt contemplated the wisdom of spilling his guts to Paul. But who else did he have to talk with? No one. He'd built his life around his job to the exclusion of everything else. When he was married, he worked so hard to make a life for his family, obsessively worked. And then one day, he woke up and found that all he had left *was* his job. So he worked harder to ease the pain and loneliness. Now here he was, possibly realizing for the first time it was all for nothing.

"I met a client," Matt began, and told Paul all about the doubts he'd been having lately about his life and his profession and how it all came to a head when Della Frazier walked through the door.

"Man," Paul said, shaking his head, "you're looking for trouble. What you need to do is give her case to another examiner—quick."

"So they can tear her to shreds? No way. She's a decent woman, Paul."

"They all are—basically. But we don't take them home for drinks and dinner."

"But she's responsible for a whole staff and—"

"Do you hear yourself? You don't know this woman from a picket fence and you're willing to jeopardize not just your job, but your career on a whim, a maybe. What if we're right and she's wrong?"

Matt stared Paul straight in the eye. "This time I don't think so."

A slow smile crept across Paul's wide mouth. "Well, it must be snowing down below, 'cause Matt Hawkins finally found his lost conscience. Let the choir say, 'Amen!' This day deserves a toast, my man." Paul signaled for the waitress to bring them two more beers.

Paul leaned forward. "So, who is the mystery woman that put some soul back in Matt Hawkins?"

———————

Della lay across her mint green comforter and stared up at the ceiling, her hands pressed against her flat stomach. A light breeze blew in from the partially opened window. In the background, Billie Holiday belted out "Ain't Nobody's Business" on the CD player.

"That's the truth," Della muttered, stretching her legs toward the ceiling, part of her evening exercise ritual. "One, two, one, two," she puffed, raising and lowering them.

It wasn't anybody's business how she handled this whole tax mess. She had to do what she thought was best—for everyone.

But Ruthie and Reggie had an entirely different idea. The way they ranted and raved after the staff meeting you would have thought she'd made a pact with the devil himself, instead of a simple appointment to see Matt Hawkins.

"Dee, have you completely lost your mind?" Ruthie squealed, totally flabbergasted by Della's apparent lunacy. "This isn't like you to take up with the enemy."

Reggie strutted back and forth, periodically giving her the evil eye, his brilliant orange silk shirt and matching slacks bright as neon in Times Square. "Well, just stick me with a fork, 'cause I'm done," he suddenly burst out with an exaggerated toss of his head.

For a moment Della felt like an errant child being chastised for her misdeeds by her overbearing parents.

But the deal was, she was in charge. It was her shop. Her decision.

"Listen, if the man said he was willing to help, I'm going to take him at his word. 'Cause right now, boys and girls, we need all the help we can get. It's just that simple."

Ruthie planted her hands on her hips and peered at her longtime friend through narrowed eyes. "Did he try to put the move on you? Is that the deal?"

"Ruthie, please. Give me some credit. I—"

"I just hope that man's looks and sexy voice haven't scrambled your brain. Don't let all that get in the way of your good judgment. That's all I'm saying. You know how those fine brothers can confuse a sistah from time to time. Have you sayin' and doin' thangs that would make yo mama shame," she said heaping on a deep Southern accent. "He is fine. You know that, right?"

Della refused to laugh.

"And he smells good, too," Reggie added.

They all burst out laughing.

# CHAPTER SIX

For reasons she didn't want to contemplate, Della dressed with extra care. She'd spent the better part of the morning rifling through her extensive wardrobe to select the perfect outfit.

She certainly didn't want to come off too flashy, but she didn't want to appear too stiff and formal, either.

Finally, she settled on a magenta-colored linen coat dress, with gold buttons down its center with an appropriate V-neck—and the perfect length, right at her knees. Strappy, cream-colored sandals with an easy-walking two-inch heel and matching purse completed her attire.

She'd set her hair on jumbo rollers the night before and it tumbled in soft curls around her face, gently caressing her shoulders. A stroke of coral lipstick and a quick brush of mascara and she was ready.

Blowing out a breath, she appraised her image in the full-length mirror. She smiled—satisfied.

As she drove along the Manhattan streets heading for Midtown, she realized that part of her anxiety had nothing to do with the reason for their clandestine meeting, but more to do with seeing Matt Hawkins again.

She could never admit it to Ruthie and Reggie, but she was truly attracted to Matt, even in the midst of all that was going on. That worried her. Suppose Ruthie was right. Suppose she was letting his good looks twist her thinking. And if she was letting her underfed libido take over, she could be leaving herself totally vulnerable.

Della made the turn onto the FDR Drive and sped along the winding thoroughfare. They were right, she concluded, wheeling around a slow-moving station wagon. This was business. Her business. She had to put her irrational feelings aside and think with her head. And that's exactly what she intended to do.

---

They'd agreed to meet at B. Smith's on Eighth Avenue, the much-publicized restaurant owned by former model-turned-mega-entrepreneur Barbara Smith.

Of course, parking was impossible, and after circling the block three times, Della finally gave up and parked in the overpriced garage.

Upon arriving at the classy Midtown establishment, Della found it to be quite busy for so early in the day. She'd expect this type of crowd during the dinner hour. From her vantage point, most of the tables were full, and waiters and waitresses were in steady demand.

She walked over to the reception table to find out if Matt had arrived, and spotted him coming toward her.

Inexplicably, a warmth rode through her like a galloping pony let loose on the pasture. It built in intensity until her face was afire and her hands grew damp. How was it that he could make her feel this way with just his appearance?

Looking at her, all the tension and pent-up frustrations evaporated, Matt realized. There was a gentleness about Della Frazier that belied her strength. She'd mysteriously short-circuited his brain from the first time he'd seen her. How in the world was he going to think logically when the mere idea of her had him willing to risk it all?

He had to pull himself together. This was business, nothing more.

"You're right on time," Matt said. "I have a table in the back." He turned without further preamble and headed toward their table.

This was ridiculous, Della thought, her heels clicking rhythmically against the tiles. Here she was, a grown woman, with her heart aflutter like a schoolgirl. She put on her game face and slid into the booth.

"Would you like to order something?" Matt asked.

"An iced tea would be fine."

Matt signaled for the waitress. "One iced tea and a Perrier with lime."

Hmm. Health nut, Della observed. Probably as obsessive about his health as he was about his job. From the looks of his body beneath the midnight blue suit, it paid off.

"So, where do we begin?" Della asked, needing to land on firm ground as soon as possible.

"What I intend to do is go through our computer files, see if there was some sort of clerical error."

Della laughed derisively. "Clerical error. I thought you said the IRS didn't make mistakes, Mr. Hawkins."

"I also said I would help you. Now, if you've changed your mind—"

"Why are you doing this? Why are you helping me?"

Matt looked at her for a long, dreamy moment. The corner of his mouth flickered with the beginning of a smile. "I'm not really sure, Ms. Frazier." He gazed down at his hands, then back into her probing eyes. "This isn't something I usually do. Actually, it's not something I've ever done."

Her voice softened. "Why now?"

The softness of her voice, the sincerity in her warm eyes, stirred him. How could he tell her about the battle he'd been having with his conscience, the slow awakening from the dead state he'd been in for the past five years? How could he tell her that when he heard her voice, then met her in person, something inside him came alive—and that it frightened him? He couldn't. She'd think he was a fool. And that he couldn't have.

"I really don't see what difference that makes, Ms. Frazier. You're the one with the problem. Now, we can either fix it or discuss my reasons why. Your choice."

Della gritted her teeth. For a New York minute she'd almost thought he was human.

"Everyone has reasons for what they do, Mr. Hawkins," she said, tight-lipped. "If you don't care to share yours, that's absolutely fine with me." She picked up her menu. "I always find it best to know who I'm dealing with." She snapped the menu open and proceeded to scan what was available for lunch, totally ignoring him.

Matt blinked, struck by her sharp tone. She actually sounded hurt, offended by his comments. But why should his reasons matter to her? Anyone else in her place would be grateful to have his help, no questions asked. Not Della Frazier.

"It seems to me," she said suddenly, slapping the menu on the table, "you know everything about who I am. You know how much money I make, where I live, my dependents, how long I've been working, right down to how many pairs of panties I've bought over the years." Matt visibly flinched. "You've crept into every corner of my life, with your forms, forms, and more forms. Everything there is to know about me is laid out on your charts, graphs, and calculator tape." She swallowed and plunged ahead. "All I know about you is your name. Is it a crime to want to know more?"

He felt the bee sting of her verbal assault, and the point of entry began to throb with the truth of her accusation. Just like that she could make him take hard looks at himself. And every time he did, he didn't like who he saw. She was right, he knew it, but it had been so long since he'd been able to share himself with anyone, longer than anyone really cared to know. For the most part, people were too turned off by what he did for a living and generally steered clear of any long-term involvement. Those who did give him the time of day usually did so because of the lifestyle he could provide; great meals, mini-vacations and expensive gifts. Neither option left a good taste in his mouth. So instead he made his work his world. Numbers and papers couldn't hurt you. They couldn't leave you or make you feel that all you'd done had been for nothing.

"I live on Central Park West," he said slowly, afraid but exhilarated by the chance he was taking. "In a co-op apartment that my . . . ex-wife and I bought about fifteen years ago. I graduated from Fordham University with a master's degree in accounting." He looked across at Della, then back down at his hands, which gripped his glass. "I have a daughter, Lisa, who recently turned twenty-three. My former wife doesn't work and doesn't have intentions of remarrying. I don't date often." He chuckled. "I can't remember the last date I was on, to tell you the truth." He took a long swallow of his drink, then gazed out of the window.

"I have a daughter, too. Chauncie. She just got married to a wonderful man, Drew Lennox. Actually, they're on their honeymoon right now. In Hawaii."

Matt smiled. "I hope my daughter will settle down one day. Every week she has another career choice."

"Oh, please." Della waved her hand. "Let's not talk about our children and career choices. Chauncie swore she would be the greatest actress since Dorothy Dandridge. Couldn't concentrate on a real job to save her life. Every day I thank the Lord that she met Drew. He really had a stabilizing effect on her. I thought I was going to support her for the rest of her life."

Matt nodded in understanding. "What about . . . your husband?"

Della pressed her lips together. "He left me about eleven years ago—for his much younger administrative assistant. That's when I decided it was time for me to get my own life. I went to cosmetology school, finished, and started working at Rosie's shortly after they opened. I've been there ever since."

"And you took over the shop?"

"Yes. Not too long ago, as a matter of fact. Louis, the original owner, turned it over to me when he remarried. He was Rosie's husband, God rest her soul."

Matt frowned for a moment. Something about what she had said nagged at him, but he couldn't put his finger on it.

"I've pretty much been running the shop for years anyway." She shrugged. "But it's a great feeling to walk into your own business with your name on the door."

"Was it your idea to add on the extension?"

Della beamed with pride. "Yes. I thought it would be great to have a place for the women to relax and chat, have a light snack away from the hum of the dryers. And then in the evenings it would be open to the public. It's hooked up with a small stage, great audio equipment, and a kitchen in the back. The grand opening is scheduled in three weeks." All at once the light went out of her eyes. "At least we were planning the opening, until this came up. It will probably be postponed indefinitely now."

"Maybe not. We're going to work on this, together, remember?"

Della looked into his eyes. "Do you really think there's a chance that this is just one colossal mistake? Please tell me the truth, not what you think I want to hear. I'm a big girl."

"There are no guarantees . . . Della. Can I call you Della?"

She nodded.

"In the worst-case scenario, if we find that the shop does owe the money, we'll work out a payment plan. One that you can handle."

"I can't lose my shop . . . Matt. I can't. I've sunk everything I have into it. It means everything to me."

Matt reached across the table and touched her hand. For a moment they were riveted by the electricity that ricocheted back and forth between them.

"You won't lose your shop, Della. I promise."

She pressed forward. "But you don't know that?"

"Think positive. In my business, I've seen people in worse predicaments than this, believe me. It can be done."

"Are you ready to order now?" a waitress asked.

Matt looked to Della.

"I'd like the grilled chicken with the honey dijon sauce and a house salad."

"I'll have the same," Matt said.

The waitress retrieved the menus and walked off.

Matt raised his glass. "To the success of Della's House of Style."

"May it see many more days to come," Della added, touching her glass to his.

He gazed at her before bringing his glass to his lips. "Are you seeing anyone, Della Frazier?"

Della's hand stopped midway and her heart knocked in her chest. "No." She swallowed. "Are you, Mr. Hawkins?"

Matt smiled, slowly. "To new beginnings," he said in his rich bass voice.

*Lord have mercy,* she thought, giddy with delight. *Ruthie and Reggie are going to have a natural fit.*

# CHAPTER SEVEN

All the while that Della prepared for work, the one thing on her mind was Matt Hawkins, and their lunch-date meeting the previous day. The way he looked, the laughter that could suddenly spark in his eyes, the sensation of his hand on hers, and most of all the fact that he wasn't some callous, mean-spirited man, resonated within her. Rather, he was a man who'd been hurt, devastated by the loss of his family, and the only way he knew how to handle his pain was through his work, and sadly by transferring some of his pain onto the people he worked with. Did that make him evil, unworthy? No, it made him human. At least that's what she believed.

She got the sense from talking with Matt that since his divorce there hadn't been anyone that he was close with—not a woman, at least—in a relationship where he was able to be himself. And the longer he lived his life that way, the easier it became to lose his soul. His loneliness and withdrawal from relationships was something she could easily identify with. In her case she maintained a relationship with her daughter, she had good friends, and she had her business to sustain her. Matt wasn't that lucky.

Since her own divorce, her first goal had been to change her life. Then, when she began working at the shop, it had been to transform others. Maybe it was only in subtle ways, like a new rinse or an updated cut. It was turning a frown into a smile. Easing a long day with some girl-talk. Making everyone who walked through the door feel special. But ultimately it was about creating a level of trust between herself and the clients, which allowed her to work her magic.

She smiled as she stepped into her heels. It had been a while since she'd had to work her charm with a man. Matt Hawkins was a prime candidate for a life makeover, and she was just the one to take him through the steps of transformation.

---

O h, I get it," Reggie said. "You're going to throw him some whip appeal, jiggle his mind so bad he won't be able to add up all those numbers you owe." He pursed his lips and stared her down.

Della sucked her teeth and added insult to injury by rolling her eyes. "When have you ever known me to be *that* kind of woman, Reginald Davis?"

"Ooh, girl, when you call me by my full name, I know I'm in trouble." He sauntered across the room, plopped down in a chair, and crossed his leather-clad legs. "Consider me duly chastised. But," he added under his breath, "desperate times call for desperate measures."

"Don't think I didn't hear that, Reggie," Della countered, and rounded her desk.

"Then please explain this to me, Dee. I don't get it. This man is in the process of dismantling your life, pulling the rug out from under you, and you're talking about cooking the brother a home-cooked meal and giving him a rubdown. Tell me what's wrong with this picture."

"It's . . . it's not that simple, Reggie. I wish I could explain. It's just a gut feeling I have about him, who he really is beneath the tight collar and the red tape."

Reggie leaned forward. "But, Della, hon, think about this scenario for one minute. What if you go through all this, put your heart, your time, and your soul on the line for this man, and he still winds up being the one to take this shop from you? What then? How are you going to feel? Are you willing to risk everything on a hunch?"

Della inhaled deeply. The same questions had plagued her all night and into the morning. *What if?* "I'm not going to lose this shop, Reg. I know that in my heart. Whatever it takes to keep it, that's what I'm going to do. I won't let you all down. And yes, I'm willing to take the risk." She slowly shook her head. "It's been so long, Reggie, since I've felt anything for any man. A very long time. I've been too busy, or too scared, or too something. And then here he comes, Matt Hawkins, of all the people in the world, and my heart just stood still, Reg. I couldn't help it and I don't want to." Her eyes filled.

Reggie got up and came around to her side of the desk, draping his arm around her shoulder. She pressed her head against his chest. "Hon, if this is what you want, you know I'm behind you one hundred percent. But I'm telling you now, if Mr. Dark and Lovely breaks your heart, he'll wish I really was the Avon lady when I come knocking on his door."

Della sniffed and laughed softly against Reggie's chest. "That's why I love ya, Reg. You always know what to say."

He gently patted her shoulders. "So, Ms. Dee, what's the plan . . . ?"

---

Matt worked right through lunch, going over all the computer information he had on hand about Della's tax situation, and still couldn't find where the discrepancy arose. This one time he didn't want to be right. After talking with her and spending those few hours with her at the restaurant, he was more convinced than ever that Della Frazier was the kind of woman he wanted in his life. He wanted to be the one who rode in on the white horse to save the day. He wanted her to admire him, to think of him kindly. Della's opinion mattered. He wanted to make this right—for her.

But how? He banged his fist on his desk in utter frustration, just as Paul poked his head in the door.

"Hey, buddy, any luck?"

Matt looked up with a scowl on his face. "None."

Paul closed the door behind him and stepped in. "Maybe you're going to have to accept the truth."

Matt turned off this computer. "And what might that be?"

"That Ms. Frazier owes the money. Plain and simple. It happens, Matt. You know that as well as I do. It happens every day."

Matt massaged the back of his neck. "Yeah, I know. I just don't want to believe it, that's all."

"So what are you going to do? You know the monthly audit is coming up in two weeks. You're going to have a lot of explaining to do if you can't get this straightened out by then. Burke isn't going to sit still for some lame reasoning that you like this woman so you think she's right and we're wrong. All he wants is results."

Matt had been so preoccupied with finding a solution to Della's dilemma, he'd completely forgotten about the monthly audit. All of the examiners had to provide a verbal and written update on all of their cases for the month, with a grand total of the money expected from each client. Horace Burke would have done well in the Marines. He was ruthless and had no qualms about browbeating his staff, embarrassing them in front of everyone else, and making life as miserable as possible for those who couldn't cut it.

Fortunately, Matt had never come under Burke's gun, but he'd been witness to what Burke had done to some of his colleagues over the years and was always thankful it had never been him. There's nothing worse than seeing a grown man cry.

"I'll have it together by then," Matt said.

"I sure hope so. Anyway, if there's anything I can do, let me know. I have a pretty light week coming up."

"Thanks, man."

"So are you going to see her again?"

"We met yesterday for lunch. And I, uh asked her to join me this weekend. There's a jazz concert in Bryant Park."

Paul's eyes widened in shock. "A date? Are you crazy? It's one thing to try to work out some glitches in a client's tax statement. That's bad enough. But dating one of your clients . . . Have you totally lost your mind? If Burke finds out, he'll hang your butt out to dry."

"Then he won't find out."

"Get yourself off this case, Matt. I'm warning you. This is nothing but a disaster waiting to happen."

"I can't do that."

"Well, you better do something. What if she's just using you to make things light on herself? You ever think of that?"

"Della's not like that. She—"

"You don't know what she's like. You barely know the woman. When people's backs are against the wall, they're liable to do anything to save themselves."

Matt had no answer, no comeback. He knew what his friend was saying was true. He'd been told all kinds of lies, had all kinds of promises made to him from people in the same position as Della. But he couldn't believe that Della was that devious.

"What in the world did she do to you?" Paul asked, totally perplexed.

Matt looked at Paul. "She made me remember that I do have a heart. That I'm not this unfeeling pencil pusher. She woke me up, Paul. And to tell you the truth, I don't want to go back to sleep again."

"Hmm. Just be careful, man." Paul turned toward the door. "I'd hate to see your face on *America's Most Wanted*. 'Cause Burke will hunt you down and make your life a pure hell."

"Thanks for the words of encouragement," he said, his voice dripping with sarcasm.

"That's what friends are for. See you Monday."

"Yeah, take it easy."

Matt sat there for a few minutes more, thinking about Paul's words of caution. He knew Paul was right about Burke. And suppose he was right about Della as well. Maybe she *was* planning to use him. He'd opened himself up to her, opened himself up to hurt and possible repercussions at his job.

He grabbed his jacket from the back of his chair and headed for the door. He'd settle all the *what ifs* once and for all.

———————

D ella sat in the chair at Reggie's station. The crowd in the shop had thinned considerably since earlier in the day and several of the technicians had already finished with their last customers.

Reggie draped a black plastic cape around Della's neck and shoulders. He ran his hands through Della's mane of hair from the roots to get a better look.

"Only a few *unwanteds*," he said.

Music drifted in from the speakers tucked away in the walls.

Della leaned back and closed her eyes. "Just work your magic, Reg. When I open my eyes, I *want* them to be a distant memory."

"You got it." He reached into his cabinet of rinses and dyes and mixed a bottle of bronze and cinnamon together. Satisfied with the results, he began applying it to her hair beginning at the roots.

"So how did lunch go with Mr. Man yesterday?"

"Fine."

"Any news?" he asked.

"No changes," she answered dreamily.

"What does that mean?" he quizzed, massaging the rinse through her hair.

"We talked."

"About what?"

"Reggie," she sighed in exasperation.

"Don't keep me in suspense, Ms. Dee." He piled her hair atop her head and put a plastic cap on it, then took a seat next to her. "Inquiring minds want to know."

"Inquiring minds are just busybodies with a new name."

"Fine, don't tell me."

She could tell he was pouting, even with her eyes closed. She bit back a smile.

"We're going to listen to some music tomorrow night," she confessed. "If you must know."

"Music, hmm, that's always a way to soothe the savage beast. You go, Ms. Dee. Use everything you got. Then when you have him where you want him, go in for the kill."

"Do you really think that's what it's all about, Reggie? I'm a little too old to play those kinds of games."

"Hey, all is fair in love and war, Della. And believe me, Ms. Girl, this is war. The man is out to ruin you if he can have his way."

"I don't believe that."

"Well, tell me, what do you believe?"

"I believe he's a man doing his job. Maybe an ugly one, but doing his job nonetheless. But that doesn't make him some sort of monster. He's really a decent guy, Reggie."

"'You are what you do,' as the saying goes."

"That's not the saying, Reg. It's, 'You are what you eat.'"

"Whatever."

Della sighed. "I thought you were on my side."

"I am. I just don't want to see you get your hopes up about this guy only to get your feelings hurt."

"Why would you think I would get my feelings hurt?"

"The bottom line is, Dee, if he has to choose between his job and you, he'll choose his job. That's his bread and butter."

"Is that what you think, too, Della?"

Della's eyes flew open and she spun around in the chair, nearly knocking Reggie over. "Matt."

Matt came closer, glanced briefly at a stunned Reggie, then focused his total attention on Della. "Is it?"

Blaize peeked down the row to catch the goings-on, then nudged Melody, whose mouth dropped open.

Della stared at Matt for several moments. Every negative thing that had been said about Matt and the dismal prospects for a relationship between them buzzed in her head. And then she thought of the Matt

Hawkins who warmed her heart, who'd let her into a dark part of his life, who was willing to risk his job to help her.

"No, I don't," she answered, more sure about that than she'd ever been about anything.

A slow smile moved like daybreak across Matt's handsome face. He walked right up to her, then glanced around at the audience. "If you all would excuse us for just a moment . . ." He looked down into Della's brown eyes, lowered his head, and placed a Kodak-moment kiss on her lips.

Lights went off and on in rapid succession in Della's head and she thanked the stars above that she was sitting down. She forgot all about the fact that she was being seduced in the middle of a beauty parlor with everyone watching. All she could think about was how good his lips felt, how magnificent his hands felt caressing her face. And she didn't care who was looking.

Reluctantly Matt eased away, but he didn't release the hold he had on her face. He stared into her eyes. "I'm going to go home and change. How much time do you think you'll need?"

Della swallowed. She looked up at Reggie, as she'd lost all sense of time and space.

Reggie shrugged helplessly. "About an hour."

"I'll see you in an hour." He stepped back and turned to go, then stopped. "Do you like seafood?"

Della nodded. "Yes."

"Great. See you in an hour." He looked around at the stunned faces. "Good night, everyone." He walked out, closing the door softly behind him.

Reggie planted his hand on his hip. "Well, Ms. Dee, the only thing missing from that scene was Mr. Man sweeping you out of your chair and carrying you off to the applause of the staff," he teased.

Della slapped his arm. "Just do my hair, Reggie, and let me worry about being swept away." She looked up at him and grinned. "That would have been awesome, though."

Blaize and Melody came scurrying over.

"Who—was—that?" Blaize asked.

Della cleared her throat. "Mr. Hawkins . . . from the IRS."

"Get outta town. Well, work your magic, girl. And find out if he has any friends who look just like him."

"I wouldn't mind an audit from him, myself," Melody chimed in.

"A government man, huh?" Blaize mused, looking Della up and down. "Well, sister girl, let's give him a run for his 1040s. I'll do your nails." She spun toward Melody. "Mel, get Tricia from upstairs and tell her Ms. Dee needs an instant facial and neck massage." She glared at Reggie. "Well, don't just stand there, Reg, get the woman's hair done. We got a date with the *government man!*"

All Della could do was sit back and relax as everyone ran around waiting on her and fussing with each other. Della sighed as Tricia applied a mask to her face. It was wonderful to have friends.

# CHAPTER EIGHT

Like proud parents sending their only daughter off to the prom, Della's staff stood at the door of the shop grinning and waving as she slid into Matt's car.

"Interesting group," Matt commented once they were out of earshot.

"That they are." Della chuckled lightly, fighting down her embarrassment.

"They must love you a lot."

"It's mutual."

Matt glanced at her from the corner of his eye, while they waited for the red light to change. Each time he was in her company, his estimation and admiration for her grew. It took a special kind of person to generate the level of support and respect that Della received from her staff. They weren't just employees, they were friends. He wished he could say the same about the people he worked with. He couldn't. For the most part, it was a cutthroat kind of business. One person trying to outdo the other. Sure, people respected his ability to get his job done, but he couldn't count a true friend among them, except Paul. That was a sad testament to his life. And part of him envied the camaraderie Della shared with her staff—her friends.

"I, uh, hope I didn't embarrass you earlier," he said, not daring to look at her.

Della felt her face heat, remembering the titillating kiss in the shop. "What if I told you that you did?" She angled her body to the side.

Matt turned ready to apologize. "I—"

"And what if I told you I like it? What if I told you I wanted to try it again to make sure I wasn't imagining things?" *Did I just say what I think I said?* she thought, suddenly mortified by her uncharacteristically bold attitude. He must think she was a lonely, approaching-middle-aged woman on the prowl. Oh, Lord. She could just die.

Was that a taunting sparkle in her eyes or the gleam of real desire? He couldn't be sure. It had been a long time since a woman had interested him enough for him to care one way or the other. He'd taken a chance on everything else having to do with Della Frazier. No sense in changing now.

"What if I told you it was the real thing?" Matt asked, his voice heavy with trepidation. "And there's more where that came from . . . if you're willing to take a chance on me."

Her heart thumped mercilessly and felt as if it were stuck in her throat as she pushed the words out. "It . . . has been about taking chances since we met, Matt. Hasn't it?"

Matt reached out and stroked her cheek.

"The light's green," Della said dreamily.

"In more ways than one."

---

For the balance of the ride to lower Manhattan, Matt drove with one hand on the wheel and held Della's with the other.

It was a gentle touch, Della thought, enjoying the tiny charges that scurried up and down her arm—secure, not overpowering or controlling. And that single gesture gave her a new look at Matt Hawkins. He had a tender side, a side she was certain he rarely displayed. She wondered what other secrets rested beneath his tough-guy exterior.

---

Much to Della's delight, Matt drove them downtown to the South Street Seaport. It was a perfect night to be on the boardwalk, watching the lights from the multitude of cafés and shops glimmer along the folds of the sea. Couples of all ages and ethnicities walked hand-in-hand, hugging and stealing kisses. Frazzled fathers and mothers chased their children in and out of stores as they searched for the perfect family spot to have dinner. Music drifted along the night air coming from the open doorways of the restaurants and music outlets.

At first Matt and Della walked companionably beside each other, taking in the sights, enjoying the atmosphere. It seemed only natural that he would take her hand, ease her close, and that she would look up at him, her eyes bright with acceptance, and gently squeeze his hand in hers. It was easy, comfortable, and exhilarating all at the same time. Most of all, it was new.

"This was a wonderful idea," Della said. "I love the water."

"So do I. I spent the first ten years of my life in the Caribbean."

Della's eyes widened. "Really? Which island?"

"Barbados."

"Get outta here. You'd never know it. There's not a trace of an accent."

"I've been here most of my life. I guess I learned to adapt, so I could fit in."

"Yeah, I guess you would have to. Kids can be so cruel sometimes."

"You get used to it. But I had my share of torture before my skin toughened. I can still go back to my roots, when need be, mon," he said with the perfect combination of island charm and musical lilt.

Della tossed her head back and laughed. "You're good . . . almost authentic," she teased.

"I'm better than good," he tossed back, stopping suddenly and pulling Della close. He looked down into her startled eyes, letting his gaze trail across her face, down the slender column of her neck, then back up again. "I'm the real thing, Della." His thumb delicately stroked her bottom lip.

Della's body began to tremble from the inside out and she didn't care who was looking or what they thought about a woman her age being seduced in the middle of the boardwalk in New York on a big Friday night.

His kiss was like finding an oasis in the middle of the desert, Della thought when his lips touched hers and his muscled arms wrapped comfortably around her waist. She sank into him, drinking him in, inhaling his scent, the taste of him. She felt almost light-headed with joy and didn't want it to stop, but knew that it should.

"I think we may be causing a scene, Mr. Hawkins," Della whispered against his mouth.

"Maybe some other time, with some other woman, I might have cared," he responded, his voice low and intimate, settling down in the center of her. His gaze continued to heat her flesh. "Not with you."

"I'm not sure I know what's happening anymore between us, with me. I—I've never—"

"Felt this way so suddenly about anyone before," Matt said, finishing her sentence.

Della flashed a coy smile. "Or met anyone who could read my mind."

Matt ran his finger down her nose. "I was going to say the very same thing," he teased, hugging her to him, relishing the feel of her body pressed against his before stepping back. "But being the gentleman that I am, I'm going to take you to dinner as promised and keep my personal wants in check."

"And what might those wants be?" Della asked, feeling totally free and daring.

"Why don't I tell you all about them over dinner and some good music under the stars?"

"I like the sound of that."

Matt took her hand and headed for a boat docked on the pier.

———

They boarded the boat and were quickly seated at a table with a glorious view of the river. From the deck above, they could hear the jazz band playing its rendition of Ellington's classic "Take the A Train."

Dinner was a seafood soufflé—the house special—with a side garden salad, saffron rice, and a bottle of chilled red wine.

Della and Matt shared the short-lived histories of their respective marriages, the effect marriage had on them, and their children.

"Chauncie grew up not being able to attach herself to anything or anyone," Della said. She took a sip of her wine. "I suppose it was her way of keeping herself from being hurt. Then she turned to the theater and acting. A world of pretend."

"But she finally settled down. She's on her honeymoon, isn't she?"

Della nodded. "Thank the stars for Drew. It was the best thing I could have done, getting the two of them together."

"My daughter swears I'm the devil in disguise," Matt said morosely.

"Why?"

"She hates what I do, but she loves what it can provide for her."

Della leaned closer, resting on her forearms. "Why do you do it, Matt? I mean, the more I talk with you, spend time with you, you seem so completely different from the kind of man you project."

"To be truthful, for a long time, especially after my marriage collapsed, I *was* that guy. I was hurt, disappointed, and alone." He looked toward the glistening water. "Everything I did, the hours I put in, was for them, my wife and daughter. I wanted to give them the best, something my father had never provided for me and my mother. I didn't want that for my family. So I worked relentlessly to the exclusion of everything, and the very thing that I was working for is what I lost. I was so consumed with providing and giving things that I ignored what they really needed—me."

"Matt . . . I'm so sorry. You don't have to talk about this."

"After they were gone," he continued as if he didn't hear her, "I threw myself into my work with a vengeance. I'm ashamed to admit this, but I enjoyed making people as miserable and unhappy as I was."

Della inwardly cringed.

"Can I get either of you anything else?" a waiter asked, suddenly appearing like an apparition.

"Nothing for me," Della said.

"No, thanks," Matt replied.

Della focused in on Matt. "Why the turnaround?"

He told her how he'd been feeling recently, the painful statement from his daughter, and then meeting her.

"I knew it was time for a change, Della. And maybe it was this job of mine that brought us together, but I damned sure don't want it to be what comes between us." He covered her hand with his.

Della looked into his eyes, a wicked smile on her full mouth. "Do they have dancing on this showboat?"

His right brow slowly lifted. "They sure do. On the top deck."

"Well, let's see if you're as good on the dance floor as you are with my W-2s."

---

For the rest of the evening they forgot about what had brought them together. They danced under the stars and talked about movies they loved and hated, books they'd read, childhood mishaps, and places they wanted to travel to—one day.

They fit when they danced, one body in tune with the other. Their laughter and soft whisperings were in perfect harmony. And their time together moved as slow and gentle as the waves that cradled the ship.

When they stood in front of Della's front door, the kiss they shared was inevitable, the only ending to an unforgettable evening.

"We've got to find a way to make things work between us, Della," Matt said with an urgency in his voice, cupping her face in his hands. "No matter what happens with this tax thing—I don't want it to come between us."

"But what if it does, Matt? How will we be able to look at each other if I lose everything? How?"

"Please, just trust me. I'll find a way—somehow." His eyes glided over her stricken expression. "I feel alive again, Della, for the first time in years. It's because of you and the possibilities that you represent. I'm not willing to let that go."

Reluctantly, Della stepped back. She looked downward, unable to face him with what she was about to say.

"You may have to, Matt. Face it. Whatever this is that's happening between us is making us lose sight of reality."

"What are you saying, Della?"

She swallowed down the knot in her throat.

"Look at me, Della, please. What are you telling me?"

Slowly she met his stare. "I'm saying . . . that I don't know if I can separate the two. A part of me wants to take this relationship and run with it as far as we can take it. Another part of me, the practical side, says to cut my losses before I get hurt—really hurt."

Matt tugged on his bottom lip with his teeth. "So, you're telling me you want out."

"Before it goes too far."

"I see. So what you said in the shop, our evening together tonight, everything I've said to you means nothing." His stomach knotted. The corner of his mouth curved in a sad half-smile. "I thought, at least I'd hoped, you were tougher than that. You don't give me the impression of being the type of woman who'd run at the first sign of trouble. I guess I was wrong."

Della stood there, unable to say what was really in her heart, the fact that she was falling too fast and too hard for Matt Hawkins, and that he had the power to not only break her spirit, but her heart. And it frightened her—frightened her even more than the possibility of losing the shop. She couldn't risk that kind of pain, that kind of loss, not at this stage of her life. She didn't know if she'd recover.

"I, uh, guess I'd better be going."

Della pressed her lips together to keep them from trembling.

"Thanks for a great evening." He turned to leave. He wanted to run before he said something really foolish. Maybe she was right, he thought, walking down the three steps to the sidewalk. Maybe they both should cut their losses. Then why did he feel so damned lousy if it was so right?

He stopped with his hand on the handle of the car door.

When his wife left him, he didn't do anything to bring her home. He turned his back on that chapter of his life and kept going, even though it was killing him inside. Maybe it was best in that situation, but he would never know, he hadn't tried. This was different. He wouldn't make the same mistake twice.

He turned back and Della was still standing in the doorway, outlined by the soft white light from the foyer. With slow but steady determination, he returned to where he'd stood only moments earlier.

Della's eyes widened and her heart raced with anticipation. She opened her mouth to speak, but Matt held up his hand to stop her.

"I don't plan to give you up this easy. I did it once and it turned me into someone even I didn't like. I don't intend to do it again." He stepped closer. "Now, maybe you think it's going to be easy to just let this go as if it never happened." He stared directly into her eyes. "I don't. And I'm going to make walking away from me the hardest thing you've ever had to do, Della Frazier."

He took her chin between his fingers, tilted it upward, and kissed her long and hard.

He let her go and stepped back, and Della would have sworn she heard fireworks, during twilight's last gleaming, stars bursting in air, the whole bit. Her head was spinning and her heart was racing so fast she could barely breathe.

"They don't call me Take-No-Prisoners Hawkins for nothing, sweetheart. Sleep well."

This time he got into his car and drove away.

Della half walked, half stumbled into her house. Her keys had fallen out of her shaky fingers so many times, the clanging was making her ears ring.

While she fumbled with the keys in the lock, she kept taking surreptitious glances over her shoulder, certain that at any moment Matt would return and assault her with another earthshaking kiss. He didn't, but she kept the feel of his lips, the power of his touch, the scent of him, the depth of his voice close to her as she prepared for bed.

When she finally drifted to sleep, it was with a smile on her lips, hope in her heart, and an itch that she desperately wanted scratched.

# CHAPTER NINE

When Della awoke Saturday morning, her first thought was of Matt and the evening they'd spent together. She felt refreshed, full of renewed energy. As she showered and got ready for her day at the shop, she hummed to herself, something she hadn't done in a while. And what she realized as she peered at her reflection in the steamed mirror was that she was happy, or at the very least on the road to happiness. Matt made her feel desirable again, a sensation that had been missing from her life for much too long. Sure, she knew she was still attractive, and there had been a few men who'd been interested in her over the years, but none had made her heart sing, her pulse pound. None had the ability to stir the embers, not the way that Matt Hawkins did.

She was taking a chance, a big chance. She was putting everything on the line in pursuit of this unexplainable sense of fulfillment. Matt did that for her, regardless of what he represented. Somehow, she decided with finality, they would find a way to work things out. They simply had to.

Now to put her own plans into action.

Della padded into her bedroom, wrapping her silk robe around her still-damp body, and reached for the phone. She punched in the seven digits and waited, tapping her foot to unheard music.

On the third ring, Matt answered.

"Hello?" he questioned, sounding suspicious.

"You don't sound like a man used to receiving calls," Della said in a teasing tone.

Matt's expression immediately softened. "To be truthful, I don't. Especially on a Saturday morning. To what do I owe the pleasure?"

"I was wondering what your schedule was like today."

"Pretty light. What did you have in mind?"

"Why don't you stop by the shop, say about noon?"

"Hmm. You're not setting me up to be attacked by your staff or anything, are you?"

"No, at least not the way you mean."

"I think I can arrange that. Are we still on for tonight at the park?"

"Absolutely."

His voice dropped a note. "How did you sleep last night?"

The question was innocuous, but the real meaning was clear.

"It was the first time in a while that I wished I hadn't spent it alone," she confessed.

"Funny," he said, "I was going to tell you the same thing."

Della smiled and felt that now-familiar rush surge through her body. "I've decided that I'm going to make it just as difficult for you to walk away from this as you were planning to do to me."

"That sounds like a challenge. I've never been one to back down from a challenge."

"I wouldn't expect anything less. So I'll see you at noon."

"Definitely."

"'Bye."

"For now." Slowly Matt hung up the phone and stretched out on his bed, cupping his hands behind his head. This was going to work out. It had to. He closed his eyes and wondered what Della had up her sleeve, just as the phone rang again. He snatched it up, sure that it was Della calling back to taunt him some more. Instead it was the last person he expected to hear from.

"Hey, man, it's Paul. Got some bad news."

Matt sat up and frowned. "What?"

"I tried to reach you last night, but I kept getting your machine. I didn't want to leave a message—"

"Spill it, Paul. What's up?"

"Horace came in after you left yesterday and went through your files. He was on some kind of tear, had a real bug up his butt. He pulled Della's file and started asking all kinds of questions as to why she hasn't started payment, and what did I know about it. He was storming through the office, carrying on like a general trying to ready his troops for battle."

"What?"

"You heard me."

"What did you tell him?"

"I didn't tell him anything. Did you think I would?" he asked, almost sounding hurt.

"Naw, man, I'm sorry. So then what?"

"He still has the file. If I were you, I'd get myself in gear and have some kind of story to tell him on Monday. He even hinted that he may move up the meeting to find out 'what the hell is going on around here,' in his own words."

"Shi—" Matt squeezed his eyes shut and tried to think.

"Have you come up with anything?" Paul asked after a pause.

"Zip."

"Hey, man, I don't know what to tell you, but your tail is on the line. You know how he can be."

"Yeah, yeah. Listen, thanks for calling. I'll figure something out."

"Talk to you later."

"Yeah."

"Matt, we've known each other a long time. I know where you've been, what you've gone through. It took you a long time to get where you are. Be careful. Think this through. With your head."

Matt heaved a sigh. "I will."

"Later."

Absently, Matt replaced the receiver. All the anticipation he'd felt for the day about to unfold went out the window. He pressed his face into his hands. What was he going to do? What was it that he'd missed? Or could it be that Della really did owe all that money? He didn't want to believe that. And he didn't want to be the one to tell her if she did. Not after all the promises he'd made. She trusted him.

He stood. There had to be something he'd missed. And he'd be damned if he didn't find it.

Quickly he threw on some clothes, put a baseball cap on his uncombed head, and dashed out.

---

Della practically floated into the shop, stopping to have a word with each and every customer, even first-time clients. She checked to make sure that they were being tended to properly and that their wait wasn't too long.

She was almost singing when she greeted the staff one by one. And even for the gregarious Della, the staff was taken aback by her high spirits and vitality—and her attire, which was entirely out of character for the stylish Della. In place of her designer suit and heels, she wore a bright white cotton shirt with the sleeves rolled half way up her arms and a pair of jeans, of all things, and sneakers. Her hair, which generally tumbled in bouncy curls to her shoulders, was pulled away from her face into a ponytail with feathery tendrils around her face, which for the most part was devoid of makeup. Della looked ten years younger.

"Mr. Man must have thrown Ms. Dee some serious whip appeal himself," Reggie muttered to Ruthie, his eyebrows rising to rigid attention.

"Shut your mouth," she said, stifling a giggle. "Good for her, is what I say. She needs somebody. Not that I'm all crazy about it being Mr. Man. But so long as he treats her right and can put that kind of smile on her face, I'm all for it."

"I suppose," Reggie said with reluctance. "I just don't want her to get hurt, that's all."

"None of us do, Reg. None of us do."

"Well, look at you, Ms. Dee," Blaize quipped, giving her a good up-and-down. "Don't we look like a new person this morning! What's the occasion?"

"Nothing special," Della replied with a sly smile. "I just thought it was time for a new look, more casual, relaxed."

"You're all that and then some, Ms. Della," said Jimmy, the delivery boy who brought the fresh supply of donuts and bagels each day.

Della turned her hundred-watt smile on him and he turned fifty shades of red. "Why, thank you, Jimmy. That's real sweet of you to notice."

"It's nothing," he mumbled, and scurried out of the door to the twittering laughter of the technicians.

"You know that young boy has a crush on you, Della," Melody said as she shampooed the head of one of her clients. "Now you almost look young enough to give him a play."

"Jailbait," one of the customers shouted from beneath a heat cap.

"You got that right," Della agreed, with laughter in her voice.

Della put her hands on her hips and surveyed the shop. Filled to the max as usual. She still couldn't believe the phenomenal business that the shop was doing. Five days a week didn't seem to be enough to accommodate everyone. They opened at ten and were there sometimes until ten at night. And when the café opened, it would get even busier. She would have to start looking for a staff, which was something she had planned to do when she got sidetracked by this tax mess. That thought brought images of Matt immediately to her mind. And instantly she felt that glow, that heat that pulsed at her center. This was crazy. She felt like an oversexed adolescent instead of a mature woman with some sense.

Well she could either stand there all day daydreaming or do what she'd intended to do. She walked over to Ruthie.

"I'm expecting Matt—"

"Oh, it's Matt now, huh?" Ruthie teased.

"Yes, miss, if you don't mind."

"Do your thing, sister. Don't mind me."

"As I was saying. I'm expecting Matt about noon. I want to give him the works, a facial, full body massage, manicure, trim, and a shave."

Ruthie fixed her face in an *Oh, yeah* expression. "Is this on the house, or what?"

"Don't worry your head about it. Just look after everything for me when he arrives and make sure he gets taken care of. I know the place is busy, but I don't want him to have to wait. Would you do that for me, please, Ruthie?"

"Sure. No problem. You're the boss."

"Thanks. You're a doll. I'll be in my office. I want to start putting together the ad for the help we'll need to get the café opened."

"Are we back on schedule?" Reggie asked.

"Matt promised he'd work it out. And I know he will."

They both watched her walk away with incredulous expressions on their faces.

"I have to admit, Reggie," Ruthie said, wrapping her client's hair around a steaming curling iron, "I've never seen her like that."

"This is better than whip appeal. I'm gonna have to look for what some of Mr. Man has myself." He chuckled.

"You need to stop," Ruthie said, laughing, but thought the very same thing.

————————

Matt sat crouched over his computer going over each detail of Della's records line by line, calculating figures, juggling numbers. He wasn't the only one working on a Saturday. Several of the other accountants were squirreled away in their offices as well. If it hadn't been for the casual attire, an observer would think it was a regular workday.

When he came in, he decided to start from the very beginning. He'd even done a search on the salon from the days when it first opened, trying to see if he could find the glitch. He even tracked Louis and Rosie Sweet's personal tax submissions to see if there was something amiss.

By the time his weary eyes looked up at the clock, it was nearly six.

Reams of paper cluttered his desk. His head pounded and his fingers were cramped from typing and scribbling.

He pressed the heel of his palm to his head. He'd totally missed his noon appointment with Della and hadn't been clear-headed enough to call and postpone. Now it was too late to go to the concert in the park. By the time he got home, showered, and shaved, it would be nearly eight o'clock.

"Damn," He shoved the papers off his desk onto the floor in a blizzard of white. He felt like hitting something. He couldn't remember being so frustrated and completely helpless.

He'd promised Della that he would work this out. She was depending on him, her staff was depending on him. And from what he could see, he'd let her down, everyone down, including himself. Big time. How was he going to explain this? Better yet, how was he going to explain his actions to his boss? And how could he ever face Della?

---

I t was nearly seven o'clock and the customers had slowed to a trickle, with only three of them left under dryers.

Della had emerged from her office every hour up until about three o'clock, when she'd stopped coming out at all.

The bounce that had been in her step, the lightness of spirit, all felt like a lead ball in her chest. Finally, when it became obvious that he wasn't going to show up and hadn't called, she'd been too embarrassed to come up front, especially after the big deal she'd made earlier.

She'd called his house several times and didn't get an answer. At first she thought maybe he'd gotten stuck in traffic, but as the hours ticked by, that notion became too ridiculous to consider. Maybe he was in an accident, she began to think, then decided that he'd better be, because no other explanation could excuse his behavior.

She felt like such a fool. She'd actually allowed herself to be swayed by his kisses, his sweet talk, and his promises of a future for the two of them. Ruthie and Reggie were right all along. She never should have let his looks and his deceptive charms rope her in. He was probably using her all along, a diversion from the drudgery of his job. She was the perfect victim. Unattached and in trouble. Thank heavens she hadn't let the relationship go further than a few passionate kisses.

Were those a put-on, too? she wondered, her heart breaking. Her stomach turned and she felt sick. Oh, Lord, she actually felt her eyes burning. She couldn't cry, she wouldn't. Not over a man. Never again.

She lowered her head onto her arms and cried anyway.

## CHAPTER TEN

Della strutted back and forth between blind rage and anguished tears. Her emotions were on a serious roller-coaster ride. Every few minutes they took another dip, another wild curve.

No one should have the power to make you feel this way, she blasted herself. She was generally in control of her emotions, kept things in perspective. But from the moment she'd met Matt Hawkins, all of her guidelines to behavior went right out the window.

She plopped down on the bed and pointed the remote toward the television, sniffing and wiping her eyes with her free hand. She'd waited until she was certain everyone had left the shop before she went home, and had only spoken to Ruthie and Reggie from behind her closed office door.

*How could he have done this to me?* she fumed. Better yet, how could she have done it to herself? She slammed the remote on the bed in concert with a Jerry Springer guest who'd just delivered a right hook to her lying boyfriend. Inexplicably Della found herself rooting and cheering for the distraught young woman. "That's it, girl, whip his tail. . . . You're right, he shouldn't have lied to you. . . . Don't listen, sister, he's just gonna lie again. . . ."

Della stared at the roaring crowd, who grew wilder by the minute as they watched the melee onstage.

"What am I doing?" she said suddenly, pointing the remote to shut off the set. "I'm just as bad as these fools on television."

She padded off to the bathroom and splashed cold water on her face. Looking up, she jerked back in alarm when she saw her reflection. Her eyes were red-rimmed and puffy and her skin looked parched.

"This is ridiculous." She splashed some more cold water on her face, then foraged around in the medicine cabinet for her cucumber cream, which she gingerly applied around her eyes. She turned on the tub and added two capfuls of almond oil and one cap of bubbles.

Out in the living room, she took a scented vanilla candle from the étagère, lit it, and placed it on the windowsill above the bathtub. Wrapping her hair in a towel, she put a Noel Pointer CD in the player and turned it up loud enough to be heard in the bathroom.

Della slipped in between the bubbles and sank down into the steamy water, letting it slowly ease the tension from her limbs. The last time she felt this way, her ex-husband David came home to tell her he was leaving her for another woman. It was that stunned, *Say what? This can't be happening to me* sensation. She'd given that man eighteen years of her life and he'd discarded it like an old shoe for a new one. But once she got herself together, David Frazier became a distant memory.

She'd taken charge of her life from that moment on and hadn't looked back. She was too old to be going through any changes about some man. So what if Matt made her feel good for a hot minute? So what if his kisses made her light-headed and his touch had her feeling like she was twenty years old again? She'd been around the block enough times to know that he was feeling it too. She emerged from the tub with a new attitude and plan. He wasn't going to get off that easy.

Pulling out her favorite fire engine–red minidress, she laid it across the bed and began to prepare for a night on the town.

---

Matt sat on the edge of his bed, staring at the phone. He'd been debating for hours about calling Della and explaining what had happened. And for each reason he came up with for calling, he found another reason not to do it. Maybe Paul was right and he should turn the case over to someone else. He was no longer thinking objectively. At least it wouldn't be him who had to drop the ax.

But that was the coward's way out, and he'd never been one to pass the buck. What he needed to do was be honest about the situation and try to explain it to Della. She had to know that he'd tried everything, and the reason why he'd been trying so hard was because he cared about her—really cared.

He supposed what was so difficult for him to deal with was the fact that he would disappoint her. He'd made a promise and failed, and failure in himself was something he couldn't swallow. But he couldn't hide out in his apartment or behind his desk. He had to face her at some point. She deserved that much.

He reached for the phone and it rang in his hand.

"Hello?"

"So you're not dead."

"Della?"

"I guess you weren't expecting to hear from me, even though I was expecting to hear from you."

"Della, I can explain everything."

"And you will. Are you dressed?"

He looked down at his jeans and wrinkled shirt, the clothes he'd been in all day. "Not really."

"Well, why don't you get yourself together and meet me in front of the Village Vanguard in an hour? Think you can do that?"

"Uh, sure. But—"

"See you in an hour. Don't be late."

Click.

Della briefly closed her eyes and prayed she knew what she was doing.

---

It was just about ten when Della pulled up in her Volvo in front of the Vanguard. Couples were filing in for the next show headlined by Wynton Marsalis and his band.

She eased into a no parking zone so she could watch the flow of traffic into the club. She was there about ten minutes when she spotted Matt coming down the block.

Her stomach started doing those little flips as she watched his approach. The man looked good, there was no denying that. He wore a cream-colored, three-button cotton knit shirt beneath a black leather jacket, with black pants. There was an assurance in his stride, the proud tilt of his head and easy body language as if he moved to a slow, intimate rhythm. She could almost hear the beat.

She smiled.

Matt stopped in front of the door and casually looked around. It was nice to know that he was looking for her, and Della wondered what he'd think when he saw her. She pulled off, drove around the block, and found a parking spot. Moments later she was turning the corner and turning heads in the process. *Yeah, she still had it.*

He turned and his mouth went dry. *Della.* She was a vision that moved toward him with total awareness as if he were the only man on earth. His hormones went on a sudden rampage and it took every ounce of willpower to keep the obvious under control.

"Glad to see you could make it," she said, stopping in front of him.

The soft, intoxicating scent of her floated to his head, invaded his pores.

"You . . . you look—"

"So do you. Ready? The show should be starting soon."

It was an exhilarating sensation to see the cool Matt Hawkins on simmer, Della thought with delight as she walked in front of him and inside the dimly lit nightclub.

They found a table and Della ordered a raspberry margarita. Matt ordered a Jack Daniel's on the rocks. Maybe a good stiff drink would take his mind off Della's legs, the dangerous dip in the front of that dress, and the come-hither look that intermittently flashed in her eyes.

He was totally confused, and suddenly felt like a pimply-faced teen in the backseat of his father's car trying to figure out what to do with the prom queen. What was going on?

"The only thing I can think of is that somehow we missed each other earlier. Or maybe I was mistaken in thinking we had plans for this evening," Della said over the rim of her glass.

"There was no mistake." He leaned forward and looked into her eyes. "I should have called."

"You ready to tell me why you didn't?" She licked her lips, enjoying the fruity taste on her mouth and the look in Matt's eyes.

He swallowed a gulp of his drink. "I have some bad news and I didn't know how to tell you, not after the promise I made."

"Whatever it is, you could have called."

He lowered his head and nodded. "You're right." He took a breath and then began to explain everything that had happened, beginning with the phone call from Paul.

With every word, Della's heart sank. Yet at the same time, her admiration for Matt grew. He wasn't a coldhearted bureaucrat, but a man who cared—cared about her. Her heart beat a bit faster in her chest.

Della reached across the table and took his hand in hers. "It's not your fault, Matt. You did everything you could. And I can't let you jeopardize your job for me. I won't let you do that." She sighed. "I'll just have to find a way to pay the money. Maybe a bank loan or something."

"I could loan you the money."

Her eyes widened in astonishment. "You can't be serious."

"Hey, if you need it, consider it done. We could work it out as a business loan. It's going to be hell for you to get a loan from the bank when they see that you owe the IRS."

"I can't let you do that." She shook her head. "I couldn't. I'll figure something out."

"At least think about it, Della. I want to help. I—I care about you. More than I realized, and I don't think I could stand it if you lost the shop, not knowing how much it means to you, to your staff."

She let out a breath. "I'll think about it. But it's my very last alternative."

"I understand."

"What are you going to tell your boss on Monday?" she asked.

"Leave it to me, I'll think of something." He smiled gently at her. "How about a dance, pretty lady?"

"I think that's just what the lady needs," she answered.

The band moved into their rendition of the Billie Holiday classic "God Bless the Child."

Della closed her eyes and rested her head on Matt's shoulder, swaying to the music. "Mama may have, papa may have, but God bless the child that's got his own," she hummed. *Isn't that the truth*, she thought.

---

Della and Matt spent the rest of the weekend together, putting their troubles aside and just enjoying each other's company. They visited museums, popped in and out of sidewalk cafés in the Village, and ended up Sunday night at Banditos wolfing down some of the best Mexican food they'd both had in a while.

"I've had a wonderful weekend, Della," Matt said on the steps of her brownstone. "I'm glad you seduced me," he teased.

"Desperate times call for desperate measures," she tossed back with a wicked grin.

"If you hadn't come to me, I would have come to you. I wouldn't have been able to stay away," Matt confessed.

"Is that true?"

"Absolutely."

She reached out and ran a finger along his jaw: "What are we going to do, Matt? Our relationship has spelled trouble from the beginning."

"First thing tomorrow, I'm going to pull myself off of your case. I have to. I can't let this job come between us." He stepped closer and slid his arm around her waist. "The only thing I ask is that you don't wear that red dress for the next examiner. I wouldn't want to have to hurt somebody."

"You sound like someone staking out a claim, Mr. Hawkins. Is that what you're doing?"

"What do you think?" he asked, seconds before moving his mouth slowly over hers, memorizing the soft texture of her lips, the taste of her, the feel of her breath as it rushed over his mouth. With great difficulty he eased away.

"So, tell me, Ms. Della, what do you think?"

Her eyes trailed up and down his face. "I'd say you have all rights reserved."

"There's no turning back for me, Della. Not now. I need you to understand that. I intend to put everything into seeing this work between us, whatever that takes. What about you?"

"It's the best proposition I've heard in a long time."

# CHAPTER ELEVEN

I called you all weekend," Ruthie complained, having finally gotten Della on the phone.

Della rolled over on her side and peeked at the clock. Seven A.M. "Girl, do you know what time it is?" she whispered.

"Yeah, I know what time it is. It's time for you to tell me where you've been. I thought you might have walked off a bridge or something."

"That's right," Reggie chimed in the background. "I just knew I was going to see you being pulled out of the Harlem River on the front page of the *Post*."

"Thanks for the confidence, guys," Della said drolly.

She and Matt hadn't gotten in the night before until nearly two and of course it didn't make sense for him to go all the way home. She looked over her shoulder and Matt was still sound asleep, and as her body came slowly awake she realized it still tingled from what they'd done to each other. After the first hour there was little left to the imagination.

"And why are you whispering?" Ruthie shouted in her ear.

"Must I tell you all of my business?"

"Della Frazier," she dragged out. "You didn't."

"And what if I did?"

"What did she do? What did she do?" Reggie asked.

"Anyway, what are you two doing together so early in the morning?" Della asked.

"Don't try to change the subject. Is he there?" Ruthie asked in a hushed voice as if Matt might hear her.

"Yes. Now good-bye. I'll talk to you later." She hung up and eased back under the warmth of Matt's body.

"Friends checking up on you, huh?" he asked, his voice still thick with sleep.

"You didn't hear that, did you?" She turned to face him.

He looked at her through partially opened lids and smiled. "Every word."

"Those two. How embarrassing is that? You would think they were my parents or something."

Matt stroked her bare hip. "They're just looking out for you."

"I suppose," she sighed.

He hugged her to him. "How are you feeling this morning?"

"Incredible. Tired, but incredible."

He kissed her mouth. "My sentiments exactly. You're wonderful. You know that, don't you?"

"How about if I take your word for it?"

He peered over her shoulder and checked the clock. "Why don't we try all the parts out again . . . just to make sure they fit?"

"I was just thinking of checking some parts myself. . . ."

A thrilling hour later, Della walked Matt to the door. She pulled her pink and white silk robe around her body.

Matt turned in the archway and tilted her chin upward, looking down into her eyes. "I've had an incredible time with you, Della. This is only the beginning for us. You know that, don't you?"

"I hope so," she said softly, wishing for the best, but preparing herself for all the possibilities.

He pulled her against him, threading his fingers through her hair. "I'm falling for you, Della. Hard and fast." His gaze traced her face. "Don't let me hurt myself, okay?"

Her heart felt as if it were going to explode in her chest. "We'll catch each other," she uttered, nearly breathless with happiness. She stroked his face. "When's the last time you had a home-cooked meal?"

"Too long."

"Come by tonight after work and we'll take care of that."

He kissed her slow and sweet. "It's going to be a long day," he said with a smile.

"And you're going to be late if you don't get a move on."

"You're right, and I still have to run home and change first."

"Maybe we should have held off our morning until tonight," she said. "I never like to rush; it unravels my day."

"Hey, for the time I spent with you this morning, I don't care if I have to play beat the clock all day."

"You're sweet."

"A man could get used to waking up with you every day, Della."

A hot flush surged through her body. "W-what are you saying— exactly?"

"Let's talk about it some more over dinner." He pecked her lips. "I'll call you later and let you know what's happening." He turned to leave.

"Good luck with your boss, Matt. And please, don't do anything foolish."

"Yes, dear," he teased in a singsong voice, and jogged down the steps.

————————

Della exhaled a long, dreamy breath and shut the door, pressing her back to it and closing her eyes. "Well, girl, you done gone and done it now." She pushed away from the door and walked back into her bedroom to survey the damage.

Picking up the bedspread, which had found its way onto the floor, she tossed it onto the chaise lounge and began pulling off the floral colored sheets, just as the phone rang.

"Ten bucks says it's Ruthie," she mumbled, picking up the phone.

"Yes, he's gone," Della said into the mouthpiece.

"Who's gone?" Chauncie asked.

Della's expression froze in alarm when she heard her daughter's voice on the other end.

"Chauncie?"

"Who did you think it was? Is everything okay? Who's gone?"

Della chuckled nervously. "You're asking an awful lot of questions, sweetheart. And in answer to all of them: Don't worry about it—everything's fine. How are you, and why are you calling so early?"

Chauncie frowned for a moment. She knew her mother wasn't telling her something. Well, she'd find out soon enough. "I called to let you know Drew and I will be leaving here on Wednesday morning to come home."

"That's wonderful, sugar."

"How's everything coming with the club? You're still having the grand opening, right? I thought I'd come back early and help out."

Della's stomach knotted. She cleared her throat. "That's really sweet of you, babe. Uh, why don't we talk about all that when you get back? These phone calls must be astronomical."

"Ma, what's wrong? You don't sound like yourself."

"Chauncie, everything's fine. Really. I'll see you in two days. Give Drew a kiss for me, and the two of you have a safe flight. I've got to run, sweetie. Love you."

Della hung up the phone. *Chauncie.* She hadn't expected her back so soon. Well, she'd have to tell her what was going on eventually. She just wished *eventually* was a little farther away.

---

awkins! I want to see you in my office in ten minutes," Horace Burke bellowed when he spotted Matt striding past his open door.

Matt's step hesitated a beat and he kept going, tossing an "I'll be right there" over his shoulder. He thought he might have gotten a reprieve until the afternoon, but that was never Horace Burke's style. He seemed to take a singular pleasure in ruining a person's day from the start.

Matt tossed his briefcase on his desk and listened to his voice mail for messages. He checked his files, and sure enough, Della's case file was missing. But he'd scanned all of her documents into his computer and put it on a disk. He flipped on his computer and slipped in the disk. Clicking on the file folder icon, he scrolled the list for the one designated "dfrazier" and opened the file. Quickly he glanced through the contents. Everything appeared to be intact. But he could never be too sure. Going through a series of commands, he made an additional disk copy—just in case.

That task completed, he stuck the extra disk in his briefcase, straightened his tie and jacket, and headed for Burke's office.

When he tapped on Burke's partially opened door, there was no answer. Sticking his head in, Matt took a quick look around. No sign of Burke. He stepped back out with the intention of returning to his own office. Burke had a standing policy that no one was permitted in his office without his presence or authority. Matt started to leave, but something stopped him—a bad case of bureaucratic indigestion. He'd swallowed enough rules and regulations to last him another lifetime. His career was on the line anyway. He felt daring. Why not push the envelope?

Matt stepped inside and boldly took a seat on the passenger side of Burke's desk.

Horace Burke had been with the IRS since before Christ, or so the rumor went. He'd risen to the top by knocking down as many people as possible and he sat on his throne with his nose turned up at all his subjects. He was a vindictive man, not only to the clients but to the staff as well. Some people who'd been with the service for twenty years or more said he wasn't always like that. And at one point he was actually a great guy with a wonderful sense of humor.

Looking around at the austere office, Matt inwardly cringed. Would Horace Burke be the man he would have eventually turned into? The thought chilled him. Yet only months ago cutting people off at the knees was as commonplace to him as watching the eleven o'clock news.

Matt stood and slowly paced the office, scanning the books in the bookcase, when a pale blue binder caught his eye. It looked like all the others, but it was the numbers on the spine that drew his attention.

Numbers were second nature to Matt. He could make them sing for their supper. He could recall strings of numbers, solve complex calculations, and compute multiple columns in his head.

He stepped closer. But maybe this time he was wrong, because if he was right, he didn't want to begin to contemplate the explanations. No wonder Burke didn't want anyone in his office.

Horace burst through the door cussing under his breath and stopped short when he saw Matt in his domain. His sallow skin turned a frightening shade of red, which began at his neck and rose to the tip of his receding hairline.

Horace Burke was a big man by anyone's standards. At six foot three and a solid 260 pounds, he wasn't someone you'd want to sneak up on you in an alley. They said he worked out every day and it was evidenced in the trunk of a neck and the biceps that threatened to burst through the arms of his suit.

"What the hell do you think you're doing in my office, Hawkins?" he bellowed, storming across the room like a raging bull. He pulled up to within inches of Matt, who stood right under his nose.

Matt didn't budge, didn't flinch. If anything, there was a light of challenge in his eyes as he stared back at Horace.

"You did say you wanted to see me," Matt said calmly, completely derailing Horace's tirade.

Horace gave him a long, steely look. "Sit down, Hawkins." Horace turned away and rounded his desk, sitting down hard and pulled open a drawer from beneath his desk. Moments later he produced a file. Della Frazier's file.

Matt leaned back in his seat and waited. By the time Horace finished berating him for incompetence, insulting his intelligence, and telling him he was lucky he wasn't getting busted down to a desk clerk, Matt had put all the numbers together in his head and they all added up to Horace Burke.

"I want, on my desk no later than Friday, a full accounting of all your cases for this month and where they stand."

"Won't all that come out in the monthly meeting?" Matt asked, the first time he'd spoken since he sat down.

"If I wanted to wait that long, Hawkins, I wouldn't ask for the report. Friday. No later. Understood?"

"Oh, absolutely," Matt said in his most condescending manner, which only infuriated Horace all the more.

"And in the meantime, I want all of your current files turned over to me. You need to concentrate on getting me that report."

"And how soon would you be needing *my* files?"

"In the time it takes you to walk down the hall to your office, collect them, and bring them back."

"Then I guess I'd better hurry," Matt said, rising from his seat.

Horace pointed his finger at Matt. "I don't like you. I never did. You think you're the hotshot around here, you're not. I've seen them come and go, Hawkins. But I'm still here," he affirmed, poking a finger at his chest.

"I'm going to gather up that information for you." Matt said, ignoring his declaration before turning and walking out the door.

———————

When Matt returned to his office his heart was racing, not from fear but exhilaration. If what he believed was true, he had the answer to Della's problem. And even more important, his discovery would shake up the entire IRS system. He took a breath. Once he made his move, there was no turning back. He must be prepared for the scrutiny that he would come under as a result. But he was ready. And if it meant losing everything to help Della, he would do it.

Matt closed and locked his office door. Horace Burke was a pompous fool, and it was going to cost him. No wonder he never wanted anyone in his office. Matt crossed the room and dialed Paul's extension.

"Paul Daniels," he answered dryly.

"Paul, listen, I found the answer. At least I think I did. But I need your help to prove it."

"What? Slow down."

"I have to get some files together for Burke to hold him off for a while. Meet me for lunch and I'll explain everything. Oh, and Paul . . ."

"Yeah?"

"I'll need to get into your files."

# CHAPTER TWELVE

How does it feel to be a celebrity?" Della asked, snuggling up to Matt on her queen-sized bed.

"It's everything it's cracked up to be," he teased, kissing her neck. "Plus I get to go home with the prize. You."

Della stroked his bare chest. "Thank you, Matt, for taking a chance, risking everything. This could have backfired on you."

"I believed in you, babe. Even though all the numbers were telling me something different."

She turned full on her side and propped her head up with her hand. "Tell me again how you cracked the case," she insisted, like a little kid wanting a bedtime story.

Matt chuckled. "Again?"

"Come on," she whined. "Just once more."

"Okay, okay. Horace Burke got to a point where he honestly believed he was beyond the reach of the law. And he was so arrogant with it, he kept the evidence right in his office. The dummy corporation that he'd set up used the same tax identification number as your shop when you took it over. The corporate number was right on the spine of the binder. When I saw it, things just clicked. I'd been running your number so often I'd memorized it."

"And Paul handled the corporate accounts?"

"Right. We went through each one, line by line, and there it was. By the time they finish investigating him, there's no telling how many more accounts he'd set up like that. You wound up paying taxes that ultimately went directly into his account."

"Wow," was all she could say. She reached down on the floor and picked up a copy of the *Daily News* and held it up in front of her.

The first two pages of the newspaper detailed the crackdown at the IRS that began with Matt Hawkins's discovery of Horace's files. And according to the initial reports, Horace Burke wasn't the only one going down.

"You look pretty good on the front page. Almost handsome." She kissed his lips. "But ain't nothing like the real thing, baby," she sang off-key.

Matt rolled her beneath him. "Don't quit your day job, love."

Della playfully pinched his thigh. "Speaking of day jobs, what are you planning to do about yours?"

"I'm not sure. They're offering me all kinds of promotions, salary increases, you name it." He sighed. "But I don't know. I didn't truly realize until you came into my life what the job had done to me over the years—what I'd allowed it to do to me."

"It's been about choices and change from the moment we met," Della said softly. "Whatever you decide to do, I'm sure it'll be the right decision, and I'll stick by you."

"Will you, Della? Really stick by me?"

"Of course, sugah, you're my hero," she whispered against his mouth. "How many women are lucky enough to say they have a real live hero as their man?"

"So, I'm your man now, huh?" he asked, stroking her hip.

"You'd better be, or else I'll have a whole lot of explaining to do to myself in the morning," she replied, locking her mouth to his.

The entire staff was in all their finery, ready to party. The DJ had arrived and was all set up. The caterer had totally outdone himself with trays of buffalo wings, deep-dish macaroni and cheese, peas and rice, collard greens, string beans, fried chicken, and six pies for dessert. None of that fake finger food for her opening night, Della had decided. This was going to be a throw-down party.

Chauncie had taken charge of decorating and the club looked fabulous. Maybe she'd find a career in interior design, Della thought as she surveyed the space.

She checked her watch. Five minutes to nine. Five more minutes and she'd open the doors to Della's Place. Her heart filled with pride. She'd done it. Actually done it. All this was hers.

She turned to where Matt stood in the corner—caged in the corner, was more like it—by all the female staff. She smiled. Since he'd decided to quit the IRS and go into his own business, everyone wanted him to be their "personal" accountant. She and Matt definitely had a rocky start, but she was sure that the road ahead would be a lot smoother.

Chauncie eased up alongside her mother and kissed her cheek. "You did good, Ma," she said, truly happy for her mother.

Della looked around. "Yes, it is great, isn't it?"

"Humph, I wasn't talking about the club. I was talking about Mr. Wonderful over there. He's a doll."

"That he is. You didn't do too bad yourself, sweetheart."

"I know. Drew is the best thing that ever happened to me," she said, looking across the room at her handsome husband.

Drew opened the door to the club and the crowd began streaming in, oohing and ahing at the decor.

The DJ played Whitney Houston's "I'm Your Baby Tonight," and the party was on.

Ruthie, Reggie, and Blaize came to stand with Della and Chauncie.

"Congratulations, girl. You did it," they shouted over the music.

Della beamed.

"And you got the man, too," Ruthie said with a smile.

Della watched Matt's steady approach. "Magic happens at Della's," she said with a wink, just before she stepped into Matt's arms. *"It could happen to you!"*

# A Matter of Trust

FRANCIS RAY

# CHAPTER ONE

Sebastian Stone was having the day from hell, and as the afternoon progressed it showed no sign of abating. But having a flat with no spare, being splashed with dirty water in his new Brioni charcoal herringbone suit as he stood on the sidewalk waiting for the auto service mechanic, then getting a speeding ticket while rushing home to change for his morning meeting at the theater, and all the other crummy things that followed, in no way compared to this latest development. "Do you mean to tell me that Gregory isn't here?"

Tianna, the young receptionist at Della's House of Style who moments earlier had greeted him with a broad smile, noticeably swallowed, the smile in her attractive nut-brown face wavering. "He had an emergency, Mr. Stone."

Concern knitted Sebastian's brow. In their six-year association, the tempestuous Gregory had never canceled. "What kind of emergency?"

"Medical." The receptionist glanced away, her right hand fluttering upward to push the shoulder-length braids off her shoulder. "He sprained his ankle last night."

Sebastian's frown deepened. As far as he knew, the most strenuous thing Gregory ever did was operating the remote control for his entertainment system. He claimed standing in his Cole Haans for hours on end, twisting and turning to get the right angle to do people's hair, was enough exercise for him. If he needed to burn calories, he had a better way. "How'd he do that?"

Tianna's gaze settled in the middle of Sebastian's blue, pinstripe-shirted chest. "Jumping off a fire escape."

Knowing Gregory lived on the first floor of his apartment complex, and knowing his passion for the ladies, Sebastian decided not to question the obviously embarrassed woman further. Apparently Gregory had been burning calories with someone he shouldn't. "I see."

Tianna's braid-covered head quickly came up. She stared at him with pleaful, big brown eyes. "But I assure you the stylist your appointment is with is well qualified to cut your hair."

"Edge," Sebastian corrected, aware that he was splitting hairs and unable to help himself. "My hair only needs to be edged."

Her smile slipped again and Sebastian felt like the demon from hell in the last play he directed. He probably sounded like an irrational fool. But, despite her position, in Sebastian's opinion few women truly understood that letting someone loose with clippers, shears, or scissors on a man's head was just as traumatic for him as for a woman getting a cut. Once the hair was gone, no amount of apology would bring it back.

Sebastian had been in that unenviable position too many times in his past thirty-seven years to take it lightly. It had taken him five long years after his move from Los Angeles to New York to find Gregory. Once Sebastian found him, he had followed the gregarious Gregory whenever he went. Della's House of Style was his third move.

Gregory might wear a foot-long ponytail, but he knew Sebastian's taste was conservative. No fades or shags for him. His haircut hadn't changed since he graduated from Howard in the early eighties.

"Gregory said to tell you he had complete confidence in Hope," the receptionist offered.

"Hope?" Sebastian repeated, foreboding sweeping through him. A woman had never cut his hair. He wasn't a chauvinist. His mother and sister could testify to that. His father would disown him if he were.

Sebastian simply believed men were more suited to some professions. This was certainly one of them.

"Hope Lassiter," Tianna finally said.

Maybe he was overreacting. Although this was only his second time in Della's, the salon had the highest reputation and it had a subdued elegance and airiness that he liked. The booths were spaced far enough apart so you didn't feel cramped or have to listen to your neighbor's conversation. . . . unless you wanted to. Mirrors abounded on the pristine white walls. A pink and blue marble floor sparkled beneath his Balleys. Fresh-cut flowers sat at every station. The setting was designed to be relaxing.

It wasn't.

Perhaps the fault was his. Even after ten years as a director in the theater, the last three mostly on Broadway, the start of a new play with all its myriad problems always put him a little on edge. He never completely settled down until after the final curtain call on opening night. With all the difficulties he was having casting the right actress for the crucial female lead in *A Matter of Trust,* if he wasn't careful, he'd be a basket case by opening night. "Which one is she?"

"Her station is the fourth one." Tianna's slim hand gestured to the left.

Sebastian's worried gaze followed. There were two women at the station, but he immediately dismissed the elderly, gray-haired woman in a trim-fitting sky blue suit. The younger woman standing by her side wasn't so easily discounted.

She was tall and shapely, and her black micro-miniskirt peeked from beneath her pink smock each time she leaned over to speak with the grinning little boy sitting in the chair. Momentarily, she glanced his way. His breath caught, then came out in a rush. The promise of her elegantly curved body and long legs was backed up with interest by her beautiful mocha-hued face.

Her pouting lower lip begged to be kissed. Chiseled cheekbones bespoke of a Scandinavian or Native American influence somewhere in her heritage. Unconsciously Sebastian took a step closer, hoping she'd turn to him again so he could see her face and determine the color of her eyes. Abruptly he stopped. His own eyes widened as the scope of his gaze broadened.

"Goodness gracious."

He might not be able to distinguish the color of her eyes, but he had no difficulty with her hair . . . black and tipped two inches in garish purple. Worse, it was spiked over her head as if she had stuck her finger in a light socket. He quickly turned to Tianna. "No way is that woman getting near my head."

---

O h, my, Hope, he's looking this way," Bridgett Swanson said, excitement ringing in her voice. "He's a handsome devil. His pictures don't do him justice."

"You gonna ask him, Mommy? Are you?" Four-year-old Jeremy Lassiter bounced in the chair with every other word.

"Of course she is," Bridgett answered, then leaned over to whisper in Hope's ear. "If I were twenty—no, make that ten—years younger, I might try out for the part myself. Next, I'd go after the man."

Hope laughed, and with the laughter, some of the tension she had fought all afternoon eased. Bridgett nodded her approval at the sound of the laughter.

Hope smiled at her two biggest supporters, Jeremy and their friend and landlady, Bridgett Swanson. Sixty years old and widowed for seven years, Bridgett was an invariable tease and absolutely wonderful with Jeremy. The best thing that could have happened to them was renting the upper floor of Bridgett's home on Shriver's Row.

Leaning over, Hope kissed Jeremy's soft cheek and winked at Bridgett. "If he turns me down for the lead in A Matter of Trust, I'll let you work on him for me."

The older woman shook her head emphatically. "He's too smart for that. Those four Tony Awards he's received in the past attest to his ability to pick winners. He needs a versatile, powerful actress for his production and you fit perfectly."

"You're the best, Mommy," Jeremy said, his eyes wide. "Everybody said so last night and all the other times."

"Listen to your son, Hope. You were the hit of the show."

"Community theater is a far, far cry from Broadway," Hope said, doubt creeping into her voice again. "Reading in *Variety* that Sebastian Stone was doing open casting for his newest play, then having Gregory call and ask me to do Sebastian's hair, seemed as if fate were working for me to get back into real theater again."

"It is," Bridgett said with complete confidence. "You said Della said it was all right for you to broach the subject with him, so all you have to do now is approach Mr. Stone."

Hope drew a deep breath. "You make it sound so easy."

"It is." Bridgett reached for Jeremy's hand. Immediately the child grasped it and jumped down from the chair to land with a solid whack on the shiny floor.

Hope frowned down at him. "Jeremy."

"Sorry," he said, an unrepentant grin on his beautiful, chubby face, his black eyes twinkling.

Hope tried to appear stern, but a smile slipped through. Douglas, the father Jeremy had never known, could always get by her with the same look. And like his father, Jeremy was perpetually happy and mischievous. "One of these days that's not going to work with me."

Jeremy's grin widened. With his free hand, he beckoned Hope closer. When she neared his face, he kissed her loudly on the cheek. "I love you, Mommy."

Hope's heart melted. Bending, she enveloped him in a hug. Thank goodness he still needed and wanted those hugs as much as she did. "I love you, too. I'll be home by six with hopefully some good news."

"He'll let you play the part, Mommy, I just know he will."

She stood. "I'll know shortly."

"Good luck, Hope," Bridgett said.

"Thanks, and thanks for coming by with Jeremy to give me a pep talk."

Bridgett waved the words aside with a surprisingly agile flick of her wrist. Diamonds and emeralds glittered. "You've given me plenty of them. About time I returned the favor."

"You do that just by being there for me and Jeremy." Reaching out, Hope briefly squeezed the older woman's fragile, blue-veined hand. "I'll walk you to the front and meet Mr. Stone." Fighting the trembling that had suddenly invaded her legs, she turned and headed toward the front of the shop and what she hoped was the key to her future, Sebastian Stone.

———————

B ut—but, Mr. Stone," Tianna spluttered. "Hope is one of our best stylists. Gregory personally selected her."

"That may be, but I want someone else." Sebastian glanced to the other side of the shop, looking for a male attendant whose hair and dress denoted some restraint. Although there were two other men there, neither inspired confidence. One wore clothes as loud as Hope's hair, the other had a pair of shears in his hand zipping over a man's head at only a fraction slower than the speed of light. "I'll reschedule."

"But—but—" Tianna stammered.

"Good afternoon, Mr. Stone. I'm Hope Lassiter. Gregory asked me to service you this afternoon."

Sebastian felt a strange, white-hot something slither down his spine. Slowly he turned. The husky, beckoning whisper of Hope Lassiter's voice went perfectly with the face and body. A combination like that had embodied man's dream of the perfect woman since the beginning of time . . . until he looked at the sobering sight of her head.

Unconsciously, he lowered his gaze to see the color of her eyes, and stared into a pair of heavily lashed almond-shaped black eyes. She was even more captivating close up. "You know who I am?"

"By reputation and from what Gregory has told me," Hope said, trying to tell herself to remain calm, that this was just another customer, albeit one who could give her back a dream that she thought was gone forever. However, his smooth, deeply compelling voice was sending her thoughts in an entirely, totally inappropriate direction.

"Gregory went to great lengths to ensure that I understood how to edge your hair correctly." Her black eyes narrowed as her expert gaze ran over his well-shaped head to give herself time to collect her thoughts.

Bridgett was right. He was a handsome devil. Devastating, in fact, with piercing black eyes, a strong jaw, a talk-me-into-anything mouth, and a no-nonsense chin. Just her luck that she was a sucker for a man with a mustache. Sebastian's was jet black and neatly trimmed.

Since Gregory hadn't mentioned it, Sebastian probably took care of it himself. However, Gregory *had* mentioned Sebastian's previous misfortunes with barbers. The way those black eyes of his were staring at her, he had lumped her in their number.

Trying to control the strange and unusual sensations swirling through her, Hope concentrated on the problem at hand, calming her potential client. This was no time to remember that the only males she had hugged lately were relatives.

"You have enough natural curl to use the scissors to shape your hair. The shears and clippers will be needed only to edge the back and sides. Moderation and restraint is what Gregory said you desired. At Della's we always give our valued customers what they desire."

Did her voice get even huskier when she said *desire,* the same way it had when she said *service*—or was it his imagination? Once he had arrogantly thought of women coming on to him as a great side benefit to being a well-known theater director, but as time passed and it happened more and more, the come-ons had quickly become an annoyance, then a nuisance. He preferred to do his own chasing. "My desire would be not to have to wear a baseball cap or a fedora for the next couple of weeks until my hair grows out," he said in a clipped tone.

In slow motion her smile withered. Her eyes narrowed and took on a distinct chill. "No one has ever been dissatisfied with my services in the past, Mr. Stone, but if you have reservations I'm sure Tianna can find someone else to assist you. As I said, at Della's we strive to give the customer what they desire. If you'll excuse me." With a slight nod of her head, she walked past him to the front of the shop, where the elderly woman and the little boy who had been with her earlier waited.

Stunned by her dismissal, Sebastian watched Hope hunker down to eye level with the young child and open her arms. The child didn't hesitate. Their shared laughter rang loud and clear. Somehow he knew the happy little boy clinging around her neck was her son.

For some odd reason he thought of his ex-wife, Celeste, who had thought children would ruin her model-thin figure. Celeste, beautiful and as selfish as they came. He had lousy taste when it came to women. That was something else his mother and sister could attest to.

"Mr. Stone, if you'd come with me, I can check the appointment book," the receptionist said.

Sebastian looked away from mother and child. "Certainly."

---

H ope was trembling, she was so angry. The compact, sturdy body of Jeremy giggling in her arms and against her body helped to calm her. The nerve of the man. To actually think she was trying to come on to him. She could tell from the sarcasm/flippancy of his statement, the piercing coldness of his gaze. She should know. She'd used a similar tone and look herself many times in the past to discourage men.

"Hope?"

Hearing the concern and question in Bridgett's voice, Hope shook her head and stood. Bridgett would understand. Many times in their long association they had had to talk out of Jeremy's hearing. With a bright smile on her face, Hope rose and said, "I'll be home earlier than I thought. Why don't we eat out tonight, my treat?"

"To celebrate?" Jeremy asked, his gaze going from Sebastian, at the receptionist desk several feet away, back to his mother. "He's gonna let you."

Hope's smile wavered, then steadied. "We'll see."

Bridgett, her mouth tight, briefly pressed her free hand to Hope's tense shoulder. "We'll talk later."

This time Jeremy didn't budge when the elderly woman tugged gently on his hand. "But you were gonna ask him, Mommy. What did he say?"

From experience, Hope knew her son wasn't easily put off when he wanted an answer. Since it was just the two of them, she had a tendency to discuss her plans with him. He had also been around adults all his life and his vocabulary and thought processes were advanced for his age.

He knew how important obtaining the part in the play was to her. To ensure that he did, she had compared it to his dream, that of becoming an astronaut and traveling to the farthest reaches of space. She hated to see the disappointment in the face she loved more than anything. "I didn't ask him, sweetheart."

"But you have to ask him, Mommy. If you don't ask him, you won't be able to—"

"Jeremy, let this *gentleman* pass," Bridgett said tightly, stepping aside and drawing Jeremy with her. This time he went, his gaze locked on Sebastian as he passed.

"He's leaving, Mommy. Mommy, he can't leave."

"It's all right, Jeremy," Hope soothed. Feeling Sebastian's hard gaze on her back, she hunkered down in front of her child again. She could easily detest him for upsetting Jeremy, but the blame wasn't his. It was hers. Somehow she had to make her son understand that sometimes dreams don't always come true, no matter how much you wanted them to.

# CHAPTER TWO

Closing the salon's door, Sebastian still felt the disapproving glare of the elderly woman and even more so the pleaful one of the little boy. The small, stark face was a drastic contrast to the giggling expression he wore earlier. Jeremy. Hope had called him Jeremy.

Hands deep in the front pockets of his navy blue slacks, Sebastian headed for his car two blocks away. There had been a parking space directly in front of the salon, but the driver of a little red sports car had zipped around him and into the space. The gloating young man, not the least disturbed by Sebastian's honking horn or his glare, had gleefully waved. Either he hadn't been taught to be courteous or had forgotten the lesson.

Sebastian's thoughts returned to Jeremy. The child seemed genuinely upset that Sebastian was leaving. His steps paused. Would Hope be reprimanded for not keeping a customer happy? Although he didn't think of himself as such, other people thought of him as important. His ex-wife certainly had. But it was only after he had married Celeste that he'd finally figured it out. They'd spent two chaotic years together before she had found someone richer and more gullible. Frowning, he paused on the tree-lined street as he tried to recall exactly what Jeremy had said.

Something about "Mommy, you won't be able to—" then the other woman had cut Jeremy off to let Sebastian pass. Sebastian had a sneaky suspicion that the interruption wasn't coincidental.

Tianna had said Hope was one of their top stylists, and he had no reason to doubt the receptionist, but something was going on. He glanced back toward the salon. Walking down the street in the opposite direction was the elderly woman and Jeremy. The child saw him and immediately stopped, bringing the woman to an abrupt halt.

From the hundred feet or so separating him, he couldn't see Jeremy's face clearly, but Sebastian had no trouble hearing the excitement ringing in the boy's voice over the traffic and other city noises. Even if he hadn't, the child was jumping up and down, his left hand pumping in the air. A lefty.

Sebastian was left-handed. If his ex-wife hadn't been so concerned with keeping her model-thin figure, partying with the rich and famous, and jetting all over the world, she might have become pregnant as Sebastian had wanted and he'd have his own child Jeremy's age. And he would've suffered the fires of hell not to disappoint him.

One step was followed by another, then another, back to Della's until he could hear Jeremy's thrilled cries of, "I knew it. I knew it." The woman trying to quiet him finally gave up. Sebastian felt himself smiling at the ecstatic boy, and hooked the thumb of his left hand upward. Grinning from ear to ear, Jeremy returned the gesture.

The day from hell had ten hours to go, but at least this time he knew what he was walking into. Wearing a baseball cap for the next couple of weeks in no way compared to disappointing a child. He opened the door and for the second time that day stepped into Della's.

---

Surprise hardly came close to describing the way Hope felt on seeing Sebastian reenter the salon. Pausing briefly at the receptionist's counter, he nodded, handed Tianna his sports coat, then started toward Hope, his long strides sure and purposeful. Despite her best efforts, Hope felt a distinct flutter in the pit of her stomach. Her hand closed tightly around the comb in her hand. No matter what an arrogant so and so she thought he was, he was an impressive so and so.

He topped six feet easily, but his physique was trim and athletic. Even without the jacket, he was a commanding figure in his blue pin-stripe shirt and navy slacks. Heads, male and female, paused to watch as he passed. Each movement was rich with an irrefutable mixture of confidence, authority, and sex appeal that announced him as a man to be reckoned with even before he opened his mouth. He stopped two feet from Hope.

"Ms. Lassiter, Tianna tells me my appointment time isn't up for another thirty minutes," Sebastian said, his gaze direct and piercing. "If you're still agreeable, I'd like for you to service me."

Hope's eyes widened, then narrowed as a ball of heat rolled through her. She had used and heard the word *service* thousands of time, but never before had an erotic image of her entwined in a man's arms popped into her head. Her hand flexed on the comb. Her breathing escalated as she fought to get Sebastian out of her mind and his slow hands off her body. What was the matter with her? As a rule, she could take or leave men. Usually she left them.

But Sebastian was a different ball game. Nervously, she moistened her dry lips. Sebastian's onyx eyes followed the movement of her tongue with rapt attention. The heat shot higher.

"Sebastian, it's a pleasure to see you again."

With difficulty Sebastian tore his gaze away from Hope's lush red mouth and greeted Della, the owner of the salon. Beautiful and stylishly dressed in a figure-flattering suit the soft color of wisteria, she extended her hand. Gladly he reached for it. "Hello, Della."

She smiled. "I'm happy to see you were able to keep your appointment."

Sebastian noted the twinkle in her eyes and smiled. The first time he came to the salon, Gregory wouldn't have it any other way except to inform Della about Sebastian's haircut horror stories. After she left, Gregory had told him about the woman's business savvy and her close monitoring of the clientele. It wouldn't surprise him if she had seen him leave, then return.

Good. At least Della didn't think Hope was the cause, but it wouldn't hurt to reinforce that notion. "I've almost come to the conclusion that it's the shape of my head and not the barber's fault."

Della shook her head, her manicured nails lightly touching the delicate sterling silver chain around her neck. "Nonsense. You have a beautifully shaped head, and from all the acclaim your plays have garnered over the years, that head possesses considerable brainpower. I look forward to seeing your next play."

"Thank you." No matter how much trepidation or problems lay ahead with *A Matter of Trust*, including the most important one of casting the female lead, Sebastian had discovered early never to let his audience know. Learning the problematic side of the production of a play often took away from patrons' enjoyment. "Open auditions are set for later this afternoon."

"Then I better let you get finished. I have the utmost confidence that Hope will meet your every need." With a reassuring nod to Hope, Della strolled away.

"If you'll take a seat, Mr. Stone, we can get started," Hope instructed.

Sebastian took his seat. His back was to the mirror, but his gaze quickly swept the line of mirrors at every station across from him until he located Hope's reflection in one and watched her step behind him. Efficiently, she placed the black cape around his shoulders and secured it at the nape of his neck. She picked up a pair of thin pointed scissors with one hand and placed the other hand on his head.

Because he knew what was coming next, her touch should have made him tense. Instead he had to stop himself from leaning closer and rubbing against her soft hand like a preening cat. Her fingertips were entirely too gentle, entirely too smooth, and entirely too disturbing. He twisted in his seat.

The next thing he knew, her splayed fingers were beneath the cape on his shoulders, massaging. He jumped and tried to turn around in the chair to face her. "What are you doing?"

"Trying to get you to loosen up. This also helps blood circulation," she told him, continuing the ministration, the pressure of her hands keeping him facing away from her.

It was a good thing he had on the cape or she could tell he didn't need the blood circulating any better in one part of his body. Annoyed with himself for his lapse and her for being the cause, he leaned away from her unsettling hands. "If you don't mind, just stick with the hair."

"Of course, Mr. Stone," she said crisply.

His cell phone rang. Sebastian grabbed for the instrument like a drowning man for a life raft. His self-imposed celibacy must be finally catching up with him. Gingerly he settled back and said, "Sebastian."

"Hi, Sebastian. It's Roscoe Carroll."

Sebastian's life preserver turned out to be an anchor in disguise. Roscoe, wealthy and with a fondness for Havana cigars and imported beer, was the producer and major backer for *A Matter of Trust*. In their past associations Roscoe had adopted a hands-off policy, but this time he wanted in on every decision. Especially choosing the female lead. Maybe it had something to do with his recent divorce from wife number three. Fifty-three years old, bald, five feet six, tipping the scales at two-thirty, Roscoe loved to be in love. "What can I do for you, Roscoe?"

"It's my pleasure to do something for you," Roscoe said, the smile in his West Coast accent easily discernible. "This afternoon when you do the auditions, you don't have to worry about the female lead."

Sebastian's grip on the phone tightened. His back came away from the chair. "I thought we agreed to make the final decision together."

Good-naturedly, Roscoe chuckled. "We will. We couldn't have better than Margot Madison."

"What?" Sebastian leaned farther forward. Gentle hands settled on his shoulders and began massaging. Telling Hope to stop ran through his head only for a second, then he felt his tense muscles loosen. He leaned back in his chair. Hope returned to his head and he almost called her soothing hands back at Roscoe's next words.

"I want Margot and we're lucky to have her. There is no way you're gonna find better at the audition," Roscoe said happily. "She can have her pick of roles. She's a star."

Sebastian knew exactly what Margot was: conniving, manipulative, egotistical . . . and those were her good points. "Have you discussed this with her?"

"That's the fantastic part. She approached me. She'll make this play a hit before it opens."

She'd also make Sebastian's and everyone else's life hell every time things didn't go her way. He glanced around the salon. A few people were already watching him. This wasn't the time or the place to go into his objections. "We've already scheduled auditions for this afternoon. Why don't you come down to the theater and we'll talk before we make any definite decisions?" Sebastian suggested, knowing there was no way he was working with Margot again. It could be financially devastating, especially if Roscoe fought him, but if pushed he'd break his contract and worry about the damage to his bank account later.

"I'll come, but my mind is made up." The line went dead.

Punching the disconnect button, Sebastian returned his phone to his shirt pocket almost at the same time Hope pulled the cape from his shoulders, then briskly brushed around his collar. As soon as she finished, he stood up, pulled out his billfold, and handed her two twenties.

Instead of taking the money, she held out a hand mirror to him. "Don't you want to see?"

"I don't have time." A lopsided head at the moment would really send him over the edge. He gestured with the money.

Curling one delicate hand around the glass and the other on the handle, Hope bought the mirror to her chest. "I didn't mean to eavesdrop, but your call sounded as if it was about your play."

"It was. The female lead." His offer of the money was again refused.

Hope moistened her dry lips. "You haven't cast the part yet, have you?"

Sebastian was watching her pink tongue disappear back into her mouth and almost missed her question. "What? No. No, we haven't."

She smiled and his breath caught. "Great, because I happen to know the perfect woman."

"Who?" he asked automatically, his attention on her mouth again.

"You're looking at her."

"What?" Sebastian quickly surfaced back to reality.

"I said you're looking at her," Hope said, trying not to be discouraged by the absolute look of disbelief on Sebastian's face. "I was with the Edgar Evans Touring Company for several years before Jeremy was born. I've played comedy and drama. Even a couple of musicals, although my voice is not very strong."

Sebastian's gaze shot up to her black hair tipped in purple, then laid the money on her service area. Hope might tempt him with her body, but he wasn't crazy enough to cast her for the lead in his play. The day from hell might be trying to drive him crazy, but he wasn't there yet. "You're not right for the part," he said emphatically.

His dismissive words stung Hope's pride. Out of the corner of her eye, she saw Lynn, the stylist next to her, taking in every word. Lynn was a nice woman, but she was also an incurable gossip. Before the afternoon was over, the entire shop would know of Sebastian's curt rejection.

Trying to negate further embarrassment, Hope lowered her voice, "But you haven't seen me act. I've played the lead part of Eleanor before and I—"

"Surely you can't be serious that you want to try out for the lead," he scoffed, causing several people around them to turn and openly stare.

Hope had been initially interested in playing Eleanor, but she would have settled for a minor role to get back into the theater after being out for so long. Now, seeing the incredulous expression on Sebastian's face, a face that had had her thinking erotic thoughts earlier, set her on a slow boil.

She might have had trepidations about asking for the role, but she had none when it came to her acting. Douglas, the loving husband she had lost unexpectedly almost five years ago to a brain aneurysm, had always maintained that if you didn't believe in yourself, you couldn't expect anyone else to.

Hope forgot all about Della's ironclad policy of deference to the clients no matter what. She forgot about the gossipy Lynn. "And why not?" she practically hissed, planting both hands on her hips.

Usually Sebastian tried to let down easy the unending number of would-be actors and actresses who approached him wanting a role, but his patience was in short supply at the moment. For some odd reason he felt betrayed that Hope and Jeremy wanted something from him like so many others.

It didn't help that Hope was also the eleventh person that day wanting him to help them get a part in his new play. Number nine and ten had done their part in continuing Sebastian's day from hell. Nine had been so busy talking, she had overflowed his water glass at lunch. He had thanked God it hadn't been coffee. Number ten had waylaid him on the elevator for fifteen excruciating floors.

And now Hope, a woman who, despite the ugly hair spiking on her head, effortlessly made his body want hers, was asking for the most difficult role he had directed in years. Well, if she wanted to know why she wasn't right for the past, he'd certainly tell her.

"Eleanor Cartwright is sophisticated, elegant, cultured one moment, then a scheming, conniving bitch the next. She can smile and cut your heart out, then cry over a sunset. She's a complex woman, and few actresses can master all the range of emotions she must carry. Certainly not a woman in your profession."

Hope's delicate nostrils flared with fury. "Are you trying to imply that because I'm a hairstylist, you don't think I have any brains or sophistication?"

"Acting is more than wanting to act," Sebastian said, fascinated in spite of himself by how anger heightened the color in her cheeks and made her beauty all the more alluring.

Snatching the money from the counter, Hope stuffed it in his shirt pocket behind the cell phone. "I can see why all the barbers messed up your hair. You head is full of hot air."

Her anger was hot, volatile. Almost tangible. He hadn't meant to hurt her, but it was better him than some slimy producer or director who would use her dream to misuse her body. Sebastian didn't like to think of Jeremy's expression when Hope told him she hadn't gotten the part. Obviously it was important to both of them.

His gaze never leaving Hope's, Sebastian slowly took the money from his pocket and placed it on the table again. It was the only thing he could think of to do to ease his own regrets, and maybe just not have Hope or Jeremy think too badly of him. Why it mattered, he wasn't sure. "I'm sorry."

Refusing to let the tears burning her eyes fall, Hope watched Sebastian and her dream walk away.

# CHAPTER THREE

Sebastian couldn't get Hope's face out of his mind. She'd looked so defiant, yet so crushed when he had told her she wasn't right for the lead. He'd made the right decision, he just wished he could have made it easier for her. Her profession had nothing to do with it. Although most stage actors and actresses preferred working in the media off-season or while waiting to get their big break, some weren't able to find employment in that area. Subsequently, they came from all types of jobs. However, he honestly couldn't think of one who had been a hairstylist.

Now, sitting five rows back in the theater, watching woman after woman try out for the lead, he was again made aware of the depth and talent needed to bring Eleanor to life. He'd hoped having an actor bound and gagged in a chair might help the women bring more emotion to the crucial confrontation scene. So far, none of the women auditioning had a clue.

Hearing conversation behind him where there was supposed to be none since auditions were in progress, Sebastian twisted in his seat and saw Roscoe's portly body coming down the middle aisle. He wasn't alone.

Sebastian stood. The hellish day was nipping at his heels again.

"Hello, Sebastian," Roscoe greeted. "You know my lawyer, Shelton Jackson."

"Yes." Sebastian extended his hand. "Shelton. I don't have to ask why you're here."

Shelton smiled, showing even white teeth, and Sebastian thought he knew exactly how a trapped animal felt as it stared into the grinning jaws of a predator about to gobble him up. "Good afternoon, Sebastian. I'm just tagging along. We all want *A Matter of Trust* to be a success."

Sebastian's brows arched at the smooth-talking Shelton, whose meticulous style of dress in a three-thousand-dollar, handmade, midnight blue Brioni suit with white stripes made Roscoe in his off-the-rack plaid golf pants and bright yellow polo shirt appear out of place and very unlikely to have the brainpower to have amassed millions in the unpredictable entertainment industry.

Not so. Roscoe was as sharp as they came and had reached the enviable point in his life where he did things to please himself—much to Sebastian's increasing dismay. "Nicely said, Shelton, but we all know you're here to remind me that the contract I signed would be costly and difficult to get out of, and that Roscoe is the major backer for the play and without his money, we close before we open."

"Now, Sebastian, there is no need to be concerned," Roscoe said, easing his hefty weight into one of the blue-cushioned chairs. "We need each other. You pull out and we both lose a lot of money. You could find another backer, but why bother when we have always worked so well together in the past?"

"I don't want Margot," Sebastian said flatly.

Shelton casually unbuttoned his suit jacket, sat down, then placed his handmade leather attachè case by his highly polished wing tips. "The contract stipulates you and Roscoe are to be in agreement, but if an agreement can't be reached, as owning sixty percent to your fifteen percent, Roscoe gets the final call."

"You never interfered before, Roscoe," Sebastian reminded him.

The older man shrugged. "So, I'm entitled."

Sebastian glanced at Shelton. Shelton smiled.

Trying to keep the expletive locked behind his teeth, Sebastian sat in the seat beside Roscoe. "Try to understand that the woman needed for this part has to be able to display a wide range of emotions. She has to be able to appear innocent and vulnerable at the beginning, then despondent when she is betrayed, vengeful and enraged when she decides to pay Lawson back for framing her for embezzlement, leery of Nolan's interest in her initially, then indecisive when she has to choose between Nolan's love or revenge against his brother, Lawson."

Stretching out his short legs in front of him, Roscoe leaned back in his seat and folded his hands over his wide girth. "That's why my money's on Margot. That woman up there now sure can't cut it."

"We've just begun the auditions," Sebastian defended, hoping somewhere offstage was an actress who would blow their socks off. "Margot is a great actress, I grant you, but she can also cause havoc on the set. If you want this production brought in on time and on budget, then scratch Margot's name."

"I don't know," Roscoe said, shaking his head as another actress took the stage and began Eleanor's monologue. "Looks like we need Margot. She told me she wants this part very much. Seems to me she'd do as you suggested."

Sebastian barely kept from cringing as the hopeful actress onstage screeched her rage and flailed her arms around at the man who had sent her to prison for five years. Subtlety wasn't her strong suit. "Margot only does what anyone says as long as it pleases her."

Roscoe glanced at Sebastian out of the corner of his eye. "She said you might not like having her. I know it's hard since she broke up—"

Sebastian came up in his seat and gave Roscoe his full attention. "I beg your pardon?"

"Don't get huffy, Sebastian," Roscoe chided gently. "Even an aficionado like you strikes out sometimes. It was bound to happen sooner or later."

"Later, maybe—because it didn't happen with Margot," Sebastian said, tired of hearing again that Margot had dumped him after the play he directed her in closed last year. Usually he didn't bother correcting the lie Margot had spread. This time was different. Margot was using the lie to try to get the lead in his play. Never. "I was the one who called the relationship off."

Roscoe appeared thoughtful as he twirled his thumbs. The woman onstage left and another took her place. "Then you don't mind if I take her out."

Sebastian's eyebrows bunched. "Don't tell me you're thinking of Margot being wife number four."

"Margot is too emotional for a wife. I like someone at home waiting for me with a nice dinner, my slippers, and my Havana," Roscoe said.

Shelton snorted. "You've been reading too many scripts, Roscoe. That woman no longer exists." He shook his dark head. "I thought my sister-in-law would make the perfect, efficient wife for me."

"You wanted to marry Gabe's wife?" Sebastian asked in astonishment. The three of them had known each other since Sebastian moved to New York. Gabe had once been Sebastian's stockbroker before he quit and became a full-time artist.

"Yeah," Shelton said, without a hint of embarrassment. "But that was before Gabe got his hands on her and turned her into Ms. Indestructible Independent. Now she's four months pregnant, on the president's list in grad school, volunteers one night a week at a shelter, and cooks the best meals you ever tasted three nights a week."

"Who cooks the other four?" Roscoe asked.

"Gabe does three and they eat out once a week at a different restaurant." Shelton shook his head. "Women. You just can't trust them to be what they seem."

All three men nodded.

"You can say that again," Sebastian said. "Just this afternoon the woman who edged my hair tried to convince me she could play the lead in *A Matter of Trust*."

"You're sure it wasn't just a come-on?" Roscoe asked with narrowed eyes.

"No. She was serious."

"Since you're not bald, you must have turned her down after she finished with your head," Shelton said jokingly.

"I did."

Sighing, Roscoe turned back to the stage. "Maybe you should have let her come. She couldn't do much worse than some of these women."

"This one may not be able to act, but with a face and body like that she doesn't have to," Shelton commented as he sat up and braced his arms on the back of the seat in front of him. "I'd like to know her better."

"My goodness." Sebastian slowly came to his feet. Even though she was wearing an auburn wig, he'd know those fantastic legs and that incredible face anywhere. "That's her."

"Her who?" Shelton asked.

"My barber," Sebastian said, unaware of his possessive tone.

"Are you sure?" Roscoe asked, leaning closer for a better look.

"I want her name and the address of the shop," Shelton said, coming to his feet as well. "That's one woman who could work on my head as well as any other part of my body she wanted to."

Not to be outdone, Roscoe rose. "You're stronger than I thought, Sebastian, if you turned her down. Maybe you were telling the truth about Margot."

Sebastian wasn't listening, he was watching as Hope, head high, shoulders erect, wearing a white blouse and little black skirt, crossed to center stage. She held something in her hand, but it was hidden behind her back. She stopped and looked straight at him.

He took an involuntary step backward. Hatred, pure and sharp, stared back at him.

---

This was it, Hope thought as she watched the shocked expression on Sebastian's face. This was her chance to prove to the snooty Mr. Hotshot Director that she had what it took to star in his play. Not good enough? She'd show him. Just thinking about his put-down made her blood begin to boil all over again.

Instead of trying to repress her anger, she used it to her benefit. Adrenaline rushed through her and she felt almost heady with its power. Fear was impossible. Her character, Eleanor, had no fear. Only a purpose.

By slow degrees, her hand came from behind her back to reveal the seven-inch blade of a mock butcher knife. Gracefully, she sank to her knees. The bound actor's shocked gaze darted from her to the gleaming blade.

"I'm going to kill you, Lawson." Eleanor's voice was icy cold and utterly controlled. "Not quickly, but slowly and with agonizing pain. You were so easy to lure here. You were actually stupid enough to think that you were such a magnificent lover that I could forget you were the reason I spent the last five years in prison. You were so eager to take me from Nolan, as you've taken all of your life from others, that you let your selfish greed lead to your destruction." Eleanor smiled, a flash of teeth and heartless black eyes.

"Struggle all you want, but the ropes around your wrists and feet won't budge. I thought it best, since before you die I intend to take that part of you that you value the most." She ran the knife in her hand up the inside of his thigh. "Are you whimpering behind your gag, Lawson? Not very manly of you. But then, you always were a coward. Worse, you're a treacherous coward, and now you have to pay."

Her voice hitched, wavered. "Nolan will be so distraught by your death, and so will I. I'll consider it my duty to console him. Comfort him."

Her head fell forward. Tears dropped on the tip of the butcher knife and slid to the wooden handle. Seconds later, laughter erupted as she threw her head back triumphantly, her eyes gleaming. "I thought I did that very well, didn't you? No one will suspect that I killed you. After you're buried, I will become Nolan's wife, sleep in his arms, and forget I ever allowed you to touch me. Now, which do you want to lose first, the right or the left?"

Eleanor brought the knife up and plunged downward again and again. Crackling laughter erupted. "You should have loved me. You should have loved me. Now you'll love no one."

———————

O n second thought, I don't want to know how to contact her," Shelton said, his words hushed and unsteady.

"Shhhh," Sebastian said, not wanting to miss one word, one gesture,
one nuance.

As gracefully as Hope had sunk to her knees, she rose. For a long
moment she and Sebastian stared at each other. Her breath trembled
over her slightly parted lips. Her reaction, she was sure, had more to do
with the man than with the rush of auditioning on Broadway. But she
had nailed the scene. She knew it from the look of rapt astonishment
on his face and the stunned relief on the bound actor's face. She had
accomplished what she had come for. Without a backward glance, she
walked off the stage.

"If I can speak now . . ." Shelton began, then continued by saying, "your barber has been wasting her talents. She's nothing short of
brilliant."

"Brilliant," Roscoe echoed.

"She's Eleanor," Sebastian said, excitement running through his
veins.

"Too bad we can't cast her," Roscoe said, taking his seat.

Sebastian rounded on him. "What are you talking about?"

"I admit she's fabulous, but we both know we need someone with
experience to play the role," the producer reminded him.

"She said she had acted before." Sebastian wanted Hope for the part
and he intended to have her.

"Then why didn't you let her audition?" Shelton wanted to know.

"Bad decision on my part, it seems. Excuse me." Exiting the row, Sebastian rushed up to the stage. He looked among the group of audition
hopefuls, but Hope wasn't among them. He went to his assistant, Roger
Kurt. "Where is Hope Lassiter?"

"She left," Roger said, glancing at his clipboard. "I tried to get her to
stay, but she said she had to go home. She was something, wasn't she?"

"Where are her credits?"

Roger handed Sebastian a neatly typed sheet of paper. "Figured you would want to see hers."

With each credit he read, Sebastian's certainty grew that Hope could play the lead. The list of New York performances and tours was impressive. The last notation was five years ago, when she had the lead in the off-Broadway production of *A Raisin in the Sun*. She must have stopped when she became pregnant with Jeremy, but why hadn't she returned? Where was the father?

Sebastian admitted his interest in the answers had nothing to do with casting her for the part of Eleanor, but asked anyway. "Do you know anything about her other than what's here?"

Roger shook his sandy head. "No. Sorry. You want me to try and find out from the union?"

"No, I'll do it," Sebastian said, studying the credits again as if that would give him the answers he sought.

"Shall we continue?" Roger asked.

Sebastian's dark head came up. He had his Eleanor, but she'd need an understudy. "Yes." The sheet of paper in his hand, he bounded down the steps off the stage, went back to Roscoe, and handed Hope's credits to him. "After you read this, you'll change your mind about casting Hope."

Roscoe scanned the page, then gave it back. "If she'll take the part."

Sebastian frowned. "Of course she'll take the part. Why wouldn't she? She approached me about it."

"And you turned her down," the producer reminded him. "I watched her doing her monologue. She was looking at you, Sebastian, and it wasn't with any fondness."

"I don't think I'd let her cut my hair again if I were you," Shelton put in.

"You're overreacting." Folding the paper, Sebastian put it in his pocket and took his seat beside Roscoe. "Hope will jump at the chance to play Eleanor."

"I hate to rain on your parade, Sebastian, but if she was as anxious as you said, she would have stuck around." Shelton nodded toward the stage as he sat back down. "I can see two other women who performed earlier, waiting offstage."

"She probably went home to see about her son, Jeremy," Sebastian said, hoping he was right. If Hope hadn't wanted the part, she wouldn't have tried out for it. Or would she have?

"Call her," Roscoe urged. "Her number is on her credits."

"She's probably not home," Sebastian hedged.

Roscoe turned around in the seat, his gaze narrowed. "I saw a mobile phone listing."

Annoyance pricked Sebastian. "Why are you pushing this?"

"Because I'm taking Margot to dinner tonight and I know she's going to ask me about the auditions." Roscoe tapped Sebastian's shirt pocket. "Make the call."

Pulling Hope's information sheet and his cell phone from his pocket at the same time, he punched in her number. She answered on the second ring. "Hello."

The husky voice came through loud and clear. Sebastian immediately thought of her lush lips, then chided himself for his lapse. "Hope. Ms. Lassiter, this is Sebast—" Click. Incredulously, Sebastian held the dead phone out in front of him.

"What happened?" Roscoe asked.

"She hung up on me," Sebastian said, still not quite believing it.

Roscoe stood. "Guess I can tell Margot she's still in the running."

"Hope will come around." Deactivating the phone, Sebastian replaced it in his pocket.

"I wouldn't put money on it if I were you, Sebastian," Shelton advised. He picked up his attaché case and came to his feet. "I thought I knew what Jessica, my sister-in-law, wanted, knew how to handle her, but as it turns out, I didn't know squat. The other women I knew got excited over diamonds and influential men. I thought she'd be the same way. She wasn't then and she isn't now.

"Gabe had a small greenhouse built for Jessica because she likes to grow her own herbs, and from the way she was crying and kissing him you would have thought he had given her a rock the size of a golf ball. His paintings are bringing in big bucks, and although she's happy people are finally recognizing what a great artist he is, she cares about Gabe, not the money. He always said she was different and had a mind of her own. I didn't believe him until it was too late. Now they're going to make me an uncle. Taught me a lesson that women are only predictable in their unpredictability."

"This is different." Sebastian came to his feet.

"I believe I said those similar words to Gabe, and instead of being the groom, I was the groomsman," Shelton said with a chuckle. "Once I got over the shock, I didn't mind losing, but I have a feeling you might."

"I'm not going to lose," Sebastian said. "I want Hope to play Eleanor."

"But does Hope want anything to do with you?" Nodding his balding head, Roscoe walked away with Shelton.

Deep in thought, Sebastian retook his seat. So he'd come down a little hard on her. It had been for her best interests.

Then he recalled the controlled hatred in her eyes and the knife in her hands, and repressed a shudder. She had ad-libbed that part of Lawson's kidnapping. Sebastian had an uneasy feeling it was for his benefit.

Hope Lassiter was turning out to be a woman as complex as Eleanor. Time would tell if she could be as vindictive.

# CHAPTER FOUR

"Hope, I can't wait another second," Bridgett confessed as she sat in Hope's chair at Della's House of Style. "All you would say last night when you came home was that you had auditioned for the part, then you had to leave to perform at the community theater and we didn't get a chance to talk. I could tell you were upset and didn't want Jeremy to find out, so I didn't press you for information. The only way I could stand not asking what happened was knowing I was coming here this morning to get my hair done."

Pausing in the act of securing a soft white dry towel around Bridgett's neck, Hope met the other woman's worried gaze in the mirror. "I ruined any chance of ever acting in any production Sebastian Stone is ever associated with, that's what happened."

Bridgett's perfectly arched brows bunched. "How?"

"By ad-libbing a scene guaranteed to make a man shudder, then hanging up the phone on him," Hope told her friend.

"You hung up on him—but why?" Bridgett asked, keeping her words hushed.

Hope paused in sectioning the other woman's wet hair. "Because he put me down earlier in the shop and I didn't want to hear him do it again."

With the edge of the white towel, Bridgett dabbed a drop of water from her temple. "Are you sure that's why he called? Maybe it was about the part. You're a marvelous actress."

Hope smiled with remembered pleasure, then spritzed the strands of hair in her hand. "Bridgett, I nailed the scene. Sebastian had this look of total awe on his face after I finished."

"Then maybe he was calling you for the part."

The smile on Hope's face faded. "No. I walked on that stage knowing I wouldn't get the part. I overheard one of the women waiting to audition say that her agent had heard that it was almost a certainty that Margot Madison was after the part and would get it."

"Didn't I read where they were involved once?"

"Yes." Hope's lips pressed into a thin line. The fact that Sebastian and Margot were once lovers shouldn't have bothered her in the least. It did. More than it should have. Reaching for a roller, Hope quickly wrapped Bridgett's hair around it, secured it with a clamp, then reached for another roller.

"Good morning, Hope."

Hope gasped and spun around. Standing there was Sebastian in all his stunning glory. No man should look that gorgeous in the morning. She caught herself before she sighed. Presenting her back to him, she picked up the roller. "Please leave."

"I apologize for what I said here yesterday, and would like very much to speak privately with you," he told her.

"I'm busy," she snapped, then clamped her teeth together. Della had been very understanding about the scene she and Sebastian had created yesterday, but she had made it clear she did not want a repeat performance.

"I see." This was not going well at all, Sebastian thought. Hope wasn't the least bit anxious to talk to him. Her hair was back to being spiked and purple-tipped. For some crazy reason, he liked it better this way. Perhaps because it showed how versatile she could be.

Trying to figure out how to proceed, he caught the glare of the woman in the chair. Instantly, he recognized her from the day before. If the elderly woman left with Jeremy, it stood to reason that she might have some influence on Hope. He smiled and extended his hand. "Good morning, I'm Sebastian Stone."

"If Hope doesn't like you, then I don't, either, and that pretty smile is not going to help," the woman said without batting a lash.

Sebastian blinked, then laughed. Up-front and outspoken, just like his mother. He liked her immediately. "I'm trying to apologize, but she won't listen."

"Half the shop is looking this way. Please leave," Hope told him, but she couldn't help taking a peek now and then at him in the mirror. He certainly knew how to wear his clothes. This morning he had on a tan linen and silk sports coat, an ivory linen shirt, and cream linen pleated trousers.

"Has Margot Madison been cast for the part of Eleanor?" Bridgett asked.

"Bridgett!" Hope screeched. More heads turned.

Sebastian's lips narrowed into a straight line. "No, she hasn't. Nor will she be, if I have anything to say about it."

Resisting Hope, the elderly woman spun in her chair until she could look Sebastian directly in the eye. "From everything I've read, you have a reputation for honesty."

"That's right, and I'm proud of it. I don't lie."

Bridgett nodded her satisfaction and let Hope swing her chair back around. "Listen to what he has to say, Hope."

"I will not." Whirling, she picked up a clipper from her workstation. "Leave or I'll give you a buzz cut."

Sebastian didn't budge, his black eyes narrowed as he studied her face. "You're even more beautiful when you're angry."

Hope gasped, surprise and delight sweeping through her. It just wasn't fair that he could turn her to mush with a look or a few words. "Leave," she repeated, but her heart wasn't in it.

"Have dinner with me and I will." From behind his back, he drew out a fresh-cut flower arrangement of miniature yellow and pink roses, a mixture of tulips, and baby's breath.

"You have style, Sebastian," Bridgett announced. "Mind your manners, Hope, and take the flowers. My hair is getting dry."

Although Hope was aware that Bridgett was conning her, she put down the clipper and took the beautiful arrangement. Her friend also gave her a gracious out. Both of them had a weakness for flowers. "Thank you." Her voice came out unsteady. Before she knew it, like a schoolgirl, she had buried her face in the sweet smell.

"The pleasure is all mine," Sebastian said, grinning like a loon.

"I'm glad we're all happy," Della announced.

Hope shoved the flowers at Bridgett, shot an annoyed look at Sebastian, and picked up the spritz bottle. "Sebastian was just leaving."

"You didn't tell me what time to pick you up," he said, unmoved.

Hope swung back around. Della and most of the people in the shop were watching her. "I—I—"

"Seven, and make reservations at the Palm Court," Bridgett told him, and gave him their address, then held out her hand. "Bridgett Swanson, and I have a fondness for flowers and Swiss chocolate."

Sebastian chuckled and shook her hand. "I'll remember. Until tonight, ladies," he said, then spoke to Della. "Please don't blame Hope. I can be pushy when I want something."

Della folded her arms across the front of her red silk dress. She was no shrinking violet herself. "And what are you after?"

Everything in the salon stopped. Everyone leaned forward to hear the answer, including Hope and Bridgett.

"I want to discuss this with Hope first, but suffice it to say, she's one of the most brilliant actresses I've ever had the pleasure to see perform and I'd consider it a pleasure to work with her."

"You do? You would?" Hope heard herself say.

"I do. Until tonight."

Hands in his pockets, he strolled from the shop whistling.

H ope was a nervous wreck. Bridgett had picked one of the most exclusive and expensive restaurants in the city and it was located in
*the* hotel of New York, The Plaza. And Hope couldn't find anything to
wear. After Jeremy was born she had added a few pounds, and the dress
she now had on was too snug in the hips. "I look like a stuffed sausage
in this."

"No you don't, Mommy," Jeremy said from where he sat in the middle
of her bed strewn with clothes.

Hope turned from the full-length mirror in her bedroom and
smiled at him. He thought it was fun seeing her small array of evening
wear scattered on the bed, when she had always insisted he hang up his
clothes after he took them off. She returned to studying her reflection
in the mirror, then trying to smooth out the puckers in the side seams
by her hips in the sheath. Yet, no matter how many times her hands
swept over the wrinkled sky blue material, the fabric refused to remain
smooth.

She barely repressed a sigh. "Jeremy, you're looking at me through
the eyes of love."

"Won't Mr. Stone love you?" Jeremy asked, climbing off the bed to
come and stare up at her.

Her heart racing, she gazed down at her son. "Why would you say
something like that?"

"We're supposed to love everybody," he said innocently. "Isn't that
what you always said I'm to do?"

Hope felt foolish, and realized she was getting in way over her head.
Her eyes closed. This night meant entirely too much to her.

"Mommy, what's the matter?"

Her eyes opened. She tried to bend from the knees, couldn't in the
tight dress, and wanted to groan. She glanced at the clock. Six-thirty.
There wasn't enough time to call and cancel even if she knew Sebastian's
phone number. "Nothing, sweetheart. Mommy is just having a little
trouble finding a dress to wear."

"Not anymore," Bridgett announced after a brisk knock on the door. "Some things of Cynthia's were packed in the attic. How about this little number?"

It was a dream, chic, black, and hand-beaded. Hope reached out, then quickly withdrew her hand. "I can't wear Cynthia's dress."

"It's not her dress anymore, it's yours." Casually throwing the dress over her shoulder, Bridgett turned Hope around and unzipped the dress she wore to the midpoint of her back. "She always did have too many clothes. I called and she said to tell you to help yourself to anything you find. She's working such long hours with her residency, she doesn't have any time to go out."

"What about Peter Johnson?" Hope asked over her shoulder. The main reason Bridgett had advertised for a female boarder was because she was lonely, with her only child in med school. Cynthia, at the top five percent of her class, was already planning to do her internship and residency in cardiology at the famed Johns Hopkins Hospital in Baltimore, Maryland. The vivacious Cynthia was one of those women who had it all, beauty, brains, charm, and like her mother, was as down-to-earth as they came.

"Struck out, like all the rest," Bridgett finally answered with a sigh. "I may never be a grandmother."

"You got me, Aunt Bridgett," Jeremy said, having heard the story many times.

"Right you are," she said, smiling down at him, then handed Hope the dress. "Let's go downstairs and let your mother get dressed."

"Thanks, Bridgett. I'll call Cynthia tomorrow and thank her as well."

"When you do, tell her how much fun you had so maybe she'll take a hint and try to keep a man for more than a couple of dates. About time too—you're worse than she is about dating."

Hope frowned. "This is business. Not a date."

"If that were the case, you would have kept on the first thing you put on." The landlady glanced from the clothes scattered on the bed to

Hope. "You didn't have this problem when you went to dinner with that school principal a couple of months ago."

"Some of them were too tight," she quickly defended.

"Some, not all," Bridgett said, then lightly touched Hope's cheek. "Tonight is important to you. Accept it and enjoy yourself. You deserve it. We'll be downstairs."

---

Sebastian got out of the backseat of the limousine, bounded up the steps, and rang the doorbell. Tonight he had pulled out all the stops. He planned on doing everything in his power to ensure Hope took the role of Eleanor. Nothing was too good for his future star.

Through the oval-shaped frosted glass in the door he saw Bridgett and Jeremy approach. The door opened.

"Good evening, Mr. Stone," Bridgett greeted with Jeremy by her side. "You're right on time. Punctuality is a good trait in a man."

"Good evening, Mrs. Swanson. These are for you." Sebastian handed her a long white box, and a small rectangular one wrapped in gold foil.

"Thank you, but you didn't forget Hope, did you?" Bridgett asked, taking the candy and flowers.

"In the limo," he said, then bent and held out his hand to Jeremy. "Sebastian Stone."

Jeremy reciprocated with all the manners he had been taught. "Jeremy Douglas Lassiter."

"Pleased to meet you, Jeremy." Since that morning Sebastian had learned that Jeremy's father, Douglas, had died while he and Hope were touring in Chicago. From all accounts, the couple had been very much in love.

"Would you care for something to drink, Mr. Stone?" Bridgett inquired, closing the door as Sebastian entered.

"No, thank you, and please call me Sebastian."

"Only if you call me Bridgett."

"I'd consider it an honor and privilege, Bridgett."

Pleased, she spoke to Jeremy. "Please show Mr. Stone into the living room and keep him company while I put these in some water."

"Yes, ma'am. It's this way," Jeremy said, unselfconsciously taking Sebastian's hand and leading him down the short hallway to the room on the left.

The room had style and warmth. The walls were painted a warm peach. Antique furniture graced the room, which was dominated by an immense bay window draped in pristine white sheers. A fresh-cut arrangement of tulips and lilies sat on the clawfoot coffee table. Photographs were everywhere. It was evident that in this home family was important.

Taking a seat on the sofa Jeremy indicated, Sebastian picked up a picture of Hope holding a baby in a long white christening gown. Tears sparkled on her cheek despite the smile on her face.

"That's when I was a baby," Jeremy said, standing by Sebastian with his hand on his leg. "Mommy said it wasn't a sad cry, but a happy one."

"She doesn't cry often, does she?" The thought disturbed Sebastian.

"No, sir. Just the time I got lost in the store and the time I fell out of the tree trying to get the cat," Jeremy confessed, then tucked his head.

Immediately concerned, Sebastian replaced the picture. "What's the matter, Jeremy?"

"Mommy might not like if I tell you," he said, his little head slowly coming up.

The black eyes were so much like his mother's, Sebastian would have done almost anything to help. But he didn't want to go against Hope's wishes. "Jeremy, we haven't known each other for long, but you can trust me. I'd like to help."

Jeremy threw a quick glance at the door, then leaned over and whispered, "I think she was crying last night."

Sebastian felt the bottom fall out of his stomach. Had he caused that?

"When she came home yesterday she wasn't happy like I thought she would be. She didn't get the part she wanted, did she?" Jeremy asked, his face somber. "She always gets me what I want. At least most of the time.

I wish I could do something to help her. I could wash your car or something to help change your mind." His small face scrunched up. "I'm not
very good at cleaning my room, so maybe we better leave that out."

Sebastian couldn't speak for a moment, his throat was so full. What
a loving, selfless child. "Jeremy, can you keep a secret for a little while?"

He nodded.

"That's why I'm here. To offer the part of Eleanor to your mother."
Jeremy opened his mouth to yell and Sebastian quickly put his fingers to
his lips. "Our secret, remember?"

"I'll remember. Thank you, Mr. Stone." Jeremy threw his arms
around Sebastian's neck.

Laughing, Sebastian hugged him back. The kid was all right. Then
the noise of heels on the hardwood floor in the hallway caused him to
turn toward the door. Hope appeared seconds later. Jeremy must have
heard her also, because he loosened his stranglehold on Sebastian's neck
and ran to his mother.

"Mommy, you're beautiful."

"Thank you," she said, her uncertain gaze going to Sebastian.

Sebastian, his heart doing a jitterbug in his chest, came to his feet.
She was stunning, absolutely stunning. But what had she done to her
hair?

# CHAPTER FIVE

"What's the matter?" Hope asked, her heart sinking at his stunned expression. "Why are you staring at me?"

"Your hair," Sebastian whispered.

Hope's hand flew up to her head. She rushed to the hall mirror, with Jeremy and Sebastian behind her. Try as she might, she didn't see anything wrong with her hair she had spent an hour styling. Finally she turned to ask him. "What's wrong with it?"

"It's not purple and sticking out all over your head," Sebastian told her, fingering the soft, sassy black curls framing her face.

Hope finally understood and would have relaxed if Sebastian hadn't continued to touch her hair. "I-it was washout dye for the play I was in. I left it in as sort of a walking advertisement. Neither Della nor my customers mind."

"Dye? Then you don't have purple hair all the time?" he asked, reluctantly drawing his hand away.

"No," she answered, trying to control her uneven breathing. The man definitely put her body into hyperdrive.

"Mommy's a motorcycle lady and gets to beat up two men," Jeremy said proudly.

Rubbing her hand across Jeremy's head, Hope smiled. "That's the scene Jeremy likes best."

"Sorry this took so long," Bridgett said, coming up to the threesome with the flower arrangement. "But I had a difficult time finding a vase big enough."

"Here let me take that." Sebastian lifted the large arrangement of mixed flowers, his gaze going back to Hope.

Bridgett frowned. "What did I miss?"

Jeremy giggled. "Mr. Stone thought Mommy's hair was purple all the time."

Sebastian looked momentarily chagrined, then laughed. "I had almost talked myself into liking the purple hair, but I have to admit you look lovely with your natural hair." The smile vanished. "That is your natural hair, isn't it?"

Hope opened her mouth, but Bridgett said, "A woman never discusses her hair color or her age."

All the adults laughed. Jeremy peered up at them, puzzled. Sebastian leaned over and said, "I'll explain it to you when you get older. Now, where shall I put this?"

———

Hope's nerves, which had been settling nicely, went haywire again. Walking down the steps to the open door of the waiting limousine, she couldn't get it out of her mind that Sebastian's words to Jeremy indicated he'd be around for a long time. Was he just mouthing words or did he plan to see them often?

She had to admit she hoped it was the latter, and she wasn't at all sure if it was just because of the play. The man was jaw-dropping gorgeous and always impeccably dressed. Any woman would be proud to be seen with him.

He had a style that denoted his wealth, authority, and power. Heads would always swivel when he entered a room. Rightly so. He possessed that special something that would forever set him apart from other men. The way he dressed added to his image. A measured fraction of crisp white shirt extended beyond the black tuxedo jacket. The collars of his shirt caressed, but did not bind, his neck. His black pants legs gently grazed the top of his immaculate shoes. Hope was both thrilled and a bit nervous about being in his company.

Thanking the uniformed chauffeur who held the door open, she got inside the car. Sebastian climbed in beside her. The door closed, enclosing them in a luxurious cocoon of comfort.

Despite the roominess of the backseat, she felt almost light-headed because of Sebastian's nearness. The heat emanating from his body where their bodies touched, from shoulder to knee, wasn't helping. The subtle fragrance of his spicy cologne whispered and teased her senses to come closer. Swallowing, she inched away.

If Sebastian noticed her moving, he didn't comment. Instead he leaned over and picked up a white box from the leather seat across from them. "For you."

Accepting the box, she tugged the intricate white-and-gold bow on top free. She glanced at Sebastian and lifted the lid. A soft sigh escaped her. Inside was a white orchid delicately tinged with pink. Trembling fingers lifted the flower. "It's beautiful. Thank you. You didn't have to."

"You're welcome, and as we get to know each other better, you'll find out that I never do anything I don't want to."

There he went again, talking as if their association would be a long one. She couldn't wait another second. "You mentioned you admired my acting. Does that mean you have a part in *A Matter of Trust* or in a future play for me?"

"*A Matter of Trust*. I want you to play Eleanor."

Hope's eyes rounded in shock. "But . . . but . . . I know what you said this morning at the salon, but I'd heard Margot Madison had a lock on the part."

"I don't lie, Hope. Ever. If they want me to direct *A Matter of Trust*, Margot will have nothing to do with the production," he said tightly. Then his voice gentled. "The major backer for the play was there yesterday when you performed. He's agreeable if you want the part."

Sebastian went on to quote a salary that had her eyes widening again. He anticipated the cast to be finalized very quickly. Rehearsals would start in three to four weeks and the play would open six weeks later. He expected the play to run on Broadway six months, perhaps longer. "All you have to do is say yes."

Hope was speechless. She had hoped, prayed, but now that it was happening, doubts began to creep in. Her temper had had time to cool and the ramifications of carrying the success of the play on her shoulders wasn't comforting.

"Well?" Sebastian prompted.

Her fingers clutched the stem of the flower. "I wanted the role at first, but now I'm not so sure." She rushed on at his hard expression. "I don't guess I really stopped to consider that I couldn't schedule rehearsals around Jeremy as I do my appointments at Della's. Then there are the nightly performances and matinees. I never agree to a community theater play that will last over a week."

"You could hire a sitter," Sebastian pointed out.

"But it wouldn't be me." She twisted in her seat toward him, trying to make him understand. "Most of my relatives and those of my late husband are in Florida. I came here after my husband died, when I was barely two months pregnant. I'd always loved New York and decided to live here. Answering Bridgett's ad for a female boarder was a godsend. She's wonderful, but it's important that I be there at night to listen to Jeremy's prayers, tuck him in, read to him."

"Jeremy wants this for you, too," Sebastian reminded her.

"He may act and sound like an adult, but he's still a little boy." Hope glanced out the window at the glowing lights as the limo sped through the night. "He'd miss me and I'd miss him."

"But think of all the advantages you could give him with your increased income," Sebastian said, determined to win this argument. "He could attend the best private schools, eat at the finest restaurants, travel extensively. The world would be his."

"If the play is a hit and I get job offers afterwards."

Sebastian jerked his head back. "I've never had a flop in my career."

Hope smiled at the affronted expression on his handsome face, then sobered. "No offense, but this could be the first time. I've had the bad experience of having a play close on me. Fortunately for us when Douglas was alive, I kept my cosmetology license current and could find work. But nothing as exclusive as Della's."

Her hand briefly fluttered to her hair. "My job there is my only source of income. The booth spaces there are at a premium and highly prized. I had to wait almost two years before a position opened up for me. If I left, I couldn't expect to just walk back in. My spot would be filled and I'd have to start over someplace else trying to build up a clientele that may not be as loyal or tip as good as those at Della's."

While Sebastian understood her rationale, he wasn't a man to take no. "What if I could guarantee your salary for a year?"

She shook her head. "And then what? I can't gamble with Jeremy's future that way."

He studied her a long time. "I watched you on that stage. You were Eleanor and you loved it."

She twisted the flower in her hand. "You're right. The bright lights, the adrenaline rush. It was wonderful being on a real stage again. But nothing is as important as Jeremy's stability and happiness."

"You're amazing."

Her brows bunched. "What?"

"I said you're amazing," he repeated.

"I heard what you said, but why did you say it?"

"Because you are. I've met only a few women who were willing to put their children—or their husbands, for that matter—before their career," he said. His ex-wife certainly wasn't one of those women. "But in this case I think you're wrong. You could have the career and Jeremy could have his mother. The play will be a success, I can feel it. Once it closed, you'll be able to have your pick of roles. You'll no longer be just an actress, you'll be a star, and Jeremy will reap the benefits. You'll be able to give him everything you've wanted for him. A pony, a swimming pool."

"How do you know what he wants?"

He shrugged. "Don't most children?"

"They grow up fine without them," she said.

"That may be, but that doesn't keep you from wanting to give them to him," Sebastian said.

Hope shook her head. "You certainly were right about being pushy when you want something."

"You haven't seen anything yet. I'm going to show you what star treatment is like." The limo pulled to a stop. Across the street was Central Park. "Starting now. Let's give people in the restaurant their first look at the next star on Broadway."

---

The restaurant was elegant and impressive. Immediately they were shown to a secluded candlelit table. The wine steward appeared after the waiter left with their food orders. Sebastian rattled off some French-sounding name of a wine to go with their filet mignon, which put a smile on the dour face of the steward. Hope bit her lip. Some star she was going to make.

"What's the matter?" Sebastian asked.

Hope saw what could have been a wonderful evening come to a screeching halt. The pads of her fingers stroked the white orchid on the table.

"Hope?" Sebastian reached across the table and covered her hand with his. She started, her gaze coming up to meet his. "If you're worried about Margot, don't."

"Actually, I have a more immediate problem." The heat of his hand was amazing and disturbing. Despite this, she felt her uneasiness increase. She'd never had this much difficulty before. Bridgett was right. Tonight did mean a great deal to her.

"What is it?"

Before she could answer, the wine steward reappeared, filled their glasses, placed the bottle in the cooler, then left. Hope pulled her hand back and watched Sebastian pick up his glass. He'd expect her to do the same. It was now or never.

"I've never developed a taste for wine. Especially dry red ones. Whites are a little better, but not much. The only one I found so far that I liked is a sweet white dessert wine one of Bridgett's friends sent her from a winery in California."

She held his gaze with difficulty. Now he'd think her gauche and probably take her home immediately. The school principal certainly had been miffed. Then she hadn't cared. Now she cared too much.

Sebastian set his wine down. "The fault is mine, not yours, Hope. I should have asked. I want you to enjoy yourself this evening, to be comfortable with me." Leaning across the table, he tipped her chin up with a long, tapered finger. "My first wine was Ripple. How's that for astute evaluation of bouquet and taste?"

Hope laughed.

His eyes darkened. "I like the sound of that."

She felt her cheeks heat. Without meaning to, she fluttered her eyelashes. Then flushed again. Goodness. She hadn't flirted since high school.

"What would you like to drink?"

"Iced tea."

He held up his hand and instantly a waiter appeared. "Please, take this away and bring two iced teas instead."

"Certainly, sir."

"See how easy that was?"

"Only because it was you," she told him.

"Probably." He glanced around the posh room. "The staff here is trained to cater to the whims of the rich and influential. To keep a straight face no matter what is asked of them."

"What about when they go in the back?"

Sebastian paused in answering as the waiter served their salad and tea. "Truth be known, I've never really thought about it and neither should you. Choosing the right wine isn't the most important thing in life. Raising a happy, well-adjusted child is infinitely more important and difficult," he said. "If I or the average person had to chose which one they'd value the most, it would be the child. You've done yourself proud. Jeremy is a wonderful little boy who shows every indication of growing into an intelligent, sensitive, and caring man."

"Thank you," she said. "He's my world. I want so much for him."

"I understand. That's why I'm going to talk you into playing Eleanor so you can show him more of it," he said, reaching for a dinner roll.

Laughing, Hope picked up her salad fork. "You never give up, do you?"

"Not when it's important." Sebastian broke his roll, but his gaze remained on Hope. "Make no mistake. You're under siege."

Her eyes widened. Her hand shook so badly she laid her fork aside. "I'm not sure I like the sound of that."

His slow, knowing grin curled her toes. "You will."

# CHAPTER SIX

Sebastian proved to be a man of his word. Hope and Jeremy, and even Bridgett, reaped the benefits.

The inclusion of Bridgett in what Sebastian called "star treatment" endeared him to Hope all the more. He seemed to know instinctively that if she were to become a success, Bridgett, who had rented her a room at a tenth of what she could have gotten, would benefit as well.

Besides the fresh flowers each received every other day, a car and driver were at their disposal. To top it off, Sebastian had loaned them his own chef, Antoine. Hope and Bridgett were ready to send the arrogant little man away until they tasted his smoked salmon. It was to die for. His sinfully rich chocolate dessert was decadent and delicious. Not one word of objection was uttered when he returned the next morning to prepare breakfast. Since both women enjoyed good food, but not the preparation, he was greeted with open arms.

A couple of days later a man dressed as a sixteenth century French courtier, powdered wig, white stockings, and gold buckled shoes had entered the salon and presented her with an engraved invitation to dinner at Sebastian's penthouse apartment. She'd said yes in a flash. The trunk of Cynthia's had yielded the most divine long red dress.

She felt as beautiful as Sebastian's words and attentive gaze said she was when he picked her up. Everything—the star-kissed night, the scrumptious food, the sparkling fruit drink Antoine had prepared especially for her, the spectacular view of the city and Central Park—was absolutely perfect. But especially the man.

Sebastian could make her toes tingle just by looking at her a certain way. She'd kicked off her shoes and delighted in the experience.

The next morning Hope woke up with a smile on her face, wondering what Sebastian's next move would be. Downstairs she looked at the crepes Antoine was preparing for breakfast and worried about adding another pound to her hips. Yet somehow she let him coax her into eating two. Delicate and light, they were loaded down with freshly prepared whipped cream and plump blueberries. She asked for seconds.

At dinner that night, Antoine even did the impossible, Hope had thought, by cajoling Jeremy into eating the mushrooms that had been sautéed with tomato and goat cheese sauce on his breaded veal cutlet. The man was a culinary genius and was making all three of them into gluttons. Sebastian, who had been invited over for dinner, viewed the entire scene of them pigging out with a satisfied smile on his face.

Three weeks after Sebastian had come into her life, Hope sat in the bright lemon yellow kitchen at the breakfast table savoring the last bite of her delectable omelet loaded with cheese, ham, red and green bell peppers, and whatever else Antoine had thrown in. Finished, she sipped her freshly squeezed orange juice and vowed the next time she saw Sebastian she would tell him not to exploit her weakness and to take Antoine away.

Leaving the house fifteen minutes later to take Jeremy to preschool, she had her chance. Sebastian, arms folded, long legs crossed at the ankles, looking as yummy as the strawberries she had devoured the day before, leaned against his Mercedes. It quickly crossed her mind that she'd like the opportunity to devour Sebastian the same way. Instead of the flush of embarrassment that would have appeared a week ago, she thought of all the ways she'd go about tasting him.

"Sebastian," Jeremy yelled, and raced down the steps.

Laughing, Sebastian picked him up and twirled him around. It had become a ritual the two enjoyed ever since they had seen a man do the same with a little boy. The three of them had been at the park having a picnic. Sebastian had glanced over at Jeremy. Jeremy had grinned. Without exchanging a word, the two had gotten up from the blanket they were sitting on. Jeremy had run a short ways off, turned, and, grinning wildly, had run straight into Sebastian's outstretched arms. From then on, Jeremy had called him Sebastian.

Hope had been so pleased that Sebastian seemed to enjoy and understand Jeremy so well, she had taken him to task only briefly, when after leaving the park he had driven to a riding stable. Jeremy had surprised her by mounting the small pony with very little assistance from Sebastian. Jeremy had had the time of his life. Score another round to Sebastian.

Hope had no doubt that, if Bridgett weren't so proud of her prized flower garden in the backyard, Sebastian would have tried to talk her into putting in a pool. On learning Jeremy wanted to be an astronaut, he had arranged for Jeremy to talk with one of the astronauts on the last space shuttle mission. Sebastian was a tactical genius.

Shaking her head, she watched Sebastian set Jeremy on his feet, then rub his hand affectionately across the top of the official New York Yankees baseball cap on his head. Sebastian just happened to have tickets for the season opener. On Jeremy's dresser, proudly displayed, was a baseball signed by all the players. How did you fight a man who wanted to give you your heart's desire and fulfill the desire of those you loved as well?

"Morning. I'll take Eli's place and, if it's all right with you, drive Jeremy to school. I thought you might be tired, since I kept you out so late last night dancing. Eli will pick you up at ten-forty to take you to Della's," Sebastian said, his large hand resting comfortably on Jeremy's shoulder. It amazed him that he had come to care for the child so quickly, and how much he enjoyed being with and pampering Hope.

"I've tried to tell you I don't need Eli to take Jeremy to school, then me to work each day," Hope said.

"A star never walks when she can ride," Sebastian countered.

Hope wrinkled her nose. "Just the ones who don't care about their health. Walking is good for you."

"Mommy, can he take me to school? Please?" Jeremy said, his brown eyes pleaful.

"I don't know if I trust you two alone together," Hope hedged.

Sebastian smiled. "No more letting Jeremy steer the car. Right, Jeremy?"

"Right. We promised, and a man never breaks his promise," Jeremy said solemnly, quoting Sebastian verbatim. "Not even when there are no cars around like we did the other time."

"See? We promise to be good." He lifted Jeremy's Kente cloth backpack from his small shoulders. "Go back inside and relax. You said last night your first appointment isn't until eleven. I'll pick you up tonight at eight-thirty for the party at Roscoe's house."

A frown crossed her brow. "I still haven't decided about taking the part. Perhaps I shouldn't go wi—"

"You already said yes," Sebastian reminded her. "Promises shouldn't be broken."

"That's right, Mommy."

Sighing, she shook her head. "Since you two are ganging up on me, I guess I'll go."

"Great. We'll have fun. You'll see."

"Can Sebastian take me to school?" Jeremy asked again.

Hope conceded to a losing battle. Most of her son's conversation had Sebastian's name somewhere in it. He adored the man. "All right."

"Yeah!" Jeremy opened the door on the driver's side and crawled inside.

Sebastian got in behind him, not minding at all that the tennis-shoes-wearing child had crawled across the custom upholstery. Hope was unable to keep from comparing Sebastian's reaction—rather, nonreaction—to Russell's, the principal. He had been furious when Jeremy had gotten on his knees in the backseat of his BMW to look out the back window at a passing parade. Sebastian valued the person, not the car.

"Go back to sleep or have another cup of coffee," Sebastian advised, closing the car door. "Antoine makes the best."

"That's the trouble," she told Sebastian, walking to the car.

Sebastian frowned up at her. "Don't you like his cooking?"

"It's marvelous and fattening." Sighing, she put her hands on her hips. "I'll be a butterball if this continues."

Slowly, like caressing fingers, his gaze ran over her. "There's nothing wrong with your figure. All of you is absolutely perfect."

Hope flushed with pleasure and tried to keep her thoughts together. "Sebastian, I ate an omelet the size of Texas this morning. I have no willpower sometimes, but especially when it comes to food."

His gaze heated, narrowed on her lips. "I'll remember that."

Her throat dried.

"I like Antoine, Mommy." Jeremy had crawled back across the seat and was looking out Sebastian's window at her.

"Let him stay, Hope. You'd be doing me a favor." Sebastian started the motor. "He always complained in the past that I don't let him truly express himself in the kitchen because I ate the same things or was seldom at home for him to cook for me. Cooking for the three of you makes him happy. Good chefs are hard to find and harder to keep. I'd hate to lose him. Please let him stay."

"Please," Jeremy chorused.

How was she supposed to fight both of them? "He can stay, but if I get to be the size of Rhode Island, you two are to blame."

Sebastian chuckled. "You won't, but even if you did, we'd still care about you. See you tonight."

"'Bye, Mommy."

Sebastian drove off, leaving a shaky Hope on the sidewalk staring after them. Sebastian had used the word *care* so casually. But did he care about her as a woman or as an actress? She certainly cared about him, and it had nothing to do with him being a director and everything with him being a man.

H ope was running late. She had decided to lie down for a few minutes and had overslept. If Eli hadn't rung the doorbell, she'd still be
asleep. Thank goodness she only lived a couple of miles from the salon.

Not waiting for Eli to open the limo's door, Hope dashed out of the
car and rushed across the sidewalk and opened the door to Della's. Every
eye in the place converged on her. Something was up.

It didn't take a genius to figure Sebastian was behind whatever it was.
In the past week alone, Sebastian had sent a balloon-a-gram, a mime to
act out that she was to get a full body massage and aromatherapy facial
after work that day, and a ten-pound box of Swiss chocolate for her to
share with everyone in the shop. Whatever it was, she didn't have time
today. Mrs. Kent, her eleven o'clock appointment, was already there.
Hope closed the door.

The music of "You Keep Me Hanging On" filled the air. A man
with a top hat, cane, and tails came out from behind the receptionist's
counter, where he had apparently been hiding.

Taking Hope's hands, he sat her in a straight-backed chair in the
middle of the floor, handed her oversized black handbag to Tianna, and
struck up a pose. The music changed to "Fame." The trim young man
began to move his shoulders up and down, his eyes fastened on her startled face. At the first burst of "Fame" from his mouth, people in the
salon began to clap and keep time with the music.

Hope's worried gaze flew to Della standing near the receptionist's
counter. She was clapping as loud as anyone. She approved. Della had
personal knowledge of a woman wanting to be an actress. Her own
daughter, Chauncie, had been bitten by the acting bug. Settling back in
her chair, Hope prepared to enjoy herself.

The singer poured his heart into the lyrics. Whether he expected
it or not, other voices joined in. People were dancing, popping their
fingers, tapping their feet. Hope was doing the two latter and grinning
like a nutcase.

For the finale, from fifteen feet away, the singer slid to her on his knees, his upraised white-gloved hands holding his cane and top hat. The music ended as he stopped a scant five inches away. "Be Eleanor and fame is just the beginning."

Hope momentarily palmed her face, outrageously delighted.

"What shall I tell Mr. Stone?" the singer asked, lowering his arms.

"That he's getting there."

"Perhaps this will help." He snapped his fingers and stood.

The rising murmurs of oohs and aahs from behind Hope had her twisting around in her seat. Two powerfully built men in skin-tight black leather pants, their hard muscles rippling across incredible wide, bare chests, were moving through the crowd passing out long-stemmed yellow roses and candy kisses from baskets held by two attractive dark-haired women in long black dresses. If the group came to a man, one of the women would give the flower and chocolate.

Finished, they passed by her without stopping. Hope sighed. Sebastian certainly knew how to put on a production. The singer bowed and left as well.

She was about to get up when a lush white rose appeared over her left shoulder. She jerked her head around and stared up into Sebastian's piercing black eyes. "Sebastian." His name trembled over her lips.

"Hope." He handed her the rose. "Perfection for perfection."

Aahs and ohhs came again, but this time Hope barely noticed, her entire attention on Sebastian. She was unaware of rising from her seat or of reaching toward him until their hands touched. She quivered as lightning zipped from her to him and from him back to her.

Someone began to clap and others joined. They jerked and glanced around self-consciously. The sensual spell was broken.

People gathered around them, but Hope wanted to tell them all to go away.

"Sebastian, I should cry foul," Della said, putting her arm around a shaky Hope. "How am I to compete with keeping one of my best stylists if you keep tempting her this way?"

"He can tempt me any day," said a female voice. Murmurs of agreement followed.

"You can say that again," agreed another female.

Sebastian heard the conversation as if from a long distance away. He was too busy trying to deal with his own erratic emotions and trying to decide if he had actually glimpsed naked desire in Hope's black eyes or simply saw what he wanted to see. Because, heaven help him, that's exactly how he wanted to see her. Naked and flushed with desire.

The knowledge hit him like a sledgehammer. He felt light-headed and something close to fear. Why hadn't he seen this coming and what was he going to do about it?

"The floor show is over, everyone. Back to work," Della ordered, using hand motions to send everyone about their business. "And you, Sebastian, leave so Hope can do Mrs. Kent's perm."

"Certainly. Right away." With barely a glance in Hope's direction, Sebastian fled from the shop.

Della frowned. "What's got into him?"

Hope flushed and looked away. She'd embarrassed him with her wanton thoughts. Usually she was able to keep a better lock on her growing fantasies about him. "Maybe he had an appointment. I better start on Mrs. Kent's perm."

Trying to maintain a pleasant expression on her face, Hope escorted Mrs. Kent to her workstation. As she passed her coworkers and their clients, she was regaled over and over about what a fine brother Sebastian was, and if she didn't want the part or the man, give them a chance.

Having heard it all before, Hope said nothing. She had told them numerous times there was nothing remotely romantic in Sebastian's attention toward her. He was simply trying to persuade her to play Eleanor.

Sitting Mrs. Kent in the chair, then draping the young woman, Hope wished she had paid better attention to her own words. She hadn't. Now she had to face the consequences of caring deeply for a man who looked at her as a challenge, not as a woman. Worse, he knew exactly how she felt about him.

# CHAPTER SEVEN

Hands deep in the pockets of his tailored slacks, head down, Sebastian paced the front of his cherrywood desk in his Manhattan office. This couldn't be happening to him. He liked his life the way it was, uncomplicated. He went where he wanted, did what he wanted. He answered to no one in his personal life, and few people in his professional one.

His life was too full. He simply did not have time for this.

It was just a fluke. It wouldn't happen again in a hundred years. A million years.

Satisfied he had solved the problem that had caused him to flee Della's, he rounded his desk and sat down. The sight of the slender blue leather jewelry box stopped him cold. He stared at the box a long time before he picked it up and lifted the lid.

Diamonds winked and glittered. The ten-carat necklace and matching earrings were stunning. He'd seen them yesterday while shopping for his mother's birthday gift. It had been a simple matter of obtaining the jewelry on loan for Hope to wear to the party tonight. Stars did it all the time. But this was the first time he had initiated the request.

All the time that the papers were being prepared, he had envisioned the surprise delight on Hope's face, then her resistance to wearing them. He already had a story made up that they were fake. He'd take great pleasure in putting the stones around her neck, feeling her soft skin beneath his fingertips.

He enjoyed introducing her to new and different things, enjoyed seeing the open pleasure in her face, enjoyed making life a little easier for her. He'd catch himself smiling at her for no particular reason except it just felt good.

It felt right.

Rearing back in his chair, he took the box with him. That should have been his first clue. He tended to be serious. Everyone, including his baby sister, who thought he was "da bomb," often told him he needed to lighten up. And while he'd like to think he had treated the women in his life well, he couldn't truthfully say he relished each and every moment with them. Even during the last couple of days when he went a little overboard in trying to persuade Hope to take the role and she became annoyed with him, he was smiling inside.

"Face it, Sebastian, this has gone way beyond you trying to entice an actress to play a part."

The door to his office burst open and his dark head came up abruptly. Dana, his secretary, glanced at him briefly, then brought her very perturbed gaze back to the woman beside her, Margot Madison.

"Mr. Stone, I'm sorry. I tried to tell Ms. Madison you were busy."

Leaning forward in his seat, Sebastian snapped the top closed on the jewelry box and set it aside. "That's all right, Dana. I'll take care of it."

With one last glare at the other woman, Dana left, closing the door behind her. Margot didn't move. Sebastian knew it was calculated on her part.

In the theater, timing was everything. So were the effects.

She had gone all out today to present herself as a theatrical star and a temptress. She was a striking woman with long auburn hair. At five feet nine, she still had enough confidence to wear four-inch heels. Her mahogany skin was flawless, her body voluptuous. Over the years she had learned how to use every asset she possessed to her full and merciless advantage.

The one rectangular pearl button on the severely tailored jacket of her Valentino ivory suit positioned just above her navel provided an unimpeded view of the curve of her generous breasts and flat abdomen.

Most men would have probably been salivating. Sebastian was pleased to note he wasn't among them.

He dispassionately studied the jaunty hat with a curved ostrich feather, the Kieselstein-Cord brushed gold metal sunglasses with faux tortoise plastic temples, the textured calfskin bag and heels from Hermes. Dangling from her ears were sterling silver jewelry with rectangular mabe pearls set in fourteen-karat gold. On her wrist was a hinged cuff bracelet to match. On the other wrist a twenty-four-karat gold Cartier watch. Not counting the diamond rings she loved to wear on almost every finger, he was probably looking at forty thousand on the hoof. He'd take Hope's simplicity and honesty in a heartbeat.

"What is it, Margot? As Dana told you, I'm busy."

Taking the shades from her eyes, she crossed to him and leaned over his desk. The jacket opening widened. The scent of her cloying perfume wafted out. "There was a time when I could make you forget about being busy."

"Long ago and long forgotten."

Her practiced smile slipped for an instant, then blossomed again. Her voice lowered to a suggestive purr. "Why don't I refresh your memory?"

"I'd rather not." He leaned away from her and the heavy scent. He'd forgotten how much he hated her perfume. Hope smelled of sunshine and a scent that was uniquely hers.

Margot's attractive face hardened. She came upright and sneered, "I suppose it's that nobody little hairdresser you've been seen with lately."

A muscle leaped in his jaw. "Watch it, Margot."

The practiced smile returned. "Sebastian, you can't possibly be thinking of letting that woman star in your play. I was born to play the role of Eleanor. It's ludicrous to risk millions on a nobody because you're angry with me."

"Margot, this may surprise you, but the world does not revolve around you," Sebastian said.

She came around the desk, her attractive face filled with entreaty. "I've never stopped caring for you. If—"

He laughed and watched shock, then anger sweep over her. "Give it up, Margot. Even if Hope doesn't take the part, I'd break my contract before working with you again."

"I want that part," she practically hissed.

"Read my lips. You're not getting it." He picked up the signed contract for the male lead from his desk. "You know the way out."

"What's this?" Before he could stop her, she snatched the jewelry box from his desk and opened it. A strangled gasp escaped her. "Is this for her?"

Standing, Sebastian held out his hand for Margot to return the case. "That is none of your concern."

"They are, aren't they?" At his continued silence her expression went from fury to scorn, then hatred. "She must be really something in bed."

Angrily, Sebastian plucked the box from her hands and slipped it into his coat pocket. "Unlike you, she has enough character and talent not to stoop that low to get a part."

"Why, you!" Margot's bejeweled hand swept back in a wide arch.

"Don't let dramatics ruin your career, Margot," Sebastian warned coldly. "Try to keep what dignity you have left and leave quietly."

Her raised hand clenched, then lowered. Her eyes chilled. "I promise you. I'll find a way to make you pay for treating me like this."

"You have no one to blame but yourself. I'm one man you don't want to have as an enemy." Planting both hands on the desk, he stared across its wide expanse at her. "Don't make the mistake of taking weakness as the reason why I never bothered to try and correct the lie you spread about who broke off the relationship. It simply didn't matter. This does."

Without another word, she stalked angrily from the room. Seconds later he heard the outer office door slam.

Dana appeared in his office doorway. "I'm sorry, Mr. Stone. Is there anything you need at the moment?"

He started to say no, then felt the jewelry box in his pocket. "Yes. See that this is returned."

"Yes, sir." The door closed behind her.

If nothing else, Margot's visit had helped him remember he had lousy taste in women.

---

Getting ready for her date with Sebastian, Hope vacillated between panic, fear, and hope. She didn't want to look into Sebastian's eyes and see pity or, heaven forbid, wariness that she'd pounce on him. Perhaps he really did leave in a hurry because he'd had an important appointment.

She didn't understand what came over her when she was around him, she thought as she straightened her sheer lace top stockings, then snapped them to the garter belt. Who would have believed the quiet and proper Hope would turn into a love-starved, aggressive woman in her mid-thirties? She'd loved Douglas as much as she thought any woman could love a man, enjoyed their lovemaking, yet somehow her feelings for Sebastian were more intense, more needy.

Sighing, she reached for the shimmering gold dress with none of the enthusiasm she'd experienced when she had first seen it in the store. While thankful to Cynthia for her generosity in giving her carte blanche with her clothes, tonight Hope wanted to wear a gown no one else had worn.

The reason made her sigh again. She wanted her friendship with Sebastian to blossom into a new and exciting experience for both of them.

The long dress slid over her head and bare skin, shaping itself to the contours of her body as it drifted downward, then flaring out dramatically at the knee. Reaching behind her, Hope zipped, snapped, then stepped into her heels.

The doorbell rang.

Her gaze went to the clock on the radio. Eight-thirty. Sebastian was prompt as usual.

Trembling fingers gathered the silk organza stole and small gold beaded bag from the dresser. Without giving herself time to think, she swept out of the room, cutting the light off as she went. At least she didn't have to meet him with Bridgett and Jeremy watching.

Thankfully Bridgett had gone to her weekly Friday night bridge party and taken Jeremy with her. A couple of the other players had grandchildren and the women enjoyed spoiling the children when they got together. Jeremy had probably already eaten his third powdered-sugar lemon cookie, a batch of which Antoine had made for the occasion.

Halfway down the stairs, her hand paused on the hardwood rail. Through the frosted etched glass in the front door she saw the silhouette of a large man. Too large to be Sebastian. She stood poised on the stairs until the peal of the doorbell had her moving again.

Opening the door, her gaze went beyond Eli's burly body to the black limo parked at the curb. Sebastian wasn't standing by the car. The tinted glass prevented her from seeing inside. Her heart began to race.

He tipped his hat. "Good evening, Mrs. Lassiter."

"Hello, Eli. Where's Sebastian?" She hated the almost panicky note in her voice, but she couldn't seem to help it.

"He sends his apologies," the chauffeur informed her. "Work kept him at his office. He'll meet you at Mr. Carroll's house."

"He expects me to meet all those people by myself?"

"No, Mrs. Lassiter," the chauffeur quickly said. "He's taking a taxi. As soon as I pick you up, I'm to call him."

Something didn't jibe. "I know his penthouse is only a short distance away from Mr. Carroll's, but it doesn't seem possible that he'll have enough time to go home, dress, then meet us there. Besides, it's only a thirty-minute drive from his office to here. How much work could he have accomplished in that short length of time?"

The young man appeared flustered. Clearly, he wasn't used to people questioning Sebastian's dictates. "If you wish, once we're rolling I'll call to let him know, then you can talk to him personally."

"Why wait?" Picking up the hem of her gown, she went to the nearest phone located on the end table in the living room and dialed Sebastian's private number at his office. After the tenth unanswered ring, she hung up the phone and turned to the chauffeur hovering in the doorway. "What number were you to call?"

"The one for his cell phone."

She swallowed the growing lump of fear in her throat. "If he's in his office, why would he ask you to call him on his cell phone?"

"Mrs. Lassiter, I'm sure Mr. Stone has his reasons," he said. "If you'll just come with me, he'll explain everything when you see him at Mr. Carroll's house."

"No," she said softly.

"No?"

"I'm not going," her determination grew with each erratic thud of her heart. She had her answer.

There had been no appointment. Sebastian had left hurriedly because she had embarrassed him. He'd keep his promise to see that she went to the party because he had given his word, not because he wanted to. He'd probably continue to try and entice her to play Eleanor, but at arm's length. The wrenching pain of loss was almost crippling.

"But Mrs. Lassiter . . . Mr. Stone is expecting you," Eli said with some alarm in his voice.

"I'm sorry, Eli, that you had to drive down here for nothing, but I'm staying here," she said, desperately trying to keep her voice normal. Sweeping past him, she went to the front door and held it open until he reluctantly walked past her.

"Good night, Mrs. Lassiter."

"Good night." Her entire body shaking as if from a chill, she closed the door, her head falling forward in despair.

---

She did what?" Sebastian yelled into the cell phone.

"She refused to come after she called your office and no one answered," Eli repeated as he sat inside the limo.

Sebastian said one crude word.

"I think she was about to cry, boss."

"Hell . . ." Sebastian sank heavily down on the padded bench on Roscoe's balcony. It had been so noisy inside, he hadn't been able to hear. "Where are you now?"

"Still outside the house."

"Good. Stay there. I'll be there in thirty minutes."

"Boss, you know taxis aren't fond of coming down here."

Sebastian stood, a determined look on his face. "With all the limos downstairs, I should be able to borrow one. Don't move, I'm on my way. If Hope tries to leave before I get there, stop her."

"How am I supposed to do that?"

"Cry. Appeal to her goodness. Tell her I'll fire you if she does."

The man laughed, then sobered. "You wouldn't do that, would you, boss?"

"I'm on my way." The phone clicked dead.

---

Sebastian had no difficulty obtaining a car. Because they were used to seeing him calm no matter what, his frantic request had his friends quickly volunteering their cars and drivers. In minutes he was on his way and had Eli back on the phone. It didn't make Sebastian any less anxious to hear the man say he had gone back and looked through the glass door, to see Hope, head bowed, sitting at the foot of the stairs.

Hanging up, Sebastian called Hope, as he had been doing since he'd gotten into the elevator to ride down to the front of Roscoe's apartment building, but at the sound of his voice she hung up. Her actions would have irritated him if he wasn't so worried.

Exactly twenty-seven minutes after he had gotten off the phone the first time with Eli, the limo Sebastian was riding in braked sharply beside Eli. Thanking the driver and handing him a hundred, Sebastian climbed out of the car. "She's still in there?"

"Yes, sir."

Sebastian rushed up the steps. The sight of her continuing to just sit there, head bowed, in a shimmering pool of gold tore at his heart. He jabbed the doorbell. "Hope. Let me in."

Her head lifted. Misery and the glimmer of tears were in her eyes. From out of nowhere he recalled Jeremy saying that he'd only seen his mother cry twice. Sebastian had known her for less three weeks and he had doubled that number.

"I'm sorry. So sorry," he said, not knowing what the problem was but instinctively knowing he was the cause of her unhappiness.

Slowly she came to her feet. His pulse raced. She was going to answer the door. Lifting her skirt, she started up the stairs.

The sight of her turning away from him shook him to the core. "No," he yelled, twisting the doorknob. To his surprise, the door opened. He didn't waste time questioning his good fortune. He rushed through the door and toward her. He'd lecture her later on keeping the door locked.

She pivoted sharply on hearing his running steps. "Leave me alone."

He kept coming until she was in his arms despite her protests. "Whatever I did, I'm sorry."

She looked away from him. "Please, just leave."

"I'm not leaving. I can't leave," he said softly, his hand gently turning her face toward his. "I thought I could."

Hope was afraid to believe. "What are you saying?"

Tenderly, he palmed her face. "That I care about you very much, but I was afraid of getting in over my head. In the past I haven't had such a good track record with women. This morning at Della's I wanted to sweep you away and make love to you."

Her breath trembled over her lips. "You didn't come for me tonight."

"Because I was afraid I'd crack under the pressure of the close confines of the car and kiss you."

"I affect you that much?" she asked, going soft in his arms.

"More than you know."

Her bare arms wound around his neck. "Then why aren't you kissing me?"

His lips fastened to hers, hot and sweet and gentle. A mating of tongues and spirits. After a long time he lifted his head. "I hate that I waited so long."

She nipped his chin. "Same here."

"You're tempting a weak man," he warned, nibbling on her ear. "A very weak man."

Her breath hitched. "Is it going to get your mouth back on mine?"

"Come on, let's see." Taking her hand, he started down the stairs. Outside, he made sure the door was securely locked. Hand in hand, laughing like school children let out for the summer, they raced toward the limo. A grinning Eli held the door open for them.

Inside, Sebastian took Hope in his arms. "Now. Where were we?"

# CHAPTER EIGHT

When Sebastian and Hope entered Roscoe's penthouse, she was blushing and he was grinning broadly. He had taken shameful advantage of the private elevator to explore the softness of Hope's sweet mouth. Each taste tempted, tantalized, beckoned him to return for another kiss, then another.

Hope was uniquely different from any other woman. Quite simply, he trusted her, and his feelings for her deepened with every beat of his heart. The only fear in his mind was the fear of never hearing the breathless catch in her voice when his arms were wrapped around her, never hearing her laughter or seeing her smile.

His arm curved possessively around her slim waist, he led her past the butler and entered the immense formal living area where the guests were gathered. Seeing him, several stopped and openly stared. Roscoe, standing with a small group of people in front of a large-scale fireplace with marble surrounds and a hand-carved mantel, excused himself, then crossed the plush white-carpeted floor to them.

"Roscoe Carroll, meet Hope Lassiter," Sebastian introduced. "The only woman, in my opinion, who can do Eleanor justice."

"Welcome, Ms. Lassiter," Roscoe greeted warmly. "I was in the theater the afternoon you did the monologue and you were nothing short of brilliant."

"Told you," Sebastian murmured, a note of satisfaction in his deep voice.

Ignoring Sebastian, Hope smiled at their host. "Hello, Mr. Carroll. That's quite an honor, coming from you."

"Simply the truth," Roscoe said. "Might I add that you're even more stunning close up?"

Sebastian's arms around Hope tightened a fraction, bringing her closer to his side. The jealousy he felt caught him off guard, but he didn't shy away from it. Hope was his. "We don't want to keep you from your other guests, Roscoe."

Instead of leaving, the rotund man folded his arms, rocked back on the heels of his gently worn shoes, and smiled. "Trying to get rid of me, huh?"

"Yes," Sebastian said flatly. He'd never been jealous because of a woman before, but he had never been a lot of things until Hope came into his life.

The older man chuckled. "Never thought I'd see it, but I guess I should have known when you were demanding the loan of a car and driver. Never seen you so frantic."

Hope should have felt badly for putting Sebastian in such an awkward situation. Instead she was immensely pleased she had been able to crack through his legendary control, but she couldn't allow him to be cast in a bad light. "My fault. There was a mix-up in communication."

"Judging by your faces when you came in, I'd say everything was resolved," Roscoe stated.

A soft smile on her face, Hope gazed adoringly up at Sebastian. "Yes, it was." His arm tightened.

"Does that mean you're going to take the part?" Roscoe asked.

Hope felt the stare of both men. "I haven't decided. I've told Sebastian that I'll give him an answer on Monday."

"Let's hope it's the one we all want," Roscoe said.

"It will be," Sebastian said emphatically.

Hope remained silent.

"Come on and I'll introduce you to some of the other guests," Roscoe said.

I t wasn't long before the room was buzzing. Sebastian left no doubt in the minds of anyone they met that he wanted Hope for the part of Eleanor. As the evening progressed, she felt the heavy weight of the burden he had placed on her. Sebastian might believe in her talent, but it was obvious the others in the room didn't. Excusing herself, she climbed the spiral staircase to the second-floor bathroom.

Her arm clutched around her churning stomach, she stared into the ornate gold mirror. If she took the part and the play flopped because of her, she had no doubts the critics would crucify both her and Sebastian. She'd damage both of their careers. Failure to a proud man like Sebastian would wound him deeply.

Failure would be just as devastating to her. She'd have to give up her dream of ever returning to the legitimate theater. No director would take the chance of letting her star in another production. The roles she'd be relegated to, if she could find them, would be few and the pay scale low. And by then she would have lost her secure job at Della's and have to take whatever cosmetologist job she could find.

Sebastian had offered her a year's salary, but as she told him, she couldn't accept the money. As a result, if the play flopped, the secure life she had worked so hard to obtain for Jeremy would be gone.

All because she had let her heart rule her head. Her feelings for Sebastian went beyond caring. From the very beginning she was aware that she had allowed him to be a part of her life more for personal reasons than professional ones.

He simply overwhelmed her. She wanted to please him, make him happy, give him that which he most desired. She loved him. Denial was impossible. The gut-wrenching pain she felt told her more definitively than the misery in her eyes. With acceptance came fear. If she didn't accept the role, would he still want to be a part of Jeremy's and her life, or would he walk?

She was ninety-eight percent sure the man she had come to know in the past weeks had more honor than to walk out on them. The other two percent was tying her in knots. And if he did stick around, could their new relationship stand up to the test? Sebastian might continue to see her, but each time he did, she instinctively knew she'd see the disappointment in his eyes. She didn't want that, wasn't sure she could live with it.

She was damned if she did and damned if she didn't. But hiding wouldn't solve anything.

Straightening, she left the bathroom and started down the curved staircase. From across the room, Sebastian looked up and their eyes met. She couldn't lose him when they had just found each other.

Her gaze fastened on Sebastian's, she was almost upon the woman in her path before she realized it. Abruptly, Hope stopped. Recognition of the woman in the revealing, skin-tight red gown came almost immediately. "I'm sorry, Ms. Madison. I wasn't watching where I was going."

"Obviously," Margot said coldly, tossing her long auburn hair back. "So you're the little hairdresser who thinks she can act."

The statuesque black woman with short blond hair standing next to Margot giggled.

Hope never took her eyes from Margot Madison's face. Beautiful and vicious. "I'm proud to be a professional hairstylist."

"Really?" Margot said. She glanced at her companion. The two looked at each other and burst out laughing.

"Do tell us more," the blonde said, derision heavy in each word.

Hope folded her arms and smiled sweetly. "I'm not surprised you'd want to know. Your gray roots are showing and, Margot, your overprocessed hair looks like straw."

The women gasped.

"You're all right, Hope?" Sebastian asked, coming to her side and sliding his arm possessively around her waist. Margot watched the movement with tightly compressed lips and furious eyes.

"Fine. We were just discussing the merits of a good hairstylist. My schedule is full, but if you'd call Della's House of Style in Harlem on 125th, I'm sure you could get an appointment with another stylist." Hope waved her fingers. "'Bye now."

Nodding, Sebastian started down the stairs with Hope. "Margot looked mad enough to go for blood. You're sure she didn't bother you?"

"Why talk about Margot when I hear there is a scrumptious buffet around here someplace?" she said evasively. With all the doubts running through her head, she didn't want a reminder of the relationship Margot and Sebastian once shared.

Sebastian peered at her closely, but all he said was, "Do you think you could wait for about fifteen minutes to eat?" They stepped off the last step of the stairs.

"Sure."

"Good night, Roscoe," Sebastian called as they passed their host.

"Good night, Sebastian, Hope. Thanks for coming."

"Good night," Hope said automatically, then frowned. Sebastian was heading straight for the front door. "We're leaving?"

"Yes," he said, going past the butler.

"You're taking me home?" Hope asked in disbelief as they stepped onto the elevator. The gleaming wood-paneled door silently closed behind them.

Sebastian pulled her into his arms. His eyes were fiercely possessive as he stared down at her. "No. I'm taking you to my place, where we can enjoy a quiet meal together and I can kiss you to our hearts' content. Any questions?"

"The same one I always have." She lifted her face to his. "What took you so long?"

---

It's lovely," Hope said looking at the candlelit table on the terrace. On the pristine white linen tablecloth beside her plate was an orchid. Her finger glided over the lush, soft petal. "You always make me feel special."

"You are," he said, tipping her bowed chin upward to brush his lips across hers.

She'd promised herself she wouldn't ask, but somehow the question slipped out anyway. "Will I still be special if I don't take the part?"

His face harshened. "You think this has anything to do with the play?"

Now that she began, she couldn't seem to back down. "I'm almost positive it doesn't."

He backed up a step. "You think I'd stoop to something that low?"

"I don't want to think that," she cried, hating the flatness in his deep voice.

"I'll take you home."

A chill swept through her. She gathered the shawl closer to her body. "I can call a cab or Bridgett."

A muscle leaped in his brown jaw. "I brought you, I'll take you. I'll call Eli."

Hope watched a stiff-backed Sebastian walk back inside the penthouse. A stab of anguish pierced her. There was no way she could share the limo with him. Taking her courage in hand, she followed and saw him pick up the phone.

"Please tell Eli that I'll meet him downstairs. Good night, Sebastian. I'm sorry about everything." Not giving him a chance to reply, she hurried toward the front door.

When she was halfway across the room, an unrelenting hand closed around her forearm and turned her around. She stared up into a pair of stormy black eyes. "I said I'll take you home."

She shook her head from side to side. "Please don't."

"You're trembling. What's the matter?" Anger swiftly yielded to concern.

"I—I want to go home."

"You think I'd hurt you?" he asked in mounting disbelief.

"That's not why I'm trembling," she said, her voice husky and unsteady.

His eyes widened with the knowledge. Desire, not fear. His head swooped down, his lips fastening on hers. Her lips parted on a whimpering sigh, allowing him full access to her mouth. He didn't hesitate.

Bold and greedy one moment, gentle and persuasive the next, his tongue stroked, tasted, teased. With each brush of his tongue, each touch of his sure hand on her heated flesh, the need for more intensified.

Her hands clutched the lapels of his jacket both to draw him closer and to give stability to her swirling world. This kiss was like no other they had shared. It burned. It demanded. It inflamed.

Hope moaned.

Sebastian shuddered.

His arms locked around her slim body, he lifted his head. "Do you trust me?"

Air rushing though her lungs, her thoughts scattered, Hope marveled that he had the presence of mind to form and ask a coherent question.

"Do you?" he rasped.

Pressed close to him, she felt the anger of his gaze, the rapid rise and fall of his chest, his hard arousal. Yet she also felt the tender way in which he held her despite his anger, but more than anything she felt the absolute rightness of being in his arms.

On tiptoes, she brushed her mouth across his lower lip, then bit. "Yes."

A hard shudder racked his body. His arms pulled her closer. "Thank goodness. Thank goodness."

His mouth found hers again. His hands were everywhere on her. They seemed to know instinctively the places to bring the most pleasure. Hope reveled in the pleasure sweeping through her body. Clothes were hastily cast aside in a feverish rush to be as one. The pace was fast and wild and glorious. When completion came, the exquisite ecstasy brought tears to Hope's eyes. Holding her, Sebastian kissed each one away.

"What time does Bridgett get up on Saturday mornings?" he asked, his mouth moving across the damp skin on her shoulder.

"A-around seven." She arched her neck to give him greater access.

"Good," he murmured. "Then we have all night to enjoy each other."

Hope's answer was a broken whimper of need as Sebastian's hot mouth moved purposefully down the taut slope of her breast.

# CHAPTER NINE

Hope had made her decision.

Her arms wrapped around her bent legs, her chin resting on her knee, she sat on the stone steps of Bridgett's house and waited for Sebastian to arrive. Like the schoolgirl she had compared herself to early in their relationship, she was too excited to wait inside for him. She didn't want to miss one second of looking at him, of being with him.

Lifting her head, she laughed out loud with the sheer pleasure of loving and being in love. The past three days had been magical. Saturday morning before dawn, Sebastian had awakened her with a kiss and breakfast, since they'd never gotten around to eating the night before. Sitting up, she had gasped in delight. Red, pink, and white rose petals were scattered all around her. After eating, they had made love. The fragrant scent of the flowers enveloped them. Never again would she be able to see or smell a rose without remembering that morning.

After taking her home, he'd returned after Hope had gotten off work a little after twelve, to take them—Bridgett included—to his estate near Long Island. The Tudor-style home, with two formal gardens, a sweeping green lawn, and mature trees, was incredible. She wasn't surprised to see a stable. They'd gone horseback riding, then swimming in the beautiful pool.

Late that evening, while Bridgett and Jeremy took a nap, Hope and Sebastian, hand in hand, had strolled the winding stone path in the formal gardens and talked about her good marriage, his bad one; the devastation of her husband's sudden death, his relief when his wife filed for divorce and, once it was final, she married a wealthy banker three times her age. Both Hope and Sebastian had caught the acting bug while in high school, but while she continued to act, he had gone behind the scenes to direct. She was the youngest of three girls from Miami. He had grown up in Los Angeles and had a sister ten years younger. Sharing these details had brought Hope and Sebastian closer.

When they returned to Harlem late that night, Sebastian had carried a worn-out Jeremy up to his room, looked at her with longing and regret, then kissed her and left. Neither had wanted to say good night.

An hour later, her phone rang. It was Sebastian. They'd talked for two hours before she started yawning and he'd said good night.

He had spent Sunday afternoon with them playing board games. But today, Monday, was just for them. Jeremy was in school and Bridgett planned to work in her flower garden. Hope and Sebastian would have the penthouse to themselves with a wonderful lunch Antoine had prepared.

She couldn't wait.

A black limo turned onto her street. Hope shot up from her perch, then ran down to the sidewalk. There was no sense playing coy.

The car stopped. Grinning, she quickly bent and opened the door. "Goo—" Shock had her straightening abruptly and stepping back.

"Hello, Hope," Margot said.

"What are you doing here?"

"Get in and I'll tell you."

"Never mind. There's nothing you can say that I want to hear." Hope swung around.

"What about the ruination of Sebastian's career?"

Whirling back, Hope returned to the car, her heart thudding crazily in her chest. "What are you talking about?"

"Get in," Margot said, her voice demanding.

Hope got in and closed the door.

"Very smart of you. We both know what I want, so I won't waste time.

After seeing a picture of you with Sebastian in the paper this morning, I thought you needed to hear some hard facts."

"Our picture was in the paper?" Hope questioned, unsure how she felt about it.

Margot's lips curled. "Don't flatter yourself. It was taken Friday night when you left Roscoe's. Apparently *Variety* had a need to fill space."

"Was your picture in the paper?" Hope asked, reasonably sure she knew the answer.

"My picture has been in newspapers and magazines all over the world," Margot snapped. "My fans adore me. I've proven what I can do on Broadway. You haven't, and if you try to play Eleanor you'll ruin Sebastian's career."

Hope's pulse leaped. "Sebastian has a fantastic career."

"You could ruin it. People were laughing after you two left."

Not by one flicker of emotion did Hope show her rising fear. She was as good an actress as Margot. "People like to talk. Roscoe is the major backer and he thinks I'm brilliant."

"One scene does not make a play," Margot said in a dismissive tone. "Did Roscoe actually say he wanted you for the part?"

"No," Hope had to admit.

"Of course he didn't. Roscoe is a smart businessman. Sebastian is a hell of a director, but even he can be led around by his pants."

Hope hadn't been expecting such a tasteless comment. She flushed. Margot had been watching her closely.

"Did he fix you breakfast in bed?" Margot wanted to know. "Sebastian is an inventive, exuberant lover, and always attentive."

This time Hope was ready for the vindictive woman. Jealousy clawed at her, but she refused to give vent to it. Her expression remained flat. "Sebastian believes in me as an actress. He wants me, not you, for the part of Eleanor."

The earlier satisfaction in Margot's eyes disappeared. Her mouth tightened. "Maybe so, but if the play fails, he's going to lose more than face. He's invested his own money. I know you care about him, so do him a favor and tell him no today."

"You know about the deadline?"

Margot's laugh scraped against Hope's frayed nerves like fingernails on a chalkboard. "Of course. Roscoe told me. He and I are very close. He wants a sure thing. If you think I'm lying, call him." Giving Hope the phone number, she had one last parting shot. "I have a lot of influence in this town and my friends have even more. We can do this the hard or the easy way. Tell Sebastian no and get out of his life, or try to hold on to him and play Eleanor, and I'll do everything in my power to discredit both of you. The next time you see your picture it might be in the tabloids, and I can guarantee the reading won't be tame."

Hope got out of the car, not noticing when the limo pulled away from the curb. She tried to dismiss Margot's words as jealousy, but deep down Hope had to admit there was truth in them as well. One short scene didn't make the play. Friday night she had seen the disbelief in people's faces.

Margot was one of them. Hope was an outsider.

Turning, she walked back into the house and started up the stairs, stumbled, and went down on her knees. Trembling, tears burning the back of her eyes, her throat stinging, she wasn't sure she had the will or the energy to stand. For the second time in her life she had lost the man she loved.

"Hope?" Bridgett called, concern in her voice.

Hope heard her friend, but she wasn't able to make herself move.

"Hope?" Bridgett repeated, joining Hope on the stairs, her hand going around her waist. "What's the matter? Hope, you're frightening me."

"I—"

The peal of the doorbell cut her off. Sebastian. The trembling of her body increased. "T-tell him I'm not here."

"Why?" Bridgett questioned, her anxiety increasing.

"Please." With an effort, Hope pulled away and started up the stairs. "I thought—"

"Please, Bridgett. I don't want to see him. Please." The doorbell chimed again. "Please."

"All right."

Hope's nod was almost imperceptible.

Bridgett watched Hope's slow, measured steps as she climbed the stairs. The doorbell chimed for a third time. Tugging off her garden gloves, Bridgett went to answer the door. The anger in Sebastian's face took her aback.

"Did you and Hope have a fight?" Her hand remained on the doorknob, blocking entrance into the house.

"Why do you ask?" he rasped, unease sweeping through him.

"Because she looked to be in worse shape than you," Bridgett answered.

His face contorted with fury. "Then that *was* Margot's limo Eli recognized."

"Margot Madison was here?"

"Where's Hope? I need to talk with her."

"Upstairs, but she doesn't want to see you," Bridgett said. "I'm sorry, but I have to respect her wishes."

"I need to know what she told Hope," Sebastian said, dread quickly overruling every other emotion. "You've got to let me see her. Margot is a vicious shrew. She'd do anything or say anything to hurt Hope and try to stop her from playing Eleanor."

"I—"

"Please, Bridgett. I've never begged for anything in my life, but I'm begging now." Hope meant too much to him to lose. He wanted her to be a part of his life, and that desire had nothing to do with her taking the part of Eleanor. But the decision should be hers. Not one influenced by Margot's lies.

"Ground rules," Bridgett began. "You talk from outside her bedroom door unless she asks you inside. No shouting. She's upset enough. And lastly, I'm going with you and if I feel Hope is becoming too upset, you'll have to leave. Take it or leave it."

"I'll take it."

Bridgett stepped aside. Sebastian rushed past her. His foot was on the fourth step before he stopped. He almost vibrated with impatience.

"Go on up. But remember, I have excellent hearing."

Giving her a smile of gratitude, Sebastian continued up the stairs. He rapped on the door. "Hope, it's me. Please let me in."

Silence.

"Hope, please. Margot is a shrew. She wants to play Eleanor and knows I'll walk before I direct her." His hand closed around the doorknob and clenched. "Hope, open the door."

The silence was painful and frightening.

His head and the flat of his palm rested on the door. "Hope, don't do this to me, to us."

"Sebastian," Bridgett said, her own voice unsteady.

Slowly he straightened. "Hope, I've always had lousy taste in women. Now that I've finally got it right, I'm not letting you toss away what we have. Sooner or later we're going to talk. I care about you. Just remember that, instead of the lies Margot told you."

His hand flexed on the door. He turned, started down the hallway, then stopped. "Take care of her, Bridgett. Neither Jeremy nor I like to see her cry."

"I will."

His hands deep in his pockets, he started down the stairs, then he whipped them out. Fury darkened his eyes. If he couldn't talk to Hope, he'd find Margot, and heaven help her when he did.

———

Curled up on the bed, Hope heard a soft knock on the door. Bridgett. Sebastian's knock had been sharp, and a bit desperate. "Are you alone?"

"Yes."

"Come in." The door slowly opened.

"Hope, you have a right to be angry with me, but Sebastian was so worried about you I had to let him come up. He cares about you."

She spoke without opening her eyes. "I know. That's why I can't see him ever again."

Easing down on the bed beside her, Bridgett stroked her hair. "You want to talk about it?"

Hope told Bridgett about Margot's threats, and ended by saying, "If it was just me, I'd spit in her eye and tell her to take her best shot."

"Hope, Sebastian is an influential man in his own right and can take care of himself," Bridgett reminded her.

Rolling over on her back, Hope crossed her arm over her eyes. "I know that, but you didn't see the hate in Margot's eyes. There's no telling what she'd do, the horrible lies she'd spread. There is going to be enough pressure on him without Margot stirring up problems. Sebastian was adamant about not giving Margot the part, but maybe if I'm not in the picture she'll calm down."

"So your mind is made up."

"Yes." Lifting her arm away, she rose and called Sebastian's secretary. "Dana, this is Hope Lassiter. Please tell Sebastian the answer is no and that I don't want him to contact me again." Slowly, she hung up the phone.

---

The short leash on Sebastian's temper shortened considerably when his secretary contacted him about Hope's decision. He called immediately, but she refused to talk with him. And the person who had started this mess wasn't to be found. After hours of fruitless searching, Sebastian went to the one person who would get a message to her.

"Roscoe, when you see Margot, tell her I'm putting the word out. I won't work with her ever. I don't even want to be in the same room with her. So if she's invited, don't expect me."

Sitting behind his massive desk in his home study, Roscoe jerked the cigar out of his mouth. "Now, wait a minute, Sebastian. You just said Hope wasn't going to take the part. What about the play?"

"I could give a flying leap."

"Let's be reasonable," Roscoe soothed, coming from behind his desk.

"Believe me, I'm trying. I warned you about Margot and you wouldn't listen," Sebastian accused. "Find yourself another director."

"What? I can't be held responsible for what Margot did. You can't walk out like this. I'll lose millions. I'll sue you."

"You know where to send the papers." Sebastian started from the room.

"Wait," Roscoe yelled, and quickly caught up with him and saw the determination in Sebastian's face. "You'd really toss away millions on this?"

"Yes." The answer was sharp and final.

"She means that much to you?"

"Yes, and unless you help me get her back, I'm seriously considering putting your name on the list beside Margot."

"How am I supposed to do that?" Roscoe railed, stuffing his cigar back in his mouth and mangling it badly. "You said she won't talk to you. Why is she going to listen to me?"

"I have a plan," Sebastian said, feeling the vise that had been constricting his chest since he'd left Hope that morning ease. "There's one place she can't run away from me."

---

Hope made herself crawl out of bed Tuesday morning, walk Jeremy to school, then go to work and get the inquisition over. She'd left work Saturday running to be with Sebastian. They'd see the dramatic difference as soon as they caught a glimpse of her face. Taking a deep breath, she opened the door and walked inside.

It wasn't until she was halfway across the floor that she noticed the absolute quiet. Her head came around. She spotted Sebastian immediately. Her heart leaped, then tumbled back to earth. Whirling, she started for the door. Bridgett, Antoine, and Eli blocked her path.

Sebastian stepped in front of her. "I told you we'd talk sooner or later."

Her hands clamped around her oversized handbag; it was that or fling them around Sebastian's neck and never let go. "Mrs. Fulton is due any minute."

"Lydia is going to take care of her. The charming woman graciously consented to change stylists even before I offered to send her and her husband out tonight for dinner and dancing. Now, about us."

"There is no us."

He stepped closer until his heat, his hardness, and the spicy scent of his cologne filled her nostrils. Her breathing quickened. "You want to say that again?"

She licked her lips. This time it was Sebastian's breathing that quickened.

"Hope." He uttered her name with reverence. "How did Margot get you to leave me?"

Margot's name effectively killed the sensual spell he had created. "I don't want to talk about it." She tried to leave and found herself without her bag, which was now pressed against Sebastian's very disturbing chest.

"What lies did Margot say?" he questioned, rubbing his cheek against hers.

Weak woman that she was, Hope told him everything, her voice so breathless and soft, her words so disjointed she was't sure he heard her until she saw the rage in his black eyes. "I'm sorry."

"Margot will be the one who's sorry once she surfaces." He spoke without looking away from her. "Roscoe. Shelton."

Two men appeared on either side of her. "Roscoe, you're up first."

"I'm sorry for any unhappiness you might have been subjected to, and as the major backer for *A Matter of Trust*, I implore you to reconsider. You have my utmost support."

"Shelton."

"Good morning, Ms. Lassiter," Shelton said, holding up a sheet of paper. "This is the addendum to the contract that was drawn up between Roscoe and Sebastian three months ago. In essence it says that Sebastian has sole power to cast the female lead in *A Matter of Trust,* and unless he's completely satisfied, the production will be canceled."

Hope thought she heard Roscoe gulp. The rotund man looked greenish.

"As for Margot's other threats, they're just that: threats." Sebastian's eyes were sad. "You should have trusted me."

Misery welled inside her. "I'm sorry. It wasn't that I didn't trust you enough, it was that I cared so much."

"For a relationship to be strong, there has to be both." Touching her cheek with unsteady fingertips, he stepped back. "Margot's lies can't hurt me. Your leaving can." He held out his hand. "It's a matter of trust. The choice is yours. Take my hand and I promise you to never let go. For as long as I live, you'll be in my heart and by my side."

Hope blinked. Sebastian's words were the same ones Nolan said to Eleanor in the last scene in the play when he asked her to choose between a life with him or extracting revenge against his brother. Eleanor had been ruled by hate; Hope had been ruled by fear. For both, love was the one answer that would set them free.

"Then I choose you."

Sebastian roughly pulled Hope into his arms to the wild applause in the shop, his lips finding hers for a long, satisfying time. How he loved this woman! He'd stopped fighting his feelings the night of Roscoe's party. Very soon he'd be able to show and tell her how much. "Does that mean you'll be my Eleanor?"

She grinned up into his face. "I'm going to knock their socks off."

# EPILOGUE

The applause lasted for a full thirty minutes. Hope took curtain call after curtain call. Her prediction was correct. She had knocked their socks off.

Holding the large bouquet of red roses Sebastian had given to Jeremy to present to her at her fifth curtain call, Hope glanced in the wings where Sebastian stood with one hand on her son's shoulder. Happiness flooded her, but not contentment. She had her dream, yet there was something else she needed to make her life complete: Sebastian's love.

---

May I have your attention, please?" Sebastian said into the stage mike at Della's Place. "First, I'd like to thank Della for allowing me to rent this fabulous nightclub for the opening night after-party of *A Matter of Trust*. I'll always have fond memories of the connecting salon."

"As long as no one else but Gregory tries to cut your hair," one of the stylists teased.

Laughter erupted. "True. I don't think I'd be lucky enough to find a woman like Hope twice."

Hope, sitting at the front table in a white Valentino gown, graciously accepted the many teasing comments from the women in the club.

Next to her, Bridgett leaned over and said, "I knew Sebastian had style. Aren't you glad I told you to accept his flower, then later helped him make you listen to reason?"

"More than you'll ever know," Hope said, her gaze locked on Sebastian.

"And thanks also to all of you for being here to help celebrate." He held up several newspapers. "In my hand I have some reviews. They all confirm what I've known from the start." His warm, proud gaze settled on Hope. "Because of the brilliant performance of Hope Lassiter, *A Matter of Trust* is a smash hit and a star is born."

The club erupted into another round of applause. Hope stood up, waved, and blew kisses. "I always wanted to do that."

Laughter joined the applause.

Sebastian silenced the audience. "I've been a director for thirteen years and seen hundreds of auditions. During that time I've never cast a role without seeing the work of the actor or actress first. Until tonight. Tonight I'm going to cast the most important role in my lifetime. "Shelton."

People in the room turned to see a tall, good-looking black man enter the room from between two white columns. Murmurs grew as Shelton made his way around the tables to the front of the stage. He stopped directly beside Hope. In his hands was a blue velvet pillow with gold tassels. On top was a white orchid and next to it was a blue porcelain Limoges egg with twenty-four-karat gold feet and hinge closure.

Sebastian left the stage, walked the short distance to a stunned Hope, then went down on one knee in front of her. Opening the egg, strands of Puccini's Aria to Madame Butterfly drifted upward. Inside gleamed a fancy yellow star-burst diamond set in eighteen-karat gold. "I love you, Hope. I can't imagine living my life without you. I've already spoken with Jeremy and he is crazy about the idea of us becoming a family. Please mar—"

"Yes," she yelled, throwing her arms around him. "What took you so long?"

"I had to special-ord—"

"Never mind. Just kiss me."

He did.

Applause erupted again. This time it was thunderous.

Shelton shook his head. "She didn't even look at the ring."

"She has the man," Bridgett said. "That's what's important."

"Then I'd say Sebastian is one of the lucky ones."

"They both are." Bridgett glanced up at Shelton, a gleam in her eyes. "By the way, are you married?"

Shelton blinked, then spluttered, "N-no."

"Well, isn't that nice," Bridgett said, a speculative smile on her face.

Hope wasn't listening to anything but the joyous singing of her heart. She was where she belonged. Where she wanted to be, in Sebastian's arms, and the most marvelous part was that he loved her. Dreams did come true. All it took was a matter of trust.

# Sweet Surrender

ROCHELLE ALERS

# CHAPTER ONE

Maria Ynez Parker watched the tall man approach her manicure station, her penetrating gaze measuring his fluid stride, the precise break of his tailored trousers over a pair of highly polished black wing tip loafers, the casual drape of a matching navy blue suit jacket over his broad shoulders, and the crisp fabric of a pale blue cotton button-down shirt he had paired with a solid navy blue silk tie.

Her large brown eyes were fixed on the lines furrowing his high, intelligent forehead and compressed lips. His grim expression indicated annoyance. And she knew instinctively that his displeasure had something to do with the young woman who had come with him into Della's House of Style for a complete makeover for her high school prom.

Maria was also aware of all the female gazes following the man's retreat from the front of the upscale, full-service salon to an area where tables and chairs were set up for manicure and pedicure services.

All conversation tapered off, then stopped completely inside the renowned salon, with its stark white walls and a distinctive pastel pink and blue marble-tiled flooring. The swollen hush was as smothering as the heat inside a crowded New York City subway car during the summer, as stylists, shampoo girls, the receptionist, the masseur, and the aesthetician, who were waiting patiently for their next clients, watched Cameron King bear down on the incredibly talented nail technician.

He had come into the salon a week ago, requesting to speak to the new owner, Della Frazier. Even before he left Della's private office, gossip swirled throughout the salon as to what he did for a living, as well as his marital status. The more resourceful salon employees had uncovered that Mr. Cameron King was CEO of King Financial Services, an accounting and investment company that had recently relocated from a prestigious Wall Street address to a town house in one of Harlem's historic districts popularly known as Striver's Row. The amateur sleuths thought themselves quite clever once they had unearthed this information, but were frustrated because a week after Cameron had walked into Della's for the first time, they still had not uncovered whether there was a Mrs. King.

*If there is a Mrs. King, then she's a lucky woman,* Maria told herself as the object of her musings stopped several feet from her. *He's perfect,* she thought. A *little too perfect,* she added.

---

Cameron King tilted his head at an angle, staring down at the woman who had been selected to do his niece's nails. The woman Della had identified as Maria Parker was sensuously stunning, even though his impassive expression indicated total indifference to her looks. His eyes narrowed slightly behind the lenses of his thin black wire-framed glasses as he took in everything about her in one sweeping glance. Her short, naturally curly dark hair was brushed off her face, showing off her delicately carved facial bones. Her questioning eyes were a mysterious brown, reminding him of a smoky topaz. Her nose was short and rounded on the tip, and claimed a light sprinkle of cinnamon-colored freckles over the bridge. Her cheekbones were high, exotic. But it was her mouth, full, pouting, and outlined in a soft orange-brown that captured his rapt attention. The shade of her lipstick complemented the shimmering gold undertones in her khaki-hued complexion.

"Ms. Frazier informed me that you've been assigned to do my niece's nails," Cameron said, addressing Maria for the first time.

Stunned by the rich vibrancy of his mellifluous voice, she nodded, finding herself momentarily mute. And there were not too many times when she had to struggle to get words to flow from her lips. His deep, velvet voice seemed to float up from the depths of his diaphragm, swirling around her like a comforting, cloaking mist.

"I have a slight problem," he continued, lowering his head and his voice further.

Maria shivered noticeably as if he had trailed his fingertips over her bare flesh, but recovered quickly with the newest revelation. So, the young woman wasn't his daughter, but his niece.

"What kind of problem?" she asked, speaking for the first time.

It was Cameron's turn to react, to the sound of her voice. He never would have expected the petite woman to claim a husky voice—one that suggested the taste of smooth, dark, rich sherry. His frown vanished quickly, replaced by an expression of inquisitiveness. Maria Parker had earned two points on the asset side of the balance sheet: He was attracted to her face *and* her voice.

"Valerie claims she wants a full set of nail extensions, decorated with gaudy designs and rhinestones."

Maria shrugged a delicate shoulder under her black smock. "It's quite popular with teenage girls to have their nails airbrushed."

"Not the teenage girls in *my* family," Cameron retorted. There was no mistaking his annoyance as his scowl returned.

Crossing her arms under her breasts, Maria tilted her chin in a haughty manner. "What do you propose I *do* about your niece?"

"Give her a set of nails, but leave off the graffiti."

*The pompous buffoon!* Maria sputtered inwardly. How dare he call her nail art 'graffiti'? In fact, she had grown up with boys who scrawled their graffiti art on any flat surface they could find, and some had gone on to become legitimate artists with a sizable following.

Counting slowly to three, she managed a polite smile. "Look, Mr. . . ."

"King," he supplied.

"King." She practically spat out the name. "I am a licensed nail technician, and I will execute whatever it is you want for your niece. But I'm also here to satisfy the clients who walk into Della's. And once your niece sits down in *my* chair she *will* become *my* client. Given her *tender* age, I am certain I can come up with something that should please you and her."

Cameron compressed his lips, successfully curbing his temper while acknowledging the manicurist's facetiousness. Since he had unofficially claimed paternal responsibility for his deceased brother's teenage daughter, he found his stress levels escalating appreciably. And seventeen-year-old Valerie had subtly manipulated him for the past two years. It was as if she were angry with the world because of her father's unexpected passing. Her grades had slipped, she openly challenged her mother and any other authority figure, and there were times when her behavior was totally inappropriate for a young woman. His sister-in-law was at her wits' end until Cameron suggested she include grief counseling with their regularly scheduled family group counseling sessions.

After less than a dozen counseling sessions, Valerie accepted the fact that her father would have wanted her to follow through with the plans her parents had made for her future. She apologized to her mother, improved her grades, and scored above thirteen hundred on her SATs. She had applied to and been accepted to attend her mother's alma mater. And in another eight weeks she would leave New York to enter Spelman College as an incoming freshman. And one of Cameron's graduation gifts to her was that he would underwrite the expense of her senior prom.

Once he committed to the undertaking, he could not believe that the cost of all of the incidentals for a successful senior prom had escalated so appreciably. When he graduated from high school, his senior class celebrated in the ballroom of a catering hall, then gathered on the beach at Sag Harbor before returning to their homes. Valerie had given him a staggering total for the cost of her dress, accessories, limousine service, and a complete beauty makeover.

"I'm certain you will please Valerie, Miss . . ."

"Parker," Maria supplied. Everyone usually referred to her as Maria.

However, the very pretentious Mr. Cameron King would not be given the privilege to become that familiar with her.

Cameron inclined his head in acknowledgment. "Miss Parker. As I was saying, I'm certain you will please my niece, but the final results must please *me*."

Maria managed a supercilious grin. "I'll see what I can do."

He gave her a lingering glance, then turned on his heel and retraced his steps, stopping at the station where a stylist was pinning up Valerie King's thick dark hair in an elaborate twist. He spoke briefly with his niece, offering her a gentle smile while leaning over to kiss her forehead before he walked off the salon floor.

Kimm Gilmore, Della's full-time aesthetician, moved over to Maria's station, watching the manicurist's narrowed gaze. "What did he say?"

"He felt the need to warn me not to put any graffiti on his niece's nails."

Kimm folded her hands on her ample hips, shaking her head at the same time she clucked her tongue against her teeth. "That man better ask somebody about who he's dealing with. I'm sure Della told him that you're the best in the business when it comes to doing nails."

"It probably would not have mattered even if she had. Mr. Cameron King came in here with his own preconceived opinions, and I doubt whether anyone can change his mind."

This time Kimm nodded in agreement. "You're probably right. The brother is sure fine enough to give a second look, but he appears a little too stuffy for my tastes." She glanced down at the watch on her wrist, frowning. "Mrs. Nichols promised me the last time she was here that she would be on time for her next appointment."

"How late is she this time?"

"Fifteen minutes."

Maria spied the eccentric elderly woman as she made her way past the reception area, stopping to exchange greetings with each stylist, as well as the stylists' assistants and shampoo girls.

"She's here," she whispered to Kimm.

Kimm's gaze narrowed. "By the time she makes it back to me, she'll be half an hour late."

Leaning closer, Maria crooned, "Patience, girlfriend."

"Pray for me," Kimm retorted. "After you finish up with Clark Kent's niece, send her to me for her makeup session."

Maria smothered a bubbling laugh. "He does remind you of Clark Kent. Especially with the glasses."

"I call them as I see them," Kimm stated confidently. She waved to Maria, then returned to the area where she performed her hydrating European facials, while Maria waited for the stylist to put the finishing touches on Valerie King's expertly coiffed hair before she applied a holding spray.

Valerie surveyed her swept-up hairdo in the mirror, nodding her approval. Less than a minute later she made her way to the back of the salon.

---

Maria stared at Valerie King's youthful face, smiling. The resemblance between the girl and her uncle was startling. She looked enough like Cameron to be his daughter. They shared the same clear brown coloring, reminiscent of polished rosewood, and the shape of their large, deep-set dark eyes was an exact match. And, Maria thought, if she learned to use her eyes effectively Valerie would be certain to make many a young man weak in the knees.

"Hello, Valerie. I'm Maria."

Reaching across the table, she grasped the teenager's hands, visually examining her fingers. They were long, slender, and well-shaped. Her nails were cut short, but the nail on the thumb of one hand appeared to be bitten away.

"Hi," Valerie said shyly.

"What happened with this one?" the manicurist questioned, pointing to the thumb.

Valerie grimaced, lowering her gaze. "I was stressed and—and sorta bit it off."

Maria gave her a you've-got-to-be-kidding-me look. What did the child have to be stressed about? "I hope you've gotten over your anxiety, because once I glue your nails on, it is going to be a little difficult to bite them off."

"I'm okay now. I won't bite them off." Valerie's even, white-toothed smile was dazzling.

Maria returned her smile. "Good for you." She glanced over at her appointment book. Valerie King was scheduled for a manicure and pedicure. "I'm going to put your nails on first, and while the polish is drying I'll give you a pedicure." She pointed to a carousel filled with rows of nail polish in every shade and hue. "What color do you want?"

Valerie shrugged her shoulder under an oversized baggy T-shirt. "I don't know."

"What color is your dress?"

"I have a picture of it," the teenager volunteered, opening the black crocheted-woven bag she had placed on the floor beside the table. Unfolding a page from a boutique advertisement, she handed it to Maria.

The dress was exquisite—perfect for a high school prom. It was a Jessica McClintock ball gown with narrow straps, pale pink butterflies and green vines embroidered on a bodice of ivory silk, and trimmed in satin with a flowing skirt of ivory organza.

"Very, very nice," Maria stated softly. She met Valerie's expectant gaze. "I'll give you nail tips—"

"I want them long," Valerie interrupted.

"How long is long?"

"An inch," she replied sheepishly.

"An inch? You don't want nails, but talons or claws."

"I don't want them short," Valerie argued softly. "And I want them airbrushed."

"Your uncle—"

"My uncle is living back in the day," Valerie interrupted again.

A shadow of annoyance crossed Maria's delicate features. There was no doubt Cameron King had his work cut out for him when dealing with his niece. "Your uncle may be living, as you say, 'back in the day,' but that doesn't give you the right to be rude. You've interrupted me twice." Valerie recoiled as if Maria had slapped her, her eyes widening in shock. "Now, if you let me finish what I was going to say . . ." she continued, this time in a softer tone.

The young woman managed to look contrite. "I'm sorry, Miss Maria."

"Apology noted. I'm going to give you acrylic tips, then I'm going to cut them down to a length where you'll be able to manage dressing yourself and anything else you'll need to get you through the night without embarrassing yourself. Then I'll give you a French manicure with a soft beige and pink combination to complement the colors in your dress. How does that sound to you?"

She barely nodded her head. Her disappointment was apparent by the set of her tightly compressed lips.

Her expression so mirrored Cameron King's that it was uncanny. *Like uncle, like niece,* Maria mused as she began the task of filing Valerie King's nails before she pushed back her cuticles.

An hour and fifteen minutes later, Valerie surveyed her hands, surprise and delight crinkling her eyes and parting her lips. Her nails were beautiful. The frosted pale pearl pink shade shimmering over her extensions was accented with the application of a sheer beige on the tips in an inverted V design. Maria Parker had not airbrushed her nails, but had added a minute rhinestone near the tip on each of her little fingers.

"Do you like it?" Maria questioned.

"I love it," Valerie gushed.

"Good. Now for your toes."

# CHAPTER TWO

Valerie, silent the entire time Maria had quickly and expertly transformed her hands, chatted incessantly while her feet were pampered.

"I can't believe that in another two months I'll be a college freshman," she sputtered, waving her hands to facilitate drying her fingernail polish.

Maria did not look at Valerie as she applied a layer of thick oil over her legs and feet before she massaged the muscles to stimulate blood flow. "Where are you going?"

"Spelman. My mother went there."

"Excellent school. What's your major?"

A slight frown furrowed Valerie's forehead. "I haven't decided on a major. I don't know if I want to follow in my parents' footsteps. My mom is a lawyer and my dad was a dentist."

This time Maria's head came up as she met her client's direct gaze. "Was?"

Closing her eyes, Valerie slowly nodded her head. "He died two years ago. He was waiting to cross a street and a taxi driver tried to pass a bus, lost control of his cab, and jumped the curb. Daddy died instantly."

Maria's fingers tightened slightly around Valerie's slender ankles. She could not imagine her own father not being alive. Even though Raymond Parker was now sixty-five, she never thought of a time when she could not pick up a telephone and hear his voice. From the time she drew her first breath to cry, she had become her father's little princess.

He had been the proud father of three sons, but yearned for a daughter. After two years of relentless urging, Raymond had finally convinced Ynez Rivera-Parker to agree to having a fourth child, and when they were told it was a girl, he celebrated for a month.

"I'm so sorry, Valerie."

Nodding, the teenager opened her eyes while biting down on her lower lip. "My Uncle Ronnie acts like my father now."

Maria flashed a reassuring smile. "You're very lucky to have an uncle like him."

"I don't know about that, because I think he's more strict than my father ever was. Daddy was ten years older than Uncle Ronnie, but everyone says that Uncle Ronnie always acted like the older brother."

The topic of conversation switched abruptly from Cameron King to the names of the celebrities who frequented Della's House of Style for their extensive beauty services. Valerie revealed that she had read a two-page spread about the salon in a back issue of *Essence* magazine, and decided she wanted to come to Della's for a beauty makeover for her prom.

And there was no doubt after Kimm Gilmore completed her facial regimen and applied makeup to the young woman's face that she would definitely turn heads. She was tall, standing five-seven, and claimed the supple, slender body of an adolescent girl on the threshold of full womanhood.

Her manicure completed and her feet ensconced in the rubber thongs she had worn into the salon, Valerie was shown to the area where she would undergo the last service of what had turned into a half day of beauty.

———

I t was nearing five-thirty when Maria sat in the employees' lounge area with a colorist and a stylist, her bare, professionally groomed feet propped up on another chair, waiting for the arrival of her last client, when a shampoo girl stuck her head in the door.

"Maria, there's a man out here who wants to see you."

Running her fingers through her curly hair, she shifted on the chair and stared up at Kiki. "Who is he?"

"He sure *ain't* one of your brothers," she drawled sarcastically, visually examining her airbrushed nails. "He's that stiff dude that came in earlier with his niece."

Reecie DuBois, Della's chief colorist, sat up quickly, slipping his bare feet into a pair of clogs. Brilliant streaks of a flamingo pink blared from the straightened, blunt-cut strands of hair secured off his long neck by a neon green elastic band.

Maurice "Reecie" DuBois, formerly known as Michael Dixon, was Della's resident cause célèbre. A brilliant, non-practicing attorney, Maurice won a high-profile discrimination case when he sued a very conservative law firm who summarily fired him because he favored wearing colorful suits to court for a trial. The partners at the firm were willing to overlook the expertly tailor-made garments in varying colors of yellow, orange, red, and green, but drew the line when Michael Dixon appeared before the bench sporting a matching shade of hair dye. He settled out of court for a high six-figure sum, invested it, then went to school for cosmetology.

"I just need one peek at him to see if he's real."

"Don't bother yourself, Maurice. He's real, all right," the stylist remarked, not moving or opening her eyes. "He's the type of man who will spend the rest of his life by his lonesome because he will claim that he can't find a woman to come up to his standards."

"How do you know he isn't married?" Maria asked at the same time she pushed her feet into a pair of sand-colored espadrilles.

"Is he?" the colorist and stylist questioned in unison.

"I'll find out for you," she teased as she left the lounge and walked through the salon to the reception area. She noticed the noble tilt of Cameron King's head as he studied some of the signed head shots of many well-known celebrities who had passed through the doors of Della's House of Style.

Her gaze was drawn to his hands clasped behind his back. Again, she admired the impeccable cut of his double-breasted jacket, doubting whether the suit had come off a department store rack. She surveyed him from head to toe and found him lacking for nothing. He was fastidiously groomed and his bearing indicated that he was in control—at all times.

"Mr. King."

Cameron turned at the sound of Maria's voice, his gaze narrowing in concentration behind the lenses of his glasses. He smiled at her, the gentle expression transforming and softening his stoic features. She did not know how she had missed it, but she had not noticed the attractive cleft in his strong chin.

He inclined his head. "Miss Parker. I came back to see you because when I returned to pick up Valerie, the receptionist said you had stepped out."

"Did you come back to let me know that you're not pleased with my work?"

His smile widened, the gesture displaying a mouth filled with large, sparkling white teeth. Seeing his teeth prompted her to wonder if his late brother had been his dentist.

"Quite the contrary, Miss Parker." Reaching into the breast pocket of his jacket, he withdrew a white envelope and held it out to her. "Please take it," he urged softly when she stared at his long, slender brown fingers.

Chancing a quick glance at the receptionist, she frowned at Ramona, who had put down the telephone receiver to listen to the interchange between her and Cameron. Ramona did not seem the least bit embarrassed that she had been caught eavesdropping.

Maria took the envelope and slipped it into the large pocket of her black smock. A small smile of enchantment caressed her lush mouth. "Thank you, Mr. King."

Cameron inclined his head again, sucking in his breath. Her smile was radiant, reminiscent of a sunrise where all of her face lit up with the sensual gesture.

"You're quite welcome, Miss Parker. Have a good evening."

"You, too."

He hesitated, then said, "Thank you." He turned to walk out of Della's, leaving her staring at his back at the same time her heart pumped wildly against her ribs.

A slow, knowing smile curved Ramona's mouth. She could not wait to tell everyone what she saw. The normally loquacious Maria Parker was practically a mute, and she knew it was because of Cameron King.

"Maria, your five-thirty says she'll be ten minutes late."

Cameron overheard the receptionist as he opened the door and stepped out onto the crowded avenue. Now he knew Miss Parker's first name. He had wanted to question his niece about the woman who had worked her artistic magic on Valerie's hands, but did not want to appear overzealous about a woman whose very presence elicited a spark of desire in him for the first time in more than five years.

Those who were familiar with Cameron King would have been surprised to know that a woman had garnered his attention. What would shock them more was the fact that she was a manicurist.

---

M aria ignored the questions thrown at her about Cameron King's marital status as she prepared for her next client.

"Leave me alone, Maurice," she hissed under her breath. "I didn't ask him if he was married."

"Well, why didn't you?" he questioned.

"Because that's too personal. And besides, why would you want to know? You wouldn't be interested in *him*."

Despite the fact that the former Michael Dixon dressed flamboyantly, he was *all* man under the flashy threads and brightly colored hair. He had confessed he dressed the way he did because he liked shocking people. And most times he was very successful.

Maurice folded his hands on his slim hips, shaking his head vigorously, ponytail swaying. "I'm just trying to help out the single sisters.

You know a *good man* is hard to find, and your Mr. Cameron King looks like a very good one."

"He's not *mine*," she argued softly, removing her cuticle clippers from a sterilizing tray.

"He could be."

Maria's head came up and she stared up at Maurice. A slight frown furrowed her forehead. She liked Maurice—a lot. He was the only one of two stylists at Della's she permitted to cut her hair. He badgered her incessantly to allow him to highlight her very dark hair, but she refused. She liked her sable brown hair color.

"Why would you say that?"

Leaning in closer, Maurice curved an arm around her waist. "Many people look at my clothes and hair, forgetting that I am a man. And because you've been without one for so long, you've forgotten how a man looks at a woman when he's interested in her. And despite the fact that your Mr. King exhibits as much emotion as a robot, that still doesn't stop his testosterone from going into overdrive."

Her large eyes widened until they resembled silver dollars. "You saw *all* that?"

Maurice hugged her, the top of her head coming under his chin. "That and a lot more, Maria. Girl, you know I like you," he continued, whispering close to her ear. "Now, if you'd give me the chance to show you how much I like you, I'd cut my hair, get rid of the color, pull my conservative Brioni suits out of my closet, and trade in my hair dye, scissors, and bumper curler for a cubicle in any rinky-dink law firm."

Tilting her chin, she smiled up at him and wrinkled her delicate nose. "No, thank you, friend."

"Don't you want to see what I look like without the costume?"

Her gaze swept over his perfectly balanced features and smooth nut-brown face. Even wearing his "costume," Maurice DuBois was an extremely attractive man. He stood six-two and weighed an even one hundred seventy-five pounds, and whenever he walked down the street he always turned heads—male and female.

Maria patted his clean-shaven jaw. "Not at all. I happen to like what I see." She knew she liked Maurice DuBois, whereas she was not certain whether she would have liked the former Michael Dixon.

Pulling her closer, he brushed a gentle kiss over her parted lips. "Thank you, friend."

"I'm sorry to break up this very tender moment, but you know what Miss Della says about fraternizing on the salon floor."

Maurice glared at KiKi. They got along like oil and water. "Did you want something, *Miss Furor Loquendi*?"

The shampoo girl rolled her eyes. "Don't you be calling me names in your lawyer language, Moe-reese."

"It's Reecie to you."

Waving her hand, KiKi drawled, "Whatever. Miss Della wants to see you, *Reecie*. And I gonna tell her that you're callin' me names."

Winking at Maria, Maurice followed the shampoo girl to Della's private office. "Well, you do have diarrhea of the mouth," he mumbled under his breath, translating the Latin.

Maria smiled to herself as she sat down and waited patiently for her last client for the day. All she wanted was to finish up and go home. Her work schedule for the past three weeks had been exhausting. All of the salon's services were utilized, with a steady flow of clients coming in for full sets of nails, perms, braids, weaves, facials, and massages for weddings, graduations, confirmations, communions, and proms.

Perusing her appointment book, she breathed a sigh of relief. There were a number of days over the next two months she had crossed out; she made it a practice to work only four days a week during the summer. Della had finally hired two additional backup manicurists, which allowed Maria to work a Tuesday-through-Friday schedule during July and August.

She spied her client, offering her a warm smile. "How are you, Mrs. Austin?"

An attractive middle-aged woman with flawless ebony-hued skin sat down on the other side of the manicure table, dropping her handbag on the floor beside her chair. "Fine, thank you. I'm sorry about being late."

Maria reached for her hands, quickly assessing what needed to be done. There was no way she could repair the tattered silk wraps. The woman would need a complete new set, and knew it would be close to seven o'clock before she would leave Della's House of Style to go home.

---

At exactly seven-fifteen Maria walked into the two-bedroom apartment, which was twenty stories above the streets of East Harlem. Kicking off her shoes, she walked on bare feet across the cool, highly polished parquet floor; she placed her handbag on a massive beveled glass-topped table positioned between two matching love seats before making her way to the narrow utility kitchen. She withdrew from a small shopping bag several containers filled with prepared shrimp, cucumber, and pasta salads she had purchased at Della's adjoining café and stored them in the refrigerator.

Then she performed what had become a ritual since she had moved into the spacious, modern apartment building—she lit dozens of candles—oil and scent-filled ones. The ritual was one she had established once she had married Tyree Johnston. She had fallen in love with Tyree on sight, married him less than a year later, then buried him within six months of becoming his wife. Their time together was short, but filled with an overflow of love, passion, and pain. A lasting pain she had not recovered from, even though she had been widowed for nearly seven years.

She was twenty-one when she met Tyree. Both were attending Baruch College as business majors. They married a month after graduating, and a week after Tyree celebrated his twenty-fourth birthday he was diagnosed with testicular cancer. His suffering was merciful because he did not survive the year, and when Maria stood at his graveside to say good-bye for the last time, she felt as if she had buried part of herself with her young husband.

Each time she lit a candle she felt reconnected to the light Tyree had radiated whenever they were together. She loved everything about him: his smile, voice, sensitivity, humor, and most of all his passion. And it had taken years for her to realize that she had not permitted another man in her life because she still wasn't willing to let Tyree go. She was still in love with her dead husband.

Returning to the living room, she stood at the floor-to-ceiling, wall-to-wall window and stared down at the traffic moving along the FDR Drive. Her gaze shifted upward to the many bridges connecting Manhattan with the other boroughs. It was one of those rare New York City late spring days when a light breeze and low humidity swept away the smog that made the city's air quality so unhealthy. This would be one night when she would be able to see many of the constellations with the naked eye.

Turning away from the window, she moved over to the table, picked up her handbag, and removed the envelope Cameron King had given her. She slipped a fingernail under the flap and withdrew a crisp new fifty-dollar bill.

A slow smile parted her moist lips as she chuckled softly. He had given her a fifty-dollar tip! There was no doubt that she had pleased not only Valerie but also her uncle.

# CHAPTER THREE

Maria walked into Della's the following morning, forty-five minutes earlier than her first client. She greeted three stylists with a barely audible "Good morning," not stopping to chat as she usually did whenever she came in early. She continued toward the rear of the salon, still wearing her sunglasses.

"What's up with her?" Deirdre Lee mumbled under her breath, staring at Maria's retreating back.

"Maybe she had a fight with her man," another stylist suggested.

Deirdre's expression suddenly went grim at the same time Wilma Rogers, the salon's senior employee, placed a forefinger over her lips and shook her head at the other two, who managed to look contrite. Most who worked at Della's knew Maria Parker had been widowed before she was twenty-five, and in the five years she had worked at the salon no one had ever seen her with a man. Even when everyone gathered for their annual holiday festivities, she attended alone.

---

Maria made her way to the room set up for facials, inhaling the sensual fragrance of vanilla, jasmine, patchouli, and bergamot wafting from burning candles set up on several tables.

"Kimm?"

The aesthetician's head appeared around a screen decorated with Japanese characters. "Give me a minute and I'll be right with you." Kimm moved from behind the screen, walking into the middle of the room. She had exchanged her street clothes for a pair of white slacks and a matching loose-fitting blouse. She glanced at the clock on the wall. "You're in early this morning."

Maria nodded. "I need your help." She removed her sunglasses.

"What happened to your eyes? Allergies?"

She touched her swollen eyelids gingerly. "No. Insomnia."

Kimm wagged her head. "Sit down and let me see if I can bring down some of the swelling."

Maria lay down on the facial chair, permitting Kimm to work her restorative magic to lessen the puffiness around her eyes. What she did not tell her was that she had spent the night crying—crying because she missed Tyree, and crying because she felt totally isolated for the first time in her life.

She had lain in bed, tossing restlessly, trying to remember how it was to have a man sleep beside her, hold her close, inhale his male scent, and welcome him into her body. The images were so vivid that her body reacted violently to a repressed passion that left her shaking and crying with its pulsing aftermath.

She was thirty-one years old, widowed, solvent, owned her own cooperative apartment, and had earned an undergraduate degree in business; she also was a licensed hairstylist, cosmetologist, and nail technician. She had everything and still she was despondent.

But her state of loneliness was of her own doing. She had rejected advances from more men than she could remember, because she had held on to everything that had been Tyree Johnston except his name. They had planned to go into business together, therefore she and Tyree had agreed that she would retain her maiden name.

There was one thing she knew she was, and that was a realist. Maurice mentioning Cameron King's interest in her had triggered an awareness that she wanted a man interested in her; she wanted to date, and she wanted to experience the milestones many women her age sought. And that meant becoming a wife and a mother.

She lay on the facial chair, savoring the coolness of two ice-soaked tea bags placed over her eyes. The taped music coming through concealed speakers lulled her into a state of complete relaxation as she lost track of time. She hadn't realized she had drifted off to sleep until Kimm shook her gently.

"Wake up, Maria. There's a delivery for you at the reception desk."

Sitting up, she waited for Kimm to remove the tea bags from her eyes and blot away the moisture. Staring at her reflection in the mirrored wall, she smiled.

"Thanks for the quick fix."

Kimm nodded, smiling. "Anytime, girlfriend."

Her brow furrowing in concentration, she tried remembering what she had ordered from one of the many catalogues that were stuffed into her apartment building mailbox. Her frown deepened when she saw that everyone from the salon floor had gathered in the reception area.

She caught the glimpse of something wrapped in cellophane. "Excuse me, please. Her voice was barely audible above the excited babble as the staff of Della's crowded closer to the perplexed deliveryman. Clearing her throat, Maria said loudly, "How many Maria Parkers do we have working here?" The throng parted in a manner that reminded her of Charlton Heston parting the Red Sea in *The Ten Commandments*.

Ramona waved at her, grinning broadly. "Maria. You have a delivery."

She felt eight pairs of eyes watching her as she stepped forward and smiled at the deliveryman, who cradled a magnificent crystal vase filled with a profusion of pale pink lilies, roses, tulips, hydrangeas, orchids, and peonies.

The man returned her smile. "Miss Parker?" Maria nodded. "I need your signature." There was total silence as she scrawled her name on a typed receipt.

"Please wait here while I get you a tip," she said softly. Her heart started up a rapid pumping when she read the name of the sender: King Financial Services.

"That's all right, Miss Parker. Mr. King took care of that."

"Well, all right!" Kimm drawled as she peered around Maria's shoulder. "It looks as if I'm going to have to change my opinion of Mr. Clark Kent. There *is* hope for the brother."

"It's rather heavy, Miss Parker. Where do you want me to put this?" the deliveryman asked Maria.

Folding her hands on her hips, she met the expectant gazes of everyone staring back at her. There was no room in her area of the salon for the massive vase. "Leave them here. That way everyone can enjoy them." What she did not say was that at the end of the day she would take her flowers home with her.

Plucking the card off the cellophane, she slipped it into the pocket of her loose-fitting Laura Ashley print dress. A mysterious smile softened her mouth as she turned and made her way to her manicure station to await her first client.

Her day, which had begun miserably, had suddenly brightened with the arrival of these flowers. Taking a surreptitious peek at the card, her smile widened. Scrawled across the back of a business card belonging to King Financial Services were the words, "THANKS AGAIN—CK."

She returned the card to her pocket and had just slipped on her black smock when Maurice approached her. "What did I tell you about his testosterone? The M-A-N wants you B-A-D."

Tilting her chin, Maria wrinkled her nose. "Stop being a drama queen, Maurice. He's only a satisfied customer."

"How many of us have gotten a bouquet of flowers from a *satisfied* customer? Tips, yes. Flowers, no."

She shrugged a delicate shoulder. "Maybe he's different."

"You've got that right—"

"Maria, you're needed up front," a shampoo girl interrupted. "Ramona has someone on the phone who only speaks Spanish."

"We'll continue this later, *chica*," Maurice promised Maria as she walked to the reception area to communicate with the Spanish-speaking caller.

Her being fully bilingual had been a major consideration for Louis Sweet, the former owner of Rosie's Curl and Weave, when he hired her a week after she had graduated from beauty school. Her facility with both languages and the fact that she was born, raised, and still resided in East Harlem were contributing factors that supported his decision to offer Maria Parker a position at one of Harlem's most notable salons.

———————

Cameron did not know why, but he found himself on 125th Street and several feet from the door to Della's House of Style. He knew the salon offered an array of services catering to both male and female, but the fact remained that he had had his hair cut by the same barber for more than ten years, so there was no need for him to seek out their haircutting services.

Standing motionless, he stared at the receptionist through the plate-glass window, trying to fathom why he had left his 139th Street office to come to 125th Street.

He was cognizant of the changes in his personality over the past two weeks. Changes that were not only apparent to himself, but also to his employees. And the change had come the day he met Maria Parker for the first time.

He had tried rationalizing it was the recent tax season's twelve-hour workday that had left him feeling burned out, mentally drained. He'd closed his office for two weeks following the April fifteenth midnight filing deadline, giving everyone a much-needed break. Everyone but himself. His niece was scheduled to graduate from high school, and he had delayed his own vacation to assist his sister-in-law with the preparations for Valerie's prom and her inevitable move to Atlanta, Georgia.

However, that did not explain his daydreaming about Maria Parker or his impulsive decision to send her flowers. And the flowers had nothing to do with her services—the monetary tip had taken care of that—but were an overture from a man who was interested in a woman. When he picked up the telephone to call the florist and order the bouquet, he had not considered whether she was married, engaged, or committed to dating another man.

Subsequent to his action, he agonized over her marital status until his secretary handed him a small blue envelope with Maria Parker's return address embossed on the flap in a dark blue script; he read the enclosed note card, his anxiety easing. She had written to thank him for the flowers, signing it, "Fondly, Maria P."

He pondered the word *fondly*, comparing it to synonyms like *affectionately*, *lovingly*, or *tenderly*, then spent the next hour wondering why he had spent the time analyzing a single word. And what was it about the manicurist that kept him coming back to see her?

He walked the remaining six feet to the entrance of the salon, knowing all he had to do was open the door to find the answers. He did, and stepped into the expansive reception area.

The receptionist offered a warm smile as he approached the counter. He returned it, nodding. "I don't have an appointment."

"That's not a problem, Mr. King," Ramona replied, her practiced, professional smile in place. "What can we do for you today?"

"I'd like a manicure."

Ramona glanced down at the large appointment book covering most of the surface of the countertop. "Anyone in particular?"

Cameron inhaled, then let out his breath slowly. "Miss Parker."

The receptionist's head came up quickly, her expertly waxed eyebrows lifting slightly. Her suspicions were right. The man everyone at Della's had taken to calling Clark Kent liked Maria.

"Miss Parker is with a customer right now."

"I'll wait for her," he countered, not giving Ramona the opportunity to suggest another manicurist. There was a no-nonsense finality in the four words.

"Let me see how long she's going to be." Ramona had lowered her voice, being purposefully mysterious. She left her post, walking to the rear of the salon.

Cameron was willing to wait—for as long as it would take for him to uncover what it was about Maria Parker that had him leaving his office to seek her out. He sat down on a plush chair and picked up a recent issue of *Ebony* magazine from a low table filled with various periodicals. He thumbed it until his gaze lingered on an article about black love. He had not quite finished the first paragraph when Ramona returned.

"She just finished with her client. You can go on back."

Putting aside the magazine, he rose to his feet. "Thank you."

"You're welcome, Mr. King."

Cameron was hard-pressed not to smile when he noticed the questioning gazes directed at him when he stepped onto the salon floor. He acknowledged the woman who had relaxed and styled Valerie's hair with a warm, friendly smile.

"Hello there, Mr. King," she crooned, the tip of her pink tongue sliding over her lower lip.

He overheard a tall man with flaming red hair whisper, "Shameless hussy," then tuned out everything else as he came face-to-face with Maria. It had been two and a half weeks since he last saw her, but it could have been two and a half seconds. What surprised him most was that he remembered the exact shape of her exotic eyes, the enchanting sprinkle of freckles over the bridge of her nose, and the entrancing sensuality of her lush mouth. Tilting his head at an angle, his penetrating gaze moved slowly over her features, visually committing each one to memory.

"Good afternoon, Miss Parker."

A slight smile tipped her mouth at the corners. "Good afternoon, Mr. King." She motioned with a slender hand at the chair on the other side of the manicure table. "Please sit down."

Cameron shrugged out of his suit jacket, walked several feet to a brass coat tree in a corner, and hung it up while Maria retreated to a nearby sink and filled a small bowl with warm water. Turning around, he went completely still. She had returned to the table but had not sat down; she stood motionless, staring at him with a stunned expression on her face. He glanced down at the front of his shirt and slacks, thinking perhaps he had spilled something on the fabric.

"Is there something wrong, Miss Parker?"

*Yes,* she wanted to shout at him. He was wrong, and then he was so right. Everything about him was so stunningly perfect that she found it difficult to draw a normal breath. And in that instant she realized that Cameron reminded her of Tyree. She was attracted to him because he had the same effect on her as her late husband.

Something in his manner was so like Tyree's, yet he looked nothing like him. Cameron was taller, at least six-one, and his upper body was more powerfully muscled than Tyree's had been. His custom-made monogrammed white shirt and expertly tailored taupe-colored trousers fit his toned physique with an easy grace that was certain to turn any normal woman's head.

"No. Nothing's wrong," she replied much too quickly. Her legs were trembling slightly as she sank down to her chair, forcing a smile she did not quite feel. She was not comfortable with Cameron. He was a man, a stranger, who made her feel an emotion that she had not felt in years.

He made her feel a warming *desire.* His very presence reminded her that she was a woman—a woman who had at one time experienced the full range of her femininity; a woman who had and continued to deny her femininity because she feared loving and losing again.

And now that Cameron sat opposite her she knew he was the reason for her recurring bouts of insomnia. His deep, resonant voice captivated her, while his ultraconservative manner intrigued her. He claimed an intense, silent sexual magnetism that made him breathtakingly mesmerizing.

Reaching for his hands, she cradled them in her palms, examining his fingers. His hands were large, long-fingered, and strong. They were as fastidiously kept as the rest of him. His nails were short and clean.

"How was your niece's prom?" she questioned as she picked up an emery board to begin filing his nails.

Cameron smiled, staring at the short, glossy curls clinging to her small, well-shaped head. "I think she described it as the 'Bomb.'"

Her head came up slightly and she gave him a knowing smile. "Then it was a success. How are her nails holding up?"

"She had them removed after a few days because she claimed they hindered her when she tried typing a paper."

Maria wrinkled her pert nose. "They are pretty, even if they aren't very practical."

There was a comfortable silence while she filed his nails and applied a cuticle oil before she placed his fingers in the solution of warm, soapy water, grateful she could concentrate on his hands rather than his face, because whenever she met his penetrating gaze she felt as if he could see beneath her impassive expression to detect the sadness she always camouflaged with a quick smile and witty dialogue.

Cameron lowered his head and his voice. "How long have you worked at Della's?"

This time she glanced up to meet his questioning gaze. "Five years."

He shifted an eyebrow. "Have you always been a manicurist?"

"No. I began doing shampoos, then moved up to styling, cutting, and coloring. I've been doing nails exclusively for the past two years."

"You're a licensed stylist?" There was no mistaking the incredulity in his voice.

"Does that surprise you?" she questioned softly as he managed to look contrite. The expression elicited a smile from her. "Working here for five years has given me the experience I need if I ever decide to open my own full-service salon."

Now his curiosity was piqued. "Are you considering starting up a business?" She nodded. "When?"

"Hopefully next year." Her voice was soft, barely a whisper.

"Have you selected a location?"

"I have several possibilities."

Cameron felt a nagging frustration. He was trying to get Maria Parker to open up to him and she was answering his questions; however, each response was vague, nebulous. She appeared guarded, unwilling to reveal too much about herself, and he wondered if this was her normal demeanor. And if she managed to remain a private person while working in a salon, then she truly was exceptional. Beauty salons were much like barbershops and neighborhood bars—everyone knew everything about anyone who walked through their doors once they became a regular customer.

"Do you have an accountant?" he queried.

She gave him a direct stare. "Are you looking for clients, Mr. King?"

A deep frown settled into his pleasant features. "Not at all. I have more than enough clients, Miss Parker." A sudden sharp chill lingered with his retort. "I only asked because I belong to a consortium of black CPAs who volunteer free consulting services to people of color looking to start up their own businesses."

He had not lied to her. King Financial Services had retained more clients than he could handle by himself. A decade-long association with another certified public accountant ended six months go when he bought out Scott Wilson's share of their partnership. His college friend and fraternity brother had relocated to Atlanta following his wife's appointment as assistant chief of psychiatry at a municipal hospital. He had hired an accounting clerk on a part-time basis for the tax season to lighten his own workload but still needed to hire another accountant for a vacant full-time position.

Maria wanted to tell him that she did not require his assistance because she probably knew as much as he did when it came to setting up a business enterprise. Working at the salon for five years after earning a degree from New York University's School of Business had adequately prepared her for the business world.

"I'd rather not talk about it *here*." Her voice had drifted into a hushed whisper.

Cameron registered her reluctance. And he did not blame her. If someone overheard them, then her personal goals would be all over the salon within the hour.

He met her direct gaze, holding her captive as he stared at her, unblinking. "When and where?"

She blinked once. "Say what?"

"When and where do you want to discuss it?"

"Definitely not here."

"Is it top secret?" he countered in a quiet tone.

Shrugging a shoulder under the black smock, Maria shook her head. "It has nothing to do with it being a secret. It's just that I don't discuss my personal business *here*. Nothing, and I mean nothing, is sacred at Della's," she whispered. "Take yourself . . ."

He sat up straighter, a slight frown marring his smooth forehead. "What about me?"

"Before your niece even walked through the doors, everyone at Della's knew your name, your occupation, and the location of your office. The only thing they haven't uncovered is your marital status or where you live."

Cameron laughed, the sound low and sensual as it bubbled up from deep within his chest. He sobered, tilting his head at an angle. "Are you one of the curious ones?"

"You flatter yourself, Mr. King."

Quickly reversing their hands, he held hers captive within his loose grip. "We've been holding hands for the past fifteen minutes and I think we should nix the surnames. Please call me Cameron."

Her large dark eyes filled with amusement. "Only if you call me Maria."

He tightened his grip, squeezing gently. "You did not answer my question, Maria. Are you one of the inquiring minds?"

"No," she half-lied. Where he lived did not interest her; however, she had to admit to herself that she was curious as to whether he was married.

"I'm not married and I live on Long Island," he volunteered. "Is there anything else you think they'd like to know?"

"Do you want me to ask around?"

He shook his head quickly. "That's all right." He released her hands, permitting her to continue with the manicure. "I was married once."

Maria heard the pain in his voice and registered the raw hurt in his dark eyes. The barrier she had erected to keep men at a distance came crashing down with his confession. "How did you lose her?"

Leaning back on the chair, Cameron closed his eyes. He still could see Sylvia's face when she told him she had been willing to compete with another woman, but never his work. She had forced him to choose, and he had chosen his career.

He opened his eyes and his brows drew downward in a frown. "At the time I loved my work more than I loved my wife. I neglected her because I was too success-driven to give her the attention she demanded from me. I didn't realize what I had sacrificed until the divorce was final."

The obvious disappointment in his compelling voice affected Maria deeply. Like herself, he had loved and lost. "Did you try for a reconciliation?"

He flashed a wry smile, shaking his head. "No. At the time I wasn't willing to compromise."

"And now?" she asked, lifting questioning eyebrows.

"I'll admit that I'm older and hopefully a lot wiser." His statement prompted another smile from Maria, the simple gesture charming Cameron. Leaning over the table, his head only inches from hers, he crooned, "Can we meet for dinner this weekend to discuss your project?"

"Cameron, I don't know whether that's—"

"A good idea," he interrupted, finishing her statement. "I think it's a wonderful idea."

Her right hand stopped, poised in midair, before she reached for a buffer. "Are you always so aggressive?"

His eyes crinkled attractively behind his lenses. "It comes with the territory. You'll discover a similar characteristic in your own personality once you follow through with your *project*."

"What makes you think I need your assistance? I've done my research."

"And you should know that you can never get too much information if and when you decide to invest in a personal venture. What do you have to lose? Remember, my services are gratis."

Cameron could not believe that he was almost pleading with her to share dinner with him. He wasn't certain once he walked into Della's how he would convince her to see him outside the salon, but when she mentioned that she had planned to set up her own business enterprise he had been presented with the perfect opportunity.

"If you're not comfortable being alone with me, then why don't you invite your boyfriend to join us?"

Maria gave him a level stare. "I don't have a boyfriend."

"Then husband."

"I don't have a husband."

Cameron was hard-pressed not to flash a wide grin of relief. She *was* available. "How about a brother?"

His last suggestion made her laugh. "I can assure you that I can take care of myself."

"If that's the case, then when do you want to meet?"

She had to admire Cameron King's tenacity. He hadn't come to Della's for a manicure, but to see her. He hadn't sent her flowers to thank her for doing his niece's nails, but because he was attracted to and was possibly intrigued by her.

And what she had to admit to herself was that Cameron openly expressed what she sought to conceal. She'd also wanted to know whether he was single, and he was. And she wanted to see him—outside of Della's.

"What do you have planned for Saturday?"

Cameron seemed startled by her query. "Nothing. But it's the Fourth of July."

She flashed a saccharine grin. If he wanted to see her, then it would have to be on her terms. "I know," she replied smugly. "I've planned to spend the weekend on Long Island at my parents' place. You can meet me there."

He recovered quickly. "Where on Long Island?"

"Brentwood."

"What time do you want to meet?"

"Three o'clock. Before you leave, I'll give you their address and phone number. It's a holiday weekend and everyone will be very casual. You do have casual clothes?"

Cameron nodded, unable to believe his good fortune. He had never come on to a woman as aggressively as he had with Maria, but he had to admit it worked.

She had agreed to see him.

It had been a little more than two weeks since he met Maria Parker for the first time, and he had found himself waiting and counting the weeks when he would see her again.

Now the wait would only be four days.

# CHAPTER FOUR

The weather for the July Fourth celebration was perfect. The day had dawned with a clear blue sky, blazing sun, and a soothing, gentle breeze that rustled leaves and flowers while cooling bared flesh.

Maria arrived in Brentwood at eleven-thirty with her brother Rafael, his wife, and their daughters, joining her parents and grandmother in helping to set up the expansive backyard for a day of dining, dancing, and relaxing. Within the hour the other two sons of Raymond and Ynez Parker arrived with their families, the noise increasing appreciably with their young children chasing and teasing the elder Parkers' dog and cat.

Hours later, platters of precooked entrées and accompanying side dishes lined the many shelves of a walk-in refrigerator in an expansive eat-in kitchen, while half a dozen other platters were piled high with basted and marinated meats awaiting the time when they would be cooked on the outdoor grill.

Maria had just put the finishing touches on a large bowl filled with a mixed green salad when her brother's voice came through the open windows.

"Yo, Maria! There's someone out here asking for you."

She grimaced, her pulse racing. The *someone* had to be Cameron. She glanced at the clock over the stove. It was exactly three o'clock.

Ynez Rivera-Parker shook her graying head. "Must that boy be so loud?"

"Maria! Don't keep the man waiting."

Ynez walked over to the screen door leading to the backyard and opened it. "*¡Bastante!* She heard you, Pepito." Turning back to Maria, she flashed a smile. "It appears that your company is as impatient as your brother."

Reaching for her sunglasses off a countertop, she squared her shoulders, walked out of the kitchen, and down a flight of half a dozen stairs to the backyard. Her shrouded gaze adjusted quickly to the brilliant sunlight, and she saw Cameron shaking hands with Rafael Parker, followed by her middle brother, Marcus. She waited until Peter—or, as everyone continued to call him, Pepito—introduced himself before she approached him.

Cameron's penetrating gaze narrowed slightly behind his sun-darkened lenses when he saw Maria. He had wanted to wring her beautiful little neck when he arrived earlier and counted the number of vehicles parked in the driveway of her parents' home. She had invited him to Brentwood without disclosing that her family had planned to celebrate the holiday together. He had driven past the house and returned to the local road to find a store where he could purchase something to add to the festivities.

The slight frown marring his smooth forehead vanished, his eyes widening, as he took in everything about the woman who continued to haunt his days *and* his nights. She had paired a navy blue–and–white-striped cotton shell with a pair of white capri pants that ended below her knees. A slight smile touched his strong mouth. The first time he saw her she had worn a pair of slacks, and the second time she had selected a dress which had concealed most of her legs.

Her legs were perfect—well-shaped curvy calves and slender ankles. Her tiny feet were encased in a pair of black ballet slippers. She was petite, much shorter and smaller than women he was usually attracted to. He doubted whether she was more than five four. However, her diminutive size was not enough to lessen his enthusiasm for wanting to be with her.

Holding out both hands, Maria gave him a warm smile. "Welcome. I'm glad you made it." Rising on tiptoe, she pressed a kiss on his smooth-shaven cheek. The sensual fragrance of his sandalwood cologne swept over her.

Tightening his grip on her fingers, Cameron lowered his head and pressed his lips only inches from her lush mouth. "Thank you for inviting me." He felt her warm, moist breath feather over his lips, and he quelled the urge to take full possession of her mouth. "I need to get back to my car. I have a few watermelons and several varieties of cheesecake in the trunk."

She inhaled sharply, pulling back and staring up at him. "You didn't have to bring anything."

He arched an eyebrow. "And you forgot to tell me that your family would be in attendance."

She felt her face heat up. "You said you wanted to get together this weekend."

Releasing her hands, Cameron crossed his arms over his chest. "Do you actually think we'll have the opportunity to *talk*?"

Maria rested both hands on her narrow hips, then tilted her chin to give him the haughty look he found so entrancing. "Did you really want to *talk,* or was that just an excuse to see me?"

He recoiled as if she had jolted him with an electrical shock. Gone was the shy, reticent manicurist, and in her place was a woman who radiated an air of calm self-confidence. A self-confidence he admired.

Arching an eyebrow, he stared down at her. "So, you knew what I was up to?"

The enchanting smile he had come to look for appeared. "I have to admit that you were very transparent, Mr. King."

He wagged his head from side to side, staring down at the toes of his shiny black Gucci loafers. "I must be slipping," he mumbled under his breath.

Her hand went to his muscled forearm. "Don't beat up on yourself. Only I knew it," Maria reassured him with a saucy wink.

His head came up and a flash of humor crossed his face. "Then it will remain our secret. But I'm still willing to help you set up your business."

Her admiring gaze swept over the black golf shirt stretched over Cameron's broad chest, moving slowly down to his freshly laundered khakis and imported loafers. So much for his casual attire. He looked as if he had just stepped out of a Ralph Lauren ad, while her brothers' casual look was a pair of jeans, T-shirt, and running shoes.

Winding her bare arm through his, she said, "We'll talk about that another time. Come, let me introduce you to my parents."

Cameron walked past Rafael Parker, handing him the keys to his car to unload his contribution to the holiday festivities, then followed Maria into the house to meet her parents.

Raymond Parker stood at the cooking island, his right arm circling his wife's narrow waist. "Do you think you put in enough mushrooms?"

Ynez glanced up at her husband of forty-two years. "Not everyone inhales mushrooms the way you do, Ray."

"Pop, Mom, I'd like to introduce you to a friend of mine. This is Cameron King." The elder Parkers turned, smiling at their daughter and her guest.

Raymond wiped his hands on a terry cloth towel before extending the right one. He was a tall, dark skinned man who proudly sported a head of thick white hair even though he had recently celebrated his sixty-fifth birthday. A friendly smile crinkled the minute lines around his eyes.

"Welcome, son. It's been a long time since my princess has invited her boyfriend over to meet her family."

"Pop!" Maria wished she had magical powers so she could disappear on the spot. She did not have to look at Cameron to see the triumphant smile curving his mouth.

"Pop, he's not—"

"I'm honored that Maria invited me to meet her family," Cameron said quickly, stopping her protest as he shook Raymond's proffered hand.

Ynez Rivera–Parker's hazel eyes assessed the tall man standing beside her daughter. Her husband was right. It had been a long time since Maria had invited a man to their home, but the wait appeared to be worth it. Everything about Cameron King radiated breeding and success.

"Welcome, Cameron. I hope you won't make this your last visit," Ynez said softly.

He inclined his head. "I'll try not to, Mrs. Parker."

Ynez shook her finger at him. "None of that 'Mrs. Parker' business. Around here it's Ynez and Ray."

An elderly woman walked slowly into the kitchen, wiping her hands on the flowery voile apron tied around her plump waist. Straight iron-gray hair was secured in a thick braided coil on the nape of her neck. She squinted behind the lenses of her glasses at Cameron. "I came to see my granddaughter's *novio*."

Maria moved over to her maternal grandmother's side. "*Abuela*, he's not my fiancé," she whispered close to her ear. "He's just a friend."

"In my day a girl did not bring a man home to meet her family unless she was going to marry him," the elderly woman stated in rapid Spanish.

Leaning over, Maria kissed the paper-thin cheek. "We'll talk later, *Abuela*," she promised, replying in the same language. "I have to introduce Cameron to the rest of the family."

She returned to Cameron, urging him to follow her. "Let's go outside."

What she wanted to do was get him away from her parents and grandmother and what was certain to become the Rivera–Parker inquisition. Each time she came to Brentwood she ran a gauntlet of questions as to her love life. Her parents wanted to know who she was dating, and when was the last time she had shared dinner or a movie with a man. And her response was always the same: She hadn't gone out with anyone since becoming a widow.

Maria and Cameron stopped in a breezeway before making their way to the backyard. He threaded his fingers through hers, squeezing gently.

His gaze lingered on her upturned face. "When was the last time a man accompanied you to your parents' home?"

She glanced away. "It was a long time ago."

He released her hand, cradling her face between his palms. "How long?"

She closed her eyes. "Seven years."

He heard the pain in her voice, wanting to hold her close, but resisted the impulse. He didn't know her, and he did not want to do anything that would jeopardize his seeing her again.

"Look at me, Maria. Please."

Squaring her narrow shoulders, she raised her chin, opened her eyes, and forced a smile. "I'm all right."

Cameron gave her a questioning look, searching her smoky brown eyes for a hint of guile. "Are you sure?"

"Very sure."

He dropped his hands and she led him toward a group of adults who had settled down on webbed chairs under a portable tent, while their swimsuit-clad children cavorted and squealed under the cooling spray of a lawn sprinkler.

Reaching out, she grasped Cameron's hand. "You've already met my brothers, so I'll introduce you to their wives."

He savored the velvet softness of her fingers. "How was it growing up with three brothers?"

The three men had inherited the height and muscular physique of their African American father and the coloring, hair texture, and features of their Puerto Rican mother. However, the inherited physical traits had changed with Maria. She claimed her mother's petite figure with an attractive blending of coloring, hair, and features from both parents. The result was a sensually beautiful woman.

"It was rather nice."

"Didn't they chase away the guys who were interested in you?"

She nodded, smiling. "Most times I did not want to be bothered with any of the boys from the neighborhood."

"Where did you grow up?"

"East Harlem. While I was growing up there, everyone referred to it as 'El Barrio.'"

"I've only driven through it on my way to the Triborough Bridge. There has been a lot of urban renewal going on in both Harlems."

She smiled up at him. "You have to let me take you on a walking tour and show you all of my favorite hangout spots. My father grew up in Harlem, but hung out in El Barrio because he attended the now-defunct Benjamin Franklin High School. His best friend was Eddie Rivera. I think he was tight with Eddie because of his twin sister, Ynez. He fell in love with Ynez as a freshman, and the year they turned twenty-three they were married.

"My father worked construction for several years before he borrowed some money from his father to open a *bodegal* deli at 115th Street and Pleasant Avenue. He rented an apartment in a row house on 115th between First and Pleasant Avenues, so all he had to do was walk about a thousand feet to get to his store. After several years he bought the building, then the entire south side of the street."

Cameron stared numbly at Maria with this disclosure. It was no wonder she was reluctant to accept his offer to help her set up her business. She did not need him when she had Raymond Parker as her mentor.

"Does your father still work in the store?"

"No. He's retired. He bought this house about ten years ago, and after commuting for five years he decided to give up work. He usually left the house at four-thirty to open the store for six A.M., and he didn't close until eight at night, which meant he usually did not get back to Brentwood until nine-thirty. The only time my mother saw him was when he was asleep.

"He gave it all up at sixty, hung around the house for six months, then enrolled in a cooking school. He takes one or two courses a year, messes up my mother's kitchen whenever he tries out a new dish, and spends the rest of his time in his vegetable and flower gardens."

"What does your mother do?"

"She used to help Pop in the store when they lived in El Barrio, but after moving out here she became involved with a local senior citizens center. She volunteers her time at least three days a week. Other than that she loves traveling. She always spends a month in Puerto Rico visiting relatives. She's a lot more relaxed than she used to be because she finally convinced her elderly, widowed mother to give up her apartment in the Bronx and move in with her and Pop. *Abuela* occupies her own apartment in the extension my father put on the side of the house."

Rafael met them before they stepped under the coolness of the tent. He dangled Cameron's car keys between his thumb and forefinger. "Your Porsche is a beaut. How long have you had it?"

Cameron retrieved the keys, slipping them into the pocket of his khakis. "Less than six months. I still haven't taken it on the road to blow out the engine."

Rafael ran a hand over his short, graying head. "Let me know if you want company."

"You're on. But your sister has first preference."

Rafael winked at Maria. "I'm sure she does."

Maria wrinkled her nose at her brother, then led Cameron into the tent, registering the admiring, questioning glances her sisters-in-law directed at the man beside her.

"Cameron, I'd like you to meet my sisters-in-law. Yvonne is married to Rafael, Deanna is Marcus's wife, and Joycelyn is married to Peter."

The three women fluttered their lashes, showed an inordinate amount of teeth, and crooned their greetings when Cameron acknowledged them in the deep, mellow baritone voice that never failed to send a shiver up and down Maria's spine.

Two of her preteen nieces stared at Cameron before they giggled behind their hands. His masculine appeal was devastatingly sensual, and she realized it would serve no purpose for her to continue to hide behind the facade she had erected to keep all men at a distance. Her vow not to become involved with another man had been challenged the moment Cameron King walked into Della's to instruct her about his niece's nails. And the vow was shattered completely when she opened her mouth to invite him to her parents' home.

Peter stuck his head through the mesh covering of the tent. "Cameron, can you help us out? We need a bit more muscle out here."

"Give him a break, Pepito. He's a guest," Joycelyn complained softly.

"Nobody's ever a guest at a Parker cookout, beautiful. Cameron will learn quickly that if he wants to eat, then he'll have to work for his food," Peter retorted with a wide grin. His admiring gaze swept over his wife's ripening figure.

Joycelyn was in the full throes of her last trimester. The couple looked forward to the imminent birth of their first child after what they had declared was an extended ten-year honeymoon. Both thirty-five, Peter and Joycelyn declared firmly that they were now ready for parenthood.

Best friends, Yvonne and Deanna married the Parker brothers in a double-wedding ceremony. The women had grown up in the same Brooklyn neighborhood. They met Rafael and Marcus when the two brothers came to their rescue after their racy sports car broke down along I-95 on a return drive to New York after a week-long vacation in Virginia Beach. After a whirlwind romance, the two couples married within six months of their initial meeting. Each twosome had given their parents two grandchildren. Yvonne and Rafael claimed two girls, and Deanna and Marcus two boys.

Cameron gave Maria a lingering stare. "I'll be right back."

"Please hurry back," Deanna whispered to Cameron's departing figure. She tossed back a profusion of braided hair framing her perfectly rounded medium-brown face; her very large dark eyes crinkled in a beguiling smile. "Maria, I can't believe you've been holding out on us. He's adorable. Where did you find him?"

Dropping down into a webbed chair, Maria studied her cuticles rather than meet Deanna's questioning gaze. "He found me."

"At Della's?" the three women chorused.

She nodded, flashing a mysterious smile. "I do his nails."

Yvonne folded her hands on her hips. "Is that all you do?"

"Don't pry, Yvonne," Maria warned.

A flash of humor crossed Yvonne White-Parker's even features. She had recently celebrated her fortieth birthday and Maria had given her a gift certificate for a full day of beauty at Della's. Yvonne's transformation was startlingly dramatic after she had elected to have her chemically relaxed, shoulder-length hair styled into a becoming close-cut natural trend that showed off the exquisite bones in her face to their best advantage.

"Get your mind out of the gutter, girlfriend. I was talking about you cutting his hair."

Maria shook her head. "I just do his nails."

Deanna waved her hand. "Give her time. First it will be the nails, then the feet. After a while it will be his hair, then a shave. I suppose she'll save the full-body massage for last."

Heat suffused Maria's face and she found herself temporarily at a loss for words. "Don't even go there, Deanna," she countered, finding her voice. "He's just a client."

Deanna sucked her teeth. "He won't be a client for long," she drawled. "Not the way he stares at you. Your very conservative-looking brother-man's eyes say it all."

Maria remembered Reecie's comment about the way Cameron looked at her. There were times when she caught him staring, but she found it wasn't any different from any other man who looked at her.

"What do his eyes say, Miss Know-It-All?"

"I want some of *that!*" Deanna replied. "And you know better than to argue with me, because you know I'm right."

Yvonne rolled her eyes at Deanna. "Don't start in with that psychic foolishness again. I've said it a thousand times, if you're that clairvoyant, then you should call Dionne Warwick and ask to work for the psychic network. The money would be a lot better than what you earn teaching second graders."

"Don't be catty, Mrs. Parker. You're just jealous because I tell you things before they come true."

"Tell us about Maria and Cameron, Deanna," Joycelyn suggested,

interrupting the good-natured banter between the two women who had
been friends since childhood.

Maria felt a flicker of apprehension course through her, and she
chided herself for inviting Cameron to celebrate the holiday with her
family. She should have agreed to meet him at his office.

"There's nothing much to tell," Maria explained quickly. "He's a client
at Della's."

Joycelyn shifted professionally waxed eyebrows. "He's a client whom
you just happened to invite to meet your family?"

Deanna shook her recently braided hair. "The brother's about to become more than a client." She closed her eyes and pressed the thumb
and forefinger of her left hand to her forehead. "You're going to marry
him, Maria," she predicted sagely.

It was Maria's turn to close her eyes. "Don't say that."

"It's not going to be like it was with—"

"Don't tell me any more!" she practically shouted, cutting off whatever Deanna was going to say.

Opening her eyes, Maria stared numbly at her sister-in-law. The
pain of loving, marrying, and losing Tyree came rushing back with such
clarity that she felt as if she were watching a film. She was mesmerized
by the images of the last time she stared at the cold, still, lifeless corpse
of the man who had been her husband.

Not waiting to hear whatever Deanna offered as a prediction, she
moved off the chair and walked out of the tent.

*Bruja!* Her sister-in-law was a witch. And what bothered her most was
that most of Deanna's predictions were accurate.

Her breath was coming quickly and she tried slowing down her runaway pulse by forcing air into her lungs. What she did not want to do was
marry Cameron, or for that matter any other man. She loved Tyree and
even after seven years she still was not willing to let him go.

# CHAPTER FIVE

Five hours later Cameron lay on a webbed chaise, eyes closed, while he listened to the soft sounds of conversations in Spanish and English floating around him as everyone waited for their food to digest before sampling the many desserts lining the table in an enclosed patio. He could not remember when he had eaten so much. Turning to his right, he detected the now-familiar fragrance of Maria's perfume and opened his eyes. She lay beside him on a matching chaise, her eyes shrouded behind a pair of oversized sunglasses.

Reaching over, he placed a hand on her shoulder. "How about a walk to help settle the food?"

She turned her head slowly and smiled at him. "You're going to have to roll me down the street."

Swinging his legs over the side of the chaise, he pushed to his feet. She took the hand he extended to her, savoring its protective warmth.

Maria tilted her chin, her enchanting smile still in place. "I should have warned you about the Parkers and the Riveras. When they say they are going to cook a little something, that something always becomes a banquet."

Cameron had to agree with her. He had consumed ample portions of white rice and beans, grilled chicken, spareribs, fried plantains, *arroz con gandules,* potato salad, and two portions of the most succulent, flavorful collard greens he had ever eaten. The appetizers were too numerous to name or remember.

Raymond had proudly shown him the commercial cart grill he had purchased for his backyard galas. The majestic cooking appliance claimed a grilling surface with an impressive one hundred thousand BTU maximum output, a smoker that enhanced foods with genuine smoked flavors, and two rotisseries that could handle two twenty-pound turkeys or six chickens simultaneously. The grill cart also had two range-top burners.

"Where do you want to walk?"

Her low, haunting voice washed over him like a seductive whisper, and Cameron wanted to be anywhere but in the Parkers' backyard with more than two dozen pairs of eyes watching him.

At that moment he wanted to take her into his arms and sample the honeyed sweetness of her lush mouth. He wanted to bury his nose against her breasts and inhale the natural scent of her flesh under the seductive fragrance of her delicate perfume.

He shrugged a broad shoulder under his black cotton shirt. "Why don't you show me the neighborhood?"

She led him across the professionally manicured lawn, feeling the heat of everyone's gaze following her and Cameron.

Marcus strolled across the grass, cradling his young son to his chest. He winked at Maria. "Don't forget to tell your boyfriend that you have a ten o'clock curfew."

She stuck her tongue out at him. "From what Raffle says, it's you who has the curfew. He mentioned something about Deanna having a fit because you stayed out all night playing cards with your so-called friends."

"My brother talks too much," he said between clenched teeth.

Cameron glanced down at the watch on his wrist. "I'll be certain to have her back before ten."

Maria gasped audibly. "Don't you dare listen to him."

Lowering his head, his mouth close her ear, he said softly, "Does that mean I can keep you out all night?"

"No. It means I'm only going for a walk with you."

There was a comfortable silence as they made their way to the tree-lined sidewalk. She offered him a saucy smile when he released her fingers and tucked her hand into the bend of his elbow.

Lengthening evening shadows signaled the approach of dusk with a hushed stillness that added a magical quality to the quiet community filled with single-family homes boasting perfectly manicured lawns and driveways filled with shiny late-model cars.

There was only the sound of rubber tires slapping the roadway as an occasional car moved slowly down the tree-lined streets as the couple strolled side by side, each lost in personal thoughts.

Maria felt a warm, fuzzy feeling sweep over her—an emotion she had not felt in years. It was a sense of completeness. Her life was on track, she wanted for nothing materially, yet she was always aware of an elusive something that was missing. And only now that she strolled along a quiet suburban street with Cameron did she realize that it was love. She wanted to fall in love and be loved in return.

Each time a man had approached her to ask her out, she balked, wondering whether she would be unfaithful to Tyree's memory. Her brothers had tried matching her up with their friends and business associates so many times that they had stopped altogether after several of the men openly verbalized that they believed their sister was "not into men." Rafael, Marcus, and Peter met with Raymond and Ynez, expressing their concern, but the elder Parkers discounted their suspicions, concluding that Maria was still grieving.

And now she realized that she had been. For nearly seven years she had held on to the memory of a man who had been her first love, lover, and husband. Since Tyree's death she had been content to lie in bed alone, recalling the whispered conversations they had shared after a passionate session of lovemaking.

All of the memories came rushing back whenever she recalled their first date, the first time she offered him her innocence, and the day and the hour he asked her to become his wife. But all of their good memories were shattered by the two words that claimed Tyree Johnston's life before it had even begun.

Could she open up to Cameron? Open up enough to permit herself to share a little of her existence with him? Closing her eyes briefly, she mumbled a prayer for strength.

"Where do you live on Long Island?" she asked him, her husky voice punctuating the comfortable silence.

"Old Westbury." Cameron had slowed his stride to match her shorter legs.

Her expression did not change with this disclosure. Cameron King lived in one of the most exclusive communities on Long Island. "Did you grow up there?"

"No. I was raised in Sag Harbor. I moved to Old Westbury earlier this year."

She stared up at his perfect profile. "You used to commute from Sag Harbor to Manhattan?" She could not imagine him driving more than a hundred miles a day—in each direction.

He shook his head. "I had an apartment in the city. I should say that I still have an apartment in Manhattan. I make good use of it during the tax season. My office and apartment are located in a building that was owned by my deceased brother, and now belongs to his widow and daughter."

"Valerie told me about her father."

"His death affected everyone, most of all Valerie."

"Does she live in Manhattan with her mother?"

"No. They moved back to Long Island six years ago when Lorena began teaching at Hofstra Law School. Greg and Lorena lived in the city when they were first married, then he purchased the building on 139th the year he established his private practice. At that time there weren't too many black pediatric dentists in Harlem."

Cameron covered Maria's delicate fingers with his free hand. He could not remember the last time he felt the gentle peace eddying throughout his mind and body. It was as if Maria Parker had become his personal amulet, her gentle existence offering him a soothing, healing balm; and despite his outward appearance of being in control of every phase in his life, there were times when he was afraid that he would not be able to grasp the love he wanted to offer a woman.

He had married Sylvia Hilton, believing he loved her totally, but in the end realized he had lied to himself. If he had loved her selfishly, then he would not have neglected her for his work; perpetuating his family's penchant for success had become all-encompassing, not allowing him to see beyond what he was forced to sacrifice for the sake of establishing a lucrative accounting firm.

It took him five years to realize that he had sacrificed his marriage, as well as experiencing ostracism from an exclusive social coterie who prided themselves in accepting only married couples into their milieu, and a schism that severed a generational association between the Kings and Hiltons.

A slow, easy smile crinkled his eyes when he thought of how different the Parkers were from the Hiltons. Maria's family was warm, outgoing, friendly, and overtly affectionate. Her brothers spoiled and adored their wives, and their children were also spoiled yet had remained respectful to their elders and appeared very secure within the extended family unit. Maria related that her nieces and nephews were bilingual even though their mothers did not speak or understand Spanish. Ynez had insisted her grandchildren spend at least a month of their summer vacations with her each year in order that she teach them the language. She also alternated taking them to Puerto Rico with her to visit their many relatives who had elected not to leave the island for the mainland.

Maria and Cameron continued walking for another quarter of an hour until Cameron's deep, powerful voice ended the silence. "Why haven't you married?"

Maria halted in midstride, forcing him to stop. She felt as if he had reached inside her and squeezed her heart until it was close to exploding. She swallowed painfully, her eyelids fluttering wildly.

"I was married." Her voice was a hoarse whisper.

Cameron released her hand, his fingers tightening on her shoulders and forcing her to face him. "What happened?"

"He left me." The three words were torn from the back of her throat at the same time her eyes flooded with unshed tears. "We were married less than a year and—and he died."

Holding her to his heart, he listened, stunned, while Maria bared her soul. She tearfully revealed how Tyree Johnston had come home early one day to tell her that a visit to a urologist had resulted in heart-breaking news. What he had suspected for more than a year had been confirmed.

"I was hysterical when he told me," Maria confessed through tears. "I screamed at him because he had hidden it from me. Instead of seeking out a doctor when he first suspected something was wrong, he hid it from me. Tyree broke down, admitting that he was afraid that I wouldn't have married him if I had known. He didn't know me at all, Cameron. He did not know that I loved him enough to marry him even a second before he drew his last breath. I loved him just that much," she mumbled over and over, burying her face against his chest.

At that moment Maria needed to be comforted, and he held her, stroking her hair. "It's all right, darling. You loved him and he loved you."

A fresh wave of tears ensued. "But I miss him so much."

Cameron closed his eyes, not knowing how, but he felt her pain. "You miss him because you haven't let him go."

"I don't want to let him go," she countered.

"You have to. Otherwise you will never heal or allow yourself to fall in love again."

"I'm afraid to fall in love again. I don't want to go through loving and losing a second time."

"It doesn't have to be the same. Let me help you, Maria," he crooned in a soft, comforting voice. "I want to love you."

He was offering her the love she sought, needed, but she was afraid. "I can't," she cried, her breath coming in hiccuping sobs.

Closing his eyes, Cameron mumbled a silent prayer, asking a higher power to heal her. It was the same prayer he had said on behalf of his parents, sister-in-law, niece, and himself after they had buried his brother.

"Yes, you can. I promise I will be here to help you."

There was something in his tone and entreaty that said that she should believe him. Her sobbing quieted as she raised her tearstained face to stare up at him. The grief and despair that had nagged her for years eased when she registered understanding and tenderness in his penetrating gaze. Could she take the chance, the risk? Could she let go of her painful past and allow the man holding her to his heart into her life?

Cameron cradled her with one arm while searching the pocket of his slacks for a handkerchief. A trembling smile parted her lips as he blotted the moisture from her delicate face. Sighing heavily, she nodded. "I can't promise you anything except that I will try."

He returned her smile. Her eyes were swollen and her nose was red from weeping, but she still was enchanting—enchanting and so vulnerable.

She needed him and he needed her; he needed her to give him a second chance to love again.

Lowering his head, he brushed his mouth over hers, capturing her jaw and increasing the pressure when she attempted to pull away. His tongue traced the soft fullness of her mouth, savoring its sweetness. He had fantasized over and over about kissing her, but had not come close to the heated honey she offered him. Raising his mouth from hers, he gazed into her startled eyes, seeking approval that he continue.

She ran the tip of her pink tongue over her lower lip, tasting him again, and when she closed her eyes against his intense stare he interpreted it as a sign of surrender.

This time when he reclaimed her mouth it was with the force of a sirocco blowing across the desert. His tongue plunged into her mouth, sampling, savoring, and devouring the passion she had locked away for years.

The rhythm of his runaway pulse matched hers, as well as his passion. All Maria had to do was touch him . . . *there,* and he would give in to the sensual spell she had woven over him without her being aware of it. He, Cameron Grant King, who prided himself on his iron-willed control, was shaking uncontrollably because he feared losing himself in the soft, scented body crushed against his own.

The kiss ended, both of them breathing heavily. Pulling apart, they shared a secret smile, a smile reserved for lovers, then turned and retraced their steps.

Everyone had retreated into the house during their stroll, and when Cameron and Maria walked into the family room, Raymond Parker noticed the signs that indicated that his daughter had been crying, and he headed in their direction.

Cameron let go of Maria's hand and met her father halfway across the room. Leaning close to the older man, he whispered, "She's okay now. I'm going to take care of her."

A knowing smile lifted the corners of Raymond Parker's strong mouth. His gaze shifted, lingering on his daughter before returning to analyze Cameron's stoic expression.

He inclined his head, acknowledging the younger man's claim to his daughter's future. "Thank you, son."

# CHAPTER SIX

Maria walked into Della's, her familiar smile in place as she greeted stylists, their assistants, and various shampoo girls.

"Good morning, everyone."

"Morning, Maria," they chorused in unison, returning her smile.

"She must have had a bumpin' weekend," KiKi mumbled under her breath.

"I know you didn't, because a man would have to be blind to be seen with you. Your hair is busted," Maurice volunteered. He gave her a knowing look as he mixed and measured colors over a sink.

KiKi folded her hands on her hips and moved closer to the colorist. "Don't be gettin' in my business, Moe-reese," she retorted. She rolled her head and glared at him from under her lashes. "Dee Dee's about to do my hair today."

Maria bit back a smile, slipping into her smock at the same time Maurice leaned in closer to KiKi and quietly explained the rudiments of proper grammar, which sent the shampoo girl fleeing toward Della Frazier's office.

Most times the good-natured rivalries among Della's employees amused Maria, but there were times when it spilled over and the clients were made aware of an undercurrent of hostility. And she knew this was something she would never tolerate once she established her own salon.

She would hold weekly staff meetings in which everyone would be encouraged to air their differences.

Retrieving her calendar from the drawer of the manicure table, she noted the date. It was July 27, and three weeks had passed since she and Cameron began seeing each other. She also had begun counting down the months because she now had less than six months before she tendered her resignation at Della's House of Style. Then she would start the new year planning and setting up her own house of style.

A dreamy expression settled into her features when she thought of Cameron. They had returned to her parents' house from their Fourth of July stroll and spent the next few hours in the family room, talking, laughing, and listening to music. She had surprised him when Peter pulled her up to dance to an upbeat salsa by the recording star India. Yvonne had tried getting Cameron to dance with her, but he refused, saying he found the steps too intricate to follow. But they did share a dance when Rafael put on a CD featuring classic soul and R&B favorites from the *body + soul love serenade* compilation.

Dancing together had become commonplace because whenever he called her for a date he usually selected a venue that included dinner, music, and dancing. They had eaten dinner at the Rainbow Room, Sunday brunch at Tito Puente's Restaurant in the City Island section of the Bronx, and had taken a Tuesday evening jazz cruise along the Hudson River.

Each time they met, it was with the intent to discuss her establishing her salon business, but the meetings always ended without either of them broaching the subject. And each time Cameron escorted her into the lobby of her apartment building she realized the meetings were a foil for the beginning of a comfortable friendship with deepening feelings for each other.

There was an occasion when she met Cameron at his office in a row house along Striver's Row. The space that had contained offices for a lucrative dental practice was renovated to accommodate Cameron's accounting and investment firm. A very proper middle-aged receptionist greeted her warmly, then requested that she have a seat in the reception area because Mr. Cameron was on the telephone with an overseas client.

She had been impressed with the tasteful elegance of the offices of King Financial Services. The softly diffused lighting cast by recessed lights and handsome porcelain lamps bathed the space with warmth. The sienna hue in the petaled lamp bases picked up the color of a coffee table constructed of lacquered wood covered with linen. The walls, sofa, and two love seats were covered in a cream slubbed wool. An Oriental rug repeated the colors of a hand-woven wall hanging, creating the illusion that the two were one continuous, harmonious element. Live potted plants on the table and in a corner brought the outside indoors and added color to the very sophisticated furnishings.

Retrieving the materials she needed for a client who had requested silk wraps, she banished her musings of Cameron to the back of her mind—temporarily.

---

The morning and afternoon sped by quickly, affording her only fifteen minutes to eat a tuna salad and drink a glass of refreshing lemonade from the adjoining café. She finished up her last client at four forty-five and looked forward to going home to enjoy a quiet evening relaxing on her terrace.

Ramona met her as she walked out of the employees lounge. "Maria, I'm sorry, but I meant to tell you that Mr. King has a five o'clock manicure."

Her pulse quickened at the mention of his name.

"When were you going to tell me? And when did he make the appointment?" she questioned the receptionist.

Ramona managed to look remorseful. "His secretary called and made it late yesterday afternoon."

Maria wagged her head in disbelief. Cameron had continued to come in for her to do his nails, but most times he had his receptionist call for an opening if his schedule permitted it. "I checked your book this morning and I didn't see his name."

"That's because I forgot to write it down."

Kimm Gilmore glared at the receptionist while sucking her teeth. It was the third time in less than a week that Ramona had neglected to write down an appointment. "If you'd stop eyeballin' the man so hard when he walks in here, you'd remember to *do* your job."

Ramona tossed her shoulder-length relaxed hair over one shoulder, rolled her eyes at the aesthetician, then strolled to the front of the salon with a deliberate sway of her generous hips.

Maria returned to the lounge, put away her handbag, picked up her smock, and returned to her manicure station. Her pulse raced a little faster when she spied Cameron approaching. He was impeccably dressed in a celery-hued linen suit, white cotton shirt, and a patterned tie with geometric designs in contrasting colors of brown, green, and yellow.

Her bright smile indicated she was glad to see him after a two-day separation. "Good afternoon, Mr. King."

He nodded, returning her smile. "Good afternoon, Miss Parker. He removed his jacket, hanging it on the nearby coat tree.

She motioned to the chair opposite her. "Please sit down."

Cameron complied, placing his hands in her outstretched ones. A mysterious smile played at the corners of his mobile mouth as he stared at her lowered head. Leaning closer, he whispered, "I've missed you."

Maria did not raise her head but glanced up at him through her lashes. "I've missed you, too."

She felt the heat of his gaze on her face as she went through the motion of filing his nails, pushing back the cuticles, then buffing the nails to a natural shine.

Her head came up and she smiled at him. "You're finished."

Reaching into the breast pocket of his shirt, he placed a bill on the table. He always overtipped her.

Her professional smile did not falter. "Thank you, Mr. King."

His eyes crinkled attractively behind his glasses. "You're quite welcome, Miss Parker. I hope to see you again next week."

She nodded, watching him retrieve his jacket, then make his way across the salon floor to the reception area, her gaze following him until he disappeared from her line of vision.

"Careful, *chica*," Maurice warned close to her ear. "It's only a matter of time before everyone at Della's will know that you and your Mr. King have something going on."

Her head swung around and she stared numbly at the colorist. "Is it that obvious?"

"To me it is."

She patted his solid shoulder. "That's because you're more perceptive than the others."

Maurice ran his hand through her hair, the ends curling around his fingers. "When are you going to let me highlight your hair before you cut it again?"

"Never, Reecie."

"Come on, *chica*. Just a few warm gold-brown highlights. It will match the gold undertones in your skin."

Maria shook her head. "No."

"I'm certain your man would like it."

"He's not my man," she hissed through her teeth.

"Quit lying, Maria. It's not an attractive trait."

Her temper flared. "Just because we've gone out a few times, that doesn't make him my man."

"Who are you going out with?" Deirdre Lee questioned as she approached them.

"Clark Kent," Maurice drawled, ignoring Maria as she shook her head vigorously. She did not want anyone at Della's to know that she was dating Cameron.

"Ah, sookie, sookie," Dee Dee crooned, snapping her fingers over her head.

"What's up?" KiKi asked.

"Maria is dating Clark Kent," Dee Dee announced in a voice loud enough for everyone at Della's to hear.

The heat flared in Maria's cheeks as a few of the stylists applauded.

She swept off her smock, picked up her handbag, and made her way across the salon floor. She did not have to turn around to feel the gazes following her retreat.

"How is your Superman, Lois Lane?" KiKi shouted over the din whirling around the shop with the latest piece of gossip.

Maria stopped suddenly, then turned slowly. She glared at the nosy shampoo girl, retracing her steps as KiKi back-pedaled until a styling chair stopped her escape.

Maria had not wanted to advertise her private life, even though she had nothing to be ashamed of. Cameron claimed everything most women sought in a man—and then some. But then, she did not want whatever she did with Cameron to be bantered about the shop as if they were public figures, either.

All conversation came to a complete halt, only the soft sounds of smooth jazz coming through audio speakers, and all gazes were trained on Maria and KiKi. For the first time since KiKi Jackson walked into Della's House of Style as a permanent employee, she feared that she had stepped over the line.

Maria saw a flash of fear fill KiKi's eyes, and she felt sorry for the younger woman. Even though the shampoo girl had recently celebrated her twenty-first birthday, she still had a lot of maturing to do.

"Do you really want to know, Miss Mouth Almighty?" The younger woman bobbed her head up and down, eyes round as saucers. "He's good," Maria crooned, inches from her moist face. "Damn good!"

"You go, girl!" Dee Dee shouted to Maria, who waved her hand above her head in acknowledgment. Turning her attention to KiKi, she snapped her fingers at her. "Stay out of other folks' business, KiKi," she warned. "You also better clean up the shampoo area before Della comes out of her office and gets all over you."

"You tell her about it, Dee Dee," an assistant mumbled angrily, echoing the other employees who also had had enough of KiKi's constant meddling.

Ramona stared at Maria's ramrod-straight back and closed expression as she stalked through the reception area and pushed open the door. "Good night, Maria. I'm sorry about forgetting to pencil in Mr. King for his appointment."

She wasn't disappointed when Maria stopped, turned, and smiled at her. "It's okay, Ramona. No harm done. Good night."

Ramona's mishap did not annoy her as much as KiKi's constant insinuations. She made a mental note to talk to Della Frazier about the shampoo girl's lack of professionalism on the salon floor. There were occasions when everyone joked and teased one another, yet they had always managed to project a modicum of decorum in the presence of the clients who came to Della's House of Style not only for its many services, but because of its reputation for being one of the most professional, upscale full-service salons in New York City. Once the customers walked through the doors of Della's, they were afforded the most up-to-date services with an unwritten guarantee of competent, undivided attention.

---

Walking out onto 125th Street, Maria fell in step with the throng of pedestrians moving quickly toward the east side. *They know about you and Cameron,* a voice echoed in her head. She had sought to keep her liaison with him a secret, knowing sooner or later someone would uncover their clandestine meetings. And each time Cameron came into Della's and sat down at her manicure table, she had to struggle to remain indifferent to his presence. She always greeted him as she did her other clients, but unlike her other clients she kept the conversation between them to a minimum.

She skirted an elderly woman who seemed intent on walking directly into her. She looked up, and then she saw him. Cameron stood on a corner of Adam Clayton Powell Boulevard, waiting for her. The rays of the afternoon sun had darkened the lenses of his glasses where he could observe her without her seeing his penetrating gaze.

His mouth curved into a beguiling smile as he moved over and took her hand. "Good evening, Miss Parker."

Tilting her chin, she returned his smile. "Good evening, Mr. King. Have you taken to waiting on street corners to drum up business?"

He chuckled deep in his chest. "Let's hope I'll never have to resort to that method." His fingers tightened slightly on her delicate hand. "There was a time when you promised to take me on a tour of your neighborhood. If you don't have a prior engagement, I'd like to take that tour now."

His suggestion startled her as she stared at him in astonishment. "But aren't you scheduled to work late tonight?"

"I was until I managed to switch an appointment."

"Why?"

He took a step closer and Maria felt the heat radiating from his large body; she inhaled the sensual scent of his aftershave, and she was swallowed whole by the energy and power that made him so undeniably attractive.

"Why, Maria? Because I don't want to see you once a week. That's just not enough for me. And coming to Della's for a manicure doesn't count."

Curving her free arm around his waist inside his jacket, she pressed her face against his chest. He had freely admitted what she had felt and had been feeling since their Fourth of July encounter. She had opened up her heart to Cameron King and in doing so she had let go of her fear of loving and losing.

Whenever he took her in his arms to dance, she was always astonished at the sense of fulfillment she experienced. And after each dance they shared a tender kiss that managed to convey more gratitude than any word either of them could summon.

She found Cameron patient, gentle, attentive, and what she had tried to deny from their first encounter was that she was falling in love with him. She had admitted it to herself the night they shared the jazz cruise. Sitting together, holding hands, listening to live music while the majestic ship sailed along the Hudson River under a star-littered summer sky stripped her of all of her fears and inhibitions so that she wanted to shout to the world that she had fallen in love with Cameron King.

She was certain he felt her slight trembling when she asked, "What is it you want from me?"

"I want whatever it is you are willing to offer me." What he did not say was that he wanted her—all of her—for a lifetime. She had changed him. Since meeting Maria Parker he had reexamined his life and his priorities. He had proven he could manage a successful business, but that was no longer as important as finding and securing personal happiness.

After she completed his manicure he'd walked out of Della's, stood on the corner, retrieved his cellular phone, and called his administrative assistant to tell her to reschedule his seven o'clock meeting for the following week. It was the first time in his life that he had rearranged a business meeting for a woman. And as soon as he pushed the button, ending the call, he knew he had made the right decision.

Maria bit down on her lower lip, composing her thoughts. "I'm not certain what I can offer you, Cameron. But whatever I give you will come from my heart."

Cameron cradled her to his chest and buried his face in her hair. "Thank you," he whispered against her ear.

"You're welcome," she replied, laughing softly. "I'll take you on the tour, then we can have dinner at my apartment."

Pulling back, Cameron stared down at Maria, complete surprise freezing his features. He drove her home after their dates, but she had never invited him up to her apartment. He usually waited in the lobby until she boarded the elevator, and once the door closed behind her he felt the detachment, knowing instinctively that she was not ready for him to encroach upon the memories of her life and the lingering love she still shared with her late husband.

It was not his intent to wipe away her memories of Tyree Johnston, but to set up new ones that included Cameron King.

"I like that idea," he stated, delight radiating from his shrouded gaze.

Reaching for her hand again, he escorted her across the wide boulevard.

# CHAPTER SEVEN

Cameron savored the husky timbre of Maria's voice as she pointed out buildings she was familiar with, while offering amusing anecdotes.

"Let's go down this block. I want to show you the building where my grandparents lived. My father used to play stickball in the street." She steered him down 123rd Street between Adam Clayton Powell and Malcolm X Boulevards. Colorful banners fluttering from lampposts identified the area as the Mt. Morris Park Historic District. They stopped in front of a brownstone that had been restored to its former magnificence.

"Do your grandparents still live here?"

Maria shook her head. "They moved back to North Carolina fifteen years ago. They're in their mid-eighties and show no signs of slowing down."

"Is your father an only child?"

"No. He has a sister who lives less than two miles from Grammy and Gramps. She looks in on them every day."

They continued down Malcolm X Boulevard to 116th Street. As soon as they crossed Fifth Avenue, the flavor of the neighborhood changed. "We leave Harlem and now enter El Barrio," Maria explained.

Cameron noticed the abundance of jewelry stores nestled between hair and nail salons, independent supermarkets, and a row of storefront businesses displaying the latest trend in street attire. He did not miss the ubiquitous Dunkin' Donuts, Burger King, and Banco Popular.

A dark-skinned woman dressed in a long colorful skirt, blouse, and matching turban gestured to them as they strolled past her *botanica*. She fingered the many strands of colored beads hanging from her neck.

"Come, *muchacha*, and have your fortune told," she crooned in musical Spanish.

Maria shook her head. "No, *gracias*."

"If not you, then your *novio*. I'm certain he would want to know his future."

Cameron stopped, listening, but not understanding the interchange between the woman and Maria. "What is she saying?"

"She wants to read your palm." He stared down at his left hand. "She wants to tell you what's going to happen in your future."

He lifted his eyebrows. "Can she really do that?"

Maria shrugged a bare shoulder under her slim tangerine orange tank dress. "Some people believe in it."

Walking to the entrance of the tiny store, he peered in. There were shelves filled with candles in every color, statues of saints, bottles of oils, and hooks overflowing with colorful beads.

He offered the shopkeeper a friendly smile. "Tell her I'll stop another time." Maria translated, and the woman returned his smile.

They continued walking, turning southward. Cameron really did not need anyone to tell him his future, because he knew exactly who he wanted in it.

Maria continued their walking tour, pointing out the renowned La Marqueta. It was an enclosed market situated under the trestle of the Metro North commuter railway. The block-long structures, divided into booths, were the precursors to the now-popular flea markets.

"Pop used to come here to buy a whole pig whenever we had a holiday celebration. My mother wouldn't come out of the house until it was completely cooked. He had to remove the head because she couldn't stand looking at the poor creature's eyes."

"You must have had a lot of fun growing up in this neighborhood," Cameron remarked as they crossed the street. He noticed a group of elderly men standing around a duo seated on wooden crates, concentrating intently on a game of dominoes.

"It was wonderful. Of course, we had our share of crime, poverty, and pollution, but that did not affect us directly. Growing up here wasn't much different than growing up in most neighborhoods in New York City. Most residents are hardworking, God-fearing, law-abiding, moral citizens."

Cameron lost count of the number of public housing developments interspersed with row houses, brownstones, and other apartment buildings making up the East Harlem neighborhood. He stopped counting after he noted the Taft, Martin Luther King, George Washington Carver, James Weldon Johnson, and Thomas Jefferson houses. Maria showed him the block and building where she had grown up, the parochial school she attended, and the adjoining church where she was baptized, made her first Holy Communion, received her Confirmation, and where she had exchanged vows with Tyree Johnston. He discovered she could now talk about her deceased husband without dissolving into tears, and knew his association with Maria had reached the point where their relationship had to be resolved.

Maria did not take him down the block where the Parker brothers ran their family-owned business enterprises. Marcus and Peter oversaw the day-to-day operations of Three Brothers Auto Body, while Rafael was responsible for *Tres Hermanos Viaje*. Rafael's outgoing personality had tripled his travel agency's revenue because he always managed to secure the lowest fares for his predominately Spanish-speaking customers. His familiar greeting, *Tres Hermanos Viaje. ¡Dígame!* was recognized throughout El Barrio.

They arrived at her high-rise apartment building as dusk was beginning to descend on the island of Manhattan. Cameron waited for Maria to retrieve her mail, then for the first time he escorted her into the elevator for a swift ascent to the twentieth floor.

She unlocked the door to her apartment, pushed it open, and stepped aside to let him enter. The sight that greeted him would be imprinted on his brain for an eternity. He felt as if he had walked into a sanctuary when his gaze moved slowly over the number of candles lining tables and shelves. A portable fountain rested on a marble table in a corner, the rush of flowing water gurgling musically over colorful rocks.

Maria kicked off her espadrilles, leaving them on a mat near the door. She walked through the entryway into the living room. "Come and sit down. If you want to, you can hang your jacket in the closet near the door. I'm going to change into something more comfortable before I begin dinner."

Shrugging out of his jacket, Cameron hung it in the closet, then followed by removing his loafers and tie. Maria had disappeared through an archway leading to another section of the spacious apartment.

His penetrating gaze took in all of the furnishings in the L-shaped living/dining area. He liked the seating grouped around a glass-topped table. Live potted plants flanked the wall-to-wall, floor-to-ceiling window overlooking the FDR Drive. Oatmeal-colored fabric vertical blinds were drawn back to take advantage of the spectacular view of the East River and the many bridges linking Manhattan with the outer boroughs.

The furnishings in the living and dining rooms were a blend of Art Deco and Oriental. Jade sculptures ranging in color from a translucent white to the more identifiable dark green sat atop black lacquered tables, a buffet server, and lined the shelves of an enormous armoire whose doors were opened to display an exquisite collection of crystal stemware, china, and several lower shelves filled with racks of wines, cordials, and other spirits.

Cameron was still standing at the window when Maria returned to the living room. She had exchanged her dress for a loose-fitting black sleeveless top she had paired with matching pants with a drawstring waist.

She stared at the fabric of his shirt stretched over his broad shoulders, and the precise fit of his slacks falling from his waist to his ankles. Her lips parted in a smile. He also had removed his shoes.

"Would you mind preparing a predinner cocktail?" He jumped slightly at the sound of her voice. It was apparent she had startled him.

Turning away from the window, he smiled at her. "Not at all. Where I can wash my hands?"

"The bathroom is down the hall and on the right."

He walked out of the living room and Maria made her way over to a wall and adjusted the central air-conditioning. She then busied herself lighting the many candles on the tables and shelves before she retreated to the kitchen.

Opening the refrigerator/freezer, she stared at the contents. She would prepare something that would require a minimum of effort. She removed a plastic bag filled with jumbo shrimp from the freezer along with two bags containing boned chicken breasts. She gathered several new potatoes from a vegetable bin and a bag filled with fresh spinach.

She set everything out on the countertop, deciding that they would share their drinks with a shrimp cocktail on the patio. The sultry afternoon temperature had dropped to the mid-seventies, making for a comfortable night for dining under the stars.

Reaching into an overhead cabinet, she pushed a button on a CD player and the soothing, tinkling sound of a piano filled every room in the apartment.

Cameron entered the narrow utility kitchen, and suddenly the space seemed too small for the both of them. He stood less than two feet away and it was the first time that Maria was aware of the marked differences in their height. Without her shoes, the top of her head came only to his shoulder. He had unbuttoned his shirt and rolled back the cuffs, and there was something rakishly attractive about seeing him so relaxed.

"The music is nice. Who's playing the piano?"

"David Osborne. The CD is called *Music of the Night*. It's one of my favorites."

"It makes you want to turn down the lights, close your eyes, and just relax."

She nodded in agreement. "That's exactly what I do the moment I come home. It takes me about an hour to purge myself of all of the goings-on at Della's. Speaking of Della's, I think you should know that everyone knows about us."

He shifted an eyebrow. "They know we're seeing each other?"

"Yes."

"Does it bother you?"

"At first it did."

"And now?"

A sensual smile softened her lush mouth, drawing Cameron's attention to the spot. "Not in the least."

Reaching out, he pulled her gently to his chest. "Good for you," he whispered, seconds before he took possession of her mouth.

His lips parted hers in a soul-searching rapture, taking her beyond herself. His tongue moved tentatively into her mouth, tasting, testing her response.

Maria's knees weakened as she opened her mouth and gave him silent permission to claim the passion she had buried with Tyree. He showered soft, shivery kisses around her lips, along her jaw, and down her throat before returning to her mouth.

His hands moved up and down her back, gathering fabric and baring her back for his exploration. She curled into the curve of his body, wanting to get closer. Her heart was pumping so hard she felt faint; her emotions whirled and skidded, heating her body as shivers of delight left her limp in Cameron's embrace.

A gasp of erotic shock escaped her parted lips when his fingers closed over her breasts, squeezing gently and triggering a strong throbbing between her thighs.

"Cam . . ." His name caught in her throat as she gave in to the pleasure rippling up and down her body. His touch was light, teasing, transporting her to a place she had forgotten existed.

She had waited for seven years for a man to remind her that she was a woman whose passions ran strong and deep. Her hands moved from his neck to his back, pulling his shirt from the confines of the waistband of his slacks.

It was Cameron's turn to gasp when he felt Maria's small hand sweeping up his chest and over his pecs. He wanted her! He wanted her in bed, with his hardness buried deep in the velvet softness of her body.

His kisses became more reckless as he lowered his head and suckled her small, firm breasts. Her knees buckled and he swept her up in his arms, his mouth fastened to her nipple. She moaned as if in pain and he raised his head and stared down at her flushed face. Her pupils were dilated.

"Maria." He did not recognize his own voice. She had aroused him so much, he doubted whether his legs would support his own weight.

Closing her eyes against his intense gaze, she whispered, "Yes?"

Gasping, he swallowed to force air into his labored lungs. "Will—will you . . ." His words trailed off as he caught his breath. He feared losing control and spilling his passions while standing in her kitchen.

Tightening her grip around his strong neck, Maria decided to make it easy—for the both of them. "My bedroom is down the hall to the left."

Cameron forced himself to go slow. Finding the bedroom and undressing Maria and himself would give him the pause he needed to bring his volatile passions under control.

The piano composition flowing from the concealed speakers in the bedroom set the stage for a passionate encounter that had endured years of denial as he parted the sheer panels draped around the towering wrought-iron, four-poster bed, pulled back the embroidered coverlet, and placed Maria on the matching embroidered sheet.

Reaching into the pocket of his trousers, he placed a small packet on the bedside table before he unbuttoned his shirt. He studied the emotions flickering across her face as he slowly, methodically removed his clothing. His eyebrows lifted slightly when her gaze moved lower, then reversed itself to linger on his face. He removed his glasses and placed them on the table seconds before he lay down on the bed beside her.

Pulling her into an embrace, he dropped a kiss on her forehead.

"Are you all right? Let me know if you don't want to do it." His deep voice rumbled in his chest.

Maria curved an arm over his flat belly. "If you don't finish what you've started, I promise I'll hurt you real bad, Mr. King."

Moving over her body, his perfect teeth flashing in a broad smile, he straddled her and unbuttoned her top and slipped it gently off her shoulders. His smile faded with each piece of fabric he removed, and when she was completely nude, he leaned over and kissed her.

His kisses set her body aflame as she writhed sensuously, wanting to get closer. She pleaded with him to release her pent-up passions, but he ignored her as his mouth and tongue charted and claimed every inch of her flesh in his journey to make her his own.

He stopped his sensual assault on her senses long enough to ease the latex protection over his tumescent sex before he slowly and deliberately pushed into her celibate body.

Her gasp of discomfort was soon replaced by moans of pure, unbridled sexual pleasure as Cameron King's lovemaking swept away the grief she had carried for years and she gave in to the sweet surrender of falling in love again.

# CHAPTER EIGHT

Maria lay atop her lover's chest, feeling the runaway pumping of his heart under her breasts.

*It was worth the wait.* Having waited for a man like Cameron King to share her bed was worth all of the endless nights she had slept alone, because she never suspected the very conservative-looking accountant would be so uninhibited. He had taken her to a height of passion she had never known before, wherein their lovemaking had become a raw act of possession, both delaying fulfillment until it threatened to tear them asunder with its intensity. But she had to let it go, and when she did, the screams were torn from the back of her throat with the force of a tidal wave sweeping away everything in its wake.

Shifting her head, she pressed her open mouth to Cameron's moist chest, eliciting a smile from him even though he did not open his eyes.

"Would you really have hurt me?" he questioned with a thread of laughter in his voice.

"No."

"That's gratifying to know, because you had me frightened for a moment."

Her head came up and she rested her chin on his breastbone. She stared up at him staring down at her. "Why?"

He picked at the damp curls clinging to her forehead. "What would it look like if a woman who probably doesn't weigh more than a hundred five pounds were to beat the crap out of a man who tops the scales at one seventy-eight?"

"It wouldn't be so funny if that woman had a black belt in jujitsu."

Cameron's body stiffened in shock. "Are you joking?"

"Nope. I don't know about you, but I need food," she said, quickly changing the topic. "But first I'm going to take a shower."

Tightening his hold on her waist, Cameron reversed their positions, looming over her. "Would you mind company?"

She flashed a sexy smile. "Not at all."

They left the bed and made their way to an adjoining bathroom. Cameron stood under the spray of a lukewarm shower, thinking about the woman whose bed and body he had just shared. He poured a small glob of scented liquid bath gel onto a sponge and drew it slowly over her breasts and down her flat belly.

"You're a black belt and what else? Is there anything else I should know about you?" he whispered near her ear.

"There's nothing else," she whispered back. *Nothing at all except that I love you,* she admitted silently.

---

Maria awoke each morning, praying that what she shared with Cameron would not come to an end—not for a long time. He had gotten his wish to see her more than once a week. He slept at her apartment on Mondays and she returned the favor when she shared his bed at his Striver's Row apartment on Thursdays. They had fallen into the habit of eating brunch at a tiny eatery along Adam Clayton Powell Boulevard on Saturday mornings before Cameron drove to Long Island, where they spent the weekend at his magnificent house in Old Westbury.

She had grown to love the structure with a cathedral ceiling rising thirty feet above gleaming wood floors. Walking into the house gave her a sense of endless space. Walls made entirely of glass opened out to vistas of sky, towering trees, and sloping lawns set on more than two lush, verdant acres.

She had invited him to Sunday dinner with the elder Parkers, and her mother fussed over Cameron as if he were a returning prodigal son. Even though she had yet to tell Cameron she loved him, it was Ynez who broached the subject. She admitted to her mother that she had fallen in love with the accountant, and loved him enough to want to spend the rest of her life with him.

---

She did not know when she awoke the first Saturday in August that the day would change her life—forever. She and Cameron did not spend Friday night in Manhattan, but had endured the bumper-to-bumper Long Island traffic to stay at his house. Cameron had invited her to accompany him to Sag Harbor for a festive family send-off for Valerie. He explained that the normal hour's ride from Old Westbury to Sag Harbor could possibly become twice that long if they did not leave early.

They had their first disagreement when she showed him the gift she had bought for his niece. She had purchased a Coach leather-bound diary for the college freshman and Cameron said he had already selected a gift for Valerie, which would be from the both of them. She told him firmly and quietly never to make a decision for her without consulting her first. He opened his mouth to come back at her, but she gave him a look that said, *Don't start with me, because you'll lose.* And the expression she had come to recognize as annoyance narrowed his eyes and compressed his lips, and it was an hour before they exchanged another word.

---

Maria was charmed with the quaint beauty of Sag Harbor. It was reminiscent of many Long Island communities claiming structures that were erected before colonial America became the United States.

Cameron indulged her when she urged him to stop along Main Street, and he waited patiently while she browsed in the many specialty shops. She lingered in an art gallery, looking for a print to go on the wall in the room she had set up as her study. Built-in shelves were filled with books, CDs, and videocassettes. She had begun her voluminous collection when she and Tyree had decided to open a supper club with an adjoining sports bar and lounge.

She picked up a small framed Monet print titled *Palazzo da Mula, VENICE 1908*. Turning the print over, she winced when noting the amount written on a small sticker affixed to the frame.

"Do you like it?" Cameron asked softly, as he stood behind her.

"Not the price." The gallery owner had inflated the price to at least three times its worth.

Cameron eased the print from her loose grip, stared at the price tag, then handed it to the gallery owner. "We'll take it."

Maria rounded on him, her mouth gaping. "Cameron!"

Reaching into the pocket of his slacks, he withdrew a credit card case, pulled out a card, and handed it to the proprietor with a smile. He turned back to Maria and curved an arm around her waist.

"Please don't make a scene," he warned in a quiet, no-nonsense tone.

She went completely still, her gaze narrowing. "You're paying me back for buying Valerie a gift, aren't you?"

Leaning down, he kissed her cheek. "Not only are you beautiful, but you're also very, very smart."

Crossing her arms under her breasts, she showed him her clenched teeth. It was apparent that Cameron King did not like to be bested. He had surreptitiously shown her another quirk of what she thought was his very predictable personality.

They left the gallery with the print after the owner had wrapped it carefully in a burlap sack. Ten minutes later Cameron steered his Porsche along a quiet residential street, crowded with late-model cars, and into a driveway of a pale gray, three-story beachfront house that claimed the beach, water, and sky as its backyard. He parked behind two Mercedes-Benz sports cars in a contrasting black and white, both bearing MD plates.

He turned off the engine and stared at Maria's impassive face. "Are you still angry with me?"

Turning to her left, she stared at him. There was something about his expression that she had not seen before. There was a vulnerability about him that she found difficult to acknowledge. He had always seemed so in control, so sure of himself.

He gave her a smile that sent her pulse racing, and she found it impossible not to return it with one of her own. "No, Cameron. I'm not angry with you."

His right hand curved around her neck as he leaned over and pressed his lips against her, then gently covered her mouth with his, leaving her gasping for breath. "Thank you, my love."

Maria was shaking when he pulled away. She closed her eyes and waited for him to assist her from the low-slung sports car.

She did not realize how fast her heart was beating when Cameron led her up the steps to his parents' home. As she walked into an entryway that was as large as her living/dining area, she thought of her grandmother's statement: *In my day a girl did not bring a man home to meet her family unless she was going to marry him.* Was it, she asked herself, the same with a man?

Her apprehension was belayed once she was introduced to Drs. Endicott and Margaret King. Cameron had inherited his height and deep voice from his obstetrician/gynecologist father, and his features from his pediatrician mother. The Kings had met and married while in medical school and had run a successful partnership practice for more than forty years until they both retired two years ago.

Margaret, white-haired, smooth-skinned, was beautifully attired in a white silk pants suit. She offered a friendly smile as she took Maria's hand. "Cameron said he was going to bring a surprise, but I never thought it would be a woman. And a very lovely one at that."

"Thank you, Mrs. King."

Margaret shifted a delicate eyebrow, her clear brown eyes narrowing behind the lenses of her gold-rimmed glasses. "If I'm going to call you Maria, then you should call me Margaret. I hope my son told you to bring a swimsuit, because it would be a shame not to take advantage

of the water on such a warm day," she continued, not giving Maria the
opportunity to respond.

"Yes, he did."

"Good. Now let me take you out back where I can introduce you to
everyone." She led her to an open patio that overlooked the beach.

Valerie spied Maria and squealed with excitement. "Mommy," she
called to Lorena King. "Come meet Miss Maria. She did my nails for
the prom."

Lorena rose slowly from her chaise, a warm smile softening her attractive features. Valerie looked nothing like her mother, who was of
medium height with a rounded face that matched her rounded body.

"I'm Lorena. I want to thank you for making my daughter's prom
night even more special with your artistic handiwork."

Marie returned the smile. "You're quite welcome."

Valerie smoothed back a wealth of braided hair falling to her shoulders.
"Are you dating my Uncle Ronnie?"

"Valerie! Mind your manners," Margaret chastised in a quiet voice.

"Well, didn't he bring her, Grandma?"

Maria laughed. "Yes, he did."

Valerie bobbed her head up and down. "Now I know why he's not so
grumpy anymore."

"That's enough, young lady," Lorena warned softly. "It's nice meeting
you, Maria," she said over her shoulder as she steered her daughter to
the other end of the patio.

"How did you and my son meet?" Margaret questioned as she took
Maria's arm.

"I'm Cameron's manicurist."

Margaret eyes widened with this revelation. "You do his nails?"

Squaring her shoulders and tilting her chin, Maria gave the older
woman a level stare. "Yes, I do."

Margaret recovered quickly, forcing a tremulous smile. "That's quite
interesting."

*Isn't it!* Maria mused as she found herself smiling even when she did not want to as Margaret introduced her to family members and friends who had come to celebrate Valerie King's pursuit of a higher education.

*They're snobs!* That was the only word she could come up with to describe the Kings. Stuffy, supercilious snobs!

---

Endicott King waited until his wife escorted Maria through a passage that led to the rear of the house, then turned to his son. He recognized an expression on Cameron's face that indicated that Maria Parker was special, special enough to introduce to his parents.

"You're in love with her." His question came out like a statement.

Cameron gave his father a level stare. "Totally."

Endicott smiled and dropped a hand on his son's shoulder. "Good. You've waited a long time to find someone."

Cameron nodded. "The wait has been worth it," he stated, unknowingly echoing Maria's sentiments. He placed an arm over his father's shoulders and told him of the plans he had made for his future.

---

Maria lay on a chaise on an outdoor patio, wearing only a navy blue maillot. The moisture on her skin and hair had evaporated quickly with the heat of the blazing summer sun.

Opening her eyes, she stared at a profusion of pink and green balloons, secured by streamers of ribbons to the slates enclosing the patio, bobbing in a warm breeze coming in from the water. The afternoon had been filled with lively conversation, sand, sea, and an abundance of seafood.

Margaret King had a caterer prepare monstrous platters of king crab legs, steamers, mussels, boiled crabs, broiled lobsters, and clams on the half-shell. For those who did not eat seafood, there were differently prepared varieties of chicken, with accompanying side dishes of marinated vegetables, roasted corn on the cob, potato salad, and cole slaw.

Cameron assumed the role of bartender, serving potent concoctions as well as nonalcoholic drinks to the assembled. The gathering numbered thirty, including a few of Valerie's friends who had graduated from high school with her.

Despite her initial assessment of the Kings and their guests, Maria had to admit that she had enjoyed herself when earlier that afternoon she'd found herself clutching Cameron's waist as they skimmed over the water on a Jet Ski. It had taken more than half an hour of pleading before she agreed to accompany him. He'd reassured her that they both would wear life vests, which had finally convinced her to join him.

Sitting up, she brushed the remnants of sand off her feet, then made her way to the half-bath off the patio. She knocked on the door, then pushed it open when no one answered.

She did not recognize the reflection staring back at her from the mirror. The hot sun had darkened her face, concealing the spray of freckles over her nose. It had also lightened her hair with liberal streaks of red running over the crown. The deep rich brown on her face made her eyes appear lighter, a smoky gray-brown.

She washed her face and hands in the sink, and as she was blotting the moisture from her face with a delicate linen towel, she heard voices and her name mentioned.

Going completely still, she listened, stunned, as she heard two women wondering how Cameron could even think that he could get away with bringing a manicurist to meet his parents.

"She's nothing more than a shop girl," one woman declared vehemently. "He could have any professional woman he wants, so why would he stoop to someone in a service industry?"

"I don't know. Maybe he's taken with her looks. She is tiny and very cute," came another female voice. "Even though he and Sylvia did not stay together, at least she did graduate from college."

"Margaret must be devastated," the first woman countered.

Closing her eyes, Maria counted to ten, then flung open the door. If she had not been so angry, she would've laughed at the startled expressions on the women's faces. They hadn't known she was in the bathroom.

"Excuse me, *please!*"

She retraced her steps to the patio, head held high, when all she wanted to do was scream and throw things. How dare they! What right did they have to talk about her as if she were disposable trash?

She found Cameron standing with Lorena's brother. The two men were engaged in a lively conversation about baseball. She tapped him on the back, garnering his attention.

"Excuse me. May I have a word with you?"

Cameron excused himself; he held Maria's hand, leading her down to the beach. Valerie and half a dozen of her friends sat on the sand, building a castle. When they were far enough away not to be overhead, he turned to her.

"What is it?"

Biting down hard on her lower lip, Maria stared out at the water through the dark lenses of her sunglasses. She had calmed down enough to tell Cameron what she had overheard.

He angled his head, listening as she repeated verbatim what the two women said about her. His mouth curved into a smile when she finished. "You're upset about that? They're just two narrow-minded women who think they're better than everyone else."

Her temper flared. "You don't think I have a right to be upset?"

He shrugged his bare, tanned shoulders. "No, I don't."

She recoiled as if he had slapped her. "I suppose not," she retorted slowly. "It wasn't you they were denigrating."

He caught her shoulders, pulling her to his chest. "Maria, it was nothing."

"Take your hands off me. And don't you dare tell me again that it was nothing."

He dropped his hands, taking a backward step. "I don't intend to minimize what they said about you, but I can forgive them because they don't know you."

"They called me a shop girl, Cameron! They compared me to your ex-wife, and I came up as the inferior choice."

He frowned in exasperation. "What do you want me to do, Maria? Do you want me to call them out and take them to task for their pettiness? Do you think that would change their opinion of you?" He threw up both hands and let out an audible sigh. "It only matters what I think of you. It only matters how I feel about you," he added in a softer tone.

Turning her back on him, she compressed her lips in a tight line. "Whenever you're ready to leave, I want you to take me home."

"You want me to drive more than a hundred miles back to Manhattan tonight?"

She had forgotten how far they were from the city. "You can drop me off in Brentwood."

Cameron did not want to take her anywhere but to his house. He took several steps, pressing his bare chest to her back. "Come home with me, darling. We'll talk about it later."

"There's nothing to talk about," she countered stubbornly.

Suddenly his face went grim, becoming a mask of stone. "If that's the case, then I'll drive you back to Manhattan—*tonight*."

# CHAPTER NINE

There was only the sound of the car's radio filling the Porsche's interior as Cameron and Maria made the return trip to Manhattan. They had left Sag Harbor at nine-fifteen, and had made it across the Triborough Bridge at eleven. It was exactly eleven-fifteen when he found a parking space near Maria's building.

It had taken Cameron two hours to conclude that he loved her enough to shed whatever pride he had to let her know the depths of his feelings. Shutting off the ignition, he got out of the car and came around to the passenger's side to help her out. Extending his hand, he caught hers, holding it for several seconds before pulling her to her feet. Curving a protective arm around her tiny waist, he led her to her building, waiting until she opened the door to the lobby. They still did not exchange a word as they rode the elevator to the twentieth floor.

Maria slipped a key in the lock to her apartment, stopping before she turned it. "I want to thank you for a lovely weekend." Her voice was barely a whisper. She completed the motion, turning the key and pushing open the door.

Cameron braced an arm over her head, stopping her from entering the apartment. "I love you, Maria," he stated with a staid calmness that chilled her to the bone. "I love you more than I've ever loved any woman."

Maria did not move, nor did she turn around. She did not trust herself or her legs. Closing her eyes, she waited. And when she opened them, Cameron had removed his arm and had disappeared into the elevator.

*You've lost him,* a silent voice chided her.

---

Maria lost track of time, reacting to stimuli that she was familiar with. She made it through the weekend without wallowing in self-pity or giving in to tears. She woke up Monday morning, showered, dressed, then headed for her brother's travel agency, and it wasn't until she walked through the door and into his air-conditioned office that she realized she was repeating what she had done as a child. Whenever she was hurting, it was Rafael Parker who calmed her fears and soothed her pain.

Nine years her senior, forty-year-old Rafael Parker now counted more gray hairs on his head than black. He motioned to her to come in as he sat behind his desk, gesturing while speaking rapid Spanish.

Sitting down, she smiled at her double-talking, silver-tongued brother. He had won the distinction of travel agent of the year three consecutive years running. She stared at him, smiling, and he winked at her.

He finished with his call, removing the headset and placing it on the desk. Rising to his feet, he came around the desk, arms outstretched. "Now, to what do I owe this honor of a visit from my sister, who I've heard from a very reliable source has fallen in love?"

She fell against her brother's solid body, holding on to him as if he were her lifeline. "I need to talk to you, Raffle."

Pulling back, Rafael surveyed his sister's darkly tanned face. A slight smile crinkled his hazel eyes. She looked good—no, better than good. She looked beautiful.

He glanced down at his watch. "Give me another ten minutes. Norma is expected in at any minute. She can cover the phones while we talk."

As if on cue, Norma Ocasio walked in. She greeted her boss and his sister, then sat down at her desk and picked up the headset to her telephone. She nodded when Rafael told her that he was going out and would be back within half an hour.

"Have you had breakfast?" Rafael asked, heading toward a coffee shop in the middle of the block.

"No."

"That makes two of us. We'll discuss whatever it is you need to talk about over breakfast."

Rafael held the door, following Maria and greeting everyone as if he were the mayor of the city. He escorted her to a booth in the rear. Within minutes a waitress sauntered over with a pot of coffee and filled two mugs with the strong brew. She waited while Rafael ordered for himself and his sister, then went to the counter to put in their selections.

Maria drank a glass of orange juice, feeling more revived than she had in hours. When she bit into a slice of buttered toast, she recalled that she hadn't eaten any solid food since leaving Sag Harbor Saturday afternoon.

Rafael stared across the table at her, his coffee mug poised in midair. "What's up, Maria?"

She told him everything, amazed that she could recall with such clarity everything the two women had said about her. She did not leave out Cameron's reaction to their disparaging remarks. Her brother's expression did not change until her voice faded away.

Shifting to his left, Rafael Parker reached for the cellular phone clipped to his waist. Punching in a button, he listened for the ringing, then a break in the connection. "Pepito, tell Markie that we have to take care of some trouble. It concerns Maria. It looks as if we have to teach Mr. Cameron King a lesson about messin' over our sister."

"No!" Maria screamed, reaching for the small, palm-sized telephone. She knew what her brother meant by *taking care of some trouble*. That meant doing bodily harm to someone, and that someone would be one Cameron King. Everyone in the coffee shop turned and stared at her. She sat back down, offering an apologetic smile.

Rafael stared at her. "Hold on, Pepito." He placed a hand over the phone's mouthpiece. "Do you or don't you want me to take care of this?"

"I don't want you to beat him up," she said in a shaky whisper. "If he deserved a butt-kicking, I think I could do a better job than any of you."

Rafael smiled, nodding in agreement. He did not think he would ever get used to the fact that his little sister had earned a black belt in jujitsu. He and his brothers had taken her to a neighborhood movie theater to see a Bruce Lee film, and when she returned home she badgered her parents to let her take martial arts instruction. Ray and Ynez finally gave in to her whining and the year she turned nine she began taking jujitsu.

Putting the phone to his ear, he said quietly, "Forget it, Pepito. She's all right. Of course I'm sure. I'm sitting here looking at her. I'll call you later and fill you in on everything." Pressing a button, he ended the call.

Vertical lines marred Rafael's forehead. "What's going on, sis? You come to me because you're upset about how your boyfriend treats you, then when I want to take care of him you tell me no."

Pressing her head against the booth's worn back, she wagged her head. "I came to you because I needed someone to talk to. I need to know if I overreacted. I know who I am and what I can do. I don't need the approval of anyone, and that includes Cameron King."

There was a full minute of silence. "Do you love him, Maria?"

Closing her eyes, she smiled. "Oh, yes."

"Does he know that?"

Her eyes opened. "No."

"Does he love you?"

She met her brother's direct stare. "He said he did."

"Smart man. Cameron is not responsible for his family's behavior any more than you'd be responsible if Pepito, Markie, and I decided to tighten your boyfriend up."

Reaching across the table, Maria caught Rafael's hand. "Promise me you won't touch him."

"Maria," he drawled, not meeting her gaze.

Her nails dug into the tender flesh on the back of his hand. "Promise me, Rafael Parker."

Nodding slowly, he looked over her head. "I promise. I'd hate to have to jack him up, then call him brother one of these days." What he didn't promise was that he wouldn't meet with Cameron.

Her eyes darkening in pain, she shook her head. "I doubt that will ever happen."

---

Cameron was somewhat surprised when the receptionist buzzed his office late Monday afternoon and informed him that a Rafael Parker wanted to meet with him.

"He doesn't have an appointment. I asked him the nature of his business and he says he needs some help with investing some of his business income. Will you see him?"

A frown marred his smooth forehead. If his instincts were correct, then he supposed Rafael Parker had come to see him about his sister, not investments. "Send him in."

Cameron was waiting at the door to his office when Rafael Parker made his way down the hall. Extending his right hand, he offered a professional smile. "It's nice seeing you again."

Rafael took the proffered hand. "Same here. Even before we begin I want to tell you that my sister knows nothing about this meeting."

"There is such a thing as client confidentiality." He arched an eyebrow. "Do you intend to become a client of King Financial Services?"

"I'll let you know after we've talked."

"Please come in and sit down."

Rafael surveyed the furnishings in the large office, admiring the sophisticated opulence. Every article of furniture, each accessory appeared to be selected with the utmost care, the style harmonizing with the personality and individuality of the company's CEO. He had to admit that Maria had chosen well.

He took a plush armchair, and to his surprise Cameron pulled over a matching chair and sat opposite him instead of retreating behind his desk.

Cameron draped a leg over his knee. "You've come to talk about your sister." A slight smile curved his mouth when Rafael nodded. "Did she tell you that I love her?" Rafael nodded again. "I need your help."

"My help?"

"Yes. You know Maria a lot better than I do. I need you to help me convince her that she should marry me."

"Damn, bro," Rafael mumbled under his breath. "Are you always this direct?"

Cameron's impassive expression did not change. "When I have to be."

"She's very stubborn."

"I know that firsthand," Cameron confirmed.

Leaning forward, Rafael disclosed things about his sister that he had never told another man. He watched an expression of shock freeze Cameron King's features. After a while the shock gave way to confidence, then laughter.

Both men laughed until they found it hard to catch their breath. Then they agreed that their ingenious plan to become brothers-in-law had to work.

---

Maria walked into Della's Tuesday morning tanned and smiling. She had promised herself that no one would know that while she smiled outwardly she cried for the loss of a man who offered her everything she needed as a female.

Maurice winked at her as she walked past him. "You look marvelous, chica. I have to assume you had a wonderful weekend."

"The best," she lied smoothly.

"Love will do it every time."

She checked her appointment book with the one on the front desk, penciling in appointments Ramona had set up in her absence. It promised to be a full four days.

The morning sped by quickly, and it was nearly three o'clock when the receptionist came to the rear to tell her that there was a delivery of flowers at the reception desk.

"Hey, Clark Kent is at it again," a stylist called out when she saw the exquisite bouquet of long-stemmed red roses.

Maria plucked the card off the cellophane, a slight frown furrowing her brow. The card was plain except for the typed letter W. Shrugging her shoulders, she stared at Ramona. "Who left these?"

"The guy was the same one who left the humongous bouquet from King Financial Services. Are you going to leave them here?"

Slipping the card into the pocket of her smock, she smiled. "Enjoy them."

Later that evening she decided not to take the roses home with her and left them on a table in the reception area. Cameron was sadly mistaken if he thought she was going to forgive him for his insensitivity just because he sent a bouquet of flowers.

*Out of sight, out of mind,* she told herself as she unlocked the door to her apartment. Kicking off her shoes, she went through the ritual of lighting her candles, then checked the messages on her answering machine.

There was one message—and it was from Cameron. He wanted her to call him so they could talk.

"Never," she whispered to the machine when his deep voice ended.

---

The delivery of roses was the first of what was to become a daily occurrence. It began with roses, then lilies. These were followed by foxgloves and chrysanthemums. Each was accompanied by a blank card with a typed letter. She laid the cards out on her coffee table. The four letters spelled the word *WILL.*

Along with the delivery of flowers there were daily messages on her answering machine from Cameron. The message was always the same: "Please call me, Maria, so we can talk."

She survived the first week, but the pattern continued the second week, and along with the delivery of flowers was the unexpected appearance of Cameron when he came into Della's for a manicure.

Maria was glad she was sitting because she was certain her legs would not have been able to support her body when he walked over and sat down with one of the other manicurists. He did not bother to look at her as he flashed his dazzling smile for the flustered woman.

She managed to steal surreptitious glances at him as she concentrated on applying a set of linen wraps. Even though he sat more than six feet away, she could make out the sensual fragrance of his sandalwood cologne. Not seeing him for a week made her aware of his masculine beauty. The sun had darkened his skin, enhancing the deep red undertones. And she noticed for the first time a sprinkling of gray in his close-cut hair at the temples. He was impeccably attired, as usual, and she marveled that he managed to appear so unwrinkled at the end of a work day.

She'd received seven deliveries of flowers with seven cards attached, each with a single typed letter. The seven cards spelled out the words *WILL YOU.* Cameron had also left seven identical messages on her answering machine.

Maria sat on a chair on her terrace, staring out at the night. It had begun raining, but she did not want to go inside. She did not want to read the cryptic message the twelve cards had spelled out. She did not need the last two letters to know what Cameron wanted. And she did not have to be a *bruja* to know what the last two letters would be. The twelve letters spelled *WILL YOU MARRY.*

"Me," she whispered to the velvet night.

Pulling her knees to her chest, she lowered her head and cried. She cried for shutting him out, and she cried for being a fool. He had sent so many flowers that everyone at Della's had begun placing bets as to when she would fly off with her Clark Kent. It had not mattered to them that she no longer did his nails, or that when he came into the salon he did not deign to give her even a cursory glance.

She had not returned his calls and there was no reason she could offer for waiting two weeks to call him. Raising her head, she sucked in a lungful of oppressive humidity. Cameron King had thrown down the gauntlet and she would accept his challenge.

She would wait for him to send the last two letters.

# CHAPTER TEN

All of the employees at Della's gathered around Maurice. "Put up or shut up," he hissed at Dee Dee's assistant. "What day do you want?"

"Put me down for Wednesday the twenty-ninth."

"How about you, Mighty Mouth?"

KiKi chewed on the tip of her forefinger. "How much are the bets?"

"Five dollars!" everyone chorused.

"What's going on here?"

Everyone jumped at the sound of Della Frazier's voice. All eyes were trained on the face of the woman who bore an uncanny resemblance to Diahann Carroll. All gazes shifted from Della to Maurice.

"We're placing bets," he stated candidly.

Della folded her beautiful hands on her slender hips. "You know the rules. No gambling and no hustling in my salon."

"We ain't gambling, Miss Della," KiKi announced. "We just taking bets on when Clark Kent will ask Maria to marry him."

She arched a questioning eyebrow. "Clark Kent?"

Everyone looked at KiKi, unofficially making her the spokesperson. Realizing all gazes were on her, the shampoo girl offered a dramatic narrative of the latest salon romance.

Much to everyone's surprise, Della doubled over in laughter. She recovered enough to ask, "How much is everyone betting?"

"Five dollars for each day."

Della glanced at the calendar, then smiled at Maurice. "Let me go and get my money from my office. Reecie, put me down for Thursday and Friday."

KiKi stuck out her tongue, giving Reecie a high-five fingertip handshake.

Maurice marked the names on the calendar, then counted the money. "If he pops the question after Labor Day, then someone will have a nice post-holiday stash." He glanced up at everyone standing around him. "If anyone breathes a word of this, I'll sue them."

"You ain't practicing lawyering," KiKi retorted.

Reaching over, he patted her cheek. "Honey, do me a favor."

Her eyes widened in delight. "What?"

"Just don't talk."

KiKi's mouth fell open, then closed as she rolled her eyes.

Della gave her a knowing look. "KiKi, just this one time why don't you listen to Maurice?"

"Yes, Miss Della."

Della glanced up at the clock. In less than five minutes the door would open for another day of beauty at Della's House of Style. "Everyone to their stations. You know we never keep anyone waiting."

---

Maria walked into Della's Thursday morning with a mysterious smile curving her mouth. She had taken special care with her appearance. Dee Dee had trimmed her hair the day before, Kimm Gilmore had waxed her eyebrows, and she had given herself a manicure and a pedicure.

Cameron had sent her another bouquet of flowers with a card, this one bearing the letter *E*. She had checked with Ramona, who told her that he was expected in at four-thirty for a manicure, so she intended to be ready for him.

"Who you looking sexy for today, *chica*?" Maurice had never seen Maria dress so provocatively. She wore a black tank dress that hugged every curve of her petite, compact body. The bodice revealed a soft swell of tanned breasts and the hem a generous amount of shapely legs. She had added several inches to her height with a pair of black patent leather sling-strap heels.

Folding her hands on her hips, she ran her tongue over her crimson-colored lips, grinning. "Clark Kent."

Maurice placed a hand over his heart. "Please don't hurt the poor brother."

She laughed, remembering her threat to hurt Cameron real bad if he did not make love to her. "I'll try not to."

A pregnant hush descended over the salon, and before Maria could pick up her smock and cover her revealing attire, Cameron King stood in front of her.

Leaning against a column, he crossed his arms over his chest and stared at her. His gaze moved slowly from her face down to her feet, then reversed itself. Reaching into the breast pocket of his suit jacket, he withdrew a small card and handed it to her.

Maria knew her hands were shaking, but she couldn't control them as she took the square of vellum. Her lids fluttered wildly as she stared at a question mark.

Her head came up, her eyes widening when she saw Cameron slip out of his suit jacket and hand it to Maurice. Her jaw dropped when he removed his tie, then slowly unbuttoned his shirt.

She took a step, stopping less than a foot from him. "Cameron. No!"

He stopped long enough to hand Maurice his glasses, then resumed unbuttoning his shirt. Maria covered her face with her hands, unable to look at him disrobing in front of the salon staff and their clients.

"Don't do this to me," she pleaded through her fingers.

"Do what to you?" he questioned as he shrugged the buttoned-down pale blue shirt off his shoulders. "Think about what you've done to me." He caught her wrists. "You've cost me a small fortune sending you flowers. You've just about destroyed whatever male ego I've managed to salvage when you ignored the messages I left on your answering machine."

She lowered her fingers, her eyes bright with unshed tears. "Not here," she whispered.

"Why not here? Why not at Della's? Isn't this where I met you? Isn't this where I fell in love with you?"

"You tell her, Clark Kent!" someone shouted.

"And you think I didn't know everyone called me Clark Kent behind my back? And why didn't you tell me that you graduated with a degree in accounting? Were you laughing at me when I offered to help you with your *project*? Well, the last laugh is on you, Miss Parker, because it's my time to put on a show."

Maria's gaze slipped from his face to his chest, and she couldn't stop the laughter bubbling up in her throat. Under his shirt Cameron wore a blue T-shirt with a big red *S* emblazoned on the front. His stoic expression softened as he went to his knees. Closing his eyes, he sang the opening line to "Maria" from *West Side Story*.

She did not know whether to laugh or cry as Cameron sang the beautifully haunting song in perfect pitch, his baritone voice filling the salon.

Reaching for his arm, she tried easing him to his feet. "Cameron, let's go outside," she whispered when he finished singing.

He stood up, bowing from the waist and waving as if he were onstage before thousands of his adoring fans. He retrieved his glasses from Maurice. Turning to Maria, he cradled her face between his hands and kissed her tenderly on the lips.

"You have all of the cards, my darling. Do you have an answer for me?"

Forgetting that she was in Della's, she curved her arms around his neck and kissed him passionately. "The answer is yes."

Cameron's arms tightened around her waist as he lifted her effortlessly off her feet. He shifted her slightly and swung her up in his arms and walked across the salon floor amid whistling and applause.

KiKi raced to the reception area, tugging at his arm. "Did you propose to her, Clark—I mean Mr. King?"

He smiled down at the shampoo girl. "Yes, I did."

KiKi turned and pointed her airbrushed forefinger at Maurice. "Pay up, Moe-reese!"

Della, who had come out of her office to observe the romantic, passionate interchange between her nail technician and Cameron King, shook her head. She had stopped counting the number of clients and employees who had fallen in love at the salon.

Raising her expressive eyebrows, she returned to her office, wondering who would be next.

# EPILOGUE

Maria stood at the railing of the cruise ship, staring out at the endless expanse of the Caribbean. Less than twenty-four hours ago she had exchanged vows with Cameron King in a New Year's Eve candlelight ceremony, with both families in attendance along with many of the staff at Della's. Maurice had surprised everyone when he cut his hair, removed the garish color, and put on an expertly tailored handmade Brioni suit. Most of the single women took one look at him, quickly abandoned their demure demeanor, and flirted shamelessly with him.

Maria had handed in her resignation and when she and Cameron returned from their honeymoon they would meet with a contractor to begin construction for her full-service salon and adjoining supper club. Cameron had suggested a location where the diners would have a view of the water from a rooftop garden restaurant. She had not planned on opening her salon on Long Island, but relented after she found the perfect location on the North Shore.

She closed her eyes, a sensual smile parting her lips when she felt the heat of her husband's body sweep over her back. His hand curved around her waist, moving up until it rested over her left breast. She felt him shudder as he drew in a sharp breath when her nipple swelled against the delicate silk dress.

Relaxing, she sank back against his cushioning embrace. Her hand moved and covered his, the eerie light of a full moon glinting off the brilliant blue-white diamonds circling her wedding band.

"The sky down here is beautiful, isn't it, Cameron?"

His warm breath swept over her ear. "Not as beautiful as you are."

Opening her eyes, she turned in his loose embrace. Her gaze caressed his face, committing each feature to memory. "I love you," she whispered reverently.

"And I, you," he confessed. Lowering his head, he kissed her mouth, giving in to the sweetest surrender he had ever known.

# Truly, Honestly

FELICIA MASON

For Michelle and for Lee, the critique partners

# PROLOGUE

One with the music, she swayed along with the rhythm of the bass, the sweet whine of the saxophone, and the teasing melody played out on the ivories. With eyes closed, she let the music take her to smooth places, sensual places . . . places she hadn't visited in oh, so long.

As the notes of the song faded away, she smiled like a woman well pleased by her man.

"That was a little sumthin' for the lovely lady in the blue and white dress at the side table."

Without opening her eyes, she reached for the glass of Kendall-Jackson chardonnay.

"Any special requests tonight, love?"

"Something mellow, Mr. DJ. Something smooth and mellow."

"It's yours for the asking, baby. Here's the piano man to take us on home here at Della's Place."

She smiled, pleased with herself. She had a regular table, a regular drink, and a regular special place in the DJ's playlist.

*Now all you need is a regular life,* she thought as she finished off her wine. But that sort of thinking wasn't allowed, at least not right now. In a few minutes, maybe, but not right now.

She signaled for the waitress to take the DJ his usual glass of ice water with lemon. He didn't drink alcohol. She'd discovered that the first time she'd sent him a drink. As the waitress delivered his bottle of water and glass of ice, the woman enjoyed a few more bars of the mellow tones. Then, as was her custom, she left a big tip on the small table and slipped from the lounge before the song ended.

Outside, she hailed a cab and quickly stepped inside. She gave the driver her Central Park address, and after they were what she considered a safe distance away, she pulled off the long, curly wig and took out the bobby pins that kept her own flat brown hair tucked securely out of sight.

The cabbie glanced at her in the rearview mirror, but she paid him no mind. This was, after all, New York. Strange things happened in cabs all the time and the driver had probably seen stranger as he drove the city streets.

Slipping off the strappy high heels, she swapped them for a pair of comfortable blue flats that she pulled from the small tote bag she carried. Then, leaning her head back on the seat, she took a deep, calming breath. By the time the driver reached her apartment building, the physical and mental metamorphosis was complete.

# CHAPTER ONE

You're such a stick-in-the-mud, Sheila. Look at you."

Sheila Landon stared at her reflection in the three-way mirror while her so-called best friend hurled insults one after the other. Not for the first time, Sheila wondered why she'd invited Tracy along on this shopping trip.

"That skirt makes you look like an 1890s scrubwoman," Tracy proclaimed.

Sheila turned one way and then the other, assessing the ankle-length wraparound skirt. "You're the one who said brown was in," she said.

Tracy sighed. "Two years ago, Sheila. Brown was in for about four months two years ago. It's a new millennium, a new day."

"Well, I'm right on time for the retro look," Sheila said with a wry smile.

"Besides, I *just* got a VCR and CD player, remember."

The grunt Tracy emitted was so typical that Sheila grinned. Her lack of stylishness—style by Tracy's definition—had been a point of dispute between them since the days they shared an apartment while in college.

"And you should be able to sell both of them at a yard sale for about forty bucks, seeing that the rest of the world is moving to DVD."

"Cut me some slack, Trace. I'm on vacation," Sheila said as she reached for a dove gray double-breasted suit. "Besides, I'm in banking, remember. I don't have to look like a showpiece 24–7 like you real estate brokers. I just have to look honest and dependable."

Tracy snatched the dull gray suit from Sheila's hands, shoved it behind her back, and held high a chartreuse miniskirt with a matching bolero jacket.

Sheila's eyebrows rose. "You have got to be kidding."

"You have the legs and the figure. There are women who would kill to have your body, and you walk around looking for sackcloth to wear."

"That's because sackcloth is comfortable," Sheila said with a pointed look at Tracy's three-inch heels. On Tracy's fashion meter her own sensible flats, suitable for extended shopping and walking, wouldn't claim even a two on a scale of ten. Sheila unwrapped the brown skirt from her waist and handed it out to a hovering attendant.

Tracy's pager went off. She glanced at it, then reached into her bag for her phone. "I need to answer this."

Used to the real estate agent's frequent calls and pages, Sheila turned her attention back to the selection of clothes. She'd mentally discarded more than half of them—all Tracy's picks—without trying them on. With Tracy distracted on her call, Sheila retrieved the dove gray suit and held it against her body in front of the mirror. She had a meeting with the bank's board of directors in a few weeks. The suit would be ideal.

Tracy caught her eye in the mirror and frowned as she shook her head.

Sheila stuck her tongue out at her friend.

A few minutes later, Tracy clicked off the line. "I have to go meet a client," she said. "And I swear, Sheila. If you buy that dull suit, I'll stop being your friend."

"Promises, promises."

Sheila shimmied into the skirt, its length a little short for banking, but not short enough to raise eyebrows in her conservative workplace. As a matter of fact, she decided after a moment, it was exactly what a vice-president-to-be might wear.

"Perfect," she declared.

"Horrendous," Tracy pronounced.

"Aren't you going to be late for an appointment?"

With a quick glance at her watch, Tracy groaned. "Call me."

Sheila waved her away. The attendant cleared her throat. "Is there anything else you'd like to see, Ms. Landon?"

Sheila peeked around the clerk's shoulders, making sure Tracy was, indeed, gone and out of earshot. A moment later, satisfied that her friend had departed, Sheila turned back to the sales clerk.

"I saw a gold sheath dress as I came in. It had purple, or maybe red shimmering highlights in it. I'd like to see that."

If the flamboyant choice from her staid customer surprised the saleswoman, she hid it well. With a demure "Yes, ma'am, I know the one," the clerk disappeared.

Sheila grinned in the mirror.

Tracy thought she was a dull person with a dull job that matched her dull lifestyle. Unfortunately, Tracy was right on at least two of those points. But Sheila knew herself better than anyone else.

"And the freaks come out at night," she said with a grin into the mirror.

Closing her eyes, she swayed to a tune playing in her head. For the next three weeks she was a free agent. She'd more than earned the comp time working eighteen-hour days the last six months on a multinational deal that would eventually earn her firm close to six billion dollars.

Some of her own six-figure bonus for her work on the project was already invested and earning fat dividends. The rest she'd earmarked for her pet project, the thing she most wanted to do these days. Sheila had come a long way in the world and took pride in her accomplishments. But the pace had been wearing on her lately.

She longed for extended time—not just a vacation or comp time—to enjoy the fruit of her labor. She'd met and exceeded all of the financial goals she'd set for herself. And she'd more than earned the vice presidency that was headed her way. But there was something she wanted even more than that coveted position with all its perks and benefits.

Not even Tracy knew about the calling Sheila yearned to answer. The time had never seemed right, the people not available or in place. But now . . . maybe she'd take part of her vacation and map out a business plan.

Before she could dwell on that, though, the sales clerk returned with the naughty dress. Sheila slipped it on and stared at her reflection in the mirror. It fit like a second skin, every curve a smooth line. She had just the right shoes for it, too.

"I'll take it."

She didn't even glance at the small, discreet price tag.

---

A re you sure about this?" LaTonya asked. "What you're describing is a pretty drastic change."

Sheila nodded. "I've been wearing a very long, curly wig every weekend for almost the past month getting myself ready for this. I'm sure."

She didn't add that she'd been sporting the look at Della's Place for the last two weekends. The fewer people who recognized her, the better, Sheila figured.

Her plan to live wild and free for the next three weeks had been spawned by a comment she'd accidentally overheard at work. Two colleagues were describing her to a new employee.

"Landon. You know, she's the one who banned the words *fun* and *lighten up* from her personal vocabulary. She wouldn't know how to let her hair down if somebody gave her a million bucks to do it."

Sheila had stopped in her tracks when she heard her name. Then, standing quietly just out of sight, she listened to her coworkers' description of her. The rest had been highly complimentary of her business skills and her hunches about the market. Then one of them even pointed out that the reason she was on her way to a vice presidency was because she was so focused on the job.

But in the way of such things, Sheila honed in not on the positive, but on her so-called deficiencies.

"I know how to let my hair down," she said.

"You sure do," her stylist said in response. "This full weave is going to be a lot of hair you can let down or put up. And I mean *a lot* of hair," she added.

"Good," Sheila said. "That's the way I want it."

She settled into the chair while her stylist braided her natural hair, the first step toward the total transformation. Sheila's plan was to spend her entire vacation letting her hair down, literally and figuratively. She'd go to clubs, parties, and hang out like the rest of the population. She wanted to catch up on the life she'd been missing while zipping along in the accelerated lane of the fast track.

In the office at Della's House of Style, DJ Daryl Desmond was having a time of it trying to convince Della, the salon owner, to let him play some of his own music in the attached lounge, Della's Place.

"I'm not talking about the whole night. Please come on, now. Help a brother out."

Della Frazier leaned back in her chair to think about it. The lounge was the newest addition to the salon. So far, things had been going well, very well, thanks to word of mouth about the mellow jazz, easy food, and moderate prices. It had been her baby from the get-go and she wanted to make sure that it, like the salon, was a hit.

"Daryl, you've been doing a good job with the music, sticking to the playlist and making sure customers' requests follow the mission. I just don't know about introducing someone foreign so early in the game."

"Foreign? I've been making my own music for three years now and playing it all over the city. Shoot, I've even been into D.C. and Philly. And my stuff fits the format for the lounge. It's mellow, laid-back, like George Benson."

"You don't play the guitar," Della pointed out.

Daryl sighed. "That was just an illustration, Della."

"So, what, exactly do you have in mind?"

Daryl unbuttoned the jacket on his blue uniform as he loosened up to make his argument. "It'll be sweet. I can play some smooth jazz, some old stuff, you know, Miles, Bird, and then segue into a Desmond tune or two."

She smiled. Standing, Della went to the window that overlooked the salon floor. The lounge drew a clientele that capitalized on the success of the shop. Della wasn't afraid to take risks, but she was afraid of Daryl messing with a good thing before its time.

"Let me think about it," she told him.

He sighed. "Okay. That's the least you can do." He pulled a plastic case from the briefcase he carried. "While you're thinking, listen to this. It's my demo CD. I think you'll like it. The work speaks for itself. It's perfect for Della's Place."

He put the CD on her desk. "Promise you'll listen to it?"

"I'll listen," she assured him.

Daryl glanced at his watch. "I better get a move on. My lunch break is almost over. I'm driving a double today, too."

"And did you eat any lunch?"

He smiled. "No time to waste on food, Miss Della. I got places to go and people to meet in every free moment." Closing his briefcase, Daryl looked at her. "I have a question for you about Della's Place."

"Um-hmm?"

"Do you know all of the customers who come in?"

"Not really. We're drawing more than the salon's regular customers," she said. "And that's the way I like it. Why do you ask?"

He shrugged. "There's a woman who's been in the last couple of weekends. I was just, you know, interested." He shrugged again. "I thought you might have known her."

Della smiled. "Another romance blooming here?"

Daryl grinned. "It's not like that. I don't even know her name. I was just curious, you know. Maybe she'll come back Friday night. If she does, I'll ask her."

From the window, Della watched him make his way through the salon. He high-fived several of the customers. Daryl had been driving a city bus for almost eight years now. When he'd interviewed for the DJ job at Della's he'd said he got a lot of inspiration for his music from the commuters and others who took public transportation.

"Just about everybody I've ever seen on a bus looks stressed out," he'd said. "The music I make is meant to relax them. Help them unwind."

Unwinding is exactly what Della wanted people to do at Della's Place. The mix of smooth jazz, mellow tones, and professional clientele made the lounge the perfect after-work stop. And on the weekends, after the shop was closed, they got a different crowd.

She'd already made up her mind about his music. She wouldn't have hired him if she hadn't been familiar with it. Daryl was good. Really good.

"But the hunger has to be there," Della said, one arm folded and a finger at her chin. Daryl Desmond wanted to go places. And Della hoped to assist him if she could. She'd do the same for any of her employees.

Back at her desk, she picked at the day's mail. Bills, styling magazines, and . . . the letter she'd been waiting for! The return address was Los Angeles, but Della knew it had been sent from New York. She'd been approached about having a music video shot at the salon. A producer had seen a couple of the salon's stylists at work at a hair show and tracked Della down. They'd talked and she'd said she would give it some thought. He'd promised to send the project outline.

"The fact that we get paid doesn't hurt one bit, either," she said with a smile.

Della tucked the letter in her purse to review at home. One of the shop's assistant managers could stumble across it if she left it in the office. She didn't want word about the video out yet, particularly since she hadn't decided if it was a good thing to do.

"Although the publicity couldn't hurt one bit," she surmised. Particularly not with music videos played twenty-four hours on television. Daryl's situation was another reason to go for it. She might be in a position to, as he put it, help a brother out.

She sorted through the rest of the mail, then spied something tucked in the middle.

"A postcard from Sweet!"

She pulled it from the stack and scanned the image of a tropical beach before reading the message:

> Hawaii is beautiful. Having a fabulous time. Flew over a volcano in a helicopter yesterday. Elaine kept her eyes closed the entire time. (I did not!) Hope you're having fun being boss.

Della chuckled at Elaine's scribbled-in message. The postcard was signed "Sweet and Elaine."

Louis Sweet wasted no time acting like a retiree. After marrying Elaine Webster, a salon customer he'd met and fallen in love with, the two started a honeymoon that was still going strong. Shortly after their wedding Sweet sold his hair and beauty salon, Rosie's Curl and Weave, to Della, its manager and his longtime friend.

"Della, change the name," he'd suggested. "Make it yours. Hell, you've run the place for years. It's already yours." Then he whisked his bride away for a year-long vacation that would take them all over the globe.

After thinking about it for a long time, Della did change the name of the salon. It wasn't easy. The shop had been Rosie's Curl and Weave for forever and she didn't want to lose the cachet the name carried. It had, after all, taken Sweet years to build that reputation. She and her daughter, Chauncie, talked about it. Sweet and Elaine had even offered up a couple of suggestions. But the final decision was in Della's hands.

Off and on throughout the years, she'd contemplated striking out on her own. But loyalty to Louis Sweet and a genuine love of Rosie's had kept her in place. That dedication ended up paying off in a way she never would or could have imagined: She owned her own business.

Della Frazier was known for her sense of style and flair, so when she hit on the right name, it seemed as though it had always been there, just waiting for her to wake up and discover it: Della's House of Style.

The Rosie's moniker would always be associated with the shop, named for Sweet's deceased first wife. But the new lounge was Della's baby, and she christened it with the name Della's Place. A picture of Sweet and Rosie hung in there, right next to one of Sweet and Elaine.

Della smiled as she looked at the palm trees on the postcard. "Sweet, you're an angel."

She propped the postcard on a pencil holder on the desk, then picked up the phone. Della planned to capitalize on the talents of the DJ who made the atmosphere in the lounge. First she wanted to order up some more fliers about the lounge, then they'd have a party.

"A party is always good," she said as she waited for the line to connect.

She'd decide later what it was they'd be celebrating.

## CHAPTER TWO

Daryl saw her the moment she stepped into the lounge. He smiled. She looked good, real good. She had attitude, like she knew how to take care of business. He liked that in a woman.

Just as soon as he could, he played Miles's "'Round Midnight" for her. She'd requested that before, so Daryl knew she liked Miles Davis. And Daryl liked what he saw in her: the wild hair all over the place, the tight dresses, and those sexy high-heeled shoes. She didn't wear a lot of makeup, but she obviously loved jewelry. Tonight, long dangling earrings matched her red dress.

At his first break, he made his way to her table.

"You're not going to escape on me tonight, Cinderella."

She smiled. "I promise I won't turn into a pumpkin or anything like that."

He held a hand out toward the second chair at her table. "Do you mind?"

"Not if you don't," she said.

Daryl smiled. This was working out just fine. Just fine, indeed. He took a seat. The waitress put a glass of ice water in front of him and left another glass of white wine for the lady.

"My name's Daryl. Daryl Desmond."

"Sheila," she said, extending a hand to him. "I've enjoyed listening to you these last few weeks."

"Thanks. I enjoy playing music for people who appreciate it. You like Miles Davis, huh?"

She nodded. "Among others."

Daryl looked around. The place was starting to fill up. "I'll be pretty busy the rest of the night," he told her. "I wanted to take a moment to say hello before things got really busy."

"I'm glad you did."

He nodded. "So, like, would you like to go out afterward? This is a good place for people to meet. But it's a little difficult for me, you know, doing the music and all."

She glanced around, then faced him again. "I'd like that."

"Bet. We can grab a bite and talk a little."

Smiling, she lifted her glass. "It's a date, then." She smiled as she sipped, peeking at him above the rim.

Daryl nodded. Yeah, man. This was gonna be right.

The night passed in slow motion as far as Daryl was concerned. At one point, Sheila left, but she held up a finger, then tapped her wrist. Daryl assumed that meant she'd be back. Apparently he was right, because she appeared again about forty-five minutes before closing.

The music had been perfect all evening. He'd even made quite a bit in tips, if looking at the jar was any indication. This gig at Della's Place gave him the creative outlet he needed. He also got to meet interesting people. And soon, if Della went for it, he'd be able to play some of his own music and showcase his true skills.

He closed the night with a mellow Luther Vandross tune, then packed up the equipment that he traveled with. Sheila sat at her table waiting for him. He'd noticed that she could make two glasses of wine last a long time. That was a good sign.

"Don't need to be bothered with any drunks," he said.

"What was that, Daryl?"

He looked up. "Oh, hi, Della. I didn't see you tonight."

Della glanced around. "I just came over a little while ago after finishing up some paperwork. Thought I'd drop in and see how things were going. I think I'm going to wire the salon office so I hear the music when I work late."

"Speaking of listening to music . . ." Daryl said.

Della chuckled and tapped him on the arm. "I did. And you're right. It would be perfect for the playlist here."

"Yes!" He grabbed Della, hugged her, and planted a big kiss on her cheek. "Della, you are the woman."

Laughing, she nodded toward the table where a customer still sat. "Looks like someone's waiting for you."

He leaned in and lowered his voice. "That's the woman I was asking you about."

Della surreptitiously glanced at her. "That's . . ." She paused taking a good, closer look. An elegant eyebrow rose. "Well, I'll be."

"What?" Daryl said. "Something I need to know?"

Shaking her head, Della continued to stare at the woman. "Good set tonight, Daryl. When you get a chance, stop by the office next week. There's something I want you to know about."

"Night," he said, as he watched Della approach Sheila. They exchanged a few words, but he couldn't hear what was said.

"Women sure know how to whisper when they want to," he said as he coiled an extension cord.

---

This is awesome," he said. They'd found a little Italian restaurant still open. Sheila nibbled on antipasto while Daryl did serious damage to a big dish of lasagna. A bottle of red wine had gone mostly untouched, but the basket of Italian bread had been replenished twice.

"You sure you don't want any?" he said, indicating the lasagna. "There's enough for about four people."

"It looks good," she said. "But I'm dieting."

"Why? You look fine—better than fine."

She smiled. "Thank you. But I could stand to lose a few pounds."

He shook his head and put his fork down. "Men like to put their arms around some flesh. How come you women worry about that stuff? There's a commercial, I think for some cereal, where a bunch of guys stand around asking, 'Do you think this makes my butt look big?' They sound crazy. And that's how you all sound. Crazy."

Seeing the amusement in his eyes, she laughed. "Well, we want to look our best for the fellas. Gotta keep up the feminine wiles, you know."

A chuckle started deep in his throat and worked its way up until a big burst of laughter came out. "Well, if that's the case," he said, "eat those olives, baby, and throw some of your wiles on me."

Laughing, she finally relented. Daryl served her some of the lasagna from the deep dish and nodded when she sopped up a bit of tomato sauce with bread.

"That's more like it." He cut himself another helping, then hefted it onto his own plate. Tearing off a piece of bread, he buttered it and popped it in his mouth.

"As long as you know I'm going to have to work off these calories," Sheila said. She glanced at him. "It'll take some strenuous exercise."

His eyes widened and he paused with his fork in midair. A vaguely sensuous light passed between them. His gaze dipped to her cleavage.

Daryl cleared his throat. Sheila smiled.

"You coming on to me?" he said.

"What do you think?"

"I think we're gonna skip dessert."

Sheila smiled. But her smile wavered a bit under his intense scrutiny. Things were moving a bit too fast. She'd gotten totally wrapped up in her sexy alter ego persona. She'd been buttoned up and closed down so long that all those pent-up emotions and urges were just bubbling and churning, like a volcano about to erupt.

Her feet hurt from the heels she'd been in for too many hours. But she couldn't very well take them off. She'd never be able to put them back on. Besides, she'd left her flats at home.

Even more important than that, though, she needed to apply the brakes to the runaway train she'd set on a collision course with this man.

"Daryl, there's something I need to tell you."

He nodded as he chewed.

Sheila studied him for a moment. Daryl was a good-looking brother, but not in the way of Madison Avenue ad agencies, his face too square and his nose larger than the features found on models. She guessed him to be on the better side of thirty. Of medium height, he stood just a couple of inches taller than her own five foot six. But he carried himself with a commanding air of self-confidence. That, she realized, was why she'd been attracted to him the first time she'd seen him at Della's Place.

If anything, she'd describe Daryl Desmond as all-American. And he had that all-male way of honing right in on what appeared to be an easy lay. But Sheila wasn't easy. She just didn't know how to change the course she'd set them on. All the men she worked with liked to talk about themselves—incessantly. If Daryl could sit there and stereotype women as all being obsessed with weight, she could assume he'd want to talk about himself.

"What do you do?" she asked.

He looked at her. What seemed like a small sigh slumped his shoulders. Then he straightened. "Doing music is my thing," he said. "I work for the city during the day."

That was a good sign, Sheila thought. He carried himself well, was well-spoken. Maybe he was an administrator or department head.

He nodded. "I've put in almost eight years. It's a good job with good money. I have my own little world that I'm responsible for every day. I've got no complaints," he said on a shrug.

Sheila sensed he had something else to say. "But?"

He smiled. "Perceptive, huh? The *but* is that there's more I want to do with my life. Don't get me wrong, my job has its rewards. I get to meet some really incredible people. There's just more out there for me."

"You mean your DJ role?"

He shook his head. "That's just part of it. I enjoy doing DJ work. I've been at it so long it's second nature. But I make music, too. That's my real passion. I've been talking to Della Frazier—and I've been trying to get her to let me add my stuff to the playlist."

"What do you play?"

"A little of everything," he said. "I can work my way around an alto sax, a little horn. But I'm a keyboardist."

"I'd like to hear you play sometime."

"That, Miss Sheila, can be arranged."

The beginning of a teasing little smile tilted the corners of her mouth. "It's a date, then."

Daryl finished off the last of the lasagna on his plate and pushed the empty plate aside. "I've been doing all the talking so far. It's your turn. Tell me about yourself."

"What do you want to know?" Sheila asked the question hoping she wouldn't have to out-and-out lie. She'd never been able to keep track of tall tales. The charade she was playing—acting like a party girl—was enough of a challenge without adding spoken untruths.

He drank from his glass of Coke. "Well, how about starting where you began with me. What do *you* do?"

Sheila smiled. The right answer came to her without any trouble. All she had to do was be evasive. Men liked a little mystery.

"Nothing right now," she said. "And that's the way I like it. The checks come in and I sit back."

Daryl's answering smile faded a bit. The last thing he needed was somebody looking for a rent payment. He'd run into her kind before. Usually they spelled trouble for a brother's bank account. The ones whose first question was "What do you do?" meant they were calculating how much they could get from a man. Daryl had been down that road before . . . with Pam, and before Pam, with Wanda. Both of them had been nothing but moochers.

No, siree. He'd been burned twice before. It didn't matter if she did like Miles Davis and Nancy Wilson, Daryl had no intention of getting taken for a ride again.

But then, he thought, she had said "Nothing right now," when he asked what she did for a living. Maybe that meant she was collecting on an accident or something. He was willing to give her the benefit of the doubt. For right now.

They finished dinner and lingered a bit over coffee and tea.

"So, what happens next?" Sheila said.

Daryl studied her. "Well, we can go back to my place."

She held up a hand. "Not so fast. We just met."

He nodded. "Okay. You just passed the first test."

Sheila raised an eyebrow at him. "Excuse me?"

"That probably didn't come out right."

"You bet it didn't," she said. "You'd better clean it up real quick."

He grinned. "So I'm getting another chance."

She flipped some of the hair off her shoulder, then folded her arms, waiting.

Daryl leaned forward. "We're both adults here," he said. "I'm sure you've had relationships where things didn't exactly go the way you thought they might have."

"This isn't a relationship. We just met," Sheila pointed out.

"And every first date is a test, so to speak. Both parties weigh the other person as they try to decide if there's . . ." He shrugged. "You know."

"Chemistry? A love connection?"

"Something like that."

"And so where are we?" she asked.

"Well, seeing that I've just buried myself in a hole over here, I think we need to start over, don't you think?"

She had to smile at that. "At least you recognize the error of your ways."

He held her chair for her as she rose. They left the restaurant and walked a bit along the avenue. It was a nice night out. New York hummed with the life and energy that was found in few other cities. Despite the rocky points during dinner, neither one seemed ready to call it a night.

"I know a place where we can hear some music," he suggested. "It's an all-night joint. A little hole in the wall, really, but the sounds are worth it."

Sheila glanced at her wrist a moment before remembering she'd decided to abandon her watches during this three-week vacation.

"Isn't it kind of late?" A second later she realized that a party girl wouldn't care about the late hour. Investment bankers who had early meetings and took work home over the weekends cared about that sort of thing. But for now, she wasn't on the fast-track to a vice presidency. Right now, her feet were aching something fierce.

Sheila lifted a foot to relieve some of the pressure. It would be a long time before she put heels like these on again.

"It is late," Daryl said. "And you're doing that fidgeting that tells me you either need to go to the bathroom or your feet hurt."

Sheila burst out laughing. She grabbed his arm for balance. "You must have a bunch of sisters or girlfriends."

He led her to the curb, where he hailed a cab. "Both. Come on." He held a door open for her and helped her in the cab.

"Whew!"

"Where to?" the cabbie asked.

Daryl shut the door and leaned inside the window. "Take the lady home," he said. "She has a date with some epsom salts."

"For sure you're right," Sheila said, chuckling. "Thanks for a nice night."

"Is there gonna be another one?" he asked. "It's your call."

"Oh, that's right," she said. "I passed your test."

"Come on, cut me some slack. I'll make that comment up to you."

Car horns honked behind them. "Lady, we ain't got all night here."

"Just a sec," she said. "You have a pen and a piece of paper?"

Shaking his head, the cab driver handed her a blank receipt and a ballpoint pen. Sheila scribbled her number on the back of the receipt and handed it out the window to Daryl.

"If you call me, I'll go out with you again," she said. "If you don't, we'll just chalk this night up to pleasant company."

He smiled. "I'll be calling."

The driver signaled. Daryl stepped back and watched the cab disappear into the night traffic.

# CHAPTER THREE

Daryl kept his promise. He called two days later. Sheila smiled at his strategic timing. She knew the unwritten rules about follow-up telephone calls. She herself had played the game too well with clients through the years. Calling the day after their date would have been a sign of anxious desperation. Calling three or more days later signaled a hope that something better would come along.

But two days after . . . well, she thought with a smile, that was just perfect. No matter what was said verbally, the unspoken message was, *I'm interested. Let's see where this might lead.*

Since Sheila found herself attracted to Daryl anyway, she was glad he called. And she readily agreed to dinner and a movie with him.

"Only if I get to pick the film," she said.

He heaved what sounded like a long-suffering sigh on the line, then laughed good-naturedly. "I suppose that means we'll be watching one of those 'relationship' films."

"You wouldn't be disparaging chick flicks, now, would you?"

His chuckle was deep, indulgent. "Not at all, Sheila Mae. Not at all."

"That's not my middle name."

"It just sounds right," he said.

She smiled. He couldn't know that that was the very nickname she'd grown up with. Only her closest and oldest friends got away with calling her Sheila Mae.

She imagined that he sat in a chair with his feet kicked up as he talked to her. Daryl seemed comfortable with his body, easy in the sense that he took care of himself, but didn't overdo it. That was something she could appreciate just as much as the fact that he'd unknowingly hit on a sweet spot with her.

"So, what shall we see and what night's good for you?"

For once, Sheila didn't have to consult her Palm Pilot or planner to make an appointment. She was free every day. They agreed on Thursday.

The two days seemed to drag by in Sheila's estimation. After spending the day working on the proposal for the nonprofit organization she wanted to establish, Sheila called it quits. She wanted lots of time to get ready for her date with Daryl Desmond. Four times now she'd decided and undecided what to wear. She listened to messages on the answering machine as she dressed.

"Hey, girl," Tracy's voice filled the air. "Don't forget we're still on for Friday night. We have box seats at the Met. And remember, we're double dating. You're going to love Perry's friend Todd. He's a lawyer. He drives one of those new cute little two-seater BMWs. Hope you're enjoying your first week of freedom. *Ciao*."

Shaking her head, Sheila could only smile. Tracy was something else. The date with Todd wasn't something Sheila really wanted to do. She'd agreed to humor Tracy and her on-again/off-again boyfriend by going out with one of Perry's fraternity brothers. She'd met Todd once before, briefly, at a cocktail party. He'd struck her as Tracy's type: wealthy, healthy, and bourgeois.

Her own taste in men had always tended toward rugged brothers, men who worked hard, played hard, and lived life to the fullest. Even though she made the bank that put her in with the country club set, Sheila never let the status, the finances, or the seedy and snooty side of the very well-to-do rub off on her. Unlike Tracy, who hadn't looked back since college, Sheila maintained ties with the community, with her sense of place and self. She believed in giving back because so much had been given to her. She knew that the success she claimed today came on the backs and through the sweat and tears and the shut doors and barred ways that her forebears faced.

Sheila's only concession to the income bracket she'd worked her way into were the clothes. A boutique could be stocked from her closets alone. She'd *always* been a clothes hound—even if her tastes ran toward the conservative.

For the movie date with Daryl, she wanted to be comfortable but fashionable. She reached for her khaki jeans and vest, then remembered she was letting her hair down.

"Wild Sheila wouldn't even own anything khaki," she said as she headed to another part of her huge closet. "Wild women wear leopard."

A pair of leopard-print leggings with black low-heeled mules were perfect. A black off-the-shoulder top and big jewelry rounded out the outfit. A riot of curls exploded from her head when she shook her new hair out. She'd picked up a bit of that glittery eye shadow she'd seen some college students wearing. That at her eyes and kiss-proof lipstick on her mouth completed her face.

When she finished dressing, Sheila wasn't even sure she recognized herself.

She twirled in front of the mirror and laughed out loud. Not only did she feel incredibly free—she felt liberated, secure, and utterly invincible.

"And sexy," she added with a Marilyn Monroe pout in the mirror.

A glance at the clock on the dresser told her it was time to go. Daryl would meet her at the movie theater.

When she got out of the cab and saw him watching her, she was glad she'd dressed the way she did. He looked pleased.

"Wow. You look great," he said.

"Thanks." She opened a little purse to pay the cabbie, but Daryl leaned down and handed the man some cash. "You didn't have to—"

Daryl took her hand in his and raised it to his mouth. He pressed a quick kiss on her hand. "Your movie's about to begin, Sheila Mae."

She smiled. Hand in hand, they entered the theater.

More than three hours later they sat across from each other at a little soul food restaurant. "I never even knew this was here," Sheila said, "and I pride myself on knowing this city."

"Well, that just goes to show that there are a few surprising things New York still has up its sleeve," he said.

She nodded. "Um-hmm. Like you."

He raised an eyebrow. "You flirting with me?"

Sheila waved a hand and touched her brow. "I must be losing my touch if he has to ask," she said in a very bad impersonation of Mae West.

They laughed together as the waiter filled their coffee cups. "Can I interest you folks in some sweet potato pie?"

"I thought you'd never ask," Sheila said.

Daryl grinned. "I think that means yes."

Then he leaned back. "So, what is it you said you do?"

The last thing Sheila wanted to do was talk about work. "Right now, I'm on something of an extended vacation. I'm, as they say, getting myself together."

His brow furrowed, but he didn't say anything.

Since he looked troubled by her less-than-forthcoming response, Sheila didn't want to just leave her explanation hanging as though she were some kind of deadbeat. "I work," she said. "I just need to get away. And this is my time."

He nodded. "I can respect that. What—"

"Oh, look!" She cut his inquiry off and pointed toward the center of the restaurant. "They're going to do a sketch."

Daryl turned as two people settled on barstools in an open area. "Everyplace in this city has turned into a performance stage."

She grinned. "Isn't it great? I read about these sketches. I've never seen one, though."

The restaurant owner made an announcement explaining that the restaurant would be showcasing local drama students, aspiring actors, and new writers every Wednesday and Friday nights.

"We want to encourage our young people."

Daryl leaned toward Sheila. "This is the sort of thing that takes away from what we're doing over at Della's. It's the same audience."

Leaning closer so they wouldn't disturb the performers and the other patrons, Sheila reached for his hand and gave her own assessment. "You're sounding jealous. This city is big enough for every venue to succeed. Let's see what they do." She squeezed his hand.

Daryl looked at their joined hands, then at Sheila before turning his attention to the performance artists.

In the next fifteen minutes, the man and woman acted out an argument and make-up scene that had been set up as the introduction to a one-act play. The actress needed to tone down the shrillness of her voice in places and the actor seemed uneasy in the moments leading up to the kiss and make-up conclusion. While a little rough around the edges, the scene had potential. When it ended, the restaurant patrons politely clapped, then turned their attention back to their meals.

"Now, what was that supposed to be?" Daryl said.

Sheila chuckled. "Creative expression."

He rolled his eyes. "Well, at least it was free. I've seen better—"

"Hi," Sheila said cutting him off. "Enjoyed your sketch."

Daryl turned around and faced the two performers, who were working the dining room, presumably for tips. Sheila waited a moment to see what Daryl would do and how he would act.

"You two in acting school?" he asked as he reached for his wallet.

The woman nodded. "I've done a couple of bit parts in commercials, mostly background work. I'd like to break into the soap opera market." She handed Sheila a flier. "We're doing the complete play at the Madison Theater. We'd love to see you. It's a Sunday matinee."

Daryl nodded as he dropped ten dollars into the Kangol cap the man held open. "Good luck to you," he said.

"Thanks."

The two moved on to the next table. Sheila sat back and smiled. "You're an old softie."

Daryl finished off the last of his pie. "No, I'm not. But I know what it's like to believe in your art—even when it's as bad as those two."

Sheila laughed. She leaned over and kissed him on the cheek.

"What was that for?" he asked.

"For being a cute softie."

Daryl lifted a hand as if to call the two performers back. "Hey, I got a fifty for you," he said just loud enough for Sheila to hear.

Her delighted laughter echoed around them and earned a few curious glances from other diners.

They shared another piece of sweet potato pie and chatted the small talk of dates. Sheila managed to either sidestep or talk around anything that might hint of what she did for a living. Her date with Todd the next night would be full of that, all of the one-upmanship and status-conscious game-playing that seemed to go along with the turf.

Being defined by what you do instead of who you are was something that bothered Sheila as much as the fact that her coworkers thought she was all business and no fun.

With Todd, she knew she'd be the future vice president of an investment banking firm, valued not for the unique person she was but for the advice and tips she could offer, the contacts and connections she could make happen.

With Daryl she could be normal, she could let her new hair down. She liked being just a regular person, a person who lived, ate, and enjoyed the sights and sounds of the city. With Daryl she could be real. That was something she hadn't really taken time to be in a long time.

After the bill was paid—by Daryl—he asked if she wanted to go listen to some music. "I know a terrific place."

The corners of her mouth tilted up in a contented smile. "I get the feeling you know lots of terrific places."

"Some of the best vibes in the city are in little out-of-the-way holes in the wall. You gotta know the way to get there, though."

"And you're the man with the directions."

"Indeed I am, you know."

"Well, lead the way, maestro."

This time they went to a smoky place playing experimental fusion. Daryl got greeted at the door like a beloved brother, then was high-fived every few feet as they made their way to a little table with a RESERVED card on it.

"You knew I'd agree to this?" Sheila asked, pointing toward the placard on the table.

He held the chair for her as she sat down. "If I had, I wouldn't be stupid enough to admit that, now, would I?"

She chuckled. "Hmm."

With a grin, Daryl slipped into the other seat. "No, this table is always available for me. You could say I'm something of a silent partner here."

She raised an eyebrow. "Oh?"

That was definitely a good sign, she thought.

"Don't read too much into that," he said. "When Dray wanted to open this place a couple of years ago, he was a little short on cash. A couple of us went in together and made sure he had the down payment."

Not only did he work for the city, he tipped well, and was now saying he owned part of a nightclub. Not too shabby at all, Sheila thought as she looked around. The lounge was small but intimate. No more than twenty tables were crammed into the space in a horseshoe around the stage, where the main attraction was a black baby grand piano surrounded by music stands, a drum set, and microphones. A short bar lined the back wall. People who didn't have seats stood around the bar or up against the walls, where small ledges just large enough for a couple of drinks and a bowl of peanuts had been conveniently installed. The acrid smell of cigarette smoke lingered in the air.

Sheila briefly wondered if her weave would pick up the scent of the smoke. Then she decided not to worry about it. She was, after all, living the life she wanted to experience while on vacation. Jazz joints and smoky bars were all a part of it.

If those judgmental coworkers of hers could see her now, they'd know she wasn't one-dimensional.

A waitress came by.

"Hey, Daryl," she said. "Hi ya doing," she greeted Sheila.

"Whazzup, Keisha? This is Sheila. Who's playing tonight?"

"Mark Bradley and his crew. They'll be back for the next set in about five minutes. The wings are slamming tonight, 'specially with some ranch dressing on the side," she said as she placed two cocktail napkins on the table. "What can I get you?"

He held an open hand to Sheila. "They have some of everything. Want a beer?" Daryl said. "Wings?"

Sheila nodded, looking forward to the treat. She didn't drink beer, and hot wings weren't exactly on the menus of the places where she usually had lunch or dinner. So both sounded just perfect.

The waitress left to put in their order. Conversation swirled around them, the buzz not unpleasant. On her left a couple huddled together making that lovey-dovey small talk. To the right sat a table of five women whose conversation whipped all around.

"And I told Jamal get the hell up outta my house."

"Girl, why you gonna be like that?"

"Hey, look. Joe Dell just came in."

"Who is that on his arm? I bet his wife doesn't know about *her*."

"You know they have one of those 'open' marriages."

"So what's Jamal gonna do now?"

"Stop hogging all the wings, Miss Thang," one of the women said as she snatched a piece of meat from the plates the table shared.

Sheila smiled. Hearing that sort of girl talk was exactly why she liked going to Della's Place. She learned so much about the things that it seemed other people took for granted. Sheila had never had a Jamal in her life, a man to kick out of the house, because she'd never taken time to get involved in relationships, be they draining *or* fulfilling.

"You're awfully quiet over there," Daryl said.

"Just enjoying the atmosphere. This is a nice place."

"I'm glad you like it."

A couple minutes later, the band members made their way to the front—a piano man, a bass guitarist, a drummer, and a sax player. They eased into a tune that put the crowd in an upbeat breezy mood. After the second number, Daryl's presence was acknowledged. The pianist urged him to join them, then slipped off the piano stool and picked up a saxophone as Daryl made his way forward.

Sheila smiled. She'd never heard him play live music. In the weeks she'd been hanging out at Della's, he'd just been DJing.

Adjusting the microphone, Daryl looked out over the crowd.

"It's nice to see all of you here tonight at Dray's. I thought I could come in and kick back a little. But y'all are putting me to work. So I guess I better get busy, huh?"

The band members chuckled and waited to follow Daryl's lead. He snapped his fingers, giving the band a beat, then placed them over the keyboard. A moment later, he held the place in awe, zipping through a couple of swinging numbers that had feet tapping all across the floor.

"We're gonna slow it down a bit now," he said after the third tune. "And then I'm gonna go back and sit with my lady."

Sheila grinned and held up her drink in salute. One of the women from the table leaned over and whispered to her, "I bet those limber fingers can do wonders in other places."

In good humor, Sheila laughed with the woman who'd jumped to a conclusion about her relationship with Daryl. But Sheila had been wondering much the same thing. She didn't know much about Daryl, but what she *did* know was that her instincts about him were right on target. Instinctively she liked him—a lot. And her gut feelings had never let her down.

Daryl eased into some mellow Erroll Garner and followed it up with the intro to Nat King Cole's "Unforgettable."

"This is for you, Sheila Mae."

He leaned into the mike and crooned the words of the classic tune to her. The smile on Sheila's face matched the one that blossomed in other parts of her. She liked the path they seemed to be on, even though she didn't know where it might lead.

As the final notes faded away, the crowd at Dray's burst into enthusiastic applause. Daryl took a bow, applauded the band, and made his way back to Sheila after more high-fives and back slapping.

When he took his seat, Sheila was waiting. She kissed him, a move that seemed to surprise him. "That was wonderful. Thank you."

He sort of shrugged, seemingly at a loss for words. She liked the sudden shyness.

"You are a maestro."

"I just like music."

"Have you ever recorded anything?"

He grinned, the shyness gone, replaced by the happy-go-lucky grin that had initially caught her eye. "As a matter of fact, I have. I'll give you one. I'm hoping to get a record deal. I have a couple of appointments coming up."

"I've never heard you play the piano or sing at Della's," she said.

"I'm working on that, too. Right now, Della Frazier's focus seems to be on building the clientele and getting the word out that the lounge is there. See the people here?" he said, indicating the packed joint. "These are regulars. People who you can always find here once a week at the very least. Della's is starting to get regulars."

"Like me?"

He smiled. "Yeah, like you. Oh, man, I should have told them to play some Miles for you."

"That's okay. I'm enjoying this." She paused and reached for his hand. "And I'm enjoying you."

His eyes darkened and his brow lifted just a little. Though they were surrounded by people, the private moment was intimate, the air around them charged with the anticipation and the knowledge that something was happening between them. Something that could be wonderful.

Daryl leaned forward. She did, too.

"Hey, hey. None of that stuff in here."

Sheila sighed as she sat back. Daryl didn't look too happy, either.

"Dray, man, you have the worst timing of anybody I know."

Since no empty chairs were around, Andre Devreaux leaned down, laughing. "Good set, man."

"Thanks. Dray, this is Sheila. Sheila, Devreaux here thinks he knows how to run a club."

Shaking Dray's hand, Sheila smiled. "I'm having a great time."

"How could you be? You're with him. Tell you what, let me go deal with something in the office and I'll come right back to rescue you from this joker."

"Man, get outta here."

The easy camaraderie between the men spoke of a long friendship. Sheila slipped her arm through Daryl's. "I think I'll keep him for a while."

Dray shook his head as if in mourning. "I tell you, the brothers who can sing and play a little get all the pretty ladies."

Looking at Daryl, Sheila then nodded up toward Dray. "I like him."

The three laughed together. Dray caught the waitress's attention. "Keisha." He held up two fingers and pointed toward Sheila and Daryl's table, indicating she should bring more food and drinks.

They stayed for two more sets, talking and munching on barbeque wings. They talked about music, about the merits of a small club like Dray's versus large ones where admission was charged and the entertainment not half as good. Sheila was having such a great time she didn't realize how late it was until Daryl suggested they call it a night.

"Believe it or not, I do have to work tomorrow," he said.

They waved to the band and to Dray as they left the club.

Outside, she turned toward him. "Did you take me there to impress me with all the people who know you?"

He smiled. "No, Miss Sheila Mae. I took you there because I wanted to share with you something that means a lot to me."

Something in his tone made Sheila look up. "You're getting serious on me," she said.

Daryl shrugged. "That bother you?"

She took a step toward him and traced the outline of the vest he wore over a white T-shirt. "No. It doesn't."

He slipped an arm around her waist. "Are we moving too fast for you?"

She gazed into his eyes, wondering what it was about Daryl Desmond that seemed to answer a yearning inside her. He wasn't exceptionally good-looking. But he wasn't what Tracy used to call a "country bama," either. Everything about Daryl was solid, average, hardworking all-American. Sheila responded to that on a level she wouldn't have guessed even existed.

"No," she finally answered him. "We're not moving too fast."

"Good," Daryl said. "'Cause what I want to do most is kiss the daylights out of you."

Sheila smiled. "Well, I'm waiting."

It was Daryl's turn to smile. "Just for that I should make you wait."

She shook her head. "I don't think so." Then she pulled him closer and pressed her lips to his.

They took the time to taste, to explore, to find a groove. Sheila felt her insides spiral in response to his touch. The warmth of him infused her with heat and with need.

No, they weren't moving too fast. In one respect, she thought, things were moving too slowly. She found herself wanting him more and more as each moment passed. But she could respect his need to get some rest. Had she been working, she would have already been in bed—with a pile of papers and reading all around her, but nonetheless in bed.

"You'd better get some rest."

He grinned. "That your way of telling me you're gonna wear me out?"

Her eyes widened and her cheeks flamed. She opened her mouth, but no words came. She'd had a relationship once, a long time ago. But she'd never considered herself experienced enough or sexy enough to wear a man out in bed.

He chuckled as he took advantage of the moment and planted a quick kiss on her.

"I'll see you home," he said.

A second later, her speech returned. She shook her head, setting the weave in motion. She absently noticed that he seemed as equally enamored with her mouth as with her hair.

"That's all right," she said. "I can hop a cab. You should do the same. I didn't realize I was keeping you out so late."

He chuckled at her spin on their evening as they stood on the sidewalk in front of Dray's. Even though their words said it was time to call it a night, he pulled her toward him. Willingly Sheila went into his arms.

"I sang that song to you tonight because I meant it," he said. "Ever since you came to Della's, I've been unable to forget you."

"Honestly?"

"What? Brothers lie to you all the time?"

A moment later, she shook her head and laughed. "I didn't mean that the way it came out. I guess I'm kind of surprised that a man like you would notice me."

He lifted an eyebrow, then cast an assessing and speculative gaze at her. "What's there not to notice? You're beautiful. You got that wild hair going on," he said as he fingered a long curly lock. "I like it when it's loose like that. And let me tell you something, just in case you didn't know."

"What?"

"I love the way you feel against me."

At that, she pressed close to him. "Well, that makes two of us."

This time when their lips met, there were no interruptions and there was no play. He framed her face with his hands and tilted her head. The taste of him was something Sheila wasn't sure she could ever get enough of. Moving his mouth over hers, he devoured her softness. She moaned and slipped her hands along his waist and up his back.

His lips left hers to nibble at her earlobes. When she leaned her head back, her hair cascaded over his arm.

"You make me want to call in sick tomorrow," he murmured against her ear.

The soft sound of amusement escaped Sheila. "Are you at Della's Saturday night?"

"Um-hmm."

"Then why don't we plan to continue this after that?"

He lifted his head and looked into her eyes. "Let's continue it tomorrow. Saturday is a long way away."

She smiled at the compliment and was about to agree when she remembered why she couldn't. "I have a . . . an appointment tomorrow night. I promised a friend—"

He put a finger at her lips. "No explanations needed. Saturday night it is."

# CHAPTER FOUR

But before Saturday came Friday night. Sheila wasn't the least bit interested in going out with Todd. But she'd promised. He was picking her up at her Central Park building. They'd meet Tracy and Perry at one of the city's newest and swankiest restaurants.

Instead of putting on airs at some too-expensive bistro, she wanted to be swaying to the music that Daryl played. Last night, he'd rocked her world in ways she hadn't expected, couldn't have anticipated. Like that kiss. The memory of it made her tingle all over.

They'd left each other with the agreement that Saturday night they'd take the time to really get to know each other, to take their budding relationship to the next intimate level. Assessing her feelings, Sheila had to admit that a part of her thought they were, indeed, moving too fast. Another part of her, though, begged to make love with him. She wanted to feel those fingers play her body.

In a slip, Sheila stared at her reflection in the full-length mirror in her dressing room. She stood in hose preparing to go out with another man while her heart wanted to be with Daryl.

"Whoa," she said. The realization that she'd made the leap from attraction to something deeper was enough to make her pause. Going out with Todd tonight was a good thing, she decided. She'd be able to determine if it was just male attention that she'd been lacking or if something else was at play.

She stared at her hair, trying to figure out what to do about it. Tracy had not yet seen the new look. Making a note to set an appointment with her stylist, she opted to tame the "wild hair" a bit. She gathered it up and twisted the curls into an upswept hairdo that could pass for a conservative banker's look. All along she'd planned to just keep the weave in for the duration of her vacation.

Another woman would have taken Daryl's comment about wild hair as an insult. Sheila knew it to be a compliment. But she wondered if he was attracted to the hair instead of to the woman.

A glance at the clock in her dressing room told her it was time to get Daryl off the brain and finish getting dressed for the evening with Todd. A little while later, though, as Todd helped her into his BMW convertible and they sat in the traffic endemic to New York, Sheila's mind was still on Daryl.

"It's great to see you again," Todd said. "I wasn't sure if you remembered me."

She glanced at him. "Oh, yes. I remembered you." What she recalled, though, was that he was one of those Type A, workaholic super achievers who cared more about bank balances and status than people and passion. Todd, she was sure, was hardly the type to eat barbeque chicken wings with ranch dressing on the side.

The comparison to Daryl made her smile.

"You have a lovely smile," Todd said.

She glanced at him. "Thank you."

He drummed his fingers on the steering wheel. "So, how's the investment world doing?"

*Uh-oh. Here it comes,* she thought. "Just fine."

"I've been thinking about diversifying my portfolio. I've had a terrific run of luck with emerging markets in Latin America, mostly Brazil and Argentina. What's your take on that trend?"

Sheila smiled wanly as she slipped into her investment banker role.

"Well, it depends on where you put your investments and for how long," she started. This she knew like the back of her hand. It was what she excelled in. That he'd ask her opinion seemed only natural. But Todd's portfolio didn't *need* diversifying, she thought as she droned on. As long as he didn't have a drug or gambling problem, he had more money than things to do with it. Sheila had been trained to help the rich grow richer. That was how she made her own money. But what she really wanted to do was help the not-so-rich and the out-and-out poor realize that they, too, could have significant savings and diversified portfolios. People like the guys in the band at Dray's and the stylists and shampoo assistants at Della's. Those were the people who really needed her expertise.

By the time they got to Peignot, the new restaurant, Sheila was starting to resent Todd's questions. And she wondered if he'd opted to drive because he knew they'd be trapped in a car for a while, long enough for him to pick her brain trying to get investment advice that would cost him thousands of dollars if he'd approached her at her firm.

"Let's talk about something else," she suggested as they waited outside for Perry and Tracy to show up. "All work makes for a dull social life. What do you do in your spare time?"

He glanced at her. "Spare time?"

The evening lasted at least twenty hours. At least that was how long it seemed. The couples' dinner conversation was the stuff of their class: summers on Martha's Vineyard, skiing in Taos and Telluride, new artists at trendy galleries. Sheila glanced at her watch more than a dozen times, willing it all to be over soon. But after dinner, they went to a show at one of those galleries. Todd introduced her to several people he recognized. The four of them chatted with the black-clad artist who'd done the work in the show, including the painting they all respectfully stared at right now, of a man staring at a blank canvas.

Immediately recognizing the symbolism of the piece, Sheila chuckled.

"Share the humor," Tracy's date Perry suggested.

Sheila shrugged. "It's just something I've been thinking about all evening."

Todd's eyes widened. "Oh, really?" He stepped away and found the gallery manager.

Tracy nudged Sheila. "He's going to buy it," she whispered.

Leaning forward as if getting a better angle on the painting next to it, Sheila whispered back, "That's because he recognizes his own empty life. How long are we going to be here? I'm ready to call it a night."

"Shh," Tracy hissed.

After the gallery, they went to a hip coffeehouse for cappuccino. As they finally departed, with hugs all around, Tracy whispered in Sheila's ear, "He's crazy about you." A grin filled her friend's face.

Tracy, Perry, and Todd all had a smashing time. Sheila found herself wondering if they realized how vacuous their lives all seemed.

She also wondered if Daryl had had a good turnout at Della's Place.

---

Daryl didn't realize how much he missed seeing Sheila in the audience until a woman sitting at the table where she normally sat sent him a drink. Daryl had the waitress discreetly replace it with his standard water, then played a song for the lady. Since it was Friday night, he took requests from his extensive collection of CDs.

Later, Della came around with paychecks.

"Good turnout tonight," she said.

Daryl nodded as he cued up the next cut. When he finished he slipped the headphones off his ears and smiled at Della. "So, have you had a chance to listen to that CD?"

"As a matter of fact, I have."

"And?" he prompted when she didn't seem inclined to say anything else.

Della smiled and patted him on the arm. "And let's talk when you finish up tonight."

A grin split Daryl's face. He planted a kiss on her cheek.

"You don't even know what I'm going to say," she said.

"Yes, I do. It's written all over your face."

Chuckling, Della looked out at the lounge, waved at people she recognized, and smiled at others. "I don't see Sheila here tonight," she said with a glance at Daryl. "Did you two hit it off?"

"We went out last night. And we have a date for tomorrow."

Della lifted an elegant, arched brow. "Really?"

"That's a fact."

"And the two of you are . . ." She paused, searching for a word. "Compatible?"

Catching the hesitancy in her voice, Daryl looked up. "What?"

Della just shrugged. "I wouldn't have put the two of you together, that's all. But then again, I'm not a matchmaker. If you don't mind my asking, what did you two do?"

"Went to a couple of clubs."

"Clubs? As in nightclubs? With Sheila Landon?"

Daryl paused in the process of reaching for a Nancy Wilson CD. "Landon. So that's her last name. I realized I didn't know it."

Della raised a questioning eyebrow. "What do you two talk about when you go out?"

Laughing, Daryl popped the CD into the player and reached for the headset to cue the music. "Now, what kind of question is that? We just talk." Then, suddenly suspicious: "Is there something I should know about her? Don't lie to me. I can take the truth, you know. Whatever it is."

"It's nothing like that. Sheila is good people. She has a good head on her shoulders. I just . . ." She shrugged. "Who am I to say? I'm glad you two have hooked up."

"So, she's not, like, a psycho or anything? That what you're saying?"

Laughing, Della turned to leave. "Sheila? Hardly. I just didn't think she'd be the type to go out with . . ."

"A bus driver?" he supplied.

Della shook her head. "No, with, to be honest, anyone. She always seems so deeply engrossed in . . . well, I've always thought she could be a little more focused on—"

"Della, there's a call for you. It's a Mr. Stencill. He says it's urgent."

"Be right there," Della told the salon assistant. "I need to take this call," she said to Daryl. "There's a note in your check about a meeting that will be here next week. I want to tell the staff about a little project we're going to be doing. Try to be here if you can."

With that, Della headed back to the salon and her office. Daryl stood where she'd left him. He pondered her words and wondered what she'd been about to say. The only thing Sheila seemed engrossed in was her hair, her clothes, and evading any direct questions about herself. Daryl already suspected that she didn't really have a job. And that, in his book, was a problem.

Women who depended on men and the government to pay their bills and put food on their tables always managed to find their way to him.

*Maybe I'm giving out some vibes,* he guessed. *Gonna have to check that at the door, though. 'Cause Daryl don't play.*

But Della said Sheila was good people, a woman with a good head on her shoulders.

*And a good head of hair.* Daryl grinned as he thought about all that sexy hair flowing over his body.

Della's opinion of Sheila had to count for something, though, because Della had never steered him wrong before. She knew half of the city and could get the scoop on just about anybody if it so suited her. Daryl grinned. Della Frazier was a powerful ally. He was glad he had her on his side. A few moments later, he turned his attention back to the job at hand and away, at least temporarily, from Sheila.

---

Tracy showed up at Sheila's door at six-thirty the next morning. Instead of going to the gym, they'd started working out together in the exclusive and well-maintained fitness room in Sheila's building.

"So what's with the hair?" Tracy asked as they pedaled side by side on stationary bikes.

Sheila laughed. She had an appointment at Della's House of Style later that afternoon, just in time for her evening date with Daryl. So for the morning workout, she didn't bother concealing the new look from her friend.

"Just something I thought I'd try for a while."

"It looks great," Tracy said. "I always wanted to suggest that you try a new look, even a temporary one."

Sheila stopped pedaling. "And why didn't you say anything? You freely criticize my clothes."

Tracy glanced at her. "It's not criticism, Sheila. Just fashion advice. And I wasn't criticizing your hair, either. The cut you keep looks great on you."

"But?"

"There's no but," Tracy said. "Sometimes, test-driving a new model gives you a thrill, even if you don't end up buying."

Chewing on that analogy, Sheila started pedaling again. "It's funny you say that."

"What?" Tracy asked as she wiped sweat from her brow with the edge of a snow-white hand towel draped around her neck.

"Test driving a new model."

"You're going to buy a new car?"

"What do I need with another car? I don't halfway drive the one I have."

"Oh, you mean Todd's Beamer. Isn't that just the cutest little thing you've ever seen? I was thinking about getting one. But it just wouldn't be practical given all the stuff I lug around with me. I need room for the laptop and the fax and the clients," she said with a laugh. "Can't have them riding shotgun on the hood."

Sheila smiled at the image. "No, I wasn't talking about Todd's car, either. You know, by the way, he didn't tip the valet."

"So he forgot. Honestly, Sheila. You make too much out of that sort of thing. He was probably so infatuated with you that it slipped his mind. Perry said Todd said one thing about you."

Interested in that opinion despite her lack of interest in the man, Sheila looked at Tracy. "And it was?"

"'Wow.' That's Wow with a capital W, too, Missy Miss." Tracy grinned. "Todd's family has been after him to settle down. He'll probably make partner in a year or two. They want him to have a trophy wife by then."

"Do I look like a trophy to you?"

Tracy gave Sheila the once-over. "Let's see. Undergrad degree from City College. They won't hold that against you because the finance degree is from Harvard. You live in an exclusive Central Park apartment, you're about to become a vice president at the investment firm. You speak fluid French and Portuguese. You're slim, trim, pretty, and you know which fork to use at a dinner function. I think that about covers it. You're in."

Sheila rolled her eyes. "I'll pass, thank you very much. The guy I finally marry or get serious about will see me for me, not for degrees on the wall or the diversification of the portfolio."

"Umm-hmm," Tracy said knowingly. "And that's why you went out with that janitor in your building who was hitting on you. His assets just made you swoon."

"I did not go out with that man."

Tracy cocked her head at Sheila. "My point exactly."

"Well, I wasn't talking about buying a car or riding a car or going out with a janitor. I was referring to a man I've been seeing."

Tracy glanced at her. "You mean a guy as in other than last night with Todd?"

"It *is* possible for me to get a date on my own, you know." She smiled as she said "you know"—the catchphrase seemed standard in Daryl's vocabulary.

"What's he do?"

Sheila thought about it a minute, her brow furrowed. "I don't know. He's never really said."

"Oh, Lord. You could be seeing a crazy person."

Then an idea hit Sheila. She'd been just as evasive when it came to talking about her own career. A smile split her face.

"What?" Tracy said.

"I think he's doing the same thing I'm doing."

"An investment banker? You go, girl."

But Sheila didn't really think he was in banking. He wanted a woman who didn't have dollar signs in her eyes or maybe one who was outside his work circle. He'd admitted working for the city. Maybe he was in the mayor's office and was keeping a low profile. Whatever the case, Sheila could respect him for keeping things on the down-low. She knew exactly where he was coming from on that particular front.

She also knew that if she didn't have a high-powered job making, as the shampoo assistants at Della's said, "serious bank," Todd wouldn't give her the time of day. And that, Sheila realized, was just fine with her.

# CHAPTER FIVE

Todd called later that morning. Since she hadn't given him her number, she knew she had Tracy or Perry to thank for that. And she gave Todd no points in the phone volley game. He was far too anxious.

*Probably to get more investment advice,* she figured. The thought of sending him a bill for the time they'd talked work the previous night did cross her mind . . . a couple of times.

"I'd like to see you again," he said.

Sheila had to think of a plausible way out of that. "Well, I'm pretty tied up with some projects right now," she said. "And I'll be heading out of the country again soon."

"That's okay. Tell you what, I'll give you a call in a week or so and we'll set something up. Maybe dinner, just the two of us."

Sheila rolled her eyes, but kept a smile in her voice. "That sounds fine," she told him. A week would give her plenty of time to come up with a real excuse to put him off permanently.

Their date as far as she'd been concerned had been a bust. The self-absorbed, status-is-everything Todd didn't strike her as the type of man who would tip mediocre performance artists ten bucks just because he related to their creative struggle. And it hadn't gone unnoticed that he didn't even thank the valets who parked and retrieved his precious car, let alone press a tip in the guys' hands.

While Tracy deemed the night a smashing success, Sheila had other things on her mind. Like getting some work done before it was time to leave for her hair appointment. The dream she'd harbored for more years than she could remember was within her power to reach right now. The timing was perfect, too. She had the unobstructed time of her vacation to put the plan on paper and the bonus from the last project at work to finance her dream of giving back to the community and the people who'd helped her achieve the success she'd garnered.

Sheila spent about three hours working on her plan. Along with a few speakers she might draft, she'd lead free seminars on personal finance, repairing credit, savings plans, smart loans, tax shelters, and investment strategy. For those who were interested, she'd start an investment club. For the young people, she could have field trips to Wall Street and a behind-the-scenes look at the banking industry.

The more she wrote, the more excited she got about the prospect of her financial services nonprofit agency. All she needed to do was come up with a name. That, for some reason, seemed to elude her.

Picking up a pen to do a little brainstorming on that, she got a couple of names down when the telephone rang.

"Hello?"

"Hey there," Daryl said. "I was, like, you know, wondering what you were up to Sunday afternoon. There's a performance—with real actors, I might add—that I think you'd like. It's at a little place off Broadway, way off Broadway."

Sheila smiled. "Well, I've been to two of your little places so far and I've enjoyed myself and the company. So I think I'm ready to trust your tastes." She thought about something. "Does that mean we're not getting together tonight?"

"Not at all, Sheila Mae. I just want to make sure all the slots on your dance card have my name on them."

Sheila smiled. "Well, being a little greedy, huh?"

"And you know that's right."

"Well, I'm looking forward to tonight."

"Me, too," he said. "I can pick you up if you're not coming to the lounge tonight."

"It will be fine to meet there. See you soon."

When Daryl got off the phone, he sighed. The woman was so embarrassed about where she lived that she didn't want him picking her up at home. This was like the third time she'd eased away from the suggestion he pick her up at her place.

*Now, stop being so suspicious, my brother,* he told himself. *She's being a streetwise New York City woman.*

He nodded. That really made more sense than what he'd been conjuring up. Meeting in a public place was smart for the first few dates. But Daryl planned to ratchet up the stakes tonight. After drinks or a light supper, they'd return to *his* place.

He looked around his one-bedroom apartment. The Shaker-style furniture lent the place a simple elegance. It had been home for a while now. Daryl wasn't one of those brothers whose apartment looked like a dorm room. Everything was ready for Sheila's visit. He had candles all around, just waiting to be lit. The sound system, one of the best on the market, was all cued with the right kind of mood music. Thanks to some of her musical requests from the lounge, he knew some of her favorites.

Walking to his small kitchen, he checked the wine he'd put in the refrigerator. Three bottles. Glasses were at the ready on the counter. His bedside table was stocked with condoms, an extra toothbrush was in the bathroom, and he'd put a spare robe on the back of the bathroom door for after the shower he hoped they'd share.

Daryl grinned as he sang a little "Let's get it on, ooh ooh ooh." He wasn't Marvin Gaye, but he knew how to set the stage for a seduction.

———

Della Frazier liked the idea of having a music video made at the salon. She'd reviewed the proposal and had listened to the song. The dance tune called "Truly Madly" had a nice little beat. The lyrics, a palatable hip-hop, put her in the mind of Will Smith's early work and the Sugar Hill Gang back in the late seventies or early eighties.

They wanted to shoot the entire production in the salon and in the lounge. Della looked at the contract. Not only did she like the nice round number they were giving her, she liked the fact that the salon and the lounge would be plugged significantly.

The group had dancers already. Della could supply up to six people who would also be in the video as extras or in scenes. She pulled a piece of paper from a drawer at her desk and wrote the numbers one through six in a line. In the first spot she put down the most obvious name: Daryl Desmond.

Even if he couldn't play his own music, Della had a feeling he'd jump at the exposure and the credit line. Tapping her pen on the desk, she thought about all the people she employed: stylists, shampoo assistants, receptionists, manicurists, massage therapists, and makeup consultants. Add the barkeepers, cooks, and waitresses in the lounge and that was a whole heap of people, not even counting her two assistant managers.

*How in the world will I ever choose?* She didn't want to show any favoritism. *But the good Lord knows I do have favorites.*

A knock on the office door interrupted her thoughts.

"Come in."

"Hi, Della. I wasn't sure if you were in today or not. I just stopped by to pick up my paycheck since I was off yesterday."

"Come on in, Joyce. I have it right here."

Della went to a file cabinet and opened the top drawer. She retrieved the shampoo assistant's check and handed it to her.

"There's a note in there about an upcoming staff meeting."

"Is the schedule for next month posted yet?"

"I'll get it up Monday," Della said.

"All right, then. I'm headed out. I need to buy a lottery ticket. It's at thirty-five million. I don't usually play until it reaches the twenty-five mark. That's some real money."

"And if you win, you'll just up and leave me high and dry, won't you?"

The girl grinned. "Yes, ma'am. I sure would."

Laughing, Della told her to have a nice weekend. When the girl left, Della went back to her desk. Joyce had given her just the solution she needed. At Tuesday's staff meeting, she'd hold a lottery. The employees who wanted to be in the video would have their names put in a hat. Five lucky winners would be chosen and Della wouldn't have to kill herself trying to decide who was worthy.

As for Daryl's spot—well, she was boss and had the last word anyway. If anyone gave any lip about it, tough.

She reached for her Rolodex and flipped to Daryl's number. She'd swear him to secrecy, then give him a heads-up about the plan.

———

"Y ou've been in an awfully good mood tonight," Sheila observed.

She and Daryl were standing in line to see a movie. They'd opted to do that instead of another club. By mutual agreement, dinner would be junk food at the movies.

"That's because I got some terrific . . . no, some fabulous news this afternoon."

"What?"

He smiled at her. "I can't tell you."

Sheila punched him in the arm. "What? Then why are you teasing me about it?"

"You'll know soon enough," he said. "It has to do with Della's."

"The hair salon or the lounge?"

"Both. Two of everything, please," he told the guy working the concession lane where they stood. "Hot dogs, nachos. What do you want to drink?" he asked Sheila.

"Coke is fine."

"Two Cokes." He looked in the candy display. "Want some?"

"We're gonna need Alka-Seltzer at the rate you're ordering."

"Nah, we'll be fine. Add a box of Goobers and a large bucket of popcorn."

He reached for his wallet, but Sheila already had money out.

"Hey, no, no, no. This is on me," he said.

"You paid for the movies. I'll do this."

He got napkins and straws while their order was being filled. "You're one of those liberated women, huh?"

"Yes and no," Sheila said. "Relationships should work two ways."

Accepting the bucket of popcorn, Daryl looked at her. He leaned in a bit. "So, you're saying we're, like, in a relationship?"

Sheila snatched a few kernels from the top. "Only if you think so."

He grinned. Then he kissed her.

The spy film they watched had enough action to please Daryl and enough romantic moments to please Sheila. During one tender scene, she reached for his hand and gave it a squeeze. They missed the next minute or so of the movie because they were too busy looking at each other.

When it ended, Daryl casually suggested they return to his place to listen to some music. Sheila agreed, and they hailed a cab.

"Do you drive in the city?"

He laughed at that. "All the time, Sheila Mae. All the time."

By the time they arrived at his apartment, they were walking hand in hand.

"I'll get us some light," Daryl said when they came in the door. He took Sheila's light wrap. She fluffed her hair out and walked to the sofa.

"Nice place," she said.

"Thanks. It's been home for about five years now. Decent rent, clean building, neighbors who aren't psychos. You can't ask for much more." With an extended butane lighter, he lit the candles in the living room and the ones along the window ledges.

Sheila wandered over to his sound system and browsed through his collection.

"Good grief. You have vinyl records. I haven't seen any of those since . . . since I can't remember when."

His grin flashed briefly. "I couldn't throw out my Sly and the Family

Stone. And where would I be without Aretha demanding respect on a 45?"

Sheila laughed as she flipped through the album jackets. "Oh, my Lord. It's Earth, Wind & Fire. Would you look at those clothes."

Daryl sat on an ottoman behind Sheila. "There are lots of kids today who don't even know that music was done any way other than CDs and cassettes."

With an album in hand, Sheila straightened. "If you stand there and tell me that you have eight-tracks *and* a working eight-track tape player, I'm just going to scream."

Smiling, Daryl went to a closed shelf on the bottom of his music collection. "The neighbors are gonna think somebody's getting murdered up in here, but . . ." He pulled an eight-track from the shelf, then opened a cabinet Sheila hadn't noticed. In it, in pristine condition, was a hi-fi player.

"This was state-of-the-art back in the day." He put the tape in.

"No," Sheila said.

He nodded.

"I don't believe it." She went to the shelf and peered through the titles. "I do not believe what I'm seeing."

A moment later KC and the Sunshine Band were singing about doing a little dance and making a little love. Sheila burst out laughing.

"Bet you don't remember how to Hustle," Daryl said.

"You'd lose that bet, brother man."

He pushed the ottoman and a table out of the way and they danced the Hustle to the song.

"Hey, remember the Bump?" he called out over the music and Sheila's off-key singing.

They quickly started that old-school dance. By the time the track ended, a modern, mellow tune was playing. Daryl stepped away to turn off the eight-track player and slipped the remote control he'd used to put the sound up a little on Brian McKnight.

He held his arms open and Sheila came into them. They slow-danced to the customized CDs, all of the tunes mellow and sensual.

"This is nice," Sheila said.

He nuzzled her neck. "It can get even nicer," he murmured. He kissed her neck and made his way up to her earlobe.

"I . . . ohhh." Whatever she'd been about to say was lost as he stoked a gently growing flame in her.

He eased her toward the sofa.

"Daryl, wait."

"What's wrong?"

"I just . . . we've only just met. This seems so sudden and all."

"Baby, we can take things as slow as you want to go."

"Really?"

"Really," he said.

She smiled and relaxed into the cushiony comfort of his sofa. He sat next to her, playing with her hair, caressing the edge of her face with a finger, gently coaxing her into sweet anticipation.

He leaned forward and kissed her, then murmured against her lips, "I have some wine. I'll go open it."

When he got up, Sheila let loose a shaky breath. She was ready for this, wanted it. Yet . . . they hardly knew each other. When it came down to it, she'd essentially flirted with him and picked him up at Della's. Looking around his apartment, though, she saw the evidence of where he expected this night to end.

And when she was truly honest with herself, she knew exactly where she wanted the night to end as well. A small smile curved her mouth.

Holding two delicate stem glasses in one hand and an opened bottle of wine in the other, Daryl returned. He smiled down at her before settling in next to her on the sofa.

He poured two glasses and offered her one. "I propose a toast," he said.

"Okay. To what?"

He stared into her eyes. For a long moment, neither of them said anything. The moment grew longer and quieter as the mutual anticipation built. Sheila licked suddenly dry lips, the motion drawing his gaze to her mouth.

"To possibilities," he finally whispered.

Before she had a chance to sip from her wineglass, he took it from her hand and placed both glasses on the table. A moment later, they were one, his mouth tasting, savoring, lingering over a wine sweeter than any that could ever come from a bottle. The kiss expanded, blossomed into an exploratory venture.

Sheila moaned and arched her back, inviting him to linger awhile.

"Come with me," he murmured.

She nodded and he led her to his bedroom. They stood at the side of his bed, staring at each other. But that didn't last very long. She reached for his shirt. He lifted a hand to her blouse. In moments, they lay tumbled together, bare skin on cool sheets. He traced the smooth brown skin of her legs, her thighs. A delicious shudder heated her body.

"You're beautiful," he said.

Had she the power of speech, Sheila would have acknowledged the compliment, but she was too full of the sensations pouring through her. His touch was magic. Pure heaven.

He pulled away for a moment and a small sound of protest escaped her lips.

"I'm not going anywhere, baby," he said. "Not when you do this to me." He guided her hand to his erection. Sheila's eyes widened a bit. Then she helped him with the condom.

They came together. Yin to yang. Alpha to Omega. He wrapped himself around her like a warm blanket and Sheila forgot everything except the touch of his hand, his mouth, his body.

A while later, Daryl got up to retrieve the wine they'd abandoned in the living room. Sheila reached for a shirt and joined him. From the sofa, sipping from his glass, Daryl watched her roam his apartment. She walked around the living and dining area, looking at his things, occasionally taking a small sip from her own glass. A mellow but jazzy instrumental tune came from the CD player. Sheila's meandering took her to a wall with several photographs and plaques.

"I like the way you're wearing that shirt," he said. She sent a smile over her shoulder at him.

"Those are pictures of some relatives and friends and some awards I've won."

"You met Quincy Jones, I see," she said taking in one photo.

"He's a cool dude. That was at a concert at the garden. I had back-stage passes."

Sheila nodded as her gaze moved on to the other items he displayed. A photo of Daryl with the mayor confirmed her assumption about his em-ployment. Until, that is, she read the engraved plaque below the photo. She leaned in closer, not believing the words right in front of her eyes.

DARYL DESMOND
New York Transit Authority
Employee of the Month
August 1999

Transit Authority? Sheila took an even closer look at the photo. The mayor was wearing a suit and tie, but Daryl, he had on a blue uniform. Like a bus driver or subway operator.

She whipped around to stare at him. Wine sloshed from her glass. "I'm sorry," she said quickly as she placed the glass on the nearest flat surface.

"Don't worry about it. What's wrong?"

The CD player switched to Miles Davis. Sheila heard it but was having a hard time registering things right now.

"You," she said pointing. "That."

He glanced at the plaque she pointed to and smiled. "Oh, yeah. That was last year. I was employee of the month. I tell you, I've been driving a bus for a lot of years now. I've been employee of the month I don't know how many times."

Sheila's eyes widened at the same moment her stomach lurched. "Driving a bus?"

He nodded as he took another sip of wine. "I told you I work for the city."

Sheila nodded. "That's right. You did."

She reached for her wineglass and proceeded to drain it.

"You like that, huh?" he asked as he got up. "I'll pour you some more."

A bus driver! The shock of it rolled through her, roiled through her. She'd assumed he was a white-collar professional. She couldn't possibly have . . . She was a vice-president-to-be. She couldn't really have . . . But a glance toward his bedroom, a glance at the lack of clothes she herself was wearing, told the story and then some.

Suddenly Sheila's head pounded, the headache attacking from nowhere. So much for her big talk with Tracy. It didn't matter when she thought that he was a city administrator or that he worked on the mayor's staff. Now, though . . . Bus drivers made what every year, thirty thousand? Maybe forty or fifty with seniority. Sheila had no clue.

Did it matter?

She was in too much of a tailspin to know right now. She needed time to think, time to deal with this new information.

Her gaze darted around his apartment as if she were seeing it with new, clearer vision. It was still nice, still clean. He still had good pieces of furniture mixed in. He seemed to like the Shaker style, although now with a second, more thorough glance, she realized she was looking at reproductions, not originals.

"Here," he said, pressing a refilled wineglass in her hands. "Let's have a seat."

She stared at him. "Uh . . ."

He peered at her from where he sat on the sofa. Placing his glass on a coaster on the coffee table, he studied her.

"You feeling all right?"

Her mind racing, Sheila just looked at him. "I, uh, no. No." She put a hand to her stomach. "Maybe I should have skipped the nachos."

"Need to go to the bathroom?"

"I beg your pardon?"

He pointed. "The bathroom's that way."

"Oh. Okay." She put her glass on the coffee table, then headed in the direction he'd pointed.

A green, gold, and burgundy shower curtain in a bold geometric design was the first thing that got her attention. Sheila shut the bathroom door and braced her hands on the sink to stare at herself.

"Are you a snob?" she asked her reflection. Since the mirror didn't answer back, she sighed.

Did it matter what a person did for a living? There was a time—like yesterday—when she would have said no. Now, when faced with the reality of her situation, Sheila found herself at a loss.

Turning the faucet on the sink, she let cool water run, then splashed a little on her face. She wouldn't have to lie about not feeling well. Her head was pounding.

She patted her face and dried her hands with a towel that said GUEST. What she needed to do was get home, get in the tub, and think this through. But before she could do that, she had to face Daryl again. She made a dash from the bathroom to the bedroom, where she quickly dressed.

He was waiting for her on the sofa.

"Feel better?"

"Not really," she said. "I think I'd better head home."

To say he looked disappointed was an understatement. But he rallied quickly. "You weren't joking earlier about maybe needing an Alka-Seltzer. I don't think I have any here."

She smiled. "That's okay. I have something at home."

He rose, got her wrap, and took her hand. "I had fun tonight."

"Me, too," she said. And she realized that was true. She did have fun with Daryl. Lots of it, every time they went out. That was more than she could say about going out with Todd. But a bus driver?

He walked her to the elevator and to the curb to hail a cab. "I'll call you in the morning," he said.

Sheila remembered that they'd set a date for the next evening. "I may need a rain check on that off-off-Broadway show," she told him.

"Not a problem. This is New York, Sheila Mae. Shows are always playing."

She smiled as she got in the cab, but her smile seemed a little sad.

"Take some seltzer. Get some sleep. You'll be right as rain tomorrow."

"You promise?"

"Yeah, I promise, Sheila." He squeezed her hand and shut the door.

As the driver pulled away, Sheila leaned her head back and sighed.

# CHAPTER SIX

The first thing Sheila did when she got home was call Tracy.

"We need to talk."

"Perry and I are going to a late movie. Can it wait till tomorrow? I'm trying to do something with this hair. I'll call you early."

Sheila paced the floor in her den, the cordless phone tucked in the crook of her shoulder and chin. "It's about the guy I told you I've been seeing."

"Oh, yeah, the mystery man. Want to do a double date?"

"Tracy, he's a bus driver."

"Excuse me?"

"You heard correctly."

"You don't like Todd, who is a lawyer, has an unbelievable salary and bonus plan, and drives that cute little car, but you'd rather hang out with a bus driver? I'll be at your place in twenty minutes."

Over a pot of tea, Sheila and Tracy talked well into the night. When it was all over, though, Sheila found herself no closer to figuring out why Daryl's place of employment mattered when it really shouldn't matter at all.

---

Della's staff meeting went well. Just two people were absent. After she finished the salon business and passed out the work schedules for the coming month, she asked everyone to gather around.

"I think I have some news you all are going to like."

She held a hand out to Daryl. "Come up here with me, Daryl. This is as much your show as mine."

Over the weekend, she'd figured out the way to let the staff know that Daryl had a shoo-in spot. When she'd told him about the video project and mentioned a couple of the names of the people she'd been working with, Daryl jumped up.

"Traymore Collins is my man. I can't believe he didn't tell me about this. Oh, just wait till I see his butt."

By Tuesday, Daryl had talked to his old friend, who didn't know that Daryl had been working for Della. He'd been immediately offered a more prominent role, which now brought the number to six, rather than five lottery slots to fill.

She quickly told the salon and lounge staff about the project. It took a good ten minutes for the excited chatter to die down long enough for her to explain what would come next.

"I thought we'd throw a party to get the word out about Della's Place," Della said. "But I think we'll get more bang for the buck by combining these events. The party will be here after the video shoot is a wrap. That's showbiz talk, you know."

She got a few laughs, then someone asked the obvious question.

"So who gets to be in the video, Della?"

"The fairest way is to pull names," she said. She nodded toward one of the receptionists to start passing out the pieces of paper. "Write your name on the paper. Maia, don't forget Nikki and Gloria, who aren't here. I'll shake 'em up really well and pull our six new music video stars."

When everyone had their name in the bowl, Della let Daryl pick.

"Close your eyes, man. I don't want you cheating," someone called out.

"Yeah, well, just for that, I won't be pulling your name, Jackson, and that'll be with my eyes closed."

But the first name Daryl pulled was Jackson Scott. The stylist did a little dance as he made his way to the front.

"Ah, suki-suki, now. I'm gonna be a star!"

The crowd laughed and urged Daryl to pull again. When it was all over, two stylists, a shampoo girl, one of the part-time receptionists, a manicurist, and the cook from the lounge were the lucky few.

Della told them the date the project would be shot and asked the six, plus Daryl, to meet her in her office after the meeting.

A little while later, they all gathered around while Della handed out a list of instructions on what their roles were to be. "They have some waivers and things for you all to read and sign. If you have any questions, the person to call is listed on that sheet."

Daryl sat on the edge of the leather sofa next to LaTonya, one of the stylists who'd won a lottery spot.

"I hear you're dating Sheila Landon," she said. "That surprised me, but I think that's really cool. You like her new hair?"

"You know Sheila?"

LaTonya nodded. "I've been her stylist for about two years, maybe three now. She's good people. She hooked me up when I was trying to figure out how to finance a couple of classes I wanted to take."

Daryl frowned. "What do you mean, hooked you up? What kind of hook-up can a woman on welfare give you?"

LaTonya sat up. "Welfare? Sheila? Maybe we're not talking about the same woman. The Sheila I'm talking about is a big-shot banker, a big muckity-muck. She works for Miller, Fitch and Hallowell."

"What is that?"

"It's one of the largest investment houses in the world," Della said. "I wondered if you knew that."

Daryl rose. "Hold up, now. You know the Sheila I've been seeing, Della. Is she the same one LaTonya's talking about?"

Della nodded.

Daryl looked from one woman to the other. "I don't get it," he said.

LaTonya folded her video instruction sheet. "What's to get? You're dating some serious bank. And she's a nice lady, to boot. I need to get running. Della, thanks so much for this opportunity. It's gonna be a lot of fun, I just know it."

Della smiled as she bade the winners good night. Daryl had thunder all over his face. "Hold up, Daryl," she said when he would have left as well. "Close the door. Have a seat."

Daryl looked at her, then plopped onto the sofa.

"Talk to me," Della said.

"What's to say? It looks like I've been played. Your Sheila was slumming. No wonder she suddenly got sick to her stomach when she saw that plaque on the wall."

"What plaque?"

He waved a hand. "It doesn't matter."

Della leaned on the edge of her desk. "Why'd you think she was on welfare?"

He shrugged. "She was always careful to meet me here. I just figured she was ashamed of where she lived. I figured the salon must have been on either an easy bus or subway line for her to get here all the time."

"She didn't tell you where she lived and you took that and jumped to the conclusion that she was on government assistance?"

"Well, she was always evasive on other things, too. Like where she worked."

"I believe I overheard her say she's been on vacation."

Daryl looked up. "Vacation? Well, what kind of banker do you know who wears slinky dresses and sexy high heels and all that hair? I figured it was a weave. But no banker I've ever seen dresses like that. They all look like librarians."

"Daryl, if she didn't tell you what she does, I'm sure there's a reason. Instead of sitting here sulking and feeling put out, why don't you give her a call?"

"Hmmph. I'm going home. I'll see you Friday night at the lounge. Kenny is working tomorrow night."

"Daryl, just remember that there's an explanation for everything.

And, more importantly, it's only been a couple of weeks. Did you tell her your complete life story in that time?"

He chewed on that thought the rest of the night.

---

But he didn't call her. As a matter of fact, the entire week went by. Friday night, about eight-thirty, he saw her slip into the lounge. A couple was sitting at the table where she usually went. She had on a fire-engine-red car-wash dress. Daryl had to admit she looked good, real good.

Then he remembered how she'd played him.

He spent the next half hour pretending he didn't see her. Then he spotted her making her way toward him with a glass of ice water and lemon in her hand. Daryl turned around and tugged the headset on as if he were about to cue some music.

"Hi, Daryl. I thought you might like a drink."

Realizing he was acting childish, he turned to greet her. She had a sweet smile on her face.

"Thanks," he said. "How are things over at Miller, Fitch and Hallowell?"

Surprise crossed her face for a moment. Daryl almost blurted out, *Aha!*

"I'm on vacation," she said. "I have another week before I go back."

"Um-hmm."

"Are you upset about something?"

"What do I have to be upset about? You just concealed a lot of information from me. You're parading around here like . . ." He paused, realizing she didn't deserve his anger. He'd had a lot of time since the staff meeting Tuesday night to think about why he was so angry with her.

When it came down to it, though, Daryl came to the realization sometime in the middle of the night last night that he wasn't angry with her. He was the one feeling inadequate. Maybe she went out with him because she liked him.

"Tell me something," he said. "Were you really sick last Saturday when you left my place or did you get sick to the stomach when you found out you'd been dating a bus driver?"

She blanched, but held her ground. "To be honest, a little of both. I wanted to talk to you about that."

Daryl's mouth thinned to an angry line. "Oh, so now I'm not good enough for you?" His voice rose enough for a couple sitting nearby to look up at them.

"I didn't say that, Daryl. Don't put words into my mouth. You don't know how I feel. I think we have something valuable here. I wouldn't want to lose it."

"You're right, Miss Investment Banker," he said as he took in her outfit with disdain. "No wonder your feet hurt that first night. I bet you don't normally wear high heels, do you?"

"There's no reason for you to get mean."

"Oh, believe me, baby, this is not mean. Now I have work to do. Some of us work more than one job."

"You're not working a second job, you're living your passion. You told me as much."

"Believe what you want," he said. With that, he slipped the earphones on and reached for a CD.

She stared at him. This was not at all how she'd expected the evening to go. She put his water on the small table he used and turned to go.

Once, she looked back at him. He studiously ignored her. Twice, she looked again. He still didn't acknowledge her.

Dejected, Sheila left. The cab ride to her apartment seemed longer than ever.

---

Daryl and Sheila didn't see each other at all the following week. She'd called him a couple of times, but he hadn't called back. On the two occasions she went to Della's Place, Daryl didn't seem inclined to talk to her. Again he pretended to be too busy to spare her a few minutes when she showed up there.

She made an appointment with LaTonya to take the weave out of her hair. It was time to return to the staid world in which she existed. During the day, she kept busy by working on her proposal. She contacted a web page designer who would be setting up her Internet site when she had everything finalized. The center—which still didn't have a name—needed to be in a central location, a place where people could easily get to it. She envisioned eventually branching out so there would be multiple centers. After mapping out details of how her nonprofit organization would work, she spent time looking at properties—anything to get her mind off Daryl. But it wasn't working.

Music on the radio reminded her of him; just looking at herself in the mirror, with the long, curly weave in her hair, reminded her of Daryl. She was going to have to decide pretty soon whether to keep the weave in or not. It really was too much hair, but she liked the way it made her feel: sexy and wanted, two things she knew she inherently wasn't.

One night, sitting at home feeling sorry for herself, Sheila picked up the telephone and called in a delivery order for barbeque wings with coleslaw and ranch dressing on the side.

Tracy called to see if she'd like to double date with Todd again. That was when Sheila realized what her problem was.

"It's not that he's a bus driver," she told Tracy. "It's that I didn't realize I was a snob."

"You're not a snob, honey. That's my department."

Sheila smiled into the phone, then nibbled on a wing. "Now he's all pissed at me for perpetrating a fraud."

"Did you explain to him why you were running around looking like Chaka Khan?"

"My hair did not make me look like Chaka, and I haven't been able to explain. He keeps shutting me out."

"Well, maybe you can start by explaining it to me, because I am clueless."

Sheila sighed. "Maybe later. I'm not up to it right now."

"Do you love him?"

"I think so," she said.

"Well, girl, it's your thing. Do what you wanna do, is what the people say."

The old song lyrics Tracy quoted reminded Sheila of the night she and Daryl had danced to eight-track tape music.

"He thinks . . ." Sheila paused. She didn't know what he thought. She hadn't talked to him since the night of their bitter confrontation.

She glanced at her watch as an idea formed. "You know what?" she said, conviction strengthening her resolve. "I like him. And he likes me. And that's all that matters."

"So you're going to do what, exactly?" Tracy said.

"If I hurry, I'll be able to catch him, if he's working tonight. Talk to you later."

She quickly dressed—this time, though, not in one of her party girl outfits, but in a pair of khaki slacks and a cotton pullover. Comfortable clothes. She felt at home and at ease, and knew that was what she'd need to feel if things went badly. If they went well, then she'd still be comfortable.

She wanted to approach him in a nonthreatening manner. Maybe he'd hear her out.

When she arrived at Della's Place, the crowd was sparse. Thursday nights seemed to be made for television. That served Sheila's purpose very well. Daryl wouldn't be able to ignore her or pretend like he had so much to do.

"Hi," she greeted him. He simply nodded. "I know you're angry, but I want you to hear me out."

He gave her the once-over. "Those your normal clothes, huh?"

She took the barb in stride. He hadn't put the headphones on, though, so she plowed ahead. "About a month ago, I overheard a couple of colleagues describe me as a stuffed shirt. They said I didn't know the meaning of fun, that I wouldn't know how to let my hair down. Hearing those things said about me hurt. A lot. Particularly since I recognized the truth in some of what they said."

"And so?"

"And so I set out to prove something to myself. A long time ago, I got caught up in my career. Things took off and I never looked back. But lately, it's all seemed to be pointless."

He placed a CD in the drive and adjusted the volume switches on his board.

"I envy you," she said.

"How's that?"

She spread her hands to encompass all the disc jockey equipment surrounding him. "You work a regular job, making a living like we all have to. And you still have time to do what you really want to do. Look at this, these people who come here, they come because you give them something they need. You play your own music. You're doing what needs to be done to pursue your passion."

"And what about you?" he said. "What are you passionate about?"

She glanced away for a moment, then met his gaze. "You, for one. I didn't realize how much until we didn't see each other. I enjoy myself with you. I can be myself."

"If this is yourself," he said, indicating her clothes, "what was with the skin-tight dresses, the shoes, the jewelry?"

"That's the part of me that I have to keep bottled up at work. Sometimes it's good to adapt to your environment. At other times, it's just, well, stifling."

"Your hair looks nice."

"I'm having the weave taken out tomorrow. I'm due back at work next week. I had some time coming to me, so I took three weeks to let my hair down."

"Why are you telling me all of this?"

"Because I don't want what we had to just disappear."

He shook his head. "It won't work."

Sheila looked crestfallen. "Why?"

"Because I did a little research into Miller, Fitch and Hallowell. That outfit is top of the line. And I found an article about you in the *Times*. You're a real hotshot."

"So?"

"So, a big-time investment banker is not going to shepherd a bus driver around to her fancy shindigs."

"You do an honest day's work for honest pay. That's something I respect."

A waitress came up and handed him a piece of paper with a request written on it. He nodded and put it to the side. "I don't know, Sheila."

Accepting the fact that she, too, had needed time to work this through in her head, she tried to be patient with him. Surely Daryl could see that they had a good thing going.

He stared at his hands for a minute. Then, "You said I was one thing you're passionate about. What else?"

She smiled. "That's where the time off comes into play. I've spent my vacation mapping out a project I've wanted to do for a long time. Yes, I make a lot of money. Yes, I've been blessed and lucky and anything else you want to call it. But I didn't get where I am today by myself. I climbed up on the shoulders of people who came before me. And they were holding me while they stood on someone else's strength." She shrugged. "You've got to give back."

"So you're gonna be handing out bags of money in Harlem?"

Sheila laughed. "Not quite, but close. I want to show people, black people in particular, that poverty doesn't have to be a life sentence. Smart investing and saving can happen no matter if you make five thousand a year, fifty thousand, or fifty million. It's a matter of being educated. That's what I can do. Teach people how to make their money work for them."

Daryl rubbed his face. "I need some time to think about all of this."

She sighed. "I understand." Looking around, she saw the crowd had thinned even more. "I can wait for you to finish up. We can grab a bite to eat or maybe go to Dray's."

"Listen to you, talking about Dray's. Like you knew it existed before I took you there."

She smiled. "That's right. You broadened my horizons. And a thing once expanded can never be the same again."

"I'll take a rain check."

"That's two, then," she said.

When his brow furrowed in confusion, she elaborated. "I took a rain check on that off-Broadway production. Now you're taking one on dinner. Dinner and a show sounds like a date to me."

He nodded. "Yeah, it does. Listen, I have some work to do here. We'll talk later. I'll call you or something."

Sheila's shoulders slumped, but she kept a smile on her face. The "or something" part sounded like his version of the polite brush-off. She'd tried everything she could think of. What happened next was up to him. Reaching in the pocket of her slacks, she pulled out a card.

"Here's the number where I can be reached at work. I hope you will call me, Daryl."

She leaned forward to kiss him, but he turned his head. The rebuff hurt. Sheila, blinking back tears, raised a hand toward him, then paused, nodded, and walked away.

Daryl watched her go and wondered if he was letting the best thing that ever happened to him walk away. He reached for the piece of paper with the request written on it. Opening the folded paper, he stared at the words, a lump rising in his throat. One of the patrons wanted to hear "Let's Just Kiss and Say Goodbye."

# CHAPTER SEVEN

The video production at Della's House of Style started early on a Saturday morning three weeks later. All of the customers had been notified that the salon would be closed that day. They'd had extended hours during the week to make up for any loss. Employees who hadn't been chosen to participate were there to watch, as were a few select customers that Della had invited.

She'd made sure to have the media on hand. "Free publicity," she'd said. "And I'm a firm believer in shameless self-promotion of the shop and the lounge."

The entire day was spent in a party atmosphere. Lights and cameras were all around. Giant speakers had been brought in as props for the video. Daryl's DJ equipment was moved from the lounge to the salon for the taping. He'd be prominently featured in just about every shot.

"Della, I can't thank you enough for this. I cannot believe that Collins is into this now. We went to school together and used to hang back in the day."

"Does that mean you have an ear for your demo CD?" Della asked.

"Nope. It means I have about ten ears for it." He kissed Della on the cheek. "Collins knows some people and he's already passed copies along. And I just got back from L.A. I was out there talking to some people. My boy put in the good word for me at a couple of record companies. You're the woman, Della. You really know how to hook a brother up."

"It wasn't me, Daryl. Things would have happened for you even if this video hadn't come along."

"Well, it might have taken longer."

Della smiled and watched as her salon was transformed. The caterer she'd hired was setting up in the lounge; the party would spill over there while the salon was put back in order.

"You know Sheila's here," she said.

Daryl grinned. "I saw her."

"And?" Della asked.

"And I'll do things in my own way and time," he said, the tone teasing.

Della raised her hands as she smiled. "I can take a hint."

The music hopped. The people bopped. The place rocked. Sheila watched from a corner. She didn't want to get in the way, but she wanted to see Daryl. Della had invited her to the party and told her about the video production. Sheila had been of a mind to decline the invitation until Della added that Daryl would be participating. He'd been "on" all day, chatting up the onlookers, teasing with the crew. He was in his element.

Hours later, after the producer and the director declared the day's work a wrap, Daryl sauntered over to where Sheila sat on a barstool.

"So were you planning to hide over here all night, too?"

"I didn't want to disturb you," she said. "You didn't call, so I took that to mean good-bye."

He took her hands in his. "Now who's jumping to conclusions and making assumptions? My not calling didn't have squat to do with you, Sheila Mae."

She looked up when he called her by the nickname.

"I had some business to attend to," he said. "I was mostly out of town."

"Oh," Sheila said, not quite sure where this was going, but glad to see he was at least willing to talk to her. "You said you needed some time to think things over. Have you come to any conclusions?"

He nodded. "I have."

She waved a hand in a forward motion. "And am I going to have to drag it out of you or should I just go ahead and tell that cameraman who asked me out that I am, indeed, available?"

Daryl scowled and took a step closer to her. "Don't even play like that."

"So, are you going to give what we have, what we've started, another chance?"

He stroked his chin. "I'm thinking about it. Knowing there's some competition on the horizon changes things a bit."

"Well, there's something else you need to consider."

"What's that?"

"If you decide that you want us to be together, you'll have to pay for all of our dates. I can't afford it anymore."

He lifted an eyebrow.

"I quit my job."

"You did what?"

"I resigned. I'll do some consulting on a case-by-case basis. But my time is going to be spent with the Second Chance for Financial Freedom Center."

He grinned. "Well, that's a mouthful."

"I'm energized by this. It's what I've wanted to do for a while."

"Truly?"

She nodded. "Honestly. I figured the only way to really do it right would be to go in and give it my all. So that's what I'm going to do."

He tucked his hands in his pockets. "So, like, that means you won't be having time for a boyfriend."

She reached for him and grabbed a bit of his shirt in each hand, pulling him to her. She opened her legs on the barstool and he stepped into the breach.

"I didn't say that at all."

"Now, wait a minute. Let me get this straight. My woman goes from being a bigshot at the firm to an unemployed lady doing volunteer work?"

She nodded.

"Baby, you gonna have to get a job."

Sheila burst into laughter. "Hey, Daryl."

"What *do* you want, Sheila Mae?"

"Well, first I was thinking we could swing by Dray's and pick up some of those wings. Then I was thinking we'd retire to your place and light all those candles again."

"Oh, you liked that, huh?"

She nodded. The grin that filled Daryl's face let her know that she'd truly found the right man. And that was an honest fact.

Donna Hill

DONNA HILL began her career in 1987 writing short stories for the *True Confessions* magazine. Since her first novel was released in 1990, she has published more than a hundred titles and is considered one of the early pioneers of the African American romance genre. Three of her novels have been adapted for television. She has been featured in *Essence,* the New York *Daily News, USA Today, Today's Black Woman,* and *Black Enterprise,* among many others. She has received numerous awards for her body of work—which cross several genres—including the *Romantic Times* Career Achievement Award; the Trailblazer Award, of which she was the first recipient; the Zora Neale Hurston Literary Award; the Gold Pen Award; as well as commendations for her community service. As an editor, she has packaged several highly successful novels and anthologies, two of which were nominated for awards. Donna is a graduate of Goddard College with an MFA in creative writing and is currently in pursuit of her doctor of arts in English pedagogy and technology. She is an assistant professor of professional writing at Medgar Evers College and lives in Brooklyn, New York, with her family. Her most recent novel, *Confessions in B-Flat,* received a starred review from *Publishers Weekly*. She can be found at donnaohill.com.

William H. Ray

FRANCIS RAY (1944–2013) was the *New York Times* and *USA Today* bestselling author of the Grayson novels, the Falcon books, the Taggart Brothers series, and *Twice the Temptation,* among many other books. Her novel *Incognito* was made into a movie, which aired on BET. A native Texan, she was a graduate of Texas Woman's University with a degree in nursing. Besides being a writer, she was a school nurse practitioner with the Dallas Independent School District. She lived in Dallas. "Francis Ray is, without a doubt, one of the Queens of Romance." —*Romance Review*

Rochelle Alers

ROCHELLE ALERS is one of today's most prolific and popular African American authors of romance and women's fiction. A regular on the *Essence* bestseller list, she has received the *Romantic Times* Career Achievement Award and many other honors. With more than eighty titles and nearly two million copies in print, Alers has been the recipient of the Emma Award, the RWA Vivian Stephens Award for Excellence in Romance Writing, and the Zora Neale Hurston Literary Award. Her novels include *Here I Am, Because of You*, and *Sweet Persuasions*. She is a member of Zeta Phi Beta Sorority, Inc., Iota Theta Zeta Chapter, and her interests include gourmet cooking, knitting, and crocheting. A full-time writer, she lives on Long Island, New York. You can contact her at www.rochellealers.org.

Duke Morse

Bestselling author FELICIA MASON has written more than twenty-five books for St. Martin's Press, Kensington Publishing, and Harlequin. She was a Romance Writers of America (RITA) award finalist in 2005 for the inspirational romantic suspense novel *Gabriel's Discovery*, and her novel *Rhapsody* was made into a TV film. For more than thirty years she has been a newspaper editor and columnist in Pennsylvania, Virginia, and now Texas. She lives in Houston, where she writes crime novels as well as mainstream fiction and romance. Her blog is at feliciamason.blogspot.com. Twitter: @FeliciaLMason

Printed in the USA
CPSIA information can be obtained
at www.ICGtesting.com
LVHW051315180324
774792LV00003B/8